No. 1 *Sunday Times* bestseller S. J. Parris is the pseudonym of the author and journalist Stephanie Merritt. It was as a student at Cambridge researching a paper on the period that Stephanie first became fascinated by the rich history of Tudor England and Renaissance Europe. Since then, her interest has grown and led her to create this series of historical thrillers featuring Giordano Bruno.

Stephanie has worked as a critic and feature writer for a variety of newspapers and magazines, as well as radio and television. She has also written the contemporary psychological thriller *While You Sleep* under her own name. She currently writes for the *Observer* and the *Guardian*, and lives in Surrey with her son.

www.sjparris.com

/sjparrisbooks

@thestephmerritt

ALSO BY S. J. PARRIS

Heresy
Prophecy
Sacrilege
Treachery
Conspiracy
The Secret Dead (a Giordano Bruno novella)
The Academy of Secrets (a Giordano Bruno novella)

AS STEPHANIE MERRITT
While You Sleep

HarperCollins*Publishers*

HarperCollins*Publishers* Ltd
1 London Bridge Street,
London SE1 9GF

www.harpercollins.co.uk

First published by HarperCollins*Publishers* 2020
1

Endpapers show 'MS 4769f.1 Execution Warrant for
Mary Queen of Scots, 1587 (ink on paper)' © Bridgeman Images

A catalogue record for this book is
available from the British Library

ISBN: 978-0-00-748129-3 (HB)
ISBN: 978-0-00-748130-9 (TPB)

Typeset in Sabon by Palimpsest Book Production Ltd,
Falkirk, Stirlingshire

Printed and bound in Great Britain by CPI Group (UK) Ltd,
Croydon CR0 4YY

MIX
Paper from
responsible sources
FSC™ C007454

This book is produced from independently certified FSC™ paper
to ensure responsible forest management.

For more information visit: www.harpercollins.co.uk/green

For the dispatch of the usurper, from the obedience of whom we are by excommunication made free, there be six gentlemen, all my private friends, who for the zeal they bear to the Catholic cause and your majesty's service, will undertake that tragic execution.

Letter from Anthony Babington to Mary, Queen of Scots, 6th July 1586

PROLOGUE

17th July 1586

Chartley Manor, Staffordshire

Six gentlemen. Six of them, ready to undertake that tragic execution in her name. She smiles at the euphemism. But then: why not call it that? Elizabeth Tudor is a heretic, a traitor and a thief, occupying a throne she has stolen; dispatching her would be no regicide, but a just and deserved punishment under the law. Not the law of England, to be sure, but God's law, which is greater.

Mary sits at the small table in her room, in her prison, thinking, thinking, turning over and over in her mind the pages of the great ledger of injustices heaped against her. Eventually, she dips her quill in the inkpot. She wears gloves with the fingers cut off, because it is always cold here, in Staffordshire; the summer so far has been bleak and grey, or at least what she can see of it from her casement, since she is not permitted to walk outside. She flexes her fingers and hears the knuckles crack; she rubs the sore and swollen joints. A pool of weak light falls on the paper before her; she has havered so long over this reply that the candle has almost burned down, and she only has one left until Paulet, her keeper, brings the new ration in the morning. Sometimes he pretends to forget, just as he does with the firewood, to see how long she will sit in the cold and dark without protesting. And when she does ask meekly for the little that is her due, he uses it against her; charges her with being demanding, spoilt, needy, and says he will tell her cousin. But should a queen plead meekly with the likes of Sir Amias Paulet, that puffed-up Puritan? Should a queen be starved of sunlight, of liberty, of respect, and endure it with patience? Twenty years of imprisonment has not taught her to bear it any better, nor will she ever accept it. The day she bows to their treatment of her, she is no longer worthy of her royal title.

She sets the quill down; she has worked herself into a fury and her shaking hand has spattered ink drops on the clean page; she will have to begin again, when she is calmer. She pushes back the chair and heaves herself with difficulty to her feet, wincing at the pain in her inflamed legs. Each step to the window hurts more than it did the day before; or perhaps she is imagining that. One imagines so much, cooped up here in these four walls. She smooths her skirts over her broad hips; and there is another injustice, that she should still be fat when she eats so little! She doesn't trust the food they bring; one day, she is certain, she will eat or drink something and not wake up. That would suit her cousin Elizabeth very well, so she will not give her the satisfaction. And yet, Mary thinks, curling her lip at her rippled reflection in the dark of the windowpane, she has grown heavy and lumpen on nothing but air, half-crippled by rheumatism, grey and faded, an old woman at forty-four. No trace left of the famous beauty that once drove men to madness. But Elizabeth is ugly too, she has heard; near-bald, teeth blackened, her skin so eaten away by the ceruse she uses to hide her age that she will not be seen by any except her closest women without a full mask of face-paint. There will be no children for her now; at least that is one contest that Mary can say she won, even if she hasn't seen her son for nearly twenty years.

She cups her hands around her face to peer out at the night, watching a barn owl ghosting over the moat, when there is a soft knock at the door. She starts, hastens back to the table to hide the papers, but it is only Claude Nau, her French secretary. He bobs a brief bow, takes in her guilty expression.

'You are writing him a reply, Your Majesty?'

'I am considering.' She draws herself up, haughty. He is going to tell her off, she knows, and she has had enough of men speaking to her as if she is a child. She is Queen of Scotland, Dowager Queen of France, and rightful Queen of England, and they should not forget it.

'I counsel against that.'

She watches Nau; a handsome man, always quietly spoken, infuriatingly self-contained, even when she works herself into one of her fits of passion.

'I know you do. But I make my own decisions.'

'Majesty.' He inclines his head. 'I smell a trap.'

'Oh, you will see conspiracies everywhere. Did you read what he promises, Claude? He has men to do the deed, and earnest assurance of foreign aid, and riders to take me to liberty. Everything is in place.' She allows herself to imagine it, as she has so many times, crossing back to the window. 'See, I have an idea' – she taps the glass, excited – 'if we know the exact date to expect him, we can have one of the servants start a fire in the stables. Everyone will rush out and in the commotion, Anthony Babington and his friends can break down my chamber door and whisk me away.' She spins around, a wide, girlish smile on her face that fades the instant she sees his look. 'What? You do not like my plan?'

'It is a very good plan, Majesty. Only . . .' He folds his hands.

'Speak.'

'We have heard such promises before. This Babington is proposing an assassination.'

'*Execution.*'

He waves a hand. 'Call it what you will. But your own cousin. England's queen. In your name.'

'She is no queen.'

He adopts the patient, pained expression that so irritates her. 'Of course not. But if you agree to their proposal, if you so much as acknowledge it in writing, you make yourself an accessory to treason, and there is only one punishment for that offence.'

'My royal cousin loves me too much to allow that.'

'She loves you.' Nau does not contradict her outright, but he allows his gaze to travel pointedly around the room in which she is held captive.

Mary's eyes flash; he has overstepped the mark. 'Leave me.' She flaps a hand to the door. 'I have my letter to write. Come back in an hour and you can encrypt it.'

'I implore you not to put anything on paper which would implicate you in this reckless business. Babington and his friends are impetuous boys. We would do better to proceed with caution, keep our options open.'

'And I order you to get out. There is no *we* here, Claude. They are *my* options, and *I* will choose. Obey your queen.'

Nau sighs audibly, bows, and backs out of the royal presence. When the door clicks shut behind him, Mary smiles, pleased with herself. She sits again at the table and dips her quill, but she cannot think how to begin. She wants Elizabeth to love her, it's true. She wants Elizabeth dead. She wants only her freedom; she wants the throne of England. She is ill, and desperate, and ready to clutch at any straw Providence tosses her way.

She glances up and sees her embroidered cloth of state hanging on the wall over her bed. Every time the snake Paulet comes into the room, he rips it down – she is not permitted the trappings of a queen, he says. And every time he leaves, her women patiently gather it up, mend the tears and hang it again. Now, this Babington is offering her the real prospect of seeing it where it belongs, above her throne at last. She has waited long enough. She is done with caution. What she wants at this moment, more than anything, is to win.

She takes a fresh sheet of paper and writes the date: 17th July 1586. It is a letter that will kill a queen.

PART ONE

ONE

27th July 1586

I am not a praying man. Thirteen years as a Dominican friar cured me of that habit, forgive the pun. But in certain situations the old instincts triumph over reason; in the teeth of mortal terror, I often find my lips forming the familiar Latin incantations before my mind has even noticed. I could wish it didn't happen; it seems disrespectful to the God I no longer believe in that some primitive part of my soul clutches at him like an infant only when I fear I am staring Death in the face, and though I willingly admit to many faults, I hope hypocrisy is not one of them. But perhaps it is only confirmation that you can never erase your past, no matter how far you try to run from it. I had caught the boat from France that summer of 1586 in the hope of finding a place of refuge. Instead – though I didn't yet know it – I had set a straight course towards a murderer.

Pater Noster qui es in caelis, sanctificetur nomen tuum—

Another wave higher than a house loomed over the small fishing vessel, tipping us so that everything not lashed to the deck slid downward and I grabbed at the rail with numb fingers to avoid being flung into the white spray as it broke.

The men grappling with the sail barked frantic orders to one another in English; I could not make out the words over the roar of the wind, but the alarm in their voices was clear enough in any language. The wave lifted the boat, allowing it to teeter for a moment on the crest, before dropping us with a thud into a trough between swelling blue-black peaks. On the next rise, I confirmed what I thought I had seen before: a wavering pinprick of light and a dark spine of shadow along the horizon.

'Is that the port?' I shouted. The captain shook his head, cupping his hand to his ear. I risked peeling one hand from the side to point. 'That light – is that Rye?'

'Rye,' he yelled back, following my finger and nodding vigorously. He pushed aside the wet hair plastered to his forehead; like the rest of us, he was soaked through from the salt spray. I was shivering so hard I had almost lost all feeling, my teeth rattling so that I feared I might bite off my tongue. The tiny dot of light from the harbour beacon did not seem to be getting any closer, no matter how the boat pitched and rolled; I felt as if we had been crossing the Narrow Sea for days, though it could only have been a matter of hours since we left France, under cover of darkness. 'You'd do better below deck,' he added, pointing to the hatch.

'I assure you I wouldn't,' I shouted back, though I was sure he couldn't hear. Below deck the half-digested remains of my supper still decorated the timbers. At least here I could see the horizon, and breathe air that smelled slightly less violently of fish. I had always confidently imagined myself at home on boats but the wind was high tonight, the swell vicious, and the last time I had sailed along the English coastline it had been on a galleon belonging to Sir Francis Drake's fleet, solid as a cathedral compared to this fishing vessel that felt with every wave as if it were a toy hurled by a petulant child. But I had embarked on this journey with no time to make preparations, and the captain was well paid to be quick and discreet.

'How long?' I yelled, pointing to the beacon as the boat rolled and the light dipped out of sight. He shot me an impatient glance and lifted one shoulder.

'Depends on the wind. If you're going to void again, stay out the way.'

I shuffled back and sat down on a coil of rope, clinging to the side of the craft with both hands, absently muttering another Pater Noster as we lurched starboard and a wave slapped over the deck to drench my feet. I was fairly sure I had nothing left in my stomach to bring up after this crossing, but I had thought that the last time I vomited, and the time before. My guts were roiling, my hands and feet raw with cold, eyes stinging from the wind, but my spirits surged each time I spotted that elusive light appearing and vanishing at intervals as the waves obscured it. For months I had waited in hope of the chance to return to England while I marked time in Paris, uncertain as to what direction my life should take next. But without a summons from the one man in London who could change my fortunes, there had been no prospect. An Italian like me could hardly turn up without a reason; the English had a deep-rooted suspicion of foreigners at the best of times, and in these days of religious unrest anyone looking and sounding as I did would be assumed to be Spanish, part of a Catholic plot, or a secret priest. Now I was within sight of Rye harbour, and in my pack below deck, safely wrapped in watertight leather, I carried a currency more valuable than an invitation: new information. The look on Sir Francis Walsingham's face when he read the letter I brought would be worth all the discomforts of this journey. He would see, beyond doubt, what I was willing to risk to protect England. But first I had to find a way to put it into his hands.

It took the best part of an hour battling the wind and tide before the boatman steered us into the channel of Rye port where the water lay calmer and I was able to let go of the boat's rail and attempt to stand on my feet. Thin mists of drizzle hung over the harbour basin. We pulled up alongside a flight of steps set in the quay wall, where one of the men flung a rope around a wooden post to hold us steady as I disembarked. I shook the owner's hand; he gave a curt nod and wished me luck. Though he didn't know my name or the nature of what I carried, he knew who had sent me and could guess at my purpose. I hoisted my bag and lurched with trembling legs on to the steps where I almost slipped, a misstep that would have sent me and my precious cargo tumbling into the black water below. Clutching at the frayed rope nailed along the wall, I righted myself to climb with excessive care to the top and into the waiting arms of two men with lanterns.

'You best come with us.' The one who had spoken gripped me by the upper arm, firmly enough to make himself clear, and began marching me towards a row of low buildings at the end of the quay. The second man, tall with a prominent Adam's apple, wrenched my bag from my shoulder and jerked it between his hands, as if assessing its weight.

I tried to appear pliant; I had expected this. In the half-light I could not see if they were armed, though I guessed they must be. In any case, I could barely make my legs move after the voyage; I could not have looked like much of a threat.

'I need to see Richard Daniel,' I said. My teeth were chattering so violently I could barely get the words out.

Adam's Apple made some noise that I supposed was a mocking attempt at my accent. 'Sorry, mate – you'll have to say that again in English.' He exchanged a smirk with his colleague.

I fought down my impatience. Deference was the only way through with men like this, puffed up with their tiny scrap of power.

'Richard Daniel,' I said, slowly and clearly. 'I was told to ask for him when I arrived.'

'He's tucked up in bed at this hour,' said the short man,

turning to face me. He had a pronounced squint in his left eye. 'You'll have to deal with us.'

'Then wake him.'

It was the wrong tone; he tightened his grip on my arm.

'You don't give orders here, you fucking – what *are* you, bastard of a Spanish whore?'

'I am Italian. But—'

I was pushed inside the door of a building with a fire burning in a small grate, filling the room with smoke.

'What's your name?' Squint asked. From the tail of my eye, I could see the other one bending to open my pack.

'I am Doctor Giordano Bruno of Nola,' I said, drawing myself up and attempting a show of dignity. 'Who are you?'

'I'm the law,' he said, stepping closer, a grim smile showing his remaining teeth.

'Well, I will need a name to give Queen Elizabeth's Secretary of State when I complain of how I was treated on arrival.'

Adam's Apple stopped rummaging and raised his head; an anxious glance flitted between them.

'Tell the Queen in person, why don't you,' said Squint, though he looked less sure of himself. 'We're only doing our job. You fetch up here in the dead of night, trying to sneak into the country, you couldn't look more like a bloody priest if you tried.'

'Then don't you think they would send someone less obvious? If I was trying to land unnoticed I would hardly come direct to the port.'

'You're bound to say that,' said Adam's Apple, crouching on the floor beside my bag. 'You'd be amazed what we find sewn in the linings of coats and hidden in false compartments. Priests' vestments, holy oil, saints' fingers – those are a favourite. Papal bulls, even.'

'There are no fingers in my belongings except yours,' I said. 'If you would just fetch Master Daniel, I could explain my business. Here—' I reached inside my doublet but before I could bring out the object I meant to show him, I felt a blow to the back of my knees; my legs crumpled and I crashed to the ground as the squinting man straddled me, pulling my left arm up behind my back.

'*Madonna porca* – what are you doing?' His weight mashed my face into the packed earth floor; I struggled to push him back enough that I could breathe.

'He was drawing a weapon,' the searcher told his colleague, who had leapt to his feet ready to join in.

'I have no weapon in my doublet,' I said, through clenched teeth. 'I only meant to show you something that might make you believe me.'

The man considered for a moment, before shifting off me, loosening his grip. 'Hands on the back of your head,' he barked, 'and stand slowly. I'll see for myself if you're armed.'

I folded my hands behind my head and rose to a crouch, my back to him. I could see them both from the corner of my eye, hovering, waiting for the smallest excuse to swing a fist at me, or worse. I began to turn; in one swift movement I bent, whipped out my dagger from the side of my boot and brought the point to the soft, pulsing skin between Squint's collarbones.

'I could cut his throat before you've even thought about drawing your knife,' I said to Adam's Apple, who froze, backing away, one hand to his belt. 'Now go and wake Master Daniel as I asked so we can all be on good terms again.' I flashed him a pleasant smile; he hesitated only briefly before lunging for the door. 'Why don't you put *your* hands on the back of your head?' I said to my captive. He glowered at me, but obeyed.

'You won't get away with this,' he muttered. 'We broke from Rome to keep people like you out.'

I let out a soft laugh. There was nothing to be gained from trying to debate with men who thought like this.

'What a curious race you are, you Englishmen,' I mused,

my dagger level at his neck. 'I never met a people who complained so bitterly about their country and at the same time believed themselves the superiors of every other nation in Europe, just because God saw fit to surround you by sea.'

'It's well known Italians are all sodomites,' he said, though quietly. I laughed again; I almost admired his defiance.

'Is that right? You must be nervous, then, the two of us alone here.' He took a step back, struggling to control his expression. I matched his movement. 'Careful you don't back yourself into a corner – who knows what I might do? And tell me – what of the Spanish?'

'Don't even get me started on the Spanish.' His squint intensified as his eyes grew animated. 'They want to invade us and rape our women, make us slaves to kiss the Pope's hole. You're all the bloody same.'

'It's a wonder you can tell us apart,' I said. 'You must enjoy your work here.' My hand was shaking with cold; I had to concentrate hard on keeping the knife steady so that I didn't cut him by mistake. I had no intention of causing more trouble than necessary.

He puffed himself up, despite the blade. 'My work is keeping England safe from the likes of you. And I am proud of that, yeah. Means I can look my son square in the eye when I go home, tell him he'll grow up a free Englishman.'

'Good for you. It must be quite a feat for you to look anyone square in the eye.'

I gave him a sympathetic smile, seeing how much he wanted to hit me. I was half-tempted to tell him of my own work, let him appreciate the irony, but I restrained myself; the truth about my journey was for Richard Daniel only. Squint subsided into silence, shooting me furious glances from the side of his good eye. I considered soliciting his view of the French, but I was too tired and the game had lost its amusement.

At length, the door opened and Adam's Apple returned in the company of a tall, broad man with black hair and beard who appeared to have dressed hastily, his doublet laced awry. He carried only a lantern, but I could see Adam's Apple had picked up a hefty stick on his way.

The newcomer held up the light and peered at me through the gloom.

'So this is the troublemaker. My man here thinks you may be a secret priest, or a spy. Do you have papers?'

'Richard Daniel?'

He nodded, impatient.

I lowered the knife, sheathed it again in my boot, and showed him my empty hands, before reaching slowly inside my doublet, where I had a pocket sewn inside the lining. I drew out a silver ring and held it out to him. He lifted it to the light, examined the emblem engraved on it, and nodded again.

'Come with me. I will take you somewhere we can talk. You look as if you need food and dry clothes.'

'What I need is a fast horse,' I said, my legs weak with relief. I couldn't help feeling a small triumph at the disappointment on the searchers' faces.

'We'll discuss it. For now you look barely able to sit upright on a chair. Your face is green. Come and eat.'

I realised the floor was swaying beneath me like the deck of the boat; I let my head hang slack and followed him, to the sound of muttered insults from the two men we left behind.

He led me uphill, along a narrow, curving street of pretty cottages, lime-washed fronts pearly in the moonlight, to a timber-framed building where the sign of The Mermaid creaked over the entrance. I followed him into an oak-panelled tap-room, empty now and silent, where stubs of candles burnt low in sconces and the embers of a fire glowed in the wide hearth. He ushered me to a stool by the fireplace and disappeared through a side door. I took off my wet cloak and huddled towards the fading warmth in the grate, catching a low exchange of voices from the passage outside.

At length Daniel returned, yawning as he drew up a chair alongside me.

'The maid will bring warm food and wine in a moment.'

'Is it your tavern?'

He shook his head. 'I have the use of a room when I'm on duty. Even the Queen's searchers must catch a few hours' sleep now and then.'

'I'm sorry to draw you from your bed,' I said, rubbing my hands over my face.

He waved the apology aside. 'It's what I'm here for. So you carry Nicholas Berden's signet ring. Why did he not come himself?'

I caught the edge of suspicion in his voice, and did not blame him for it. Berden was Sir Francis Walsingham's most trusted agent in Paris; his mark guaranteed the integrity of any document or person who carried it. But the traffic of secret letters between England and France was so fraught now, every network fearful of infiltration by double-dealers, that it was not beyond belief that I might be a Catholic conspirator who had killed Berden and stolen his ring to use as a passport.

'Berden intercepted a letter, two days ago. He wants it in the right hands without delay. He is well entrenched with the English Catholics in Paris now, they take him for one of their own – he could not leave for England in haste without arousing suspicion, and he did not want to pass it through the English embassy, because he fears it is not secure. So he asked me to deliver it myself.'

He gave me a long look, sizing me up. 'Why you?'

'There is no reason my name should mean anything to you,' I said, meeting his gaze straight on. 'But we serve the same master. You understand my meaning. I must leave for London as soon as possible.'

'This letter you carry speaks of some imminent threat, then?' He watched me carefully, doubt lingering in his eyes.

'That is for greater men than me to determine,' I said, with equal care. 'My instructions are only to put it into their hands. But Berden believes it cannot wait, and I trust his judgement.'

'He did not tell you what it contains?'

'No.' This was a lie, and I suspected he guessed it. We continued to watch one another, until we were interrupted by the arrival of a young girl, cap aslant, eyes blurry with sleep, carrying a jug of wine and a bowl of pottage. Daniel sat back in silence, arms folded, while I attempted to swallow some, my hollow stomach cramping at each mouthful until I began to relax and felt the warmth spread through my numb limbs.

'So you will give me a horse?' I asked, when I could speak again.

He pressed his lips together. 'We have post-horses ready to courier urgent messages to London. But if I may say so again, you do not look fit for the road. If your letter is so important, I should feel safer entrusting it to an experienced fast rider.' He passed a hand over his beard. 'Besides, as you have seen, your appearance attracts hostility from some Englishmen. You will have to stop for food and water along the way, and those you encounter will not give two shits for Nicholas Berden's ring. What then, if your message should be lost, and you the only one in possession of its content?'

'I know how to fight.'

'I don't doubt it. But you are only one man. And you are – forgive me, what age are you?' He frowned.

'Thirty-eight. Not quite in my dotage yet, sir.' I guessed him to be thirty at most, though likely less; sea-winds could age a man beyond his years. I leaned across the table and lowered my voice. 'I will see this letter delivered into Walsingham's hands myself, and no one will prevent me, I swear to it.' I spoke through my teeth, with more confidence than I felt; I knew that everything he said made good sense, better sense than my plan, but this letter was my passport back to Walsingham's favour and I had not come this far to entrust it to some messenger and lose the opportunity I hoped to gain by it.

Richard Daniel looked at me for a long while, weighing up my words, and finally nodded, a half-smile hovering at the corners of his mouth.

'I see you are a stubborn fellow,' he said. 'Well, then. I shall find you a horse while you change your clothes. But I must insist you take one of my men with you, for protection. He can carry food and water for your journey too.'

I hesitated, but saw this was the best deal I was likely to strike, and I had seventy miles to cover across the Sussex Weald and the Surrey hills; I would not reach London without Daniel's assistance. I nodded, drained the last of the wine and stood. 'Let us not lose any more time.'

'You do not wish to rest?'

'The enemies of England are not resting.'

He pursed his lips, as if he approved this answer. 'Then put on dry clothes, if you have them, and I will meet you outside in half an hour with everything you need.'

He clapped me on both shoulders and left. I stood and stretched my back, catching sight of myself in the darkened window. Thirty-eight, and looking haggard with it. Black hair, stiff with salt, curling past my collar; a four-day growth of beard; dark hollows under my eyes and below my cheekbones from lack of sleep, and lack of something else. Purpose? Peace of mind? These last few months in Paris had been melancholy. No wonder those two searchers at the port had suspected me of desperate measures; I looked like a vagrant – which was, I reflected, not so far from the truth. I had been living in exile for a decade now, one eye turned always over my shoulder, as a man with powerful enemies must. The Queen of England could put an end to that, if she chose, once I had proved my worth to her.

I undid my pack and pressed along the stitching of the secret compartment. I could feel the slight ridge of the leather wallet inside containing the documents. But the letter's contents were committed word for word to my memory, and its cipher too. Let it be stolen; the paper would be useless to anyone without the knowledge I alone carried in my head. I would bring it to the door of Queen Elizabeth's spymaster and lay it at his feet, to remind him – and his sovereign – what service I had done England in the past.

TWO

'Lady Sidney will see you now.'

The man who grudgingly addressed me wore a steward's chain of office, a black doublet with a blanched muslin ruff and soft leather indoor shoes; he kept his distance, halfway up the path to the entrance of the red-brick mansion on Seething Lane. I jerked my head up at his voice; we had been waiting half an hour already and I had almost given up hope of a response. I was not exactly surprised; if I had looked like a desperate man when I landed in Rye, it was fortunate I could not see myself in a glass by the time we reached London, on the evening of 29th July, our second day on the road. I must have had the appearance of a lunatic assassin: mad-eyed, unslept, unwashed, unshaven. The guards had had their weapons in my face before I had even dismounted. It fell to my taciturn companion, Richard Daniel's man, to step forward with his official messenger's livery and prove that I had not come to murder Queen Elizabeth's Secretary of State in his own home.

One of the guards held his halberd lowered towards me, the point a foot from my chest, while his colleague unlocked the tall iron gates and nodded me through.

'Just you,' the steward added. 'He can go to the servants'

quarters.' He motioned to Daniel's rider, a sturdy Sussex man who had spoken little on the journey, except to mutter occasional resentment at having his progress slowed by an incompetent foreigner half-asleep in the saddle.

Golden evening sun caught the many diamond-paned windows of Walsingham's town house. The light softened its mellow brick and glazed the tall twisted chimneys like sugar sculptures. It was a house that discreetly announced its owner's wealth. The Queen had rewarded her spymaster handsomely for his tireless service, as well she might; most of his spare funds were diverted into paying his intelligencers, since Elizabeth's Treasury was notoriously miserly with resources, preferring not to acknowledge the underground networks of information and interception that protected her realm just as surely as her warships and soldiers, with a great deal less expense.

'You will find Lady Sidney in a sombre cast of mind,' the steward informed me, with a pompous air, as the heavy oak door was drawn back by a young woman in a black dress and white coif. 'I hope it is no bad news you bring, as she should not be troubled further. Perhaps it would be best if I relayed your message to her?'

'My news is for Lady Sidney's ears alone,' I said. His moustache twitched with disapproval, but to my relief he did not press me further, only gestured for me to follow him along a panelled corridor hung with tapestries.

I had guessed Walsingham would not be here; he would likely be at court, at the Queen's right hand, or at his country house upriver in Barn Elms, near Mortlake. I had gambled on the house at Seething Lane, where his daughter lived, as the quickest way to him, wherever he was currently to be found. I barely knew Frances Sidney, as she now was, and was not at all convinced that my name would mean anything to her; I had only dared hope she might receive me for the sake of her husband, Sir Philip, who had been my closest friend when I lived in England a year ago. Sidney was now away in the Low Countries, fighting with Elizabeth's forces against the Spanish under the command of his uncle, the Earl of Leicester, but I hoped there would be a vicarious pleasure in hearing news of him from his wife.

I was ushered through a door at the end of the corridor into a wide receiving-room, flooded with light from its west-facing windows. Lady Sidney rose from a chair by the fireplace and held out a hand in greeting. She was as slight as I remembered, in a gown of dark grey satin, though it was barely eight months since her child was born. Her pale face was still almost a girl's, but as she approached I saw that her smile was brittle and shaky, her eyes puffy with traces of tears. The weight of my journey and lack of sleep seemed to land on me with one blow as I struggled with the import of her appearance. Why had the steward not warned me more clearly? Not Sidney, surely, it couldn't be? There would have been news in Paris – he was well connected among the English diplomats there – I would have heard, would I not? My knees buckled; I stumbled back a pace as I stared at her, open-mouthed, forgetting all etiquette, unable to form the words I dreaded to speak.

Frances Sidney darted forward and drew a stool from the hearth to offer me.

'Marston, fetch this man food and drink at once, can't you see the journey he's had?' She spoke sternly to the steward, but she was so young, barely twenty, and her command sounded like a child playing at running a household. The man gave a curt bow, but his look was not one of deference.

'With respect, madam – I am not sure I should leave you alone with this man. Your father—'

'My father trusts this man with his life,' she said hotly. 'Now go and do as I ask before our guest faints from hunger.' She turned to me, her hands outstretched. 'Bruno.' There was warmth in her smile, as well as sadness. 'I did not think we would see you again. You left for Paris last autumn, I thought?'

'I had good reason to return.' I took her hands in mine and kissed them briefly. 'But my lady, tell me . . .' I stood back and searched her face. 'I intrude on some private grief? I pray it is not . . .' I hesitated again '. . . news from the front?'

She gave a little gasp and pressed a hand to her mouth, then let out a brief, panicked laugh. 'Oh God, no – you thought . . . ? No, Philip is well, I am sorry to have alarmed you. If anything had happened to him, you would have heard my lament all the way from London Bridge. The whole city would be in mourning. But you are right that you find us a house of sorrow. We have suffered—' She broke off, pressing her lips together as if afraid of breaking a confidence. 'That is a story for another time. Sit – you look exhausted. Tell me in truth, though – I will wager you have not travelled from Paris without rest just to visit me.'

'I must see Sir Francis,' I said, lowering my voice. 'As soon as possible.' Lady Sidney's waiting woman stood by the window, her hands folded neatly behind her back, not observing her mistress, but nevertheless I felt I should be discreet, even in this household where secrets were a native language.

Frances nodded, her face solemn again. 'Plots?'

'What else?'

She pulled a lace handkerchief from her sleeve and worried its edges between her fingers. 'Father never sleeps now, you know – he says the Catholic plots are like the Hydra, you cut the head off one and a hundred more grow in its place. He is making himself ill with it, and still Her Majesty remains stubborn, she will not heed his advice nor pass the laws that would make her safer. She wills herself to believe that her subjects love her, and her cousin Scotch Mary would never scheme against her, despite all evidence. But you are in luck – he dines here tonight, or so he has promised. I expect he will be late, as always.' I caught a peevish edge to her voice;

the frustration of a girl sidelined by the men in her life for matters of state. 'Why cannot the damned Catholics see reason?' she burst out, so suddenly I flinched, as she brandished the kerchief in her fist towards me as if I were responsible. 'Can it be so hard for them, to worship as the Queen commands? Then they would keep their lands and titles, they would not be thrown in prison, they could cease their plotting to put that fat Scottish bitch on the throne, and innocent people wouldn't have to die for their schemes.'

I blinked, unsure how to respond; it was an unexpectedly vehement outburst, turning her face red and blotchy, her eyes bright with tears. I presumed she must be thinking of her husband, dug in with the garrison at Flushing.

'They would tell you, my lady,' I said gently, when it seemed the question was not merely rhetorical, 'that they fear the sin of heresy more than England's laws. They would say they had rather keep their immortal souls than their titles.'

'Oh, but they don't mind staining their souls with the sin of *murder*, which they say is no sin if it suits their purpose.' Her eyes blazed at me and for an instant I saw the image of her father, his anger and ruthlessness. 'Could they not just leave off their relics and rosaries and do as the law commands? It is the same God underneath it all, is it not?'

'My lady—' The maid by the window turned and stepped forward, her hands held out as if to break up a fight.

Lady Sidney sighed and seemed to subside. 'Don't worry, Alice – I will mind my speech. Besides, Doctor Bruno here is the last person in the world who would report me for heretical words, for he is a famous heretic himself. Is it not so?'

I inclined my head. 'Depends who you ask. It is not a reputation I sought.'

'But you are proud of it nonetheless,' she said, with a faint smile. 'Do not tell my father I said *bitch*. He dislikes profanity in women, even when it concerns Scotch Mary.' She regarded me with interest. 'You left the Roman Church, Bruno, did you not? Philip told me you were once in holy orders. But you ran away to become a good Protestant, at great risk to your life.'

She had half the story, at any rate; or perhaps Sidney had wanted the latter part to be true.

'I am not confident I can claim to be a good anything, my lady,' I said. 'I have been thrown in prison for heresy by both the Roman Church and the Calvinists. My ideas do not seem to please anyone who thinks their beliefs cannot be questioned.'

She looked at me, approving. 'Well, at least you are even-handed in the giving of offence. What God do you believe in, then? Philip says you have written that the universe is infinite, and full of other worlds. Then you think we are not the centre of God's creation? But how can that be? It would render the whole of Scripture uncertain. For if there are other worlds, did Christ become flesh for them too?' She jutted her chin upward, defying me to answer to her satisfaction.

I pushed my hair out of my eyes. 'My lady, I have barely slept in the past three days, and eaten less. I'm not sure I'm fit at present to dispute theology and cosmology with a mind as rapier-sharp as yours.'

Lady Sidney laughed, and her face again looked like a girl's. 'Neatly sidestepped, Bruno. Though you know you may say what you like in this house, we have no Inquisition here.'

No, I thought, though your father does not shy away from their methods when he wants to wring names from some terrified student priest in the name of England's freedom.

'You will want to wash and rest before Father arrives. Oh, but wait!' She clapped her hands together, as if an idea had just occurred – 'you must pay your respects to Elizabeth before you retire.'

I stared at her. 'The Queen is coming here?'

Her eyes danced with mischief at my amazement. 'I mean my daughter. Wait till you see her, she is the spit of Philip, with the same little tuft of hair at the front, you know? Named for her godmother, of course.' Her tone suggested this had not been her idea. 'We call her Lizzie.'

'Then the Queen has forgiven Philip?' Sidney was one of Elizabeth's favourite courtiers, and she could turn perverse and sulky as a child if he dared move out of her orbit; she had been staunchly set against him going to war, which had only made him more determined.

'Fortunately for us. She gave the baby the most generous gifts of jewels and coin. And now Philip is made Governor of Flushing, and makes us all proud with his bravery and service.' I caught it again, that tremble of her lip, a hint of sarcasm in the words. Frances Sidney was afraid; both her protectors, the men she loved, father and husband, courting death in the service of the Queen. 'Alice, fetch the baby,' she said, waving at the older maid.

As soon as the latch had clicked shut and we were left alone, Frances drew up a chair beside me and leaned in, her face grave.

'Now we may talk. Providence has sent you to my door today, I am sure of it.' I raised an eyebrow; she pressed on, her tone urgent: 'My dear friend and companion Clara was murdered by papists two days ago, most horribly.' Here she left a pause and looked at me with an expectant air.

'Are they arrested?'

'No.' She pressed her lips together and in her white face I saw the tremor of emotion, though I was not sure if it was grief or anger. I waited for her to say more but she seemed folded in on herself.

'But you know who they are?'

'Yes. Well – not exactly. It's complicated – my father has . . .' She let the thought fall away and examined me again, as if trying to read something in my face. 'Philip always said you had a talent for sniffing out a murderer.' I held up a hand to protest but she continued, 'I remember that business with the Queen's lady-in-waiting, three years ago, the autumn Philip and I married. My father was called away from the wedding feast because of it. It was you who discovered the truth of all that, was it not? Father said England owed you a great deal.'

Yes, and England has not yet seen fit to settle her debt, I thought of saying, but kept my counsel. 'Sir Francis spoke to you of that business?'

'Not *to* me, exactly.' She pushed her forefinger under the edge of her hood and scratched at her hair. 'But he often forgot I was there, and have ears, the way he has done all my life. I probably know more of what goes on than most of the Privy Council. I swear, if I turned traitor, I could sell enough secrets to sink the realm.' The flicker of a weary smile. 'I know all about that conspiracy in '83, and your part in stopping it. I'd wager you could find out what happened to Clara in no time, if my father would allow you.'

If he would *allow* me? The oddness of the phrase did not escape me, but I merely looked apologetic. 'My lady, my task is to deliver these letters to Sir Francis and see if he has any further use for me in his service. If not, I must return to my employment in Paris.' Though I hoped for Walsingham's patronage, I could not forget what I had been dragged into during that last investigation into the murder of a young woman, and the other deaths that had followed it. I was not in a hurry to involve myself in anything similar.

'I will *make* him find use for you,' she said, fixing me with a fierce glare. 'I can think of no one better to undertake this matter. Philip would wish you to help me, I am sure of it.' Her eyes glittered; invoking her husband was a clever tactic, and not one I could easily dismiss. I could see she had already made up her mind; it occurred to me that Frances had inherited all her father's stubbornness along with his name, and that both he and Sidney might have underestimated her.

Before I could quibble, the maid Alice returned carrying a chubby infant who was indeed a miniature of Sidney, swamped in a white lawn dress, her face rumpled and confused from being woken. The child looked around the company in bewilderment, then pushed her fat little fingers through her sparse hair, making it stick up at the front. I laughed in wonder, seeing an exact mirror of the gesture Sidney always made when tired or frustrated, and in that moment I felt a sharp pang for my absent friend.

Frances took the child from Alice's arms, smiling at my recognition. 'You see? The very image of him, is she not? Here.' She dumped the baby in my lap before I had a chance to object; immediately a small hand shot out and grabbed a fistful of my hair.

'You must miss him,' I said, through gritted teeth, wondering how tight I was supposed to hold the squirming bundle.

A shadow passed over Frances's face. 'None of this would have happened if he had been at home,' she said, a dark undertone to her voice. 'He would not have countenanced it.'

'None of what?' I asked, as I sensed I was supposed to.

'My lady,' Alice said, with a note of warning. The baby fixed her wide blue eyes on me, her expression uncertain, before opening her mouth and letting forth a furnace of furious noise. I jiggled her fruitlessly, sent a sidelong pleading glance to her mother, who watched me with that wry amusement women save for the spectacle of male incompetence; finally, in the absence of any other solution, I swung the child above my head and held her there. The sudden movement shocked her into silence; I made a face at her, in the air, and after a moment of suspicion she chuckled and squeaked in a manner that seemed to signify approval.

'You are a natural, Bruno,' Frances said, as if I had passed a test. 'Now when you next write to Philip, you can tell him you have held his daughter in your arms. Which is more than he has ever done. But' – her eyes lit up – 'next month, God willing, she and I sail for Flushing to join him. The Earl of Leicester himself is making the arrangements.'

'Your father will let you?' I lowered the infant, who shrieked immediately to repeat the game, confirming my theory that all children are tyrants, and tyrants merely children who have never been refused.

Frances's face darkened. 'He will not dare oppose Sir Philip and the Earl together. Besides, my husband is my master, not my father.'

I nodded quickly. In the ordinary course of events, this would be true. A woman's duty passed to her husband on her marriage, but theirs was not an ordinary situation; Walsingham had quietly dispatched thousands of pounds of Sidney's debts on the joining of the two families, and given the young couple this fine house to live in, since Sidney's youthful extravagance meant he could not afford to provide a home for his wife and daughter. I had always supposed there was little question about who was master in this household. Sidney's desire to go to war had been partly prompted by the need to escape the weight of being beholden to his father-in-law.

'But if this business with Clara is not resolved,' Frances continued, biting at the edge of her thumb, 'my father may fear further danger and hesitate to let me travel alone.' She gave me a long look, until she was certain I understood what was at stake, and the part she wanted me to play. This, I supposed, was my cue to ask why the death of her companion should prevent her from travelling to the Low Countries – I guessed it must be to do with the 'complications' she had hinted at surrounding the girl's murder – but before I could form the question, the steward Marston burst through the door carrying a silver jug and a linen towel, his face flushed with his news.

'My lady, Sir Francis has arrived early, with Thomas Phelippes.' He glanced at me, exaggerating his surprise at seeing me holding the baby aloft. 'Should I show this man out while you greet your father? He has the dust of the road on him still.'

'Certainly not. My father is not squeamish about a bit of sweat, Marston. He will be almost as delighted to see Bruno as he is to see Lizzie.' She turned to me. 'He dotes on that child. If the Queen of Scots ever saw the doe-eyed grandfather inventing rhymes, singing nursery ditties, braying like a donkey and I don't know what other nonsense, she would never fear him again.'

'You had better watch that the Catholics don't recruit the baby to wheedle her way past his defences,' I said, smiling.

Marston cut me a disapproving look. I could not picture Master Secretary's dour, terse expression softening to impersonate animals, though I had glimpsed Walsingham's more human side now and again when I was last in his service. It was not an aspect of his character he showed often; he wished to be perceived as unbending in his devotion to the security of the realm. Perhaps he needed to believe it himself. Above me, the baby gurgled and released a spool of spittle on to my forehead.

'Where is my little kitten?' called that familiar dry voice from the corridor, to the beat of quick footsteps, and here he was, striding across the chamber, dressed head to foot in black as always, his hair greyer under the close-fitting skullcap, his beard too, and his face thinner than when I had last seen him, nearly a year ago. He stopped in his tracks halfway across the room and a broad smile creased his long face.

'Good God in Heaven. Two people I never thought to see in an embrace.' He gave his daughter a perfunctory pat on the shoulder on his way past, but his attention was all for the baby, who shrieked in delighted recognition and strained out of my arms towards him. 'Well, well. Giordano Bruno. So you have come hotfoot all this way from Paris to see the newest shoot of the Walsingham tree, eh?'

'She's a Sidney,' Frances said, her voice tight. I noticed how she hung back; her father managed to command all the space in the room, though he was not a tall or broad man. He laughed and held out his arms for the child; I passed her over gladly.

'What say you, Bruno?' He pinched the baby's cheek while she tugged at his beard and burbled. 'She has the Walsingham shrewd eye, does she not, and witness the firm set of her jaw? None of your aristocratic foppishness in this little chin, is there, my dove?'

I stood, straightened my clothes, and effected a bow, though he was so absorbed in his granddaughter, he would not have noticed if I had pulled down my breeches.

'She combines the perfection of all the virtues of her illustrious forebears on both sides, Your Honour.'

'I see you have been perfecting the empty flattery that passes for diplomacy at the French court,' he said, giving me a sidelong glance at last. 'For a more honest answer I shall have to seek the opinion of Master Phelippes. Thomas, what say you – is my granddaughter a Walsingham through and through?'

The man standing patiently in the doorway now stepped forward. Thomas Phelippes, Walsingham's most trusted assistant and master cryptographer, was unremarkable in appearance – early thirties, thinning sandy hair, long face, his cheeks pitted with smallpox scars – but his looks belied a singular disposition. Phelippes boasted a phenomenal memory, a source of great fascination and envy to me, since it appeared to be the result of a natural gift rather than determined study – he had merely to glance over a cipher once and could not only commit it to mind but analyse and unpick it in the same instant. But he also had a way of not meeting your eye, and an almost comical resistance to the finer points of tact and social niceties. If Phelippes thought you were an idiot or your breath smelled, he would tell you outright, though without malice, finding no need for a polite falsehood. I found his honesty refreshing, if occasionally disconcerting, and liked him, though I sensed that being liked by me or anyone else made no difference to him either way. He put his head on one side and considered the baby.

'She has enough semblance of the Sidney family to allow for a reasonable degree of certainty about her paternity,' he said, matter-of-factly. Lady Sidney made a little noise of indignation. 'Theories of generation differ as to whether the female can imprint characteristics on the growing infant, or is merely a receptacle for the male seed, and as yet there is no conclusive evidence either way. This one is so young it is presently impossible to gauge the quality of her mind. Being female one would naturally expect it to be weaker, so if you are asking whether you can expect to see echoes of your own traits in her, Your Honour, you will probably be disappointed. But this is not really my field of expertise,' he added, with a shrug.

Walsingham chuckled, largely at his daughter's bunched fists and tight expression. 'Well, Frances, there you have it. You will want to occupy yourself with the child and supper, I expect,' he said, handing the baby back to her. 'I will speak with Bruno in my study. Call us when the food is ready.'

Lady Sidney watched us to the door, eyes dark with mute rebellion. I guessed she was biding her time before suggesting my involvement in the business of her companion to her father, and I hoped I might pre-empt her request.

Though Walsingham had given the Seething Lane house over to Sidney and his wife, he had taken care to make clear that the arrangement was temporary; all the furnishings remained Walsingham's own, and he had kept his large, book-lined study at the back of the house for use when he was in town. Now he settled himself comfortably behind his desk opposite the fireplace, cast an eye over a pile of letters, moved them to one side and motioned me to a seat. Phelippes took his place at a second desk set against the back wall and bent his head over a leather folder of papers as if no one else were present.

'So. Urgent news from Paris, I presume.' Walsingham steepled his fingers and watched me.

I reached into my pack and passed the wallet containing the letters across the desk to him. He turned it carefully between his fingers but did not open it immediately. 'Give me the meat of it. Thomas will transcribe it later.'

'Nicholas Berden intercepted a letter from Charles Paget to Mary Stuart, written four days ago. There is an English priest arrived in Paris this last fortnight disguised as a soldier – one Father John Ballard, claims he is part of a well-advanced plot to murder Queen Elizabeth and spring Mary from her prison to take the throne. Paget took him last week to the Spanish ambassador, where this Ballard assured them both that English Catholics at strategic points across the land have pledged to rise up and assist an invading army, if King Philip of Spain will commit troops and money. They believe the timing is apt, with so many of England's fighting men away in the Low Countries.' I paused for breath, amazed to see a wide smile spread slowly across Master Secretary's face.

'Well, this is excellent news, Thomas, is it not?' He appeared delighted.

'We could not have hoped for better,' Phelippes replied, without looking up from his papers.

I stared at Walsingham, thrown by his reaction.

'Forgive me, Your Honour, but Berden believes this intelligence to be credible. That is why he sent me with all speed – he dared not trust the diplomatic courier.'

'I have no doubt that Berden's intelligence is entirely accurate. He is one of my best men. This is the very letter I have waited for – and from Paget too, the horse's mouth.' He gave me a knowing nod, his eyes alight with anticipation. I grimaced. Charles Paget was the self-appointed leader of the English Catholic exiles in Paris; it was he who coordinated links between the extremist Catholic League in France, led by the Duke of Guise, and the English conspirators who wanted to replace Queen Elizabeth with her cousin. He had been behind the plot in '83, and my encounter with him in Paris had almost cost me my life before Christmas. Walsingham tapped the letter, impatient. 'What more?'

'Ballard says he has a band of devout men in London committed to carrying out the execution of Queen Elizabeth. That is the term they use to absolve themselves of regicide.'

'Good. Names?'

'Not set down in writing. But Ballard returns to London imminently to further his preparations. Ambassador Mendoza promised he would send one of his men here directly – a Jesuit priest – to bring the conspirators funds, though he has not yet gone so far as to commit Spain to military support. Paget guesses that this Jesuit's task is to sound out their seriousness and report back to Mendoza, though he tells Mary to take heart, he is sure Spain will champion her cause.'

'Marvellous. I look forward to hearing more of their progress.' Walsingham sat back in his chair and folded his hands together, smiling to himself, showing surprisingly white teeth.

'You do not seem overly concerned,' I remarked. In truth, I could not help feeling resentful at the reception of my news; I had expected a mix of shock and gratitude, and a flurry of activity as Walsingham rushed to apprehend the plotters and warn the Queen, quietly mentioning my name as the bearer of this timely intervention. Instead, even by Master Secretary's standards, this reaction seemed unusually phlegmatic.

'Ah, Bruno. Do not think I don't appreciate the efforts you have made to bring me this news – I have been waiting for it. We've been monitoring John Ballard for some time, waiting for his plans to bear fruit. And now that the game begins . . .' he paused, pulling at the point of his beard '. . . all we have worked for stands on a knife-edge. One false step could mar everything. You see?'

'I'm afraid I don't. I had not thought it was a game.' I looked across to Phelippes for a plainer explanation, but his eyes remained fixed on his scratching nib.

Walsingham sighed. 'Do you know how difficult it is to kill a queen, Bruno?'

'I have never tried.'

'Well, I have been trying for years, believe me. And now the means is almost at my fingertips. We cannot afford to fail this time.'

I watched him while his meaning gradually took shape. 'You mean the Queen of Scots.' I let my breath out slowly and felt a tremble. 'You want her dead.'

'That vixen.' He pushed his chair back abruptly and strode to the window with his back to me, but I could see the suppressed fury in the set of his shoulders. 'Every damnable conspiracy against the state and the Queen of England's person these last twenty years – who is at the heart of it? That conniving Scottish witch. There she sits like a poisonous spider at the heart of her web, under house arrest, embroidering tapestries, complaining she is not kept in regal luxury. She protests her love for her cousin Elizabeth, while her words and letters embroider plots of murder and insurrection for her devoted followers in France. She wraps every gaoler I appoint around her finger with her simpering and her flirtations. It must *end*, Bruno, do you understand?' He turned back to me, thumped his fist once on the wood panelling to make his point. 'While she lives, the Protestant Church in England will never be secure. Her name is a banner to rally every angry young man who believes his fortunes would be better if the clocks could be turned backwards to a golden England of yesteryear, before the break with Rome. An England that exists only in his imagination, but no matter – he will plunge the country into ruin to recover it.'

'But the Queen of Scots cannot be held responsible for what impetuous men do in her name, surely?'

Walsingham sank into the window seat as if the outburst had exhausted him, and I saw in his strained look why his daughter worried for his health. 'Explain it to him, Thomas.'

Phelippes lifted his head and glanced at me briefly before shifting his gaze to the bookshelves.

'Actually, she can now – Master Secretary has passed legislation this year to say exactly that. Mary Stuart is the granddaughter of the eighth King Henry's sister,' he said, in his odd, flat voice. 'So for those English Catholics who hold that Henry's divorce was not sanctioned by the Roman church and that his second marriage to the Queen's mother Anne Boleyn cannot therefore be legitimate, Mary Stuart is the only true, Catholic heir by Tudor blood to the English throne. They maintain that Queen Elizabeth is a bastard.'

'I know all this.' I tried to conceal my impatience, but Phelippes had a manner of explaining that addressed his listener as if they were a slow child. 'I was the one intercepting the letters from Mary's supporters through the French embassy three years ago, the last time they tried a plot like this. But there was no evidence that Mary had given the conspiracy her approval.'

'You understand the challenge, then,' Walsingham said, his voice soft. I looked at him; his gaze did not waver.

'You mean to entice her into betraying herself.'

'The new law states that anyone who stands to benefit from the Queen's murder is guilty of treason, even if they do not commit the deed with their own hand.'

'Then – this plan of Ballard's, that Paget mentions – it's a trick?'

'Oh, the plot is real enough.' Walsingham stood, with evident effort, and returned to his desk, taking a small sip from his glass. 'The invasion plans too, quite possibly, though

I suspect Philip of Spain will think twice before reaching into his coffers again for a rabble of hot-headed Englishmen – he has heard all this before, remember, with the Throckmorton business in '83?'

I nodded; my part in that was not an experience I would forget in a hurry.

'But none of this worries you. You appear to have it all under control, so I see I have had a wasted journey.' I heard the pique in my voice but was too tired to disguise it. As so often with Walsingham, I had the sensation of playing a hand of cards without being told the rules of the game. I wondered if Nicholas Berden knew the information he had risked so much to procure was already familiar to Walsingham, or if he too was being kept in the dark.

'Far from it, my dear Bruno. It is never a waste to see old friends.' He moved around the side of the desk and put an awkward arm around my shoulder, patting it briefly. A moment later he moved away – he was not a demonstrative man – and covered his embarrassment with a cough. 'In fact, since you are here, a thought occurs to me – but you must allow me a pause while it takes shape. Thomas' – he clicked his fingers in Phelippes's direction – 'decipher that letter as quickly as you can – I want to know about this Spanish Jesuit Mendoza is sending. In the meantime, Bruno, you must wash, and eat, and we will talk further.'

He handed me my pack and showed me to the door, patting my shoulder again for reassurance. As it closed behind me I heard Phelippes say, quite clearly, 'You cannot seriously propose the Italian?'

I waited, keeping as still as possible.

'Why not?' Walsingham replied, his tone buoyant. 'He is Catholic, or was. He can parrot their incantations without missing a word. It is the perfect solution.'

'I will tell you why not,' Phelippes said. 'Because they will kill him.'

I strained to hear more, but at the sound of footsteps I glanced up to see the steward, Marston, approaching from the other end of the corridor; I smiled and stepped towards him, trying not to look as if I had been eavesdropping. I would have to wait for the details of Walsingham's plan for my impending death.

THREE

'You will wish to leave us now, my dear.' Walsingham wiped his fingers on a linen cloth, pushed away his plate and directed a meaningful look at his daughter. 'No doubt the child needs your attention.'

Candles burned low in their sconces, a warm light touching the curves of Venetian glass and the edges of silver platters, softening our faces and the old wood of the panelling. The table was littered with the debris of a fine meal – a soup of asparagus, capons in redcurrant sauce, a custard tart with almonds and cream, sheep's cheese and soft dark bread. As with the furnishings of the house, the food had been plain, but of excellent quality. Though I had rested for an hour before supper, I could feel myself dragged by my full belly towards sleep, and hoped I might be excused before anyone – Lady Sidney or her father – could draw me into their schemes. In my somnolent state I would likely agree to anything if it would grant me an early night. I was aware that my hosts had barely touched the jug of excellent Rhenish which had been generously poured for me, and Phelippes did not drink wine at all, preferring to concentrate on consuming food methodically, one dish at a time, which he arranged on his plate in geometric patterns and ate without speaking.

Frances Sidney returned Walsingham's look with cool resistance. 'She is asleep, and her nurse is with her. I wish to speak to you, Father, in this company, on an important matter. You understand me.'

Walsingham sighed, and made a minute gesture with his head to the serving boys clearing the table. He beckoned Marston, who stood silently in the corner by the door as he had throughout the meal, alert to his master's needs; Walsingham whispered to him and the steward nodded. When the last dishes had been removed, Marston brought fresh candles and a new jug of wine, before discreetly withdrawing. The door closed softly behind him.

'I know what you are going to ask me, Frances.' Walsingham's eyes rested briefly on me, and there was a warning in his tone.

'He is the man to do it,' she said, her voice rising; she nodded at me across the table as she worked her linen cloth between her fingers, twisting and untwisting it. When Walsingham said nothing, she sat up straighter. 'You know he is. Let him find out the truth – he has done it before.'

'Frances—' Walsingham laid both hands flat on the table.

'What – because it might interfere with your plan? It's your fault she's dead!'

She threw down her cloth and glared at her father; I glanced from one to the other and was surprised to see him lower his eyes, his expression pained.

'That is not a reasonable conclusion,' Phelippes said mildly, concentrating on folding his napkin into a neat square, the corners precisely aligned. 'There are a number of factors that contributed—'

'Oh, shut up, Thomas.' Frances rounded on him. 'What would you know? You have no more feeling than a clockwork machine.'

He raised his head at this and blinked rapidly, before returning his gaze to his task.

Walsingham watched his daughter in the flickering light.

'Do not vent your anger on Thomas, my dear. This was not his doing.'

'How do you know? Maybe one of his letters gave her away.'

'Very unlikely, Lady Sidney,' Phelippes said. 'My forgeries are excellent and have never yet been detected. It is much more probable that Clara Poole was careless. I had doubts about her ability to perpetrate a deception at that level of sophistication. She was too much at the mercy of her emotions.'

'Oh, you had *doubts*? Then why did you let him send her?' She pointed a trembling finger at her father.

'Lower your voice, Daughter.' Walsingham's tone had grown sharp, the indulgence gone. 'What is it you want?'

'You know already.' She swivelled in her chair to look at me. 'Let Bruno investigate. He will tell you who killed her and whether your precious *operation* is compromised.' Her voice was tight with emotion; when she dropped her gaze I saw tears shining on her lashes. 'Then, once we know, you can tear the bastard's insides out while he's still alive to watch them drop in the flames, and I will be in the front row, applauding.'

There was little that could shock Walsingham, but I saw him flinch at her words.

'Would someone mind explaining—' I began.

'Oh, my father will tell you,' Frances said, winding the napkin around her knuckles. 'He can explain how his ward Clara Poole ended up in a whore's graveyard south of the river with her face smashed up. Oh, I see you look startled, Father – did you not realise I had heard you discuss that detail with Thomas? Perhaps you forgot I was there, as usual.' She poured herself a glass of wine and drank a deep draught; I saw how her hand shook.

Walsingham brushed down his doublet, took a moment to compose himself, and raised his eyes to fix me across the table with his steady gaze.

'These men Paget mentions in his letter,' he said, eventually. 'A band of devout Catholics sworn to carry out the Pope's death sentence on Queen Elizabeth. We know who they are.'

'Then – can you not arrest them?' I asked.

'I've been waiting for them to give us more conclusive evidence,' he said evenly.

I nodded, understanding. 'You want to use them as bait, to catch a bigger prize.'

Walsingham fetched up a faint smile, but it did not touch his eyes. 'You always were perceptive. They do this in the name of the Queen of Scots, as you know. Part of their plan is to break her from her prison at Chartley and set her on the throne. I have enough in their letters alone to hang and quarter every last one of them. What I lacked was a firm response from her hand.'

'So you mean to let this plot unfold until she gives it her explicit support in writing?'

'The instant she signs her name to any approval she will have committed high treason. The only possible sentence under the terms of my new Act for the Queen's Safety will be execution.'

Frances snorted. 'He thinks Queen Elizabeth will simply agree to that. Chop the head off a fellow queen, her own cousin. I tell you, Father – I know I have only met Her Majesty a handful of times, and you converse with her every day, but I am certain of this – she will not sign that death sentence, no matter how many letters you show her in Mary's hand. She dare not. No matter how many people you consider expendable in the process.'

'My daughter sometimes believes she sits on the Privy Council,' Walsingham said drily.

'I would talk more sense than half the blustering old men there,' Frances shot back. 'If the Privy Council and the Parliament were all women, we'd have less money wasted on war and twice as much done.'

Walsingham caught my eye with a half-smile; I tried to picture Elizabeth Tudor seeking the counsel of other women on matters of state. An unlikely scenario; it was well known she commanded most of her courtiers to leave their wives at home in the country so she did not have to share their attention.

'He had my companion, Clara Poole, working for him in this business of Babington,' Frances said to me, tilting her head towards her father. 'It ended badly for her, as you heard. He needs to know why, I want justice for her, and you want employment, so you see, we all want the same thing.'

'Who is Babington?'

Walsingham lifted his wine glass and studied it without drinking. 'The ringleader of this little band of would-be assassins is a young blood by the name of Anthony Babington. Catholic, twenty-five, made extremely wealthy by the death of his father last year. Studied in Paris not long ago, remains friendly with known conspirators there, including Mary's agents. A wife and infant daughter at the family seat in Derbyshire, but spends all his time in London now, throwing himself into the Catholic cause – more out of desire for adventure than ardent faith, I think, but he met Mary Stuart as a youth and has romantic notions of her suffering and her rightful claims.' He paused, sucked in his cheeks, as if weighing how much more to say. 'I needed someone on the inside to monitor Babington and his friends without drawing suspicion – it proved difficult to get any of my trusted men close enough. Babington is hot-headed but he is not a fool, and he is understandably cautious about this business. Clara Poole is – *was* – a beautiful young woman. It seemed an obvious solution.' He lowered his eyes and looked at the glass turning between his hands, avoiding his daughter's sharp stare.

'She was beautiful until they broke her face,' Frances said, through her teeth. She turned to me, her tone softer. 'I've known Clara since I was ten years old. She was four years older than me, and my father took her and her brother in when they were orphaned. She was my companion for four years until she married at eighteen, but she was widowed a year ago and returned to my household, since her husband had left her without means. I had thought she would work as governess to my daughter when Lizzie was old enough to take lessons. She knew French and could draw beautifully.' Her voice wavered, and she returned to twisting the napkin between her fingers.

'Clara's half-brother, Robin, has been in my service for some time,' Walsingham said. 'The Catholics trust him – he has helped import books and relics for them in the past, and served time in prison for it, without betraying that he was my man. They do not know the extent of his work for me – they think he is true to their cause and believe he spies for them. It was an easy matter to have Clara introduced to Babington's circle. I thought her charms might open doors closed to the men in my employ, and I was not deceived in that.'

'You sent her – forgive me – to seduce him?' I stared at Walsingham, thinking of the court in Paris, and the bevy of beautiful, accomplished young women trained by Catherine de Medici, the Queen Mother, to use their wiles in spying on the King's enemies; I had personal experience of their determination. I had imagined Master Secretary, whose morality leaned towards the puritanical, to be above such methods. Clearly I had been mistaken.

'Like a whoremaster,' Frances said, pointedly.

'Remember to whom you speak, Daughter.' Walsingham's tone was stern, but he looked uncomfortable. 'Clara was willing to be of service,' he added, to me. 'We must conclude that certain things are no sin when they are done to save the life of an anointed sovereign, or to protect the state. We must trust that God sees the greater picture.'

'Just as He does when my father turns the handle of the rack to make a priest confess to treason,' Frances said, with a flash of triumph in her eyes. I sensed that she enjoyed sparring with her father, and that Clara Poole's death had given her a licence to do so.

'Would you have them move freely through the realm instead?' Walsingham turned to her, his voice wound tight; her provocation was succeeding. 'If you had seen what I have seen, young lady – you were but four years old when—'

Frances rolled her eyes. 'When we were barricaded inside the English embassy in Paris on Saint Bartholomew's night, yes, yes, I have heard this story before, Father. All my life, in fact.' She sounded like a sullen child.

'So that you never take it for granted.' Walsingham leaned back in his chair. I could see that he was forcing himself not to lose his temper. 'We were a hair's breadth from being massacred along with all the other Protestants in Paris that night. And if you think the same could not happen in London if Catholic forces invade, you are nothing but a silly girl and not worthy to carry your husband's name or mine. Sacrifices must be made. Philip knows that. So did Clara. Only you seem to think the world should fall into your lap without cost, and perhaps the blame for that rests with me, and the way I have spoiled you.'

Frances coloured as if she had been slapped. Walsingham breathed out again and clasped his hands, his watchful gaze settling on me.

'You have risked your life before in England's service, Bruno,' he said, quietly. 'Would you do so again?'

I shifted in my seat. 'Your Honour, you know I am willing to offer what skills I have to secure England's freedom, be assured of it. But . . .' I hesitated, spread my hands. 'I am a philosopher. I'm not sure I am equipped for the task you mention. Besides, I have a teaching job in Paris, I am expected back—'

At this, Walsingham chuckled. 'Ah, yes. The Collège de Cambrai. And how does that suit you?'

'It's . . .' I scratched the back of my neck. It was impossible to guess quite how much Walsingham knew. 'A prestigious position. King Henri himself arranged it for me.'

'To keep you away from court after that episode last Christmas,' he said, without missing a beat. 'And does it satisfy your taste for adventure – arguing with undergraduates?'

'It gives me an income, Your Honour.' I could not quite meet his eye.

'Hmm. Thomas?'

Phelippes looked up and blinked. 'Last month you gave a lecture in which you spoke against Aristotle and the ensuing debate ended in a mass brawl which had to be broken up by the city authorities. One student was left with a cracked jaw and another with a dagger wound. They made a formal complaint. You received an official warning from the university. Since then, you have been corresponding with Professor Alberico Gentili at the University of Wittenberg, and making secret plans to travel there.' He recited this as if reading from an official report.

I looked at him; it was not even worth asking how he knew all this. It was true that I had intended to move on to Wittenberg at the end of the summer, but I had told no one.

'Gentili works for me,' Walsingham said, by way of explanation. 'I take an interest in your movements, Bruno – that should not surprise you. Once a man has been in my employ, he becomes part of a family, so to speak. Tell me honestly – would you not rather return to the service of the Queen of England, and earn her gratitude?'

Damn him. I watched him watching me; he knew so precisely how to find a man's weakness. Queen Elizabeth's patronage would be a prize more valuable than any other monarch's, since in England I had greater freedom to publish my controversial books than anywhere else in Europe. But if she had not offered it the last time I was here, after the service I had done her, I was not convinced that finding another killer would persuade her this time. I wondered if the Queen even knew of Walsingham's intricate scheme to bring her cousin Mary to the block. Somehow I doubted she would approve it.

'Her Majesty was much taken with your writing,' he continued, pushing the decanter of wine down the table towards me. 'She would be intrigued to read more, I think. I could certainly arrange that.'

I ran my tongue around my teeth to find my mouth dry. 'I had hoped to finish a new book in Wittenberg this summer,' I said, and heard how feeble the excuse sounded. 'Gentili has offered—'

'He has offered you a place there, I know. You could still take it up in the autumn, if you would spend a few weeks here and do me this one favour. I will write to Gentili – he will understand.'

I took a long drink of Walsingham's good wine, tilting the glass so that the liquid glowed ruby in the candlelight and the Murano crystal shimmered as if it were made of nothing but air. Finally I raised my head and met his eye. I had run out of excuses.

'What would you have me do?'

FOUR

Lady Sidney gave a little squeal of delight and sat back in her chair, clasping her hands together. Walsingham continued to study me, his face grave. At length, he turned to his daughter.

'You have your wish, Frances. Now you must leave this in my hands, the details are not for your ears. And make no mention of Bruno's coming here in your letters to Philip, unless you want to compromise the whole business.'

'I am not a fool, Father.' Her lip curled with scorn as she pushed her chair back. 'Do you forget I was born to double-dealing?' She stood and turned to me, bobbing a brief curtsy. 'Give you good night, Bruno. And thank you. I am more grateful than you can know.'

Born to double-dealing, I thought, as the door clicked shut behind her. It was a phrase I had heard before; Walsingham had used it of Charles Paget, whose father, Lord Paget, had been spymaster to Queen Elizabeth's father, the last King Henry. What must it be, to grow up in a world where counterfeiting is a language you learn from childhood, and everyone you know wears at least two faces? I had developed a grudging respect for Paget in my encounters with him, though I knew he would have let me die without a second thought if it had suited him.

'Bruno? Are you with us?'

I shook myself free of memories and focused on Walsingham at the other end of the table. I noticed again how thin his face had grown.

'At your service, Your Honour. You need to know who killed Clara Poole. I suppose you assume it was this Babington or one of his associates?'

He rubbed a hand across his beard and paused before answering.

'I need more than that. Clara was my most trusted source on the inside of that plot. She delivered intelligence reliably on their intentions – it was how I could be sure the business was not advancing beyond my ability to control it. You can imagine how carefully this must be balanced.'

I nodded. No wonder he looked as if he didn't sleep. It was one thing to allow an assassination plot to unfold in order to entrap Mary Stuart in an act of treason; quite another if that plot should succeed because he failed to monitor it closely enough. 'Does the Queen know of this Babington conspiracy?'

'No.' His face darkened. 'And she will have no need to, until it is all set down on paper and her royal cousin on trial, if our skill and God's Providence serve. I have one other reporting to me from among the conspirators, but lately I am not certain his loyalty is wholly mine. I need someone' – he raised a forefinger and levelled it at me – 'to join Babington and his friends. Find out why Clara was killed. I have no doubt that one among them suspected her – but I need to know if all were behind her murder, or one took it upon himself to act alone, and how much each one knows. If they think she betrayed their plot, they may change tactics, or put it off until a later date, and that we cannot afford. I don't have that kind of time.' He broke off and reached for his glass, coughing as he swallowed.

'Your Honour –' I leaned forward, alarmed – 'are you ill? I hope you don't mean—'

'Look at me, Bruno.' He slumped back in his chair, drained. 'The spirit is willing, but the flesh is weak. So damnably weak, and growing weaker by the day. If any apothecary could make me a philtre that would wind the clock back ten years, I would sell everything I own to buy it.' A ghost of a smile flickered over his lips. He examined the backs of his hands and did not meet my eye. 'I have given the best of my energies to keep this realm safe, free and Protestant, and I will do so until my last breath, but I can't go on like this forever. I must and *will* see the Queen of Scots brought to the block as my last act of service to Elizabeth.' One hand curled into a fist. 'With her death, England's enemies will be scattered. Then I could close my eyes with a degree of peace.'

They would soon regroup, I thought. Instead I said, 'Your Honour, I hope and pray these fears are premature. You are only—' I stopped to calculate his age. Barely old enough to be my father, though in some ways I had come to think of him in that role.

'This is my fifty-sixth summer, Bruno.' He sat up straighter, toying with the stem of his glass.

'Well, then. Unless a physician has told you otherwise, there is no reason to think you will not go on serving the realm for another three decades.' I tried to sound buoyant, but his eyes clouded.

'I need no physician to tell me what I feel in here.' He struck his chest. 'But enough self-pity. I tell you only so that you understand the urgency. I must know why Clara Poole was killed, and what Babington will do next. This Jesuit priest Mendoza is sending to join the conspirators . . .'

'What of him?'

'You will be him.'

I had guessed this was where he was tending. I closed my eyes to escape his intense stare.

'Your Honour, it's impossible that I could pass myself off as this man without suspicion. I am known in London—'

'Not as well as you think,' he cut in. He had clearly anticipated this objection. 'It is almost a year since you were last here. You were known at the French embassy when you lodged there, I grant, but since Ambassador Castelnau was recalled to Paris, his household staff returned with him and it's not as if the new ambassador has your portrait hanging over the mantel. There are few Londoners who could identify you if they passed you in the street.'

'I am known by some at court,' I said feebly.

'Your name is known in select circles, perhaps. But you will not be going by your own name, and it is no great work to change your appearance. Besides, you will be nowhere near the court – Babington's group hide themselves in taverns and brothels, and meet in lodging houses. There is no reason anyone should connect this Spanish Jesuit with the Italian scholar Giordano Bruno, if you remember not to provoke arguments about Aristotle.'

I noted the glint of humour in his eye.

'We don't know anything about this Jesuit. He could be seventy years old. He could be famous for having one leg. Ballard might have met him already in Paris, for God's sake – they would know I was an imposter the minute I walked through the door.'

Walsingham straightened, a knowing smile creasing his face. 'I doubt Mendoza would send a man of seventy, or one hampered by the loss of a leg, but these are matters we can check. There's no evidence from Paget's letter that either he or Ballard have met this man. There is only one person among the conspirators who would know that you are an imposter.'

'Then the plan is over before it is begun, if one of them knows me. Who?'

'You'll enjoy this. The only associate of the Babington group who will know you're not the priest is Master Gilbert Gifford.'

'Gifford?' I stared at him, incredulous. I had encountered Gifford in Paris the previous autumn; a gawky, anxious youth whose father had been imprisoned for refusing to recant his Catholic faith, and who harboured romantic notions of overthrowing Elizabeth and her government, like every other angry young Englishman who fetched up in France. 'I warned you about him before Christmas. He was planning to return to England carrying secret letters for Mary Stuart from Paget and his circle in Paris.'

'And thanks to your warning, he was intercepted by Richard Daniel in Rye,' Walsingham said, looking pleased with himself. 'Daniel rode to London to bring the boy to me in person. With a few judicious incentives, young Gifford was persuaded to see that his best interests lay with England's cause and not Mary Stuart's.'

'You didn't torture him?' The thought of Walsingham's methods of persuasion turned my gut cold; I had no great affection for Gilbert Gifford, but he had struck me as foolish and easily manipulated, rather than dangerous.

Walsingham gave me a reproving look. 'Good God, no. I am not a monster, whatever my daughter may think. Torture a creature like Gifford? I had as well take a sword to a kitten. No – he had enough on him when he arrived in Rye for me to throw him in the Tower on the spot, and he knew it. Not only the letters to Mary promising foreign support for her claim to the throne, but – can you credit it – a copy of a new papal bull of excommunication against the Queen.' He shook his head at the audacity. 'And woefully badly concealed. Gifford was on his knees begging for a reprieve before I said a word, ready to promise anything. So I offered him his liberty if he would continue in his role as courier to Mary, but under my direction.' He paused, allowing me to appreciate the achievement. 'To sweeten the deal, I released his father from prison as well. The old man was in the Counter almost a year for recusancy. The family has lands and a manor house in Staffordshire, you see.'

I shook my head, failing to see the significance.

'Mary has been transferred to Chartley Manor, nearby,' he said, impatient. 'So Gifford may take her correspondence while making visits to his family home, without arousing suspicion. It is the perfect cover, and the conspirators believe it is all down to their ingenuity. For the present, Mary Stuart thinks Gilbert Gifford is her saviour.'

'And this Babington group – they trust him too?'

'Implicitly. He came with personal letters of recommendation from Charles Paget in Paris, and Mary has vouched for him.'

'Forgive me, Your Honour, but you have said yourself that these men are not stupid. They are in regular correspondence with Paget, who keeps a close eye on me. It will not take him long to notice I have left Paris. And what happens when the real Jesuit priest turns up?'

He chuckled. 'He will not make it past the searchers, trust me. While you were resting, Thomas and I dispatched fast riders to all the southern ports giving them warning – the Jesuit must be expected any day now, posing as the son of a cloth merchant, according to Paget. The minute they have him, he will be brought safely to Barn Elms, where we can count his limbs and he can tell us everything we need to know to make your performance convincing. I assume you have Spanish among your languages, growing up in Naples?'

'Of course. It was the language of the nobility when I was educated at San Domenico. A Spaniard might detect a Neapolitan accent, though I am fluent enough to convince Englishmen. But—'

'Excellent.' The smile crept back. 'Don't worry about Paget. We will put the word out in Paris that you have taken a trip to Wittenberg.'

'What will you do with this Jesuit while I am impersonating him? You will not kill him?' I tried not to think about how the Spaniard would be persuaded to share his information. It was said that any prisoner suspected of possessing intelligence too sensitive to be heard even by the torturers at the Tower was taken under cover of darkness to Walsingham's country house near Mortlake, where he would conduct the interrogations himself in his cellar.

'The Jesuit will be my concern,' he said, with a snap of finality. He folded his hands together and leaned closer. 'But you must tell me now if the business makes you squeamish. Once it is begun, once you are in with them, you must see it through to the end. If you waver, if you hesitate even once and they suspect you, they will kill you. They have too much at stake. We have already seen what they will do to a woman.' He held my gaze, unblinking. 'And you have a tender conscience, Bruno – I have noted this in you before. As a man, it is a virtue that does you credit. As an agent, it could be your undoing. In this occupation, one is sometimes required to override conscience with duty, just as a soldier on the battlefield must.'

'I have watched a man die a traitor's death, Your Honour,' I said quietly. 'What you are asking of me – to befriend these men, eat with them, earn their trust, all to bring them to the scaffold – it is no small thing. Anyone with a conscience would think twice.'

'I expect you to think twice. But remind yourself that these men want to kill an anointed queen.'

'So do you.'

I saw his fingers flex, but his voice remained level. 'I wish to convict a traitor who conspires against England on the side of foreign invaders. What title she claims is not at issue. These people do not deserve your sympathy, Bruno. But if you need further convincing, I am happy to oblige. Marston!' He scraped back his chair and stood as he called out. The steward appeared with remarkable speed, leading me to suspect he had remained right outside the door. It was not my concern if Walsingham's servants eavesdropped, I tried to tell myself, but there was no avoiding the knowledge that, if I accepted this commission, everything surrounding it could mean the thin sliver of difference between life and death. I had seen before what could happen when a man trusted his servants unquestioningly.

'Prepare the carriage with no livery,' Walsingham said. 'Fetch my cloak too, and tell the servants to bring Bruno's bags.'

Marston nodded and left the room. Walsingham turned to me. 'You can stay with Thomas tonight in Leadenhall. Best you keep away from my house, in case you are seen. We will take you there on the way back.'

'Back from where?'

'You will see.' He set his mouth in a grim line. 'I want you to know the men you are dealing with, before you make your decision. I would also value your shrewd eye.'

I could barely keep my shrewd eyes open by this point, but I rose, gave a small bow and followed Phelippes along the corridor to a back door that gave on to a neat courtyard and kitchen garden. Cloaks and bags were brought, and we were led out to the tart chill of the summer night, the light almost gone, a fading scent of roses and woodsmoke on the air. I breathed in; I guessed at what Walsingham meant to show me, and I wanted to inhale the freshness of the night and hold it deep in my lungs against what was to come.

FIVE

'There is one thing I do not understand,' I said, bracing myself against the seat as the carriage jolted along a rutted track. Black cloth hung at the windows so I had no idea of where we were; only that we had been travelling for more than half an hour and had passed outside the city walls – we had made a brief stop while Phelippes descended and I had caught the exchange of voices before the scrape and creak of gates opening. But no one had offered any further information and we had bumped along in silence until now, Walsingham's brooding expression forbidding unnecessary questions.

He raised his head from his thoughts and nodded for me to continue.

'You've had Mary Stuart in custody for nearly twenty years. If you want so badly to be rid of her, why don't you slip something into her food? She could die quietly of an unexplained illness, without all this need for elaborate trickery and conspiracies and the spectacle of a trial with all of Europe watching.'

His shoulders slumped as a sigh escaped him and I saw him exchange a glance with Phelippes.

'Do you suppose this has not been considered?' He sat back. 'You tell him, Thomas – I am weary of making this argument. I have it with the Queen at least once a week. She favours your method, Bruno. If she could have Mary dead without sullying her own hands or her conscience, she would sleep easier than she has in two decades. So she claims.'

'Then why does she not do it?' I turned to Phelippes.

'It is more complicated than that,' he said. 'Lord Burghley wants to remake the constitution of England.'

'It has become a stand-off between the Queen and Burghley.' Walsingham leaned in again. 'You remember him, of course. England's greatest statesman, stubborn as a donkey.'

Even in the dark of the carriage, I noted the faint gleam of his teeth, a smile of affection, not mockery. I had encountered William Cecil, Lord Burghley, the last time Walsingham had asked me to investigate the murder of a young woman at court, and knew something of his reputation. He was now Lord High Treasurer, and Elizabeth's most senior and trusted advisor. He was also the man who had raised Master Secretary to his present position, and Walsingham's loyalty to him was second only to that he showed the Queen. I would need to be careful of my response.

'The very concept of the divine right of kings hangs on Mary Stuart's fate, as Queen Elizabeth knows all too well,' Walsingham continued. 'Once precedent has been established that an anointed queen may be tried and condemned by a jury like any other private citizen, part of the monarch's power will have been ceded to Parliament for good. This is Burghley's goal.' He tapped his thumbnail against his teeth. 'Her Majesty the Queen would love nothing more than a silent assassin in the night to do the job for her. But we must ensure that Mary is shown publicly – before all the kings of Europe – to have been the architect of her own downfall, else her death will always be surrounded by the suspicion of foul play. The last thing we want is to make a martyr of her. The whole point is to prove that, when it comes to treason, no one can be above the law.'

'The kings of Europe will need some convincing. Are you hoping for a letter in Mary's hand ordering the death of Elizabeth? She is too canny to trap herself like that, surely?'

His mouth grew pinched. 'Ideally, I had hoped for a letter from Babington spelling out the exact means by which it was to be done, and naming his co-conspirators, and a reply from Mary giving her explicit assent. She is desperate, and growing incautious – I think, if things had continued to unfold as they were, we might have brought her to it. But Clara's death has thrown all that into confusion. The one letter we have from Mary to Babington hints at her approval of the plan, but in abstract terms only.' He steepled his fingers together. 'I am not happy about our chances of convicting her on that alone.'

'It could be made more convincing,' Phelippes said, impassive. Walsingham did not reply.

That hardly sounded like due process to me, but I had no chance to comment, as the carriage pulled to an abrupt halt. Phelippes slammed open the door and jumped down. Walsingham gestured for me to follow and I climbed out, peering through the darkness to discover that we were among fields, a few low dwellings and hedgerows standing out along the horizon. It must have been near midnight; overhead a milky moon shone through scraps of cloud, and ahead I could make out the shape of a small building with a pointed roof. The remote bleating of sheep and the drawn-out hoot of a hunting owl carried through the dark. Phelippes had taken a torch from the coachman and knocked on the door.

'One of the old leper chapels,' Walsingham remarked, beside me. His breath steamed in the night air and he stamped his feet against the cold. 'Still has its uses.'

The door scraped open a crack, enough for a stocky figure in clerical robes to appear and demand our business. Phelippes held up his light and when the man realised who his visitors were, he bowed low and held the door wide for us.

'Any trouble?' Walsingham asked, moving briskly past him

into the shadows of the chapel. Inside, a couple of tallow candles were burning low, and I saw a bed had been made up in a far corner. The air smelled of animal fat, with a reek of piss pots and something worse hovering beneath.

'No one has been near the place,' the man said, leading us to his straw pallet, which he pulled aside to reveal a hatch set into the floor. 'Save a couple of vagrants looking for shelter. I gave them bread and threatened them with the constable if they returned. Otherwise quiet.' He drew a key from his belt and unlocked an iron padlock that secured the opening, pulled back a bolt and lifted the hatch to reveal a set of steps. Cold air and the unmistakable stench of stale blood and dead flesh rose through the gap. I recoiled, stepping backwards into Walsingham.

'Steady, Bruno.' I felt his hand rest on my shoulder a moment longer than necessary, as if to impart courage. 'Let Thomas go first with the light.' He turned to the curate, or watchman, or whatever he was. 'Fetch me a lantern and keep your eyes on the door.'

I took a deep breath and followed Phelippes into what must have once been a crude crypt beneath the chapel. The smell of death intensified and as my eyes adjusted, I saw a table had been constructed on two trestles, with a shape draped in a sheet lying on top. Phelippes approached it, his face contorted against the stink, twisting his features into a grotesque mask in the flickering light as he pulled the cloth back. It snagged in places where the body's excretions had caused it to stick to the skin. I fought down bile and pressed my sleeve to my face as I willed myself to look at the sight he had uncovered.

Her face – what remained of it – was hideous; a gaping hole where one eye and the nose had been, now collapsed in on itself as the flesh around it had begun to blacken. The head had been crudely shaved and the ears sliced off. The girl was clothed, though her feet and arms were bare, the skin mottled; the bodice of her gown was stiff with dark stains. Her remaining eye, wide and bulging, seemed to stare upwards at horrors she would never divulge.

'*Dio porco*,' I breathed, through my sleeve.

'I know.' I felt Walsingham's shoulder touch mine as he held up the lantern. 'Thoughts?'

I shook my head; my only thought at present was to escape to the cool night outside, breathe deeply, run a mile from this obscenity and everything he was asking of me. Even a boat back to France and the wilful stupidity of my students seemed preferable to what he was proposing, now that the girl's body was in front of me. Instead, I fought down my nausea and approached the table, steeling myself to examine her with a physician's impartiality. It was hardly the first time I had been in the presence of violent death; somehow I never grew inured to it. I would have made a hopeless soldier, as my father had been fond of telling me.

'She was found in a churchyard, you said?'

'A graveyard,' Walsingham corrected. 'The Cross Bones, in Southwark. No church involved – it's a scrap of wasteland, given over by the Bishop of Winchester for the burial of those who can't be put in consecrated ground. Suicides, unbaptised infants, but mostly the criminals and prostitutes who turn up dead in the borough. Saves too many questions about what happened to them.'

'The ward of Southwark is outside the legal jurisdiction of the City of London and instead falls under the governance of the Bishop of Winchester, which makes it effectively lawless,' Phelippes put in, helpfully. 'This is why it is full of bear pits, brothels and gaming houses – the Bishop turns a blind eye and the city authorities cannot intervene.'

'I know. I am familiar with Southwark,' I said, giving him a look which was lost in the dark. I turned back to Walsingham. 'Do you suppose her killers meant to bury her there, to keep her from being found?'

'I would say that was likely not their intention. She was discovered at first light by the night watchman – old fellow, getting on for seventy. If they had wanted to hide the body, there were easier ways to do it.'

'Then she was supposed to be seen,' I mused. 'And in a whores' graveyard. The face, too, and the hair – that would fit. A deliberate display, rather than merely cruel torture.'

'What do you mean?' He moved closer beside me, raising his light to illuminate that grisly mutilation. I fixed my eyes on Clara's hand, cold and white at her side, slim fingers curling gently inwards. I noticed that her nails were neatly filed and well cared for; she was evidently a woman who had taken pride in the details of her appearance. That should not have affected the degree of horror I felt at what had been done to her, but somehow it seemed to make it worse. I swallowed.

'In some ancient societies – Byzantium, for example – a woman who committed adultery was punished by having her head shaved and her nose and ears cut off.' I spoke slowly, forming the thoughts even as I voiced them. 'Though she was intended to survive the disfiguring. It was a way of marking her betrayal for life, and ensuring no other man would touch her.'

Walsingham clapped me on the shoulder. 'You see, Thomas – this is why we have need of Bruno's mind. I had supposed they meant to obscure her identity, so she could not be easily recognised, but I confess that made little sense, given that they left her clothes. I had not thought it might be symbolic.'

He fell silent and I knew his thoughts had flown back, as mine had, to the last time he and I had stood over the body of a girl whose killer had left symbols carved into her flesh.

'Perhaps I am reading too much,' I said quickly. 'I only wondered if someone was making a point about betrayal. How was she identified?'

'I have people among the night watch and the constables in every borough. Clara had gone out on the evening of the twenty-seventh and was expected back at Seething Lane later that night. When she had not appeared by the following morning, I put out word that I should be notified immediately if the body of a young woman turned up anywhere in the city. The Southwark watch sent word and I dispatched Thomas to identify her. I saw her later, after we had the body brought here.'

'And you're certain it's her?' I raised my head to look at Phelippes.

'Quite certain,' he said. 'Clara Poole had a large birthmark down the right side of her neck and her collarbone.'

I held my breath and leaned closer. Though the skin was discoloured and the light poor, I could make out the shape of a port-wine stain on the girl's neck, where the blood had been cleaned away.

'The dress is hers too,' Walsingham said, 'though the sleeves had been removed, along with her shoes.'

'How did she die?'

'I was hoping you might tell me.'

'She would have bled like a slaughtered pig,' Phelippes remarked. I heard Walsingham softly click his tongue in disapproval.

'Yes, but not enough to kill her,' I pointed out, 'not for a long time. If her attacker cut her and starting beating her, she would have been well able to scream and alert the watchman before she bled out. I would guess she was dead when she was mutilated.'

Walsingham exhaled slowly through his teeth. 'Small mercies,' he said, in a choked voice.

I steeled myself and parted the stiffened lace collar to look at the girl's neck. 'It's difficult to see by this stage if there's bruising. But the way that eye is protruding – I'd say she was strangled or smothered. No other injuries?'

'None visible, beyond the obvious.'

We contemplated the body in silence. I looked again at the

bloodied mess of her face, the lips pulled back over the teeth. It would have taken effort and strength to inflict that kind of damage; the force of the blows had splintered the bone of the eye socket. If she had been beaten like this even after she was dead, it argued a loss of control by the killer, a frenzy of rage and hate. But to shave her head and sever her ears suggested the opposite: an elaborate, planned disfigurement that would have taken time, when the murderer must have known there was a chance the watchman might hear and disturb him. Why run the risk of getting caught, unless the mutilations were meant to send a message?

'Thomas had the body brought here immediately,' Walsingham continued, 'before talk could spread. The man upstairs is the curate of the local parish church, he keeps the key to this chapel and does me loyal service when I need to use it for such purposes. He knows how to keep his mouth shut.'

I wondered how many other corpses Walsingham had stowed here, in case their discovery should prove inconvenient. Bodies moved in the dead of night from the cellar at Barn Elms, perhaps.

'So – her death is not made public?'

'No. I wanted to see if anyone came asking after her, or said anything that implied a knowledge of her killing. The watchman who found her is being held in custody for the time being, to stop him gossiping, and the constables have been paid to keep quiet.'

'Does her brother know?'

'Yes.' In the dim light I saw his face tighten. 'He has taken it hard, as you would expect, especially as I will not let him see her. It is all I can do to hold him back from running Babington through with his dagger, bringing the whole edifice crashing down, and if Robin knew the detail of what had been done to his sister I would have no hope of restraining him. I have had a great deal of work to persuade him that my way of bringing her justice will serve her memory better.' He sighed. 'Robin is a solid, loyal man, but Clara was all the family he had. His desire for revenge burns hot, and I fear it may eclipse his commitment to the greater good. You will meet him – his knowledge of Babington's group will be useful to you.'

He appeared to have forgotten – or was wilfully ignoring – the fact that I had not yet agreed to his mad scheme.

'She must have been killed south of the river, either in the Cross Bones or close by,' he continued, moving around to the other side of the body on the trestle and peering down, a sleeve pressed to his mouth, eyes narrowed as if trying to solve a cipher. 'Babington and his friends were dining together in the City on the night of the twenty-seventh, but the party broke up before midnight, so any one of them could have gone to meet Clara in Southwark without the others knowing.'

'Did she give any hint that she feared they suspected her?' I asked, keeping my eyes fixed on the girl's hands.

He glanced at the steps behind us. There was no trace of any movement, but he lowered his voice regardless. 'No. But in her last communication with Thomas she had promised to bring us a list of English Catholic nobles and gentry around the country who had committed to providing money and men for an invasion, once the Queen was dead. One of Babington's group had ridden out to gather support over the last fortnight, and was due back in London any day. It would have been invaluable in anticipating possible landing places for foreign troops. Not to mention having all those confirmed traitors by name.'

'So you think the act of stealing this list gave her away? I suppose it was not found on her?'

'We don't know that she even had the list yet. But she could have expressed too great an interest in it, and aroused suspicion that way. Or let slip any number of ways that she was spying.' Walsingham shook his head. 'You heard my daughter

– she thinks I feel no remorse for this death. She could not be more mistaken. Clara and Robin's father died in my service, I took them into my household when they had no other prospects, and they have both served me willingly. This should never have happened. But Frances cannot see that private griefs must give precedence to matters of state.'

'She is young,' I said gently.

'So was this one.' He reached out and rested his fingertips briefly on the cold flesh of the girl's hand. 'She should have made a better marriage, become a mother. I should have looked to that, instead of— No matter now.' He raised his head and his eyes gleamed black in the lantern light. 'I must find out what is happening inside this Babington conspiracy, Bruno. What her death means for its progress. If they fear betrayal and decide to hold off, we may never bring the Scottish pretender to justice.'

'How long had Clara been intimate with the Babington group?' I asked, as his words had prompted an idea.

'Robin first introduced her in March,' he said, narrowing his eyes at me. 'Why?'

'Three months. Have you checked to see if she was with child?'

'The body has not been examined by a physician. What makes you suppose that?'

'Only that, in my experience, it can be a pressing reason for a man to rid himself of an inconvenient mistress. It might be worth a look. The motive may be nothing to do with your conspiracy.'

Walsingham looked down at the girl, considering, a hand on the hilt of his knife; I half-feared he might perform the examination himself right there. 'In your experience?' he said, after a while, with an eyebrow cocked.

'My experience of murder.'

He nodded. 'Very well. Thomas, send for the physician to do what is required at dawn. She can't stay here more than a day longer. That's another confrontation I must have with her brother, who wants to take her all the way to Essex to have her buried with their father.' He sighed and rubbed the back of his neck. 'We should go to our beds now, sleep a few hours while we can. There is much work to do.'

Again, in that half-light, I saw how drawn he looked, before he turned abruptly for the steps as Phelippes pulled the sheet over the body. Upstairs Walsingham exchanged private words with the curate – I saw him slip the man a purse from his cloak – and, to my great relief, we emerged from the chapel into clean night air. I stretched up to look at the stars and breathed deep.

'Gifford will be at Thomas's lodgings when you arrive,' Walsingham said, as the carriage lurched back over the rutted road towards the city. 'Say nothing to him of our plan – I will be the one to brief him. But keep your ears open for anything Gifford has to say to you. He may be less guarded than he is with Thomas.'

'You mentioned that you had a man inside the group whose loyalty was uncertain. I presume you meant Gifford?'

Walsingham turned his face to the blacked-out window. 'Gilbert is not a steadfast young man. He will do whatever is expedient at the time, but I must work with what I have. That he was already established as courier to Mary was a gift I could not turn down – I will not find a man better placed. But his loyalty is only bought, and he is especially vulnerable to having his head turned by a pretty young woman.'

'Aren't we all?'

'No,' Phelippes said, sounding puzzled. 'He should do his job.'

Walsingham caught my eye and, for the first time since we had left Seething Lane, I saw the flicker of a genuine smile. 'Not everyone has your single-minded devotion to duty, Thomas,' he said, laying a hand on his assistant's arm. I noted how Phelippes flinched away from it, frowning as if he realised there was a joke somewhere but could not identify it. 'The lady in question,' Walsingham continued, 'is Bessie Pierrepont. I fear Gilbert has conceived a fancy for her, and that is worrying.'

'Why? Who is Bessie Pierrepont?'

'A lady-in-waiting to Queen Elizabeth. More significantly, she is the granddaughter of Bess of Hardwick.'

I shook my head. In the upper reaches of English society, everyone seemed to be related to everyone else, and it was assumed you knew them all. 'You will have to explain the significance.'

'Of course. No reason these names should mean anything to you. Tell him, Thomas.' He leaned back against the seat.

'Bess of Hardwick is wife to the Earl of Shrewsbury, who was Mary Stuart's keeper when she was first imprisoned,' Phelippes explained, obligingly. 'She and Mary became close. Sewing together, and other women's pastimes. She was supposed to relate back to Master Secretary and my lord Burghley the confidences she gleaned. Instead her loyalties transferred to Mary – Bess and her husband treated her like a house guest rather than a prisoner, and Mary's correspondence with her supporters in France went unchecked. After the last plot to free her came so near to success, Master Secretary was obliged to remove her from the Earl's care and confine her under sterner conditions.'

'In the absence of her own child, Mary conceived a great affection for Lady Shrewsbury's granddaughter, Bessie Pierrepont, who was often at the house. She would even take the girl to sleep in her bed when she was four or five years of age.' Walsingham twisted his mouth. 'Young Bessie is now nineteen and in Queen Elizabeth's service. She will utter, by rote, every profession of loyalty that she knows we expect of her, but I have lingering doubts. Childhood devotion dies hard, and Mary has sent her valuable gifts over the years. Gifford has sought an introduction to her lately, and I would like to know what that is about.'

'Why don't you ask him?'

'More interesting, I think, to see where the association tends if he thinks I know nothing of it. He has taken trouble to keep his interest in her from me and Thomas, and that in itself is reason to watch him. The boy is foolish enough to confide his secrets if he believes himself in love, and Bessie also knows Babington. I don't want our plans coming to nothing because Gifford feels the need to show off for a girl. Not something we need worry about with you, eh, Bruno?' He fixed me with a mischievous look. 'Would all my espials had the training in resisting female wiles that comes from a spell in the religious orders.'

'That does not necessarily follow, Your Honour,' I said, dipping my head. He knew well that I was as capable as anyone of recklessness for the sake of a woman – or had been, for one woman at least.

'True. By the time the religious houses were dissolved here, there was barely a monk left who knew the meaning of chastity.' He sniffed. 'See what you can find out from Gifford. I will put you in lodgings together – he may open up to you.'

I doubted this; when Gifford realised that I was behind his arrest at Rye and his forced cooperation with Walsingham, he was likely to throw the nearest heavy object at my head. They left me alone with my thoughts for the remainder of the journey. Master Secretary stared at the blacked-out window as if reading invisible secrets there. Phelippes leaned forward, rocking slightly, his gaze concentrated on the floor, muttering fervently under his breath. At first I thought he was praying, but when I listened closer, I realised he was reciting mathematical formulae. I sat back and smiled; it struck me as oddly endearing, and I caught myself thinking that, despite the absurdity of what I was being asked to do, I was back where I belonged.

SIX

'You!' Gilbert Gifford glared at me across the cramped space of Phelippes' living quarters, one trembling finger pointing as if he thought he might be seeing an apparition. From the glassy look in his eye I guessed he had spent the evening in a tavern. Besides the flush in his cheeks, he looked much as he had when I last saw him, before Christmas; skinny and mousy-haired, with pale eyelashes and darting grey-blue eyes, though the hunched, nervy posture I associated with him was gone, displaced perhaps by drink.

'Living quarters' was a generous description: Walsingham's right-hand man inhabited two large rooms with narrow leaded windows on the first floor of a house off Leadenhall Market. One was a study, the only furniture a broad desk with a chair, walls of shelves crammed floor-to-ceiling with files, parchments and boxes of papers, all neatly arranged, and a ware-bench bearing the tools of his forger's trade: inks, waxes, brass seals and an array of quills and fine-pointed knives. The other room was for sleeping, and contained only a narrow wooden bed, a wash-stand, a chest for clothes and a pallet on the floor, where I supposed Gifford stayed when he was in town. I had left my bags in the passageway; no one had yet made any mention of where I was expected to sleep.

'What a small world it is,' I said, smiling. Gifford's face darkened.

'I never trusted you. I was picked up the minute I set foot ashore in Rye. I suppose it was you sent warning ahead of me?'

I laughed. 'Master Gifford – you confided your most secret plans to a woman in order to impress her. That is always a mistake.'

He nodded, understanding. 'Of course. Mary Gifford. My so-called relative in Paris. I suppose she was spying for him too?' He jerked his head towards Phelippes, who continued to sort his papers into piles on the desk.

'In fact, the girl was not in our employ, though I wish she had been,' he remarked, without looking up. 'She delivered better intelligence than half the men we have in Paris.'

I glanced at him; I wanted to steer Phelippes away from the subject of Mary Gifford, the young woman who had worked as a governess in the English household where Gilbert had lodged in Paris, lest he take too much interest in her abilities, and her history.

'You should be grateful to her, Gilbert,' I said. 'From what I hear, your cargo was not well concealed. If your arrival had not been expected you would have been caught anyway, and you would have joined your father in prison. As it is, you both enjoy your liberty, and now you have useful employment.'

'So I should consider myself in your debt?' He tilted his chin and fixed me with a challenging look.

'You should not consider me the architect of your misfortune, at any rate,' I said, stretching out the ache in my back. 'What was your life in Paris? Moping about bemoaning the loss of your family's estate and waiting for a scrap of attention from Paget, who cared more about the letters you carried than he ever did about your safety. Now you are writing yourself into history. Think on that.'

He squinted as he attempted to work out if I was serious. 'Not the way I wanted,' he said, more soberly. 'All I do is ride back and forth to Staffordshire on filthy roads, for a deception I am ashamed to—' He broke off, casting a glance at our host and evidently thinking better of his words.

'If you must keep talking, you will have to go next door,' Phelippes said. 'I have work to do.'

'It's the middle of the night, man,' I said. 'Are you not half-mad with tiredness? I know I am.' It seemed weeks since I had set out from Rye, though it was only first light the day before.

Phelippes raised his head, surprised. 'No. If you want to sleep, take my bed.'

'Where will you sleep?'

'He never sleeps,' Gifford said, with a touch of bitterness. I guessed that part of the reason for his accommodation here was so that Phelippes could report back on his movements. I wondered if I would be subject to the same scrutiny. I believed Walsingham had faith in me, but perhaps he never fully trusted anyone. I would not either, in his position.

Gifford and I moved through to the bedchamber, where he flopped on the pallet without undressing, hands folded across his stomach, staring at the ceiling.

'I suppose you were in love with her too,' he said, after a while, as I took off my doublet and laid it at the foot of Phelippes's bed. 'Mary Gifford, I mean. If that was even her real name.'

I sat down to pull off my boots. 'No, I was not in love with her.' This was a lie, but there was no need for him to know that. Her real name was Sophia Underhill, but that was not his concern either.

'I thought I was,' Gifford said, with unexpected candour. 'Now I know it was not love – only a mere shadow of the real thing.' A dreamy smile played at the corners of his mouth. I set my boots down and leaned forward to look at him.

'You have found the real thing, then?' I asked, keeping my voice casual.

His eyes darted sideways at me and his expression hardened. 'If I had, I would not speak of it to you – you would run straight to tell Walsingham for the chink of a couple of groats in your purse.'

'Why, is it something Walsingham should know of?'

A deep colour spread instantly over the boy's face, displacing even the flush of drink. '*No*. I mean to say – I have nothing to hide from him. But some things I may keep private. He is not master of my affections, though he may have bought my service.'

'Well, whoever has command of your heart now must be a rare beauty, if she has displaced the lovely Mary Gifford in your eyes.' I leaned back on the bed, not looking at him, hoping an offhand manner would invite further confidences.

He met this with a pointed silence, continuing to stare at the ceiling. I turned my back to him and began to unlace my shirt, feigning a lack of interest.

'Her beauty is not so cheap as shows only in a glass,' he burst out, eventually. 'It also shines in her nobility of birth and character. Though, I confess, she has been blessed by nature too.'

I smiled to myself; in my experience, a young man will always find a way to boast of his conquests, even when he knows better.

'She is a lady, then?'

'The granddaughter of an earl, and serves the Queen herself in her bedchamber. Mary Gifford is nothing but a governess. I am not convinced we are even related. My father never heard of any branch of the family from Somerset.'

'How did you meet this noble beauty?' I asked, to prevent any further speculation on Mary Gifford's identity. 'The Queen keeps her women close, I thought?'

He seemed on the point of answering, but somewhere behind

the haze of drink and infatuation, a note of caution sounded; I saw his eyes sharpen. 'I will think twice before I tell you anything, Giordano Bruno. Paget warned me about you. I know you for a heretic.'

'Well, my soul is no business of yours, Gifford, but we serve the same earthly master now, so we will have to get along a little better. Give you good night.' I leaned over and blew out the candle. If I were to agree to Walsingham's absurd scheme – and I had not yet given any undertaking, though he seemed to have assumed my willingness – there would be time enough to win Gifford over. I pulled the blanket around my shoulders and allowed the exhaustion of the past two days to fall on me. The creak of boards carried from the adjoining room as Phelippes moved around, about his secret work of symbols and ciphers, saving the realm. I was about to tumble over the edge of sleep when Gifford shifted on his pallet and yawned.

'She came back to London, you know. Mary Gifford, I mean.'

I pushed myself upright instantly. 'What? When?'

He gave a soft laugh. 'What is it to you? I thought you were not in love with her.'

I ignored this. 'She spoke to me of returning to London, but in a year or so, she said. Do you know different?'

He stretched out his limbs, enjoying this small power. 'Perhaps she grew impatient. Before I left at Christmas, she had asked Paget to write her a letter of recommendation to a family he knew in London, to serve as a lady's companion.'

'And did he? What was the family's name?'

'I will have to see if I can recall. Give you good night, Bruno. Sleep well.'

I could hear the smile in his voice as he turned over. I called him a son of a whore under my breath in Italian and flung myself back on the bed, all thoughts of sleep banished. Moonlight slanted through the narrow casement; I stared at the patterns it cast on the wall while I considered that Sophia

Underhill, the woman who had troubled my dreams in all her various names since I first encountered her in Oxford three years ago, might be out there somewhere in the same city, perhaps only streets away. I turned on to my side, and heard a furtive rustling from Gifford's pallet, a sound I knew all too well from years confined as a Dominican friar; the boy was furiously frotting himself, no doubt thinking of his new love's noble character. *Madonna porca*. I was too old to be sharing a bedchamber with worked-up boys. I rolled on my back and recalled my last meeting with Sophia in Paris, when she still called herself Mary Gifford. She had fled to France to escape the law in England, but she had always meant to return; she had left behind a child, taken from her at birth because she was unmarried, but she had not given up her dream of finding him again. If she had hastened her return to London, it could only mean she had received news that gave her reason to hope. If I could see her, perhaps I could be of use to her in her quest. Then I remembered that, if I stayed in London, it would be as a Spanish Jesuit and my time would be taken up conspiring to regicide; it would be all but impossible for me to see anything of Sophia in that guise. Even so – if Gifford was telling the truth, her presence here was another reason to consider staying.

The boy made a noise like a strangled fox as he finished and was snoring within minutes. I lay awake, staring at the ceiling, wondering if any of the possible rewards of this business would be worth the price.

The next day I woke early, blinking into a chilly light, aches deep in my shoulders and thighs from two days in the saddle. Gifford lay sprawled on his pallet, twitching in dreams like a dog, but I could hear low voices from the adjoining room, so I splashed water over my face and quietly pulled on my clothes, thinking Walsingham must have come for my answer. Instead I approached the half-open door to hear Phelippes in hushed conversation with a tall man who had his back to me. I could see only that he was dark-haired and wore a rust-brown leather jerkin patched on the shoulders.

'Master Secretary mentioned nothing about this last night,' Phelippes was saying, his voice impatient.

'I have just now come from Seething Lane,' the stranger said, in an accent that sounded to my ears like that of the London boatmen. 'The Italian is to come with me to Southwark.'

'This makes no sense. Why would Master Secretary send him poking about the scene of the death in broad daylight, when the killers may be watching the place to see precisely who comes asking questions? And you, Master Poole – I would have thought you were the last person—'

'Perhaps you don't know his every thought, Thomas.' The newcomer's voice was tight. 'Master Secretary wants the Italian's view on the business. Don't ask me why – I didn't question it. But he did say for him to cover his head with a hat and his face with a kerchief. And tell him not to shave.'

'Does he decide the length of my beard now?' I said, pushing the door open. Phelippes glanced up without surprise; he was still sitting behind his desk making notes on his papers as I had left him, and it was impossible to tell from his face whether he had been there all night. The tall man turned and I saw that he was in his early thirties, good-looking in a dishevelled way, with a strong jaw and thick eyebrows that met in a V above his nose. It seemed from a soreness around his eyes that he had cried recently, or perhaps it was only the dust of the streets.

Phelippes waved a hand at him. 'Doctor Bruno, this is Master Robin Poole, supposedly come from Seething Lane to conduct you to Southwark, though I am not persuaded this is a good use of your time.'

Robin Poole met my look and rolled his eyes in what I took as a complicit comment on Phelippes and his blunt ways.

So this was the brother of the dead girl, the one who wanted to run her alleged killers through without waiting for evidence. Though his face appeared open, I could not help but concede that Phelippes might be right; it seemed unlikely that Walsingham would send this man to investigate the murder of his own sister. Master Secretary distrusted anyone who could not keep a tight rein on their emotions, especially when engaged on his business, and a man in the throes of grief was not the best judge of his own actions. I inclined my head and waited. He thrust his hand out and I shook it in the English fashion.

'Giordano Bruno.'

'I know. You are to come with me, but cover your face. I have a horse outside.'

I glanced at Phelippes. 'On what business?'

Impatience flashed across Poole's eyes, but he kept his countenance. 'I will brief you on the way. Master Secretary wants your view of things.'

'What things?' If Walsingham had given these orders, he must have a purpose. Perhaps he had considered it wise to let Poole feel he was playing some active part in the investigation, but wanted me there to ensure he didn't blunder.

'You ask a lot of questions. This murder.' Muscles tensed along his jaw, but his voice remained steady. 'He says you have a trained eye.'

I thought I caught a note of scepticism, but perhaps that was my imagination. I gave a brisk nod.

'Is there anything to eat?'

Phelippes sniffed. 'This is not an inn, Doctor Bruno. Ask Master Poole if you wish to break your fast on the way, he claims to have your needs in hand. I hope you are not being dragged on a fool's errand. We have little time to lose as it is – the girl's death has disrupted everything.'

Poole held the door for me, raising his eyebrows again to make clear his feelings about Phelippes. When I joined him on the stairs with a hat pulled down over my ears and a kerchief tied around the lower half of my face, he gave me a cursory glance of approval and signalled for me to follow him. I noticed that he walked with a slight limp in his right leg. He didn't speak until we were outside, where a boy with scabs on his lip held an old but solid-looking grey mare by a rope halter.

'You'll have to ride behind me.' Poole pulled himself into the saddle with an easy, practised movement that almost disguised the way he nudged his right leg over subtly with his hand. I climbed up behind him, wincing at my aching muscles. He slipped the boy a coin and we turned out of Leadenhall down Gracechurch Street towards London Bridge.

'There is something wrong with that man,' he said, after a while, as if challenging me to disagree.

'Phelippes? He is unusual, I grant. But I have studied the art of memory for nearly twenty years and only ever met one other with natural faculties like his.'

Poole grunted. 'I still say he is touched. The man behaves as if he has never known a human feeling. Mark how he spoke of my sister, as if her death is no more than an inconvenience. And he believes Master Secretary can't scratch his arse without he, Thomas, weighs up the cost and stamps five papers to approve it.'

I laughed, though I was not sure if it was intended as a joke, but I felt him relax. 'I'm sorry for your loss,' I said, as we passed down New Fish Street with the great gatehouse arch of the bridge in sight. The streets were already busy with traders' carts, and goodwives on their way to market, baskets jutting from their hips. Gulls wheeled overhead, loosing lonely cries. The air was cold, carrying the dirt smell of the river on a sharp breeze.

'She should never have been caught up in this,' he replied, after a long pause. 'Clara was an innocent, Doctor Bruno. She was not cut out for living a double life, the way we learn to in Walsingham's service. Women are too much led by their feelings to dissemble in that way.' He fell silent again and a shudder rippled across his back as he exhaled. I could have told him then that I had met plenty of women as skilled in the arts of duplicity as any man, and every bit as determined – I thought again of Sophia Underhill – but it was not the moment.

'You blame Walsingham, then?'

'It would be meaningless to blame him,' he said, after a moment's pause. 'Clara volunteered for this work. She was tired of a life indoors, a poor widow marking time to become a governess. She sought adventure. Now see where that has led her – pushing her way into a man's world.' He seemed about to say more, but fell silent abruptly. I wondered how much detail Walsingham had told him about the manner of her death. Poole made it sound as though he partly blamed his sister for her own end.

'Then it was her idea, to become close with the conspirators?'

His shoulders tightened. 'She only thought of carrying letters or something in that line. She badgered Walsingham to give her a task – he said he had enough couriers. I think he had misgivings, rightly, about trusting a woman with sensitive correspondence. But if the fault for her death lies with anyone, I must own it.'

'How so?'

He glanced to the side, wrinkling his nose as we approached Fish Wharf and the Fishmongers' Hall on the north bank of the river and the smell assaulted us from all sides. He dropped his voice, so that I had to lean forward to hear.

'Babington and his friends keep themselves close, as you'd expect. They do not lightly confide in outsiders – you'll find this out for yourself soon enough, though Master Secretary seems to believe you will walk into their open arms without hindrance.' His tone let me know what he thought of

Walsingham's faith, though I chose not to take it personally. 'They found me useful because they believed I brought them information about Walsingham, but my connection with him also made them wary, even though I have been working to gain the trust of the Catholics in London for years now. I was brought to the conspirators by Jack Savage, who I met in prison when I was serving time for distributing illegal books. But they still didn't invite me to their most private meetings. Walsingham grew frustrated with the lack of progress, though no more than I was with myself. Once I made the mistake of remarking to him that, with a man like Babington, a woman might have better luck drawing out his secrets. It never occurred to me that he would think to use my sister.'

'Then it was Master Secretary's idea to have her introduced to them?'

'It could have been Clara's. She would have thought it good sport.' He sighed. 'My sister was a beautiful girl, Bruno. I wish you could have seen her. Long, red curls down her back, and white skin – people said she looked like the Queen herself when she was a young princess. I don't suppose she ever intended to do any more than flirt with them, see what they would confide. I didn't like the idea, but Walsingham overruled me.'

'You could not have known how it would end.'

'I should have guessed, and put my foot down. I knew what those men were like, I'd seen what they were capable of. And Clara was soft-hearted. She married a man with no money because he won her with pretty words. She should never have gone near the like of Babington and his friends. Our father would spin in his grave. God knows when I shall even be permitted to bury her.'

'You have not seen her?'

'He won't let me, yet. Says it's vital her death does not become public knowledge too soon, the better to allow her killers to betray themselves.' He shook his head and his voice took on a dark edge. 'That's what makes me think he is keeping something from me.'

He left an expectant pause but I said nothing, and we rode on in silence, passing through the north gatehouse of London Bridge. A young man hung limply by his wrists in the pillory, glazed eyes barely noting the passers-by, who were too caught up squeezing through the archway to pay him any heed. It was only as we drew level that I realised it was a girl dressed in men's clothes, her hair cut short, her face grey with fatigue.

'What's her offence, do you think?' I asked Poole, leaning forward.

He gave her the briefest glance. 'She'll be a whore from the Bankside stews,' he said, as if this were an everyday sight. 'Some of them dress as boys for the clients. It's prohibited. If they're caught, it's a few hours in the pillory.'

The girl looked up at me from under her hooded lids, her expression neither pleading nor defiant, and I recalled the day Sophia Underhill had come looking for me disguised as a boy to escape a charge of murder. I wondered again where she might be, and whether her current identity as Mary Gifford was any more comfortable to her. If Gilbert Gifford insisted on playing games about how to find her, I was quite prepared to threaten it out of him.

Our progress slowed as we joined the flow of traffic making its way along the narrow conduit, barely twelve feet across, between the houses crammed each side of the bridge. Carts, wagons, horses and people on foot hoisting baskets or children on their shoulders were forced into a laborious shuffling procession, one lane in each direction, accompanied by cursing and shoving as those in a hurry tried to push ahead, only to be forced back, sometimes with blows, by people in front determined not to give way. The stink of horseshit rose as we inched forward; I took a deep breath through the kerchief and considered that, in my eagerness to return to London, I had forgotten how much I resented trying to get around the place.

'Where are we going?' I shouted at the back of Poole's head, as the horse flicked its ears, impatient at the throng milling about its legs.

'To search the place she was found.'

'Has that not been done already? It was two days ago, I thought.'

He made a scornful noise through his teeth. 'I wouldn't trust the London constables to search their own breeches and find their cocks.'

'And what are we looking for?'

'We'll know if we find it.'

I let this cryptic answer hang for a moment.

'This will be a difficult task for you,' I said, when he made no move to continue the conversation. The muscles across his back stiffened.

'Who has suggested that?'

'I mean only that you cannot be impartial.'

'None of us is *impartial*, in this business.' He allowed a pause. 'Oh, I see. They have told you I will blunder in and mar the project, because I cannot contain my grief. Who said that, Phelippes?'

'No one has said so.'

He glanced back over his shoulder. Even in quarter profile I could see his scorn. 'How long have you been in the Service?'

'For Walsingham? I met him in the spring of '83, shortly after I arrived in England.'

'Three years, then. Though you have been out of the country since last autumn, I understand.' He sounded pleased, as if he had won an argument. 'I have served him twelve, since he was first appointed to the Privy Council.'

'What is it you do for him, exactly?'

'I talk to people.' He set his eyes ahead so that I could not see his face, but I could tell from his voice that he was smiling. 'Listen, I've been in prison three times for his sake, once for two months, and given no special treatment that would mark me out as his man. I took my beatings like the rest of the papist suspects, and my knee has never fully recovered.' He slapped his right leg, hard, as if to punish it. 'If I did not betray myself then, I will not now, any more than you will.'

'I meant no offence,' I said hastily. 'Only that I have never lost a sister – I do not know that I could keep my countenance in your position.'

'I think you are disingenuous, my friend.' But he sounded mollified. 'If he thought you could be ruled by your emotions or betray yourself so easily, he would not have chosen you. For myself, I must put grief to one side. I know how to do that well enough. Sister or no sister, she was a pawn in a chess game played for high stakes, and I intend to find out who took her.'

I felt his metaphor was flawed, though I resisted pointing this out. He appeared to have assumed a responsibility for investigating Clara Poole's death that I suspected did not come from Walsingham, and again I wondered at Master Secretary's motive in involving him.

'Tell me of this Babington group, then,' I said, to channel his anger. 'What kind of men are they? Besides ruthless.'

He let out a bitter laugh. 'Walsingham insists on giving the business Babington's name, since Babington's money is furnishing the plans and he wants the glory. They should more properly call it the Ballard plot. That priest is the dangerous one among them. Him, I would call ruthless. Next to him, Babington is a mere fop. A pretty, rich boy looking for adventure. He wanted a cause, and in Mary Stuart he has found one. And the others can't proceed without his money, so he is flattered and made to feel important.'

'You think Babington's faith is not sincere?'

'Oh, he believes absolutely in his own sincerity, and the idea of himself as the saviour of England. But I don't think he gives two shits for the sufferings of ordinary English

Catholics. His father left him a thousand pounds a year, what would he know of hardship?'

He did not trouble to disguise his anger. I had the sense that Robin Poole's antipathy to Anthony Babington had put down roots long before the death of his sister.

'And the others?' I prompted.

'Let's see. Father John Ballard. Thirty-seven, ordained priest, goes about in the guise of a veteran soldier. Calls himself Captain Fortescue. *His* faith verges on fanatical. If he'd been born in your country, he'd have volunteered to join the Inquisition, and enjoyed it.'

'I have met the type,' I said, with feeling.

'Ballard dreams of ushering in the reign of a second Bloody Mary, turning the skies over England dark with the smoke of burning Protestants. If anyone could kill a young girl in cold blood, it would be him. Or more likely his faithful dog Jack Savage, who is justly named – he used to be a professional fighter. Then there's Chidiock Tichborne, Babington's closest friend – another rich boy who only wants England's return to Rome so he can get his father's estate back. Same with Thomas Salisbury – he's the one Ballard has riding about the country persuading Catholic nobles to let Spanish troops land on their coastline.' He gave a sceptical laugh. 'They really think Philip of Spain is going to send his Armada when they snap their fingers. They are all boys playing at holy war.'

'But they trust you?'

'I believe they do. I'm from a Catholic family, and Savage vouched for me to Ballard. They think I share their grievances.'

'But I thought your father worked for Walsingham?'

'He did.' A brief pause. 'He was an informer.'

'I see. Did the Catholics know?'

'Well. There's the question.' His voice grew tight. 'My father drowned ten years ago. Fell from the riverbank on the way home one night, they said. Assumed he was drunk. But my father knew how to hold his drink, so . . .' He lifted a shoulder, inviting me to draw my own conclusion. 'I was twenty-two, Clara fourteen, both our mothers dead. Walsingham took her into his house, and paid for me to study the law, so I could monitor my fellow students for him. Now Clara's gone too, for the same reasons. And I let it happen.'

'You can't blame yourself,' I said, hearing the emptiness of the words before they left my mouth.

'Not really for you to say,' he replied, though without rancour.

We crossed the rest of the way in silence as the crowd funnelled through the archway of the Great Stone Gate on the south bank. Poole raised his eyes as we emerged from the shadow and I followed his gaze to the sightless remains of heads on spikes high above. Crows perched on ledges nearby, shreds of matter in their beaks; I looked quickly away.

'I will see Babington and his fellows up there, whatever the cost,' he said through his teeth as the traffic eased and we turned right to follow the road along the Bank Side.

SEVEN

I remembered, in an instant, how the first thing that hit you about Southwark was the smell. To be more accurate, the collision of smells, all of them fierce enough to make your eyes water and your throat burn. The heavy scent of hops from the breweries fought with vile stinks from the tanneries and the dyers; these in turn mixed with the human odours of the gong-men's carts, and the sharp, animal musk of the bull and bear rings as we passed the church of St Mary Overy and the walled gardens of Winchester House. Beyond the bull ring, the famous Bankside Stews lined the road facing the river, with their own ripe scents behind closed doors. According to ancient laws, most of these inns and licensed brothels were painted white, their colourful signs affixed above the doors with images that announced their names to those who could not read: The Boar's Head, The Horseshoe, The Rose, The Barge, The Half Moon, The White Hart, The Olyphant, The Unicorn. Many were fine old houses with gates wide enough for coaches, and gardens with ponds and orchards stretching out to the rear. But they were separated by narrow alleys running with refuse and ordure, and when Poole turned the horse down one of these to follow it south, away from the river, I pulled the kerchief tighter around my mouth and nose and fought back the bile rising in my throat.

In the streets behind the bank, tenements crowded on one another as if they had been thrown together by drunks from whatever lay to hand: scrofulous plaster flaking from the walls, sheets of oilcloth nailed over windows in place of glass, roofs with missing tiles and greasy boards propping up lean-to shelters barely fit to keep a dog in. Despite the early hour, men in shirtsleeves stumbled along roads rutted by cartwheels, or pissed against the doorposts of alehouses under fading and splintered signs, regarding us with unfocused eyes that made me think of the girl in the stocks. It was impossible to tell if they were on their way home after a long night, or beginning again for a new day. Silent, dirty children with sores around their mouths crouched in the alleys, watching with wary, sunken eyes. Tired-looking women in low bodices and smudged face paint jutted their hips and pouted at us as we passed; one, a spotted scarf around her black hair, made a comical honking noise after us and asked, in a foreign accent, if we handsome gentlemen were hungry for a little gooseflesh this fine morning? When she stepped too close to the horse, causing it to rear its head back, Poole snapped at her to fuck herself. 'Where would be the profit in that?' she fired back, quick as blinking, with a merry laugh, and I found myself smiling. Poole muttered something about damned Winchester geese, and I recalled the nickname given to the women who worked in this lawless borough, where any pleasure or entertainment might be acquired, at a price.

Poole turned east and south again, through streets lined with half-derelict buildings, until the tenements gave way to open fields and we followed a mossy wall of crumbling brick on our left. When we reached an unmarked gate, he brought the horse to a halt and sprang down; I followed, and he handed me the reins.

'This is the place.' He slapped his palm against the slats. The gate looked as if it could be torn away with one hand, though the lock held fast as the wood juddered. 'The Cross Bones. They took this from the old keeper.' He held up a key and fitted it to the lock. 'Bring the horse in with you, or he'll be gone in two minutes round here. Nothing but thieves and whores, this whole stinking borough. Let's see where she was found.'

I followed him through the gap into an uneven patch of waste ground. There were few upright stones; those that remained listed at angles, edges worn away by time and weather, their inscriptions erased to a smooth blank. Here and there rotting wooden posts stood over other mounds, but for the most part you would hardly know the place was given over to the dead, save for its air of neglect and the crows perching with watchful eyes in the trees.

Poole looked about him, scanning the perimeter wall. It stood some ten feet high, though in places the brick was so old and worn it appeared that it would crumble to the touch. To our right, the wall was bordered by a row of cottages in poor repair. Along the side opposite the gate, a few trees remained inside the boundary, branches snaking along the top of the wall, small green apples budding on the higher reaches. Immediately to our left, on a flat patch of earth, an iron brazier stood, flakes of black ash around its feet. I pulled the kerchief down from my face, reasoning that there was no one to see me here.

'Not what you'd choose for your last resting place, is it?' He kept his voice determinedly light, though the tightness in his jaw betrayed the emotion he was fighting. 'A pit of sluts, criminals and suicides. Never thought to see her end up somewhere like this.' He turned to me. 'She loved beautiful things, my sister.'

I thought of Clara's pretty clothes, her careful manicure, that face.

'At least she won't be buried here,' I said, aware it was meagre comfort.

'She won't be buried at all till Walsingham gives his say so. She'll be left to rot till then, and I'm not even told where.' He clamped his teeth together until he had composed himself. 'The old watchman swears no one came past him through the gate all night. So they must have come over the wall. There, where the trees are – that's the only place.'

'You questioned the man yourself?'

'No, though I'd have liked to. Walsingham told me. The old boy claims he heard nothing, saw nothing, till he found her under the tree at daybreak. But he's not necessarily a reliable witness. He's thought to have a history of turning a blind eye.'

'To what?'

'All sorts. It's said bodies go missing from the Cross Bones. There's the hospital of St Thomas just upriver – plenty there would pay to get their hands on a fresh corpse. I suppose they think no one would miss a dead whore.' He gestured to the graveyard. 'Not as if anyone comes to lay flowers here.'

'This old watchman digs up the bodies to sell?'

'Takes a coin to look away while others do it, more likely. If he says he heard nothing, that might be no more than he always says.'

'He didn't sell Clara's body.'

'He's not a fool. He'd have seen from her clothes she was no Winchester goose – he probably guessed someone would come looking for her. Don't suppose that stopped him pocketing what he could first. Come on.'

He set off across the plot towards the far wall. I let the horse loose to graze on the long grass and followed, skirting clumps of nettles and the treacherous dips between graves. Ahead of me, Poole stopped and kicked at a patch of ground beneath the apple tree, scuffing up the earth with the toe of his boot.

'Look at this,' he called, gesturing with his foot. I hurried after him, gripped by a sudden horror that he might have stumbled on the girl's severed ear, tossed aside by the killer. But as I approached I saw what he had found; it was clear no rain had fallen in the past two days, and a wide rust-brown stain spread out between spikes of grass a few feet from the tree. When he lifted his head to look at me, I saw the effort it was costing him to maintain the appearance of detachment.

'Blood, no?'

I nodded. He bunched one hand slowly into a fist and wrapped it in the palm of the other.

'They told me she'd been strangled. I thought – well, at least that's quick, she wouldn't have suffered too long. So where's this much blood come from?'

'She could have wounded her attacker trying to fight him off,' I suggested, half-heartedly. I recalled how Walsingham had feared Poole's reaction if he learned what had been done to his sister's face; I had not anticipated being the one to tell him.

He considered this; I waited for another sarcastic response, but this time he nodded. 'That would mean she came in alive,' he said, looking up at the wall.

'I think you're right. I can't see anyone getting a dead body over that. It would take two men at least. But why would she be here at all?'

'Well, there's the question. She must have arranged to meet someone.'

He strode away abruptly, tearing at the tall weeds that tangled at the foot of the wall. I watched the ferocity of his movements. So much for keeping his countenance. I reached up and broke a low branch from the tree, sturdy enough to bend back the undergrowth, and swiped back and forth without conviction; I was certain that a killer organised enough to plan such a grotesque display would not have left anything to incriminate himself in the place he wanted the girl found. I wondered again why he would have chosen this spot – neither busy enough to make a public spectacle of the death, nor obscure enough to suggest they wanted to cover it up. It only made sense if my theory about the mutilation was correct, and they were making an allusion to Clara Poole being a whore, and a betrayer. Perhaps I was reading too much into it, and the location was simply convenient, but I found that hard to believe; with a lot less effort her killer could have left her in the street outside. This was Southwark; a body in the gutter was barely cause to break stride for most passers-by.

I pulled myself up into the lower branches of the tree to take a look over at the street, aware of Poole pausing to watch me. Smears of blood had stained the bricks at the top; it looked as if the killer had escaped this way after arranging the body. I was trying to calculate how long the whole business might have taken him, when I glanced down and saw an unmistakable glint of metal through the brambles beneath the tree.

'Found something?' Poole asked, straightening and wiping his hands on his breeches.

'Wait there.' I shinned down and plunged into the undergrowth to grab the object.

He was almost breathing on my neck when I emerged, hands and arms shredded by thorns and clutching a gold locket, its chain snapped. I held it out to him.

'Fuck me,' he said, letting out a slow, shaky breath.

'Is it hers?'

He nodded, turning it over in his hands. The face was engraved with scrolled letters entwined in a pattern of flowers and leaves.

'It was her mother's. She passed it on to Clara when she was dying. Look, here.' He pressed the catch and the locket sprang open to reveal a curled lock of red-gold hair tucked inside. 'Clara never took it off. But she wore it under her clothes, in case anyone got close enough to read the inscription.'

He clicked the face shut again and lifted it so that I could see more clearly. Around the edge, the engraved letters spelled out 'Veritas Temporis Filia'. I raised my eyes and met his.

'*Truth is the daughter of time*. But why should that be hidden?'

He seemed pleased by my ignorance. 'You really don't know? It was the motto of Mary Tudor, the Queen's sister, may she burn in Hell.'

'Bloody Mary? But why did Clara have that?'

'Ann – Clara's mother – served in Queen Mary's household as a young woman. Ann was twenty-five when Mary died, and Elizabeth took the throne. You didn't go about telling people you'd worked for Bloody Mary after that – you kept your mouth shut and acted like a good Protestant if you didn't want repercussions. My father forbade Ann ever to speak of it. But she used to tell her stories to Clara, as soon as she was old enough to hear.'

'So Ann was Catholic too?' I wondered what effect those old stories might have had on Clara. Could she have harboured secret sympathies for Babington and his friends, despite her debt to Walsingham?

'Ann worshipped as the law demanded, my father was careful about that. He was taking enough risks with his own double life, he didn't want his wife doing the same. But Clara said she never gave up her rosary. Nor this locket. Clara wouldn't have been parted from this lightly.' His jaw clenched. 'See here where the chain is broken? Do you suppose he tore it off her if she was resisting him?'

I rubbed the backs of my hands where the thorns had pricked them, glancing to either side with an uneasy sense of being watched. Something didn't feel right here; I had known that feeling too often not to trust my instincts. It seemed to me that Clara's locket had jumped too readily to my hand. If the girl's shoes and sleeves had been stripped from her to sell before her body was handed over, surely a piece of gold jewellery would not have been left behind unless someone wanted it found? We were the only souls in the graveyard, and yet I couldn't shake the feeling that we were playing on a stage, for the benefit of an unseen spectator. I pulled the kerchief up around my face again, just in case.

'She could have lost it climbing the wall,' I suggested, unconvinced.

'Or – wait – she could have thrown it into the brambles herself,' he countered, suddenly animated. 'Suppose she realised what was happening, that her life was in danger? She might have ripped it off and tossed it away to stop him getting his hands on it.'

'If she was intimate with Babington or one of his friends, they would have known she wore the locket,' I suggested. 'Wouldn't they have searched for it?'

Poole looked at me as if he pitied my stupidity. 'Babington and his friends were all dining together the night she was killed,' he said. 'All save Ballard, who was in France – or so we believe. They didn't necessarily murder her with their own hands. And if they paid someone to lure her here and get rid of her, he might not have known to look for a locket. Besides, there would have been nothing but moonlight to see by – he couldn't have lit a lantern for fear of disturbing the old watchman. And if the killer was hurt, he must have wanted to get away as quick as he could. He wouldn't have wasted time scrabbling through bushes.'

I held my tongue; I could not contradict this thesis without revealing that Clara's assailant had had the leisure to cut off her hair and ears, and that the blood was not his but hers. It was not for me to take from him the idea of his sister bravely resisting her attacker until her last breath. But the appearance of the locket so conveniently troubled me. Poole was staring at it, rapt, smoothing the pad of his thumb over the surface.

'Should we keep searching?'

'What?' He jerked his head up. 'Forgive me, I was . . .' He

indicated the locket with a diffident nod, as if embarrassed by his grief, before slipping it into the pouch at his belt. 'I suppose we should see if there is anything else.' But his earlier resolve seemed to have ebbed away; he looked around with the air of a man who has entered a room to find he has no memory of what he came in for. I picked up the broken branch I had discarded and pulled back the undergrowth where I had found the locket, hoping a cursory search would satisfy him so that we could make our way back across the river; there had been no mention of breaking our fast and my stomach was cramping with hunger. As I stepped closer to peer through the leaves, my foot struck something solid. I kicked it back towards me and bent to retrieve an earthenware carafe decorated with the embossed head of a unicorn. I sniffed it; the scent of spiced wine was still strong.

'What have you there?' Poole asked, snapping out of his reverie.

I held it up to show him. 'Only a pitcher. Not been there long, by the looks of it.' I shook it, to hear the dregs sloshing in the bottom. 'Perhaps whoever killed Clara brought it with him.'

Poole considered. 'Or it was thrown over the wall, or the old watchman dumped it. Can't see that it tells us much.'

I tipped the carafe and let a drop of liquid slide on to my finger. It was a cheap, sweet wine, with a bitter aftertaste beneath the sugar. 'It comes from the Unicorn, look. We passed that on the way – it's up the road, on the riverfront. Maybe we should ask there.'

'Ask what?' He gave me that same pitying look. 'Good day, did any of your customers happen to strangle a woman in the Cross Bones the other night?' He shook his head and I realised he was right. 'You don't go around the Bankside stews asking questions like you're the law, not unless you want to end up in the river. I'll mention it to Walsingham. It might be something or nothing. I'll bet these bushes are full of old bottles.'

'Will you tell him about the locket?'

'Of course. Though it's mine by rights, I'm her only family.' His hand moved protectively to the pouch where he had stowed it. I waited, hoping he would decide it was time to go, when a movement at the edge of my vision made me spin around to see a slight figure crouching on the wall across the graveyard, above the gate.

Poole followed my gaze and gave a shout; the intruder straightened, pausing long enough for me to see that it was a boy of about ten, dressed in a ragged cap and breeches. His skin was darker than usual for an English child; he would not have looked out of place on the streets of Naples.

'You there – stay where you are!' Poole yelled. The boy instantly disappeared, dropping to the far side of the wall silent as a cat. Poole swore and set off at a run across the grass towards the gate, hampered by his damaged leg. 'Cut the little fucker off the other side,' he called to me over his shoulder, pointing at the tree. I launched myself up through the branches and over the wall to the street, landing hard and narrowly missing a pile of horseshit. Cursing, I ran the length of the street towards the row of cottages, but there was no sign of the boy to left or right when I reached the end. A couple of minutes later, Poole rounded the opposite corner, slowing when he saw me. I shook my head; the child could have slipped into any number of hiding places, or simply outrun us.

'How long was he watching?' Poole breathed hard, his face rigid with anger.

'No idea. I saw him a moment before you did.' But I remember the cold sensation of being watched earlier; had the boy been there all along?

'I want to know his business.' He bunched his fists. I was surprised by his anger.

'We're not likely to find him now. He was probably just a street boy being nosy.'

'That's what I'm worried about. Why would he be watching the Cross Bones?'

'You think he was spying? For whom?'

Poole rolled his eyes. 'I wonder that Master Secretary sets such store by your wits,' he said, and I did not miss the barb in his tone. I realised then that he resented me – and that could only mean Walsingham had spoken highly enough of me for Poole to fear I threatened his standing. I confess that the thought pleased me. 'No one is supposed to know that Clara is dead, least of all me,' he continued, his voice a low growl. 'Coaxing a slip-up from Babington and his friends depends on me pretending I know nothing of her whereabouts. If I have been seen poking about the scene of her murder, my deception will be exposed.'

'Exactly as Phelippes warned,' I murmured. He shot me a hostile glare.

'He saw you too.'

I refrained from reminding him that Phelippes had foreseen that as well.

'We're not going to find the boy now. The best thing we can do is get away from here as quickly as possible. It's probably nothing,' I added as we retraced his steps past the cottages. 'Maybe he just took a fancy to the horse. You said yourself the whole borough is full of thieves.'

Poole stopped dead and stared at me. 'Shit. The gate.'

He broke into a run; I followed him around the corner and we tumbled through the open door of the Cross Bones, to find the graveyard empty. Only a fresh pile of dung by the brazier gave any indication that a horse had ever been there. Poole tore off his hat and flung it on the ground with an impressive string of oaths that would have made a Neapolitan proud. When he had exhausted all the words he knew, he looked at me.

'Are you *laughing*?'

'Sorry,' I said, leaning against the wall and clutching my

stomach. I could not even say why I found the situation so funny; the two of us, vying with each other for Walsingham's approbation as to who was the best of his espials, while a child thief had played us like a lute. Poole took a step forward and I shrank against the wall, bracing myself to dodge a punch, but he stopped abruptly and doubled over, his shoulders shaking. Eventually I realised he was laughing too.

'Oh, fuck,' he said, when he could speak, straightening up and wiping his eyes. 'It wasn't even my horse. It was Ballard's. He'll have my balls.' He laid a hand on my shoulder and burst into guffaws again. I clapped him on the back. I could see that this was a way for him to release the pent-up emotion of the past hour, and it seemed to have broken the tension between us too. But I couldn't help a glance behind me. Perhaps the boy was a mere horse thief, but he had seen my face.

EIGHT

We caught a wherry back across the river from Goat Stairs and walked back up through the city to Leadenhall. I bought a pie from a street vendor on the way, though Poole ate nothing; his fit of hilarity had passed in the boat and a morose mood had overtaken him. I wondered if he was brooding on his sister or the loss of the horse.

Back at Phelippes's rooms, we found Walsingham prowling the large study like one of the Queen's caged beasts, while his cryptographer sat in his usual place at the desk, head bowed, quill scratching.

'You took your time,' Walsingham said, not quite hiding his irritation. 'I began to think you'd gone back to France.' This last was directed at me.

'The journey took a while,' I said, not looking at Poole.

'Huh. Was it worth the trouble? Anything useful?'

'Bruno found this, Your Honour,' Poole said, holding out the locket. 'It's my sister's all right.'

Walsingham turned it over in his palm and raised an eyebrow at me. 'That's worth a bit. I'm surprised it wasn't spotted by greedy eyes. Where did you find it?'

'In the undergrowth,' I said.

'We think she might have thrown it there when she realised

her life was in danger,' Poole added. Walsingham continued to look at me, a question in his eyes. I could have voiced my reservations about Poole's theory but I was not about to make him look foolish in front of his superiors.

Walsingham nodded. 'Thomas.'

He tossed the locket to Phelippes, who snapped it open, removed the lock of hair, then inserted a fine, thin tool into the hinge. Soundlessly, the inner casing flipped up to reveal a hidden compartment. With a pair of tweezers, Phelippes removed a thin strip of paper and unfolded it, while Poole stared in amazement.

'Ingenious, no?' Walsingham allowed a brief smile. 'Bloody Mary gave these as gifts to her trusted women. Useful way to carry secret messages around unseen.'

'I have seen something similar,' I said, thinking of a woman I had known long ago, in Naples.

'Clara never showed me this,' Poole said, with a hint of indignation, his eyes wide. 'Is that how she hid messages from the conspirators?'

'One of the ways.' Walsingham pressed his lips together with a grim satisfaction. 'Get to work, Thomas. What have you there, Bruno?'

'I found this in the same place,' I said, handing him the pitcher. 'It's recent, there's a little wine left in the bottom. I don't know if it's useful. There was nothing else there that I could see.'

Poole frowned. 'Except a quantity of blood. I would speak with you alone, Your Honour. It's time I was allowed to see my sister, and bury her.'

'Long past time,' Walsingham agreed. 'But for now I need you close to Babington. Ballard is expected back in London any day and I must have Bruno prepared for his return.'

I opened my mouth to interject but he spoke to Poole over me: 'Find out what you can. Mark what they ask you about your sister, and who among them seems ill at ease. Continue to tell them you have not heard from her.'

Poole appeared to consider arguing, but subsided under the force of Walsingham's stare. In the doorway he paused, one hand on the post.

'That locket belongs to me,' he said, with a hint of warning. 'It's all I have of her.'

'And you shall have it, as soon as Thomas has finished his work,' Walsingham said, in the same reasonable tone. 'Bring your news to Seething Lane after supper and we'll speak further. I know how hard this must be, Robin. Your loyalty and obedience will be remembered, when this is done.'

Poole gave a curt nod and disappeared. Walsingham waited until his footsteps had died on the stairs before closing the door to Phelippes's chamber.

'She'll be in the ground by then. That curate you met at the leper chapel – he's burying one of his elderly parishioners this afternoon. Clara will go in the churchyard at the same time, no one will be any the wiser and with luck, Robin will never have to see the body. Especially after my physician opened her this morning, at your suggestion. No sign that she was with child.'

I felt obscurely disappointed; I had wanted to be right about that.

'Then we can rule out that theory, at least. I suppose there is no doubt that her death is connected to the conspiracy.'

'But *why*, Bruno? What did they suspect – did they know they'd been infiltrated? That is what I need to know. What did you make of your trip to Southwark?'

'I don't understand why I was there.' I jerked my thumb towards the door. 'Why did you send *him* to search the place?'

'Robin was determined to go, with my permission or without.' Walsingham walked to the window and peered out over the street. 'He came to me demanding I give him one of my men to help. Seemed convinced there must be something there to discover that would help him pin the blame. I thought it better to let him feel he was being useful, and I thought of you because you'll have to get to know each other – you'll be looking out for one another among the conspirators. And with a stranger his guard might have been down. One must always watch the watchers, eh, Bruno?'

I looked at his back as his meaning became clear. 'You don't suspect *Poole*? Of murdering his own sister?'

Walsingham turned, with a sombre smile. 'Let us rather say, I hold no one above suspicion in anything. Every man has a price. Even Thomas. Isn't that right, Thomas?'

'I would have dispatched her more efficiently,' Phelippes said, without looking up. There appeared to be no trace of irony in his words. 'Not with that absurd spectacle. Besides, I was with you at Seething Lane that night.'

Walsingham winked at me, but I could only think of Frances Sidney's remark that Phelippes had no more human feeling than a clockwork machine. There was something chilling about the man; I had no doubt that he could kill in the Queen's service if the proposal made logical sense, and that he would plan it to the last detail with a total absence of conscience.

'But you're right, it would be a stretch to suspect Poole,' Walsingham said. He looked even more exhausted than he had the day before. 'How did he seem to you?'

'Like a man fighting to remain master of his feelings,' I said.

'Which feelings, precisely?'

'Guilt. Anger. Grief, obviously. I was praying he wouldn't stumble on a severed ear – it was bad enough trying to reason away the bloodstains he found. He knows you have not told him the whole truth. You can't seriously think he would have done anything so vicious? He clearly loved her.'

'Oh, Robin loved Clara a great deal, no question,' Walsingham said, wandering over to Phelippes's desk. He let the statement hang, ripe with ambiguity. 'And this?' He picked up the locket, dangling it from the broken chain.

'It was there for the finding. I'd be surprised if that was coincidence.'

'Interesting. Who planted it, I wonder? Clara? Or her killer? And why?' He pulled at his beard. 'Is it a cipher, Thomas?'

Phelippes glanced up from the paper. He wore a pair of magnifying lenses fixed with a silver hinge over his nose; they made his eyes disturbingly fish-like. 'It's a series of symbols, very precisely drawn. But it doesn't fit with any code I recognise from the Babington group. I will need to give it more study.'

'Quick as you can. If it was meant to be found, someone wants us to read it. Perhaps the victim herself. And have the wine in that bottle tested, see if there is anything to be learned. As for you, Bruno,' he clapped me on the shoulder, 'I'm expecting news any day of our Spanish Jesuit's arrival. Time for you to stop dancing around me like a coy maiden, who may or may not. Will you return to your squabbling undergraduates and a French knife in your back, or will you lend your considerable talents to protecting Queen Elizabeth and the freedom of England?'

He spoke as if he had never doubted my decision.

'Poole says Ballard and Savage are dangerous fanatics.'

'You knew that. They wish to assassinate the Queen. You saw what was done to Clara.'

'They will cut my throat in a heartbeat if they suspect me. That would be no use to you. Or to me.'

'But we shall make sure they won't.' He smiled. 'Come, Bruno. You lived for two years at the French embassy, trusted associate of the ambassador, protégé of King Henri, all the while working for me and never suspected. You know how to play a part quite as if you were born to it.'

'But I was at least playing a version of myself. And there were those who suspected my loyalty even then – they just couldn't prove it. You want me to become someone else entirely – I have no experience of that. What if I should slip up, or be recognised?'

'No experience?' The smile grew wider, but there was

warmth in it. 'Philip Sidney told me you spent two years travelling through Italy under a false name after you abandoned the Dominican order without permission, with the Inquisition at your heels. You can become someone else when it suits you.'

'That was ten years ago. I had a greater appetite for adventure then, and no choice about it.'

'I don't believe your craving for adventure has diminished since. Else you would not have caught a midnight boat from France to bring me Berden's letter. As for choice . . .' He laid a hand on my shoulder and the smile vanished. 'Don't you see, Bruno – you are the only one who can do this for us. The arrival of the Jesuit makes it the perfect opportunity. No one else has the ability to get inside Babington's circle and make sure this conspiracy plays out as we need it to.'

'I feel as if we are reliving history,' I said, suddenly weary. 'All this happened three years ago with Throckmorton and his plot.'

'How do you think *I* feel?' He threw his hands up with a mirthless laugh. 'These plots repeat year after year, and they will keep coming, for as long as Mary Stuart lives to shout her claim to anyone who blames the government for his misfortune. The difference this time is that we have a real chance to cut off the source of them for good.' He drew the edge of his hand across his throat. It was this, more than anything he said, that betrayed his desperation; Walsingham was not given to dramatic gestures.

I hesitated. That was my mistake. His eyes hardened; I had made him doubt my commitment, and he despised above all a man who wavered.

'There is another consideration,' he said. 'Your friend Sophia Underhill.'

'What of her?' The immediacy of my response, and its defensiveness, were enough to show him that he had hit the mark.

'When did you last see her?'

'In the spring. I don't remember. February or March, perhaps.'

March 17th; it was etched in my memory. She had told me she thought it best we did not meet any more. She worried about my reputation in Paris, and hers among the English Catholics there if she should be seen with me. She feared I hoped for too much from her. It was then that I had decided to go to Wittenberg.

'Did you know she planned to return to England?'

'She mentioned the possibility, though only as a plan for the distant future.'

'She arrived in London in – when was it, Thomas?'

'Third of May,' Phelippes said, not troubling to look up.

'May.' Walsingham fixed me with a stern look. 'Charles Paget wrote and told me. He continues to try and curry favour with me, and thought the information might come in useful. He had set her up with a position, as a companion to Lady Grace Cavendish. Wife of Sir Henry Cavendish, an old gaming associate of Paget's.'

The names meant nothing to me. I held his gaze, waiting for him to reveal his purpose. Wherever he was tending, it would not be good.

'Henry Cavendish is the eldest son of Bess of Hardwick, from her first marriage. A libertine, gambler, drunk and an idiot, up to his neck in debt. He was disinherited years ago in favour of his brother. Eight bastard children and not a one with his wife. You can see why she would need a companion, poor creature.'

'Is Sophia in danger?' The thought of her living under the same roof as a man like that made the hairs stand up on my arms. Walsingham allowed a wolfish smile; my reaction seemed to have pleased him.

'Oh, I think your Sophia knows how to take care of entitled men, does she not?' He left a significant pause. 'She's still going by the name of Mary Gifford, by the way. But she had another name once – besides the one she was baptised with, I mean. She was known in Canterbury as Mrs Kate Kingsley. You remember, I'm sure.'

A chill flooded through me and I felt my throat constrict. I understood him now, and did not trust myself to speak.

'In fact,' he continued, his voice smooth, 'she was wanted for murder under that name, do you recall?'

'The case was closed. She was never convicted.'

'More accurate to say she was never brought to trial,' he said. 'Paget doesn't know about that business. He took an interest in her because he found her intelligent and he is practised enough to know when someone is hiding their past. And, of course, because he knew she was of interest to you. But it was bold of her to come back to England so soon. There's every chance of her being recognised, and even a man like Henry Cavendish wouldn't want a cold-blooded murderess playing chess with his wife.'

'She's not a murderess.' I fought to keep my voice level.

'I'm sure she is not.' His tone had grown placatory, which was always the most dangerous. 'From what you have told me, she is a most resourceful and sharp-witted girl. She must be, to have outwitted you.'

I wondered how he knew of that, and supposed Sidney must have told him the whole story: how I had acted to clear Sophia's name in Canterbury, believing she returned my feelings, only for her to flee to France after stealing a valuable book from me, as if I meant nothing to her. The betrayal still stung. I said nothing.

'I should like to make use of her talents,' Walsingham continued, as if he were merely thinking aloud.

This made me straighten. 'How?'

'Henry Cavendish is uncle to the lovely Bessie Pierrepont, who has caught our young friend Gifford's imagination, as I told you. Bessie is a frequent visitor to her aunt Lady Grace, and shares confidences. Another pair of eyes and ears in that household would be extremely useful.'

'What makes you think Sophia would work for you?' The thought of her pressed into Walsingham's service made my head ache; she would leap at the chance of a role beyond those available to her as a woman of no means, the excitement of it. Just like Clara Poole.

'Because I could have her arrested for the murder of her husband and sent to stand trial in Canterbury any time I chose,' he said, with a trace of impatience. 'But if she helps me, I will help her. She wants to find her son, does she not? The one she was forced to give up three years ago.'

I stared at him. 'You know where he is? How?'

He arched an eyebrow. 'Really, Bruno. There's not much goes on in this realm that I can't find out.'

'Does Sophia know?' Even the discovery that her son was alive would mean the world to her. But perhaps a glimmer of possibility would be worse than ignorance; as far as I was aware, the boy had been sold by Sophia's aunt to a wealthy childless couple and there was little chance that his mother, as an unmarried woman, could hope to get him back, especially if she could not reveal her true identity. Knowing Sophia, that would not stop her trying.

'I have not yet found an opportunity to speak with her. That rather depends on you.' He let the implication hang there between us.

'You mean that if I don't agree to this Babington business, you won't tell her about her son?'

'I mean, Bruno, that you risked a great deal to save her from a murder charge once before, so I have no doubt you would do so again.'

We watched one another like dogs at the start of a fight; his eyes were implacable. I wondered how long he had been keeping this ultimatum up his sleeve. If I did not agree to his proposal, he would see Sophia arrested for murder. If I did what he wanted, his generosity would extend to her as well as me. I realised, with a quickening flush of shame, how foolish I had been to think of Walsingham as a benign father figure to his agents; looking at him now, the hard line of his compressed lips, I saw the man who could turn the rack on a young priest without flinching, who would put his daughter's closest friend in an unmarked grave to save his mission, and I understood that nothing would come between him and his duty to England and the Queen.

'Her Majesty's Service is not a *hobby*, Bruno,' he said with quiet finality. 'It's not for you to pick and choose the parts that strike you as an amusing pastime. England needs your skills now. That is all there is to it. Do we have an agreement?'

My fists drew tight at my sides as I tried to outstare him; I felt the strain in my jaw as I fought to batten down the rising tide of anger, just as I had seen Poole doing earlier. At length, I bowed my head. There was nothing left to say.

'Good. I am needed at Whitehall. You will do as Thomas tells you until I return, I hope that's clear.' He paused on his way past me to the door, and laid a hand on my shoulder. 'God be with you.'

I almost responded, but I was furious with him and determined that he should know it. I turned my face away. He waited a moment, and withdrew. I stood, fixed to the spot, shaking with rage. Phelippes's quill scratched on rhythmically in the empty air.

'Do you think he'd have done it?' I asked, turning to him. 'Sent her for trial to punish me? After everything we have been through?'

The cryptographer unexpectedly looked up, took off his eyeglasses and blinked at me. 'You don't really need to ask that. He will do whatever is necessary for the good of the state.'

'Of course.' I placed my hands on the edge of his desk and leaned over him, hearing the bitterness in my voice. 'The good of the state. Why should he have a conscience over sending one girl to the gallows, when he has none over sending a queen to the block?'

'The stake,' Phelippes corrected, angling himself away from me to avoid being spat on.

'What?'

'Your woman is accused of killing her husband. In English law that is petty treason. Her punishment would be burning at the stake.'

I pictured Sophia's face engulfed by flames and closed my eyes briefly.

'You know, I once believed he had some affection for me.'

'He respects your talents.'

'But we are all pawns to him in the end. Poole was right. Even you.' When he didn't reply, I moved closer until my face was an inch from his. I wanted to provoke a reaction, but he merely blinked again.

'Truer to say we are troops in a war. A general cannot shed a tear over every soldier who falls.'

'But a good general stands by his men.'

When he did not reply, I slapped my palm on the desk, hard.

'Doesn't that make you angry, Thomas? You've devoted your whole life to him. Or do you imagine you are different?'

He returned his attention to the paper before him. 'I have never given it much thought,' he said. I realised that, unusually, Thomas Phelippes was lying.

NINE

The next day passed without incident, while we all awaited further news from Walsingham. My orders from Phelippes were to stay indoors, on the grounds that I should not be seen around London before I was ready to encounter the Babington group as the Spanish Jesuit. Gifford, too, was confined to our lodgings; he could not risk running into any of the conspirators until Phelippes had finished copying and deciphering the latest batch of letters he had brought from Mary in Staffordshire and Gifford was free to hand over the originals. I slept fitfully, since there was nothing else for me to do, though I felt no better for it; I was wound so tight that the moment I began to drift into blissful oblivion, the slightest sound snapped me back to wakefulness, where I lay on the bed considering all the ways this plan might fatally misfire. In the afternoon, Gifford and I played cards, but since I would not play for money, and he saw no point in playing without, the game soon petered out, leaving us both pacing and irritable.

By early evening I was ready to beg Phelippes to let me go at least as far as a tavern for supper instead of sending out for food again; even a low place where no one would know me was better than those four walls in the company of Gifford.

I was pulling on my boots in readiness when Phelippes's head appeared around the door to summon us into the study.

'Good news,' he said abruptly as he settled behind his desk, leaving us standing before it like two schoolboys waiting to be reprimanded. 'We've received word that Mendoza's Jesuit was apprehended the day before yesterday coming ashore at Southampton and is already on his way to London in custody. Even better news for you, Bruno – he is in his thirties with a full complement of limbs, so we are more than halfway there. His name is Xavier Prado, so you'd better get used to it. He is expected to arrive at Barn Elms some time tonight and will be interrogated immediately.'

I felt Gifford stiffen beside me. If Phelippes noticed, he ignored it, and pointed his penknife at me.

'If by tomorrow morning we have sufficient information from him to make the operation plausible, you will be introduced to the conspirators the same night, when Gilbert will deliver the latest correspondence from Mary. They are meeting for supper at The Castle tavern on Cornhill. Ballard is expected back from France today or tomorrow – they will want to discuss how to proceed in the light of her encouragement and their new-found Spanish support.'

'That hardly seems enough time to prepare,' I ventured. I did not relish another day confined in Phelippes's rooms, but the prospect of being thrown in with all the conspirators at once, especially with the famously sharp eyes of John Ballard on me, seemed suddenly alarmingly real.

'There is no time to waste.' Phelippes tapped the handle of his knife on the desk as if to reinforce the urgency. 'If Clara Poole was killed because they guessed she was a spy, they will want to reconsider their strategy as soon as possible. I would speculate that they are awaiting the return of Ballard – none of them would dare alter their course without his say-so, not even Babington. Master Secretary wants you at that table tomorrow, to observe what is said of her, and by whom. We must assume at least one of them knows of her death – but was it agreed among them all, or is the killer hiding it from his fellows?'

'They may not wish to discuss the matter in front of a newcomer,' I said. 'If they are counting on Spanish support, they will not want Spain to know the plot may be compromised.'

Phelippes considered this. 'True. But that in itself would be worth noting. Robin will be there – we can have him make some reference to his sister, you can observe their reactions.'

'This is a mad scheme.' Gifford folded his arms and crossed to the window, making his pique evident with small huffy noises through his nose. He had been regaling me with his objections all day, all of which centred on his own fear of being found out and punished. 'They'll never believe Bruno's a Spanish Jesuit.'

A crease appeared between Phelippes's brows, as it always did when he found a question irrational. 'Why would they not? Look at him. He has the looks, he speaks the language, he knows Catholic doctrine inside out – unlike you, Gilbert, Bruno did manage to get himself successfully ordained, whereas you were thrown out of the seminary, I believe.'

Gifford pushed out his lip and snorted again; I almost laughed.

'I was excommunicated later,' I said, to make him feel better.

'He will bring letters and money from Ambassador Mendoza, and the promise of Spanish troops – they will think all their prayers have been answered at once.'

Gifford hunched his shoulders, tucking his chin into his chest. 'But you don't know them, Thomas.' His voice had grown quiet, and less petulant. 'If he puts one foot wrong, one word, it would be enough to arouse their suspicion . . . It's hard enough already trying to keep on top of my own double life without having to remember to call him by the right name and not give away that I know Clara's dead.' He looked tired and pale, and very young. I felt sorry for him.

'You would find it easier to remember the detail if you stayed away from the alehouse,' Phelippes remarked, without sympathy. I watched the cryptographer arranging his papers neatly in front of him, and wondered if he had any life away from that desk. Had he ever fallen wildly and hopelessly in love, or got drunk and laughed until the sun came up, or jumped on a tavern table to dance when a musician struck up a tune? Had he even had a woman? No doubt he would go at it with the same methodical concentration he brought to everything, point by point. The image made me convulse with sudden giggles, like a schoolboy. Phelippes glanced up, frowning.

'They *meet* in alehouses, for God's sake, I can hardly avoid it.' Gifford's voice had grown plaintive again. 'If they suspect Bruno of being a spy, they will suspect me too, for bringing him to the group. They will cut both our throats before the first course is served.'

Phelippes wrinkled his nose. 'That would be inconvenient. I think it more likely they would wait until you left the tavern. Two corpses would be difficult to dispose of without attracting attention. Besides, I do not think they would cut your throats, it would be too quick. If they suspect you, they will want to question you hard to find out what you know first.'

'Why must you be so damned literal, always?' Gifford pushed both hands through his hair, made a strangled noise of frustration and wrapped his arms around his chest.

Phelippes blinked twice and returned his attention to the desk, considering.

'That is a good thought, however. Perhaps we should have a system in place which would allow you to dispatch yourselves quickly, should it come to that, before they can make you talk. A small vial of poison concealed about your person, if it were concentrated enough—'

I let out a bark of laughter, and heard a high note of panic in it. 'I do love this about you, Thomas – I can never tell when you're joking.'

He pursed his lips. 'Why would I joke about your deaths? It would make life very difficult. Especially his.' He gestured towards Gifford. 'We could not find another plausible courier at such short notice.'

Even Gifford laughed then, as he caught my eye. 'Well, I'll do my best not to add to your load by getting murdered. I am going out now.'

'Where?' Phelippes looked alarmed.

'Who are you, my mother?' Gifford pulled his short, green cloak around his shoulder and settled his sword belt. 'Must I report my every move for your approval? I am going for food and drink and company. I have friends in London, you know.'

Phelippes's gaze travelled slowly to me; Gifford raised a hand to pre-empt him.

'And no, I will not take Bruno with me. I have no need of a nursemaid. Give you good night. Leave the latch off – I don't know what time I'll be back.'

With that, he swung open the door with a great show of defiance and indignation, but his cloak became entangled with the bolt and ruined the effect. He pulled it free with a huff and swept out. I suppressed a smile.

Phelippes looked at the door as it slammed, worrying at his lip.

'Follow him,' he said, after a moment.

'*Dio mio*. All day you've had me cooped up in this room like a mad dog because I mustn't be seen in London until I am introduced to Babington tomorrow, and now you want me running around after Gifford? Leave him to his diversions. What harm if he has a few drinks with friends?'

'He is lying. He has no friends in the city that we know of, outside Babington's group.'

'Then he must be seeing them. The last thing you would want is for them to spot me trailing him.'

'So make sure they do not, if it is them. Cover your head.'

Phelippes tapped the handle of the penknife against his open palm, his brow creased in concentration. 'I find it unlikely he would meet Babington or the others tonight, since he can't take the letters yet, and to the best of my knowledge they do not know he is back in London. But if he is seeing any of them separately, we should know of it.'

'Perhaps he is meeting a girl.'

'That would be worse. He is liable to drink and brag about his secret work to impress her. Master Secretary does not trust him, as you know. But we should learn if he has other associates. Hurry, he will be gone.'

'Why can't you follow him? Might do you good to get out to a tavern for the night, Thomas.'

'I have all this to get through.' He made a sweeping motion over the piles of paper on the desk. 'Besides—' he hesitated, and his gaze dropped to his hands. 'I lack the skill for it. I cannot converse easily in a tavern – people think me odd. I would stand out.'

'You think I do not?'

'You attract attention for being foreign, I grant you. But once people see past that they warm to you, Bruno, in a way they do not with me. You can make them laugh. I do not have that talent.'

I pitied him then; for all his brilliance, there was something childlike about him, as if he did not understand how to move among men. 'Damn you,' I said, slapping him on the arm in a way that was meant to be reassuring. He flinched. I shrugged on my doublet and pulled a hat down over my forehead.

He disappeared under his desk and opened a chest, emerging with a leather purse in his hand, from which he took a handful of silver shillings. 'In case you need to buy yourself supper,' he said. 'Quick, or you will lose him.'

I paused outside the front door, trying to judge whether Gifford was likely to have turned right toward the Aldgate or left, in the direction of Bishopsgate; five minutes of walking in the wrong direction and I would have no hope of catching him up. The prospect was not unappealing; I could take Phelippes's money, buy myself a quiet supper in a tavern and claim Gifford had escaped me, rather than spend the evening skulking after him. But I had my pride; I did not want Walsingham to think I had lost any of my skills during my months in France. The road to Aldgate was busier, with more places to eat, but there had been something evasive in Gifford's manner, especially in the way he had so quickly resisted any suggestion of my company, which made me suspect that he preferred not to be seen. I took a gamble and turned left, quickening my pace until I rounded the corner of Leadenhall and, to my relief, caught a glimpse of his green cloak ahead at the end of the street, approaching the city wall. The church bells had tolled seven while we were talking in Phelippes's rooms, and evening sun glinted on windowpanes from a sky patched with white cloud, though the air was unseasonably cold. I was glad of it; London in the heat smells like a cesspool, and the chill gave me an excuse to wear my hat pulled low and my collar up without looking too out of place.

Bishopsgate Street was busy, despite the temperature; people making their way home from the markets or out of the city from a day's labouring, while others were dressed up in their finery, as if for an evening out. Now and again a carriage lurched past, causing people to scatter to either side of the street, cursing as they tried to peer in the windows. One or two passers-by glanced at me sidelong from beneath their caps or kerchiefs, but this was likely because I was intent on keeping to the sides of the street, close to doorways or alleys I could slip into unnoticed if my quarry should turn around, and must have looked as if I were stalking someone to rob them. But no one challenged me, or called me a filthy Spanish son of a whore, as had happened so many times on the streets of London. There seemed no danger of Gifford noticing me either, as I quickened my pace; he continued blithely on his way, the jaunty bounce to his walk making me suspect that I had been right in guessing that he was on his way to a romantic tryst. Would it be the famous Bessie Pierrepont, whose ample virtues he had elaborated to me the night before? But this Bessie was an attendant to the Queen; it seemed unlikely that she would have the opportunity for assignations in city alehouses.

Gifford passed under the arch of the Bishopsgate and I hung back at a safe distance, hiding myself among the crowds. On our left, the high walls of the Bedlam hospital for the mad cast long shadows over the street; occasional wild cries rose up from the interior, and I noticed people swerving away, as if they might catch the affliction on the air. Londoners in their fine clothes surrounded us, all moving in the same direction, and it was only as I overheard a couple of young gallants with bright slashed sleeves arguing about the competing talents of their favoured performers that I realised, with a sinking of my spirits, that Gifford must be headed for one of the playhouses built out here beyond the city limits, on the outskirts of the village of Shoreditch. The last thing I needed at the end of this long day, tired and hungry, was a night at the theatre.

The Curtain was set back from the main road, its dirty whitewashed walls softened by the amber glow of evening sun. The audience funnelled into a tight throng as we neared the main gates and I pressed through, despite the protests from those jostling around me, to keep Gifford's green cloak in my sights. In the yard outside, wooden stalls with bright awnings sold beer and bread; others hired out horsehair cushions to patrons rich enough to pay for a seat. A broad man stood in the entrance, collecting the fee in a ceramic box; as Gifford approached, they greeted one another with a mock salute as if they were old acquaintances and I squeezed forward until only three people stood between us, close enough to hear their conversation.

'Back again, sir? You're a glutton for punishment,' said the doorman with a grin, holding out his hand for Gifford's coin. 'You'll like this new one. *Three Ladies of London.* Tell you what, you could get that down Bankside for half the price, eh? All three at the same time.'

Gifford joined in with a gust of raucous laughter, trying hard to sound like a man of the world.

'Well, it can't be worse than the last one, the other day,' he said with feeling. 'That revenge thing. There was so much pig's blood on the stage the heroine slipped right off into the pit as she was stabbing herself.'

'Ah, that was the last night, they were having a laugh among themselves,' the doorman said, with the air of inside knowledge. 'Bleedin' actors. Drives Mr Burbage mad, but the crowds love it. There'll be none of that tonight, it's a morality play. Worst of all worlds. Any case, you young fellas only come to gawp at the real girls, am I right?'

Gifford grinned and ducked his head, but I saw a fierce blush inflame the side of his face and realised I'd guessed right.

'Get a move on, some of us want to get in before the Second Coming,' called a plump woman in front of me, and the line behind us raised a cheer in support. Gifford glanced around and I ducked behind her broad hat, heart thumping. But he looked straight past me; I paid my penny and followed him through the tall gates into the theatre yard.

The Curtain was a larger, permanent version of the old inn yard theatres I had seen on my travels through England: tiers of wooden galleries built on three sides of a rectangle around a central pit, with the stage protruding into the space where the crowds milled around, buying hot pies and rolls from vendors with trays around their necks, while girls in garish face-paint swayed their hips and batted their lashes at potential customers. Keeping half an eye on Gifford, I craned my neck to look up at the galleries, where for three or fourpence the wealthier spectators could watch the play seated. The noise of excited chatter echoed around the rafters; I wondered how the actors would ever make themselves heard. A girl wandered past with a tray of pies; I fished for more of Phelippes's money and bought two. If I was going to spend the evening on my feet watching something as appalling as the doorman made it sound, I would need to keep my strength up.

Gifford had positioned himself near the stage, leaning back against it, chewing anxiously on his thumbnail as he scanned the upper balconies. I found a spot behind a tall, red-headed man in a leather jacket where I could keep an eye on the boy and hide myself from view if he should turn his gaze on the groundlings. I had just taken a bite of pie – some unidentifiable grey meat in congealing fat, I tried not to look too closely – when the man I was using as my shield stepped back into me, knocking it out of my hand. He immediately apologised, the way the English always do in crowds, even if you barge into them.

'Don't worry.' I said, brushing pastry off my doublet. I held up the second pie. 'I already have a spare, and I think that might be one too many.'

He laughed. 'My mate swears he found a rat's tail in one of them once. I've done you a favour, eh. Mug of beer instead?' He made as if to head for the stall at the back selling ale; I grabbed his sleeve before he could move and leave me exposed to Gifford's view.

'No need, I'm fine. Have you seen this play?' I asked, to distract him.

'Nah, it only opened three nights ago. Saw the one before, though.'

'The revenge thing? I heard it was good.'

'You heard wrong. It was shit.'

'People slipping off the stage in the fake blood? Sounded funny to me.'

'Oh, that was only the last night,' he said, with an air of expertise. 'Didn't happen the other times I saw it. You're right, it was better as a comedy. The crowd thought so, anyway.'

'It was so bad you saw it more than once?'

'Mate, no one comes for the play. The toffs come to watch each other. Me, I come for the ladies, and not the ones on stage.' He nudged me and nodded towards the whores strolling around the edges of the crowd. 'Better quality than you get down Bankside, eh?'

I nodded, but my brain was racing to catch up with the implication of his words. 'So – when was the last night of that revenge play? The night they fell off the stage?'

He rubbed his chin. 'That would have been four nights ago.'

'The twenty-seventh?'

'If you say so. It was a Friday, I know that much.'

'You're sure?'

'Certain. What are you, the fucking magistrate?' He caught my expression and cuffed me on the arm, almost making me drop the other pie. 'Only kidding. I know because it was the day I got paid. I came here after I knocked off work. Had a sore head and aching balls to show for it the next morning, and not much left of my wages.' He looked briefly rueful. 'Still, a man's got to enjoy himself sometimes, eh? Otherwise, what's it all for?'

'You're a philosopher, sir,' I said, peering round him to check on Gifford. The boy had told Walsingham he returned from his most recent trip to Staffordshire on the 29th, the same day I arrived in London. But if he had been present at the last night of the revenge play, it meant he had been in town at least two days before he reported to Phelippes's lodgings, and had lied to them about it. Walsingham was not wrong to suspect that Gifford was double-dealing with him, it seemed. It also meant that Gifford had been in London on the 27th of July, the night Clara Poole was murdered. That was absurd, though; I could not see Gifford, with his mercurial, fearful, self-interested temperament, killing a woman even if his own life depended on it, let alone mustering the cruelty necessary to mutilate and break her face, nor could I see what motive he would have – unless he were acting on behalf of one of the others, so that they could keep their alibi. The more I considered the brutality of her death, the more it seemed the work of a madman who took some perverse pleasure from savagery, or else the exact opposite – a cold man who could act with complete detachment. A professional soldier, perhaps – not a failed student priest like Gifford, who could talk up his desire for revolution in a tavern with a few pots of ale inside him, but buckled the moment he faced the prospect of punishment. I studied Gifford's profile over the red-headed man's shoulder. Apparently he was not afraid of defying Walsingham when it suited him, though, so maybe I had underestimated his mettle.

An expectant ripple travelled through the crowd as an actor stepped on to the stage; some in the audience even broke off their conversations and turned to the front. He bowed low and began intoning a Prologue in lumpen verse, raising his voice to compete with the jeers and catcalls from the spectators. But his words washed over me, because at that moment I saw Gifford's face light up; he was not looking at the stage, but at one of the boxes alongside it, where the gentry paid sixpence a seat to be seen. I followed the direction of his gaze and had to fight to keep my mouth from hanging open.

In the box, three young women had arrived and begun taking their seats with a great deal of fuss, as if determined to distract attention from the performance. The one on the right wore a dark red gown with a lace shawl fastened modestly across her breast and had tied her mousy hair back in a net under a fashionable hood. Though her clothes and rings suggested money, her face was pale and pinched as if she did not eat enough, and she glanced about at the crowd with a nervous air that suggested she was uncomfortable up there on public display. The girl to her left could hardly have been more different in her manner. Her black hair hung in loose ringlets over her shoulders under her hood, a sign that she was unmarried, and she leaned forward over the wooden balustrade to give anyone who cared to look a fine view down her bodice. She was pretty, in an obvious way; her face heart-shaped with small, neat features and clear skin. Her sharp eyes scanned the spectators as she toyed with an elaborate fan, peacock-blue to match the expensive silk of her dress, and adjusted her posture to one side and then the other, well aware of the admiring glances she drew. But the third woman in the box was the most arresting, at least to me: it was Sophia Underhill.

Though it had been only a matter of months since I had last seen her, she had the same effect on me as she did every time. I always thought of Dante's description of his first sight of the divine Beatrice, in the *Vita Nuova*: 'the vital spirit, which dwells in the inmost depths of the heart, began to tremble so violently that I felt the vibration in all my pulses'. I had mentioned this to Sidney once; he had laughed, and said he knew exactly where I was feeling my vital spirits pulsing. I could curse Sophia for this power she had over me – quite without intention on her part, since she had never been a coquettish kind of girl, and almost seemed to resent the attention she attracted from men. I had risked my life for her more than once, and she had rewarded me with deception, but I had forgiven her because I understood her reasons; somehow I never managed to let go of the hope that, in different circumstances, she might come to see that she would not find another man who would respect her independent spirit the way I did. The problem with Sophia was that she was not looking to find a man at all; she had long ago lost her faith in men and God.

She leaned on the ledge of the box, chin resting in her hand, her eyes fixed on the actor with an expression of detached amusement. The last of the evening sun, almost vanished behind the roof of the theatre, caught the edge of her cheekbone, making her skin glow gold. She did not wear the pale face-paint fashionable among the ladies of the court, and kept her dark lashes and full brows as nature had made them, instead of plucking and painting them back in a thin line; her chestnut hair hung long down her back under a small white hood, though I could have vouched for the fact that she was no longer a virgin. Even before the only time she came to my bed – I still dreamed about it – she was already a mother, though of course no one among her new companions would know of that. They would take her at face value as Mary Gifford, a pious, modest maid, just as she had seemed in Paris. I guessed that the nervous woman with the pinched face must be her new employer, Lady Grace Cavendish, and judging by the way Gifford was gazing like a stunned bullock at the flirtatious girl in the centre with the dark hair, this could only be Bessie Pierrepont, showing off her noble virtues.

I moved a couple of feet from the shelter of my new friend the philosopher, to keep the women in my sights. The dark-haired girl leaned across and whispered something to Sophia from behind her fan, nodding towards Gifford with a mischievous smile; Sophia looked down and her gaze fell on me. I saw her tense, her eyes widen in shock. I shook my head and pressed a finger to my lips; Bessie frowned, and must have asked Sophia a question; Gifford noticed the women conferring and turned to see the focus of their attention; in the same instant the Prologue finished his laborious introduction and the crowd broke into applause and a volley of shouts – not necessarily of appreciation. I took advantage of the distraction to duck below the line of the stage and slip around to the other side, where I could keep Gifford and the women in my sights without being seen.

Sophia had recognised me, I knew. But I also knew that

she was clever and discreet enough not to say anything, if I warned her against it. After all, she too was here in London under false pretences and needed me to keep her secrets as much as I depended on her to keep mine. I wondered how I might find a chance to speak with her alone during the evening. A manservant in livery stood impassive behind the three women, guarding the door to the box, and I could see that he was armed; it seemed unlikely that any of the ladies would venture into the pit by themselves. Nonetheless, I determined to take any opportunity that came. I must also make sure I did not leave Gifford unattended; it was possible that he came here merely to gaze on his beloved, but if there was more to their meeting, Walsingham would want to hear of it.

The show lived down to expectations. A heavy-handed moral allegory, where actors performed characters named after virtues and vices as in the old religious plays, in verse so painfully lacking in grace or wit that I could only assume the author must be the owner of the theatre, or related to him; there was no other explanation for anyone believing the public needed to hear this. Perhaps I took against it more than most, since all the villainous characters were either foreign or Jewish, and the worst of all was an Italian merchant, who drew lusty jeers and boos from the audience whenever he appeared with his exaggerated accent, sounding like no Italian I had ever heard. No wonder the English threw stones and insults at foreigners, if this was how they were encouraged to view anyone who looked or sounded different. On the strength of the first two acts, I concluded that English theatre in the age of Queen Elizabeth did not have much of a future.

The final bow came as a mighty relief, though I was obliged to keep my wits about me as the crowd swarmed for the gate, either to use the jakes or stock up on food and beer. I saw Gifford glance up to the box, where the dark-haired girl I assumed to be Bessie had already risen from her seat; the manservant made as if to accompany her, but she held up a hand and disappeared through the door. I followed Gifford, keeping enough people between us to remain unseen. He slipped through the entrance and made his way around the side of the building, away from the stalls where the rest of the crowd were shoving one another in their haste to be served. I pressed myself close to the wall, my hat pulled down. Rounding the corner, I glimpsed Gifford's green cloak. A row of men had lined up to piss against the outer wall of the theatre; I joined them so as not to look conspicuous, and to keep my back to Gifford's tryst. Over my shoulder, I could see him loitering, trying to look casual; after a few moments I caught the blue shimmer of the girl's dress. She had pulled her shawl up around her face. Neither was looking in my direction. Gifford bobbed a brief bow; I saw her touch him lightly on the arm, her head tilted back in bright laughter that looked to me as artificial as the performers on stage, though Gifford blushed fiercely and planted his feet apart, squaring his shoulders and attempting to carry off a swagger. They conversed for a few minutes more; she must have bid him farewell because he bowed low, this time to kiss her hand, and as I watched I saw the pale flash of paper slip between her fingers and his. As he straightened, his hand slipped inside his doublet; the exchange was effected with professional dexterity in the blink of an eye, invisible to anyone not observing them as closely as I was. The girl disappeared around the side of the theatre the way she had come; Gifford joined the line of men facing the wall at the other end from me and began unlacing his breeches. I quickly finished my business and fastened my own, hoping I could lose myself in the crowd before Gifford made his way back.

As I was about to retrace my steps to the yard, I glanced up and caught sight of a figure rounding the corner, whose appearance was so unexpected that I found myself rooted to the spot with instant dread, blinking hard to convince myself that I was not conjuring him out of my worst dreams. I ducked my head down and turned away, pulse hammering in my throat, my hat pulled closer around my face, not daring to move until he had passed. He advanced slowly, taking in the scene as if he were looking for someone, but with no particular urgency; I kept my eyes turned to the ground, pretending to take my time lacing my breeches as he walked so close behind me he could have reached out and tapped me on the shoulder. When he was a few paces away, his back to me, I risked a quick glance; he stood observing the row of men against the wall, though with no more than a passing curiosity. His eyes alighted for the briefest instant on Gifford before he continued on his way, around the side of the building where Bessie Pierrepont had disappeared.

Relief sluiced through me, returning me to my senses; I had to put out a hand and lean against the wall while I caught my breath. He had not been looking for me, of that much I could be reasonably certain. There was no way he could have known that I was even in the country. But his appearance at the playhouse, at that precise moment, could not be mere chance. Who was he watching – Gifford? Bessie? It seemed so, but why? His presence so close to people I was supposed to be observing lodged a hard knot of fear in my gut; if he was interested in them, sooner or later he would find me, and when he did, he would almost certainly kill me.

He looked no different from the last time I had seen him, almost three years earlier. Medium height, not stocky, but solidly packed with muscle under his shirt, and the confident, easy gait of a man who feels at home wherever he finds himself. If you passed him in the street, you would not guess he was born into the Scottish nobility; he cultivated a kind of rough charm that allowed him to blend unnoticed in the lowest taverns, among soldiers and working men. When I had known him, during the time I lived at the French embassy, he had been a frequent dinner guest of the ambassador, though he usually looked like an itinerant hauled off the streets. He could not have been above his mid-forties, but his hair was greying and he wore it long and dishevelled, together with several days' growth of unkempt silver beard. Drink and hard weather had etched lines in his face, but his jaw and cheekbones were fine as a carved saint's and his blue eyes glittered like a wolfhound's; women apparently found him fascinating. His name was Archibald Douglas, and he had vowed revenge on me for my part in disabling the Throckmorton plot against Queen Elizabeth in 1583. I had assumed then that he worked for the cause of Mary Stuart, but I had not known the whole story. I wondered who was paying him now. He remained a wanted man and had slunk back to Scotland to avoid the Tower; it could hardly be coincidence that he had resurfaced in London just as another plot to put the Scottish queen on England's throne was gaining pace.

I decided it was time for me to leave; if Douglas was sniffing around the playhouse, for whatever reason, we would run into one another before the evening was out, and that would be the end of Walsingham's plan to insinuate me among the conspirators. The thought gave me a guilty flush of relief; the Father Prado identity relied on there being no one in London who would remember me from the French embassy days, and now here was a man who would unmask me the instant he set eyes on me. All I had to do was tell Phelippes that Douglas was in town, and they would never risk using me. It was quite possible, given his connections, that he was even involved with Babington and his companions; here was my chance to have them call off the whole operation, with no shame on my part.

But as I walked briskly back along Bishopsgate Street towards the city walls, I grew less certain. If I didn't become Father Prado, would I be on the next boat back to Paris, to the drudgery of a teaching job I had grown tired of months ago, and the constant fear of footsteps at my back? Was that really what I wanted? I had waited so long to be called back to Walsingham's service, and despite my initial resistance to his lunatic idea of joining the conspirators, now that I had an easy way out, I felt a sudden perverse sense of loss at the thought of returning to Paris without proving myself.

Though the play had felt as if it lasted several days, the bells had not yet struck ten and the sky held the last of the light, striped with orange and pink cloud above the rooftops. The dusk chill in the air suggested summer was over before it had begun. Dust hung in drifts above the road. I picked up my pace, wanting to arrive at Phelippes's lodging before night settled in; London was not safe after dark, especially for someone with my looks, even without Archibald Douglas on the prowl. I had not walked for more than five minutes when I heard a woman calling.

I turned to see Sophia hurrying down the street towards me at a half-run, picking up her skirts to keep them out of the dirt, hair flying behind her. I stopped and found myself smiling, no doubt with the same stupid expression I had seen on Gifford's face earlier. As she caught up with me – breathless, pushing a stray lock of hair out of her face – I realised she was not equally pleased to see me. She planted herself in my path and squared her fists on her hips.

'You *shit*.'

I dipped a small bow. 'A good evening to you, too.'

'What in God's name do you think you're doing?'

'I'm going home,' I said, mildly, gesturing in the direction of the City.

'You know what I mean. How dare you follow me!' Her eyes blazed. 'My God, your arrogance is breathtaking.'

'So I've been told. But to an onlooker, madam, it would rather seem as if it is you who has followed me.'

'Don't be clever, Bruno. And be glad I did not call your name out in the street – I was not sure you would be using it.'

'That was thoughtful. You would know all about false names. Are you Mary here, or have you acquired another?'

'It's none of your damned business. I told you we should not see each other – did I not make that clear enough? Who do you think you are, to pursue me here from France? What is it you hope to gain?' The colour had risen in her cheeks. She blew her hair out of her face. She always looked more beautiful when she was fired up with anger; fortunate, since it seemed impossible for us to have a conversation without it becoming an argument.

'Pursue you? Seriously?' I laughed. 'And you talk of my arrogance.'

For the first time, her indignation faltered.

'What am I supposed to think? Two months after I come back to London, here you are, in the same playhouse, staring up at me like a, like a . . .' She appeared to be searching for a suitable image, but left it hanging.

'A faithful dog?' I offered. 'A lovesick youth? Go on, say what you think. So, you presume I have dropped everything in Paris and run after you, since I have nothing else in my life.' I turned away and continued walking towards Bishopsgate. Sophia was as tall as me, which always made me feel obscurely at a disadvantage. She hesitated a moment, then fell into step beside me.

'What else would you be doing here?' Her chin jutting up, defying me to contradict her.

'I arrived in England four days ago,' I said, trying to keep my voice even. 'I had work to undertake. I had no idea you had even left Paris. I don't concern myself with your movements any more.'

'You just *decided* to come to that play by yourself?' Her voice dripped with scorn.

I stopped and spun round to face her again. 'Since we know enough of one another's secrets to barter with, I will tell you this. I did follow someone to the playhouse, and it was not you.'

'Oh. Gilbert Gifford.' She clapped a hand to her mouth, realising. I was gratified to see her turn scarlet.

'Exactly. So you can flatter your vanity by interpreting my motives as you wish, but Gifford was the object of my interest tonight, and him alone. Not everything is about you, Sophia. You had better return to your companions, they will be missing you by now.' I heard how haughty I sounded, but I didn't care; I was stung that she would find the idea of my attention so repellent.

'*Shit*,' she said, clenching a fist, though I could see that her anger was directed at herself. 'I'm an idiot, Bruno. Sorry. I should have guessed you had better things to do than run after me.'

'Yes. Well. I will try to keep out of your way in future. Unfortunately young Gifford is keen to throw himself in the path of your friend Bessie, so we may see one another again. I'm sure you can learn to look past me. In fact, you will have to.'

'That's not what I meant.' She raised a hand, as if she were about to lay it on my sleeve; instead she hesitated, and let it fall to her side. 'She's no friend of mine. I must tolerate her company now and again, not by choice. Why are you following Gifford?'

'Why do you dislike Bessie?'

Her mouth twisted. 'She is one of those women who lives or dies by how many men look at her. That is why she likes to come to the playhouse.'

'Are you sure? Perhaps it is an act. I understand she is quite clever.'

'The two things are not exclusive.' She tilted her head to one side and looked at me. 'You seem very interested in her.'

'Shouldn't that be a relief to you?'

She shrugged. 'I wish you luck. The other thing about Bessie Pierrepont is how much she cares about rank and title. I never hear the end of "my grandmother the Countess of Shrewsbury". I don't think you are quite the man she has in mind.'

'By that token, neither is Gilbert, and she seems to favour him with her attentions.'

'Oh, she must have someone to admire her at all times. And he is at least a gentleman.'

'No more to it than that?'

A sly smile crept across her face. 'I see. You did not answer my question about Gilbert. You are on the trail of *intrigue*.' A light dawned in her eyes, and this time she did grasp my sleeve. 'Wait – I told you before Christmas that he was carrying letters for Mary Stuart. Is that why you're in England? Is he caught up in something? Is *Bessie*?'

I drew back; the excitement in her face was confirmation enough that she would jump at any chance of adventure if Walsingham held it out to her.

'Don't play mysterious with me, Bruno – it's only thanks to me that you know anything about Gilbert and his letters. The least you could do is tell me what's going on.'

'Gilbert has been of interest since long before you mentioned him,' I said, keeping my voice low.

'Of interest. To whom, I wonder?' She tilted her chin. 'I know what work you are involved in, Bruno. Do you forget Oxford?'

The smile was gone. She gave me a long look that contained all our shared history, and I was struck again by the colour of her eyes, amber flecked with gold, a shade I had only ever seen replicated in one other creature – the lion King Henri of France kept at his menagerie in the Louvre. Sophia had something of its watchful menace in her gaze too. I had not forgotten Oxford, where I had first met her when I stayed at her father's college, nor what my work for Walsingham there had cost her. I remained convinced that my actions three years ago had saved her life; she thought they had led directly to her losing the man she loved, her son's father, and the future she believed they would have had together. I suspected that, in some deep-buried secret place of her heart, she still blamed me for everything that had happened to her since. I turned away first.

'I could help you,' she offered, casually. 'If you want to know what Gilbert is up to.'

'You see him often, then?'

She shrugged. 'Three or four times now, since I returned, always at the playhouse. But we have spoken only once. He was very formal and cool with me. I suppose I should be glad that he has turned his gaze elsewhere.' She made a small, brittle movement with her neck that conveyed her impatience. Gifford had been a lodger in the English Catholic household where she had worked in Paris, and she had spent her days constantly sidestepping his gawky attempts at courtship. To see the scorn on her face, I almost felt sorry for him.

'Does he always meet Bessie at the playhouse? What do they talk of?'

'I've never been close enough to overhear. She always contrives to leave the box between acts, without the manservant. Once I followed her, out of curiosity. She was around the back where the men go to piss, talking to Gilbert, though when she saw me she pretended to have run into him by chance. I thought she was just flirting, and embarrassed to be caught. Do you think Bessie is secretly *Catholic*?' Her eyes danced with the thrill of gossip. I guessed incident was rare in her current position.

'I've no idea. You must know her family better than I. Though on first impressions, Lady Grace looks sour enough to be a Calvinist.'

She laughed. 'That is unkind of you, Bruno. She is not the liveliest companion, it is true. But being married to a brute like Sir Henry would crush any woman's spirit.' She broke off, wrapping her arms tightly around her narrow chest; I knew she was remembering her own brief, unhappy marriage that had led to so much grief in Canterbury.

'And what of your quest?' I asked gently, to change the

subject. 'Did you have news that brought you back to England so soon?'

She pressed her lips together and looked away. 'Nothing solid. Charles Paget said he had news of my son, and he would tell me when he was sure of it, but I have heard nothing from him yet, he was probably lying. In any case, I had had enough of Paris. I wanted to be home. When I am more settled, I will begin making my own enquiries.'

'Take care you don't arouse anyone's suspicions.'

A shadow passed across her face. 'I do not need you to tell me that, Bruno. I know what's at stake.' She sighed. 'I thought no one would know me in London. And yet, here you are. It seems I cannot escape faces from my past.'

'I have the same problem. But I did not come here to find you, I assure you.'

She dropped her gaze. 'It was foolish and vain of me even to think it. I apologise. And perhaps I spoke too hastily in Paris. I was not myself then. I thought you wanted . . .'

'What?'

She lifted a shoulder. 'More than I could give. You wanted me to go to Prague with you.'

'You wanted to travel.'

'I could not risk being distracted from the only thing that matters at all in my life. Until I find my child, I have nothing to offer anyone.'

'I have never asked you for anything,' I said quietly. She could not know how close I once came to asking her to marry me, at the exact time she had been planning her escape. Even the memory made my skin prickle at how narrowly I had swerved that mistake. At least I had clung on to a shred of dignity.

'I know. You have always been good to me, and I have never deserved it . . . We could meet in secret, if you wanted,' she said, almost shyly. 'I could let you know if I learn anything about Gilbert and Bessie. It would be good to have a friend in London.'

A friend. Strange how that word could sound like an insult from the lips of a woman you are longing to push up against a wall there and then. I still remembered the sensation of her nails urgent on my back, her long legs wrapped around me.

'It would be difficult,' I said, aware that my effort to keep my voice steady made me sound clipped and cold. 'We are both pretending to be someone else. If we should meet in public, we must not acknowledge one another. People may be observing us. Even now, for instance. You should return to your company before they begin to worry and send someone looking for you.'

Confusion flickered across her eyes and I confess it gave me some satisfaction to see her process the idea of being rebuffed. But she composed herself quickly, and set her shoulders back with a tight smile.

'You're right. Well – you know where to find me. We come every week, when Bessie has her day off. She likes to chivvy her aunt into society, claiming it does her good. I have yet to see the evidence. Lady Grace only seems more despondent after a trip to the theatre.'

'I know how she feels.'

She laughed; she looked me in the eye with a frankness that seemed both knowing and hesitant, and for a moment I thought she might be about to lean in for a kiss, but she pulled her jacket around her shoulders and nodded briskly.

'Goodbye, then. Until next time.'

I made as if to set off, but when she turned to walk away I stopped and watched her to the end of the street, her long, swinging stride, the supple curve of her waist as she moved. She did not look back for me, as I had known she would not.

TEN

I was in bed and feigning sleep by the time Gifford stumbled into the room, tripping over my boots and swearing. From the smell of him, he had stopped off in a tavern on the way home; I had to hope that would be to my advantage. After servicing himself again, with a series of muffled grunts – I had to admire the boy's stamina, though he took longer this time, thanks to the drink – he fell asleep almost immediately, his breathing heavy and sated, gently snoring through his open mouth. When I could be certain he was not going to stir, I slipped out of bed and crept to the corner where he had dropped his doublet and breeches in a heap on the floor. It took a few minutes with no light, freezing every time his pallet creaked as he shifted in sleep, ready to pretend I was feeling my way to the piss pot, but I knew better than most where to look for secret letters, and I quickly found the slit in the padding of his doublet where he had hidden Bessie's note.

I found Phelippes bent over his desk in the next room, candles blazing around him, indecipherable papers spread out on the desk.

'I began to think you'd nodded off,' he whispered, with an air of reproach. He had not been pleased with me for leaving

Gifford unsupervised at the playhouse, though I had pleaded my fear of being discovered, and the news of the boy's encounter with Bessie and the note she had passed had mitigated my offence. I had not yet mentioned the appearance of Douglas; I could not decide what to do for the best about that.

'I was waiting for him to fall asleep,' I hissed back. 'Here. You'll have to copy it quickly, in case he wakes and sees my bed empty.'

He took the paper from my hand, unfolded it, skimmed it with a glance and nodded, the candle flames dancing in his eyes.

'Something interesting?' I asked.

'Oh yes. I have seen this cipher before, I'm certain. But not in this context. Most curious. You're certain the Pierrepont girl gave it to him?'

'Yes. The meeting was clearly arranged. Apparently it's not the first.' I decided against telling him that I had heard this from Sophia; I didn't want her drawn into this business any sooner than necessary. 'What is it, a letter?'

'Obviously, it's a communication of some kind.' His tone implied that I was an idiot.

I clicked my tongue. 'Well, yes. But who is it to, can you tell? Gifford, or is he an intermediary?'

'That,' Phelippes whispered, glancing up and giving me a rare direct look, so that I saw the shine of excitement in his eyes, 'is the great question. Don't distract me now – we need to replace the original before he wakes. Lucky it's short. He must not suspect anyone knows of it.' He stared at the paper again, shaking his head as if at a great marvel. It was the closest I had seen him to animated. 'This really is remarkable. Don't pace, you're making the boards creak.'

It was clear I was not going to draw any more from him until he was ready. I stood as still as I could by the dying fire, shivering with my arms wrapped around my chest, while his quill scratched frantically in the silence. At length, the sound stopped and he held out the paper.

'There. Put it back where you found it. I will work on the copy.'

'Did you get anywhere with the other paper?' I asked, tucking Bessie's note into my breeches. 'The one from Clara's locket.'

'No.' His mouth pinched. 'That one is far stranger. Unlike any code I have seen before.'

'May I look?'

'You have experience of cryptography?' He regarded me with a sceptical eye.

'A little.'

He looked unconvinced, but he reached into a wooden box on the desk and pushed a scrap of paper across to me. 'Well then. See if your little experience can help you with this, for I cannot fathom it yet.'

I picked up the tiny note and smoothed out the creases where it had been folded into the locket, curious to see what could have foxed even Phelippes's formidable powers of analysis. The message, if such it was, consisted of only four symbols, miniature but so carefully rendered that they were almost tiny sketches: a half moon, waves against a beach, what appeared to be a field ploughed into a deep furrow, and a rose.

'Concise,' I said. He did not reply. 'Not exactly a full alphabet.'

'That much I had discerned for myself,' he murmured, still bent over the copy of Bessie's letter.

'It's more like a pictogram.' I held it up at arm's length, as if that might make the meaning clearer; the paper was so small, it would have taken a fine quill and considerable skill to draw. Clara Poole had drawn beautifully, Frances Sidney had said. 'Like the Egyptians used to use. But are those images literally representative, or do they have some symbolic significance only to the person they were intended for? That is what we must determine.'

'Congratulations, I see you have understood how ciphers work.' Phelippes pushed his chair back and crossed the room to a shelf of books, ran his finger along the spines, pulled out the one he wanted with a flicker of a smile and returned to his desk, all without looking at me. But there was a companionable kind of stillness to the room, both of us concentrating, the warm, flickering light, the smell of beeswax and paper and old wood. It put me in mind of the library at San Domenico, the only place I had ever felt at home during my years in the convent, so that I felt indulgent enough to ignore his sarcasm. I even hoped for a moment that he would let me stay up working with him, sharpening our wits together on hidden meanings.

'Moon, sea, land,' I mused, tapping the paper in my hand. 'A reference to the elements? Heavens and earth? And the rose is usually a symbol of transience. So it could signify death.'

He ignored me, his eyes flitting back and forth from the book he had fetched, now propped open before him, to the copy of Bessie's letter.

'Or,' I continued, mainly to myself, 'perhaps it's more obvious than that. The rose could be a reference to the Tudor rose. Maybe the message means that they will kill Elizabeth Tudor at the next half moon. Which will be' – I crossed to the window and craned up at the night sky, to see the horns of a crescent moon poking out from behind a chimney stack – 'in a couple of days, no?'

He made a faint derisive noise. 'And will they kill her on a beach? Or in a field? Or in the village of Beechfield?'

So he was listening.

'Is that a real place?'

'I've no idea. It's as likely as your wittering.'

'I'm only trying to help.'

'You can help by making sure that letter goes back in Gifford's doublet before he wakes. I'm busy.' He stopped suddenly, very still, staring at the page in front of him. Then he scratched a few urgent notes and sat back with an air of satisfaction. 'There.'

'Already?'

'Yes. I knew I had seen that alphabet before. Bessie's correspondent is either lazy, stupid or over-confident, to re-use the same cipher.' His lips pursed, as if in disapproval at the lack of challenge. 'That, of course, is to our advantage.'

'So? Are you going to tell me who she's writing to? Is it Gifford? Babington?'

'That is for Master Secretary alone.' He did not say this with any kind of malice, or pleasure in making himself important, merely in his usual blunt factual manner. 'Go to bed.'

I had not really expected a different reply, but all the same I was reluctant to leave. Childishly, I wanted to be let in on the secret, to stay here at the heart of the business, not sent to my room. I had always been quick at ciphers; I had been taught well and I wanted to believe that I could match Phelippes's skills, given the chance, though I also knew that was not true.

'How do you do it?' I asked softly, turning to the door.

He frowned up at me, as if surprised to find me still there. 'What?'

'You looked at that for less than a minute and said you recognised the cipher. You knew exactly where to find the book you needed – I assume for the key. But with all the different codes you must have seen in your work – how could you identify it so quickly? What is your technique?'

'Technique?'

'Your memory system. I'm genuinely interested.'

He looked blank. 'No system. I just know. I may as well ask you how you understand Italian.'

'That's not the same at all. We absorb our native language

as infants, before we can even form thoughts, we can't separate it from thought. But this—'

'So with this. Even as a child I could memorise sequences of numbers at a glance, it was natural to me. I register patterns, almost before I am aware of doing so. I used to entertain myself by reciting my father's account books. I have no more understanding of how I did it than you do of learning your own tongue. My mother feared I was possessed.' This last part was barely audible.

'One day, Thomas, I will write a book on the art of memory, and you shall be in it,' I told him. 'I would give anything for your gift.'

'No,' he said, his attention already back on the paper. 'I do not think you would. Try not to wake Gifford. You did well tonight,' he added as an afterthought.

At the door I paused to watch him, head bowed in the cone of light, his face in shadow, jaw muscles twitching minutely as he worked at his secret calculations. He was right; I had thought I lived a lonely life, but there was a particular quality of solitude about Thomas Phelippes that I did not envy, in spite of his prodigious memory. How would it feel for a child to see his own mother afraid of his strange, extraordinary mind? I wondered if Queen Elizabeth would ever truly know how much she owed him, or think to show her gratitude. I suspected it would not bother him either way. A man like Phelippes – and I was not even sure what I meant by that, since I had never met anyone else quite like him – was not motivated by principle, or faith, or ambition, or the desire for recognition, as far as I could see. I thought of how he repeated that phrase, 'the good of the state', like a religious creed. It seemed a matter of sheer blind luck that he had crossed paths with Walsingham and dedicated his peculiar talents to the government's cause. I could not help thinking that, in other circumstances, with a different set of acquaintances, he could as easily have lent his skills to England's enemies. I did not know what to make of a man so apparently detached, except to think – not for the first time – that I needed to be careful of him. If I outlived my use to the operation, he would not be moved by loyalty or fellow-feeling to defend me; in fact, I had no doubt that he would consider me immediately expendable.

ELEVEN

I slept fitfully that night, troubled by wild and whirling dreams. In one, I was standing near the front of the crowd at a public execution; as the prisoner was led to the scaffold, I saw, with fearful disbelief, that it was the first man in England sent to his death as a direct result of my work for Walsingham. When he was cut down from the gallows and laid on the block, still living, he turned his head and looked straight at me, eyes fixed steady on mine with an expression of sorrow and regret, and as the knife ripped him open and the executioner pulled his guts out by the handful, his mouth formed words meant for me alone, words of great secrecy and importance, and though I shook my head and tried to push closer, I could not make them out. Behind him, slipping in his blood as they bowed their heads for the noose, there followed others who had died through my agency, each of them seeking me out with his frank, accusing gaze, while I tried to shout my justifications over the noise of the mob. In another dream – or perhaps the same one – I saw Sophia ahead of me on a busy London street, chestnut hair gleaming down her back, rippling with the confident sway of her walk. I called out to her, shoving people aside until I could tap her on the shoulder; she turned, and I cried out as I saw the gaping hole where her eye and nose had been, the bleeding stumps of her ears. From the depths of my horror I forced my mind back to the surface until I woke, slick with sweat, to find Gifford kneeling by my bed in the grey light, his face inches from mine; I shouted again as I pushed him away from me, thinking first that he belonged to my night-terrors – though the smell of stale beer on his breath quickly convinced me of his solidity.

'Are you all right? You were making a devil of a noise there, yelling all manner of things.'

'Was I?' I levered myself on to my elbows, alarmed, and pinched the corners of my eyes between finger and thumb. 'What kind of things?'

He grinned. 'No idea, it was all in Italian. You sounded near terrified, though.'

I breathed out, relieved. Christ be praised for that, at least; lucky for me that I still dreamed in my native language. I hoped to God I had not called out any names.

'Dreaming of home is not always comforting,' I said. He gave me a long look and let out a sigh.

'Don't I know it. My father guesses at the price of our freedom and despises me for it.'

'Is he not pleased to be out of prison and back in his own house?'

Gifford stood and crossed the room to the window, pulling back the shutter to let in a dull light that suggested the sun was not long up, and obscured by clouds. He reached for the piss pot. 'He feels the shame of trading his courage for his safety, when so many of his friends would not. I understand that.'

'Well, at least he has the luxury of reflecting on his shame in a feather bed. As do you.'

'Hardly feathers.' He cast a glance back at the thin mattress as he relieved himself in an aggressive stream. 'I lie awake night after night tormented by the thought of what I am helping to bring about. How God will punish me for it.'

I hoped he was speaking metaphorically; last night he had not noticeably been kept from sleep by his conscience. 'You were caught with a bull of excommunication against the Queen, Gilbert. If you weren't doing this, they'd have torn out your gizzard and stuck your head on London Bridge. Have you ever seen a traitor's execution?'

He shook his head as he rearranged his underhose. 'I have been out of the country a long time. I sometimes think I would not have the stomach for it, though it is not manly to say so. I saw a woman burned for a witch once, in Paris. I could not get the smell out of my nose for days.' He shuddered, pulling on his shirt and reaching for the doublet he had tossed in the corner the night before. Before he put it on, he ran a finger around the seam where the letter was hidden, checking for it, oblivious to the fact that I might be watching. He was supremely naïve at this subterfuge business.

'Tonight you meet them,' Gifford said, as if following my thoughts, looking out of the window as he pulled on his breeches. He did not sound enthused about the prospect. 'The conspirators. Are you afraid?'

'A little.' I sat up, wrapping my arms around my knees. In truth, I was more concerned about him making some careless slip that would see both of us with a knife in our necks. And he was not the only worry. 'Did you ever hear any of Babington's group mention the name Archibald Douglas?'

He thought for a moment. 'Not that I remember. Why, who is he?'

'Someone who used to work for Mary Stuart. I wondered if he had any connection to this plot.'

He shook his head. 'I have not heard the name. I know that Ballard was keen not to involve anyone associated with previous conspiracies, who might be known to the authorities.'

'Then forget I mentioned it. Are you worried about tonight?'

'I think it will be a miracle if we survive it.' He grabbed a fistful of his hair in both hands. 'I live in terror of saying the wrong thing. I can just about keep up with my own deceit, but now I have two people's stories to maintain. I'm not good at holding my nerve under pressure. Unlike you, I did not choose this.' His voice had grown peevish, as if his situation were all my fault. 'And John Ballard is so sharp – the way he looks at me, I sometimes think he suspects me already. It would take only the smallest thing for him to sniff a deception.'

'Do you think that's what happened to Clara Poole?'

'How should I know?' He let go of his hair and made a brief, dismissive gesture, holding both palms up, empty. 'I never even met her. Babington didn't invite women to meetings about the conspiracy – Ballard would never have stood for that. I've no idea why she was killed – I was not even in London when it happened, and I have not spoken to any of them since her body was discovered. Master Secretary has asked me all this already.'

'But if you had to guess?' I said, gently. His response seemed unusually defensive, and I knew that on the matter of not being in London, he was lying.

A quick shrug of one shoulder. 'Then I'd say it would not surprise me at all if a woman had given herself away through some carelessness. Rather, I am surprised that Master Secretary ever trusted her in the first place. She was bound to do something stupid sooner or later.'

'Because Clara was a stupid woman, or because no woman is capable of the subtlety needed for this kind of work?' I asked. I refrained from reminding him that he had just been fretting about the likelihood of doing the same thing himself.

'Most women are not.' His expression glazed over again and his eyes took on that dreamy look I recognised. 'Of course, it could be that an exceptional woman, led by her intelligence and true motivation, might have the skill to serve a cause in that way.' He paused, and his voice stiffened again. 'I don't know if Clara Poole was especially stupid, but if she managed to give herself away so easily, she was clearly not that woman. I still say it is work better left to men. We are practised at hiding our feelings.'

Straight from the book of Robin Poole, I thought. Funny how these English boys appeared so threatened by the thought that women could be effective agents. I wished I could transport them to the French court; they would be no match for the talents of Catherine de Medici's Flying Squadron. I filed away his comment about an exceptional woman to consider at more leisure; the look on his face suggested he had been thinking of Bessie Pierrepont. 'You Englishmen, perhaps. You are famed for never showing emotion. But you would not deny a woman has advantages she can use in persuading a man to talk.' I slid him a sly look.

Gifford blushed to his hairline, and I remembered from our brief acquaintance in Paris how any mention of sex rendered him as tongue-tied as a schoolboy. 'That is a dangerous approach, though,' he said, frowning to cover his embarrassment. 'Women are weak. If a woman goes to a man's bed, she will grow attached to him, and then her loyalty is compromised. Unless she is a harlot,' he added, sitting on the edge of his bed and reaching for his boots.

'Well, you seem to have their entire sex summed up. You should write a book.'

He glanced up, to see if he was being mocked. I bit down a laugh; the least skilled of Catherine's girls would eat him alive. But at the thought, his words recalled another memory from Paris, of a girl who had fallen in love with the man she was supposed to be spying on and compromised her loyalties. I wondered if there might be lessons in that story for the case of Clara Poole.

'You don't think it matters, then,' I continued, before he could take offence, 'to find out which of them killed her?'

'What difference would it make? They are all destined for the scaffold anyway, if Walsingham's plan succeeds – who cares which of them held the knife? Far more important to find out how much they know about who she worked for. If they think she was spying, they may suspect others among us, and I do not fancy being subjected to interrogation by Ballard or Savage.' He chewed at his thumbnail, looking like a boy afraid of a beating.

'Held the knife?'

'What?' He lowered his thumb and his eyes widened.

'Was she killed with a knife, then?'

His face grew wary. 'I assumed – I thought I overheard Phelippes say something about it. Why, is that not so?'

He appeared flustered, but that did not necessarily mean anything; his habitual manner was a constant switch back and forth between certainty, anxiety and self-pity. Still, I thought it unlikely that Phelippes would have elaborated any details of Clara's death in Gifford's hearing.

'I don't know. Make sure you don't let slip any mention of knives, or even of Clara, this evening. The point is for them to give themselves away, not you.'

He nodded, relieved. 'I will say nothing. In any case, it was a figure of speech. To mean the guilty party, you understand?'

'Naturally.' I flashed him a reassuring smile, and his shoulders dropped with relief. 'And don't worry, the conspirators will not suspect you, Gilbert – didn't you come personally recommended by Charles Paget, one of Mary's most trusted agents?'

He puffed up a little. 'Yes, and they have a letter in Mary's own hand vouching for me. But it has not escaped their attention that my father was released from prison shortly after I arrived back in England. They do not like the coincidence. I have been asked about it more than once, and it is no easy business being on the end of their questions, as you may well discover.'

'But, not being a weak woman, I'm sure you kept your countenance and gave nothing away,' I said.

He paused in the act of pulling on a boot. 'I did not,' he said tersely. 'Or I suppose I would have gone the same way as Clara Poole by now.' His gaze slid away.

'Still, you will be on the road again soon,' I said, aiming to cheer him. 'Then you will not be responsible for keeping my cover, at least. Perhaps the business may even be over by the time you are back.'

'Perhaps it may, one way or another.' He looked morose. 'And what then, for us, if we succeed? You think we will be any safer?'

'What do you mean?'

He jerked his head in the direction of Phelippes's room and lowered his voice. 'You ask if I am afraid. Besides Ballard, I am most afraid of them.'

'Of *Thomas*?'

He stared at me as if I were defective. 'His master, rather. They know my history – I have only their word that my part in this plot will buy my freedom and my family's – and what is that worth? They might just as easily decide to round me up with the other conspirators and send me to the scaffold once I have served my purpose. It would be no trouble to them to deny all knowledge of my work for them, and who would believe me? I've heard it's happened to others who have betrayed the cause, believing the promises of heretics were worth anything.' He set his mouth miserably as he pulled on the other boot.

I noticed the way he was talking more carelessly to me this morning, in language that made plain where his loyalties lay in the competing causes of Queen Mary and Queen Elizabeth; I wondered if fear had loosened his tongue. I could not help a shiver, nonetheless; no doubt there was some truth in the rumour that Walsingham persuaded Catholics to betray their friends with the lure of promises that were never kept. Whether he would go so far as to send Gifford to the gallows with the other conspirators, I did not know or want to believe, but the fact that the boy's worries echoed my own misgivings about Phelippes caused a knot to lodge in my throat.

'I believe they are men of their word,' I said, as blandly as I could manage. He watched me as I swung my legs out of bed in search of my shirt.

'I suppose *you* do not need to worry,' he said, with an edge of resentment. 'Since you are an enemy of the Catholic church, your loyalty is not in question. I imagine you will be glad to see Mary Stuart's head on a spike.'

'Christ's blood, Gilbert.' I turned my back to him while I dressed. 'I don't relish the prospect of anyone's head on a spike, least of all a woman's. Anyway, it is the Church that has chosen to be at odds with me – I did not seek their enmity. I want only to be left alone to write my books. The fault is theirs if they don't like my ideas.'

He laughed, as if I had confirmed a suspicion. 'Charles Paget said you were the most arrogant man he had ever met.'

'That is quite an accolade from Paget. Himself a paragon of humility, of course.'

'What are you doing here, then?' Gifford gestured to the room. His tone had grown harder. 'If all you want is to write your books, why are you taking part in this charade, *Father Prado*?'

His hostility was becoming wearing. This delicate balancing act was going to be a lot harder if one of the two men I relied on to support my cover was holding a grudge against me. I should have realised that he would not forgive me for trapping him into working for Walsingham just because we were now nominally on the same side.

I sighed. 'Because it seems to me that, one way or another, a queen must die. If I have to choose, I would rather place my bet on the one who would let me live in England and write, without burning me for heresy.'

'You would be burned if Mary takes the throne, and I will be gutted at Tyburn if Elizabeth keeps it,' he said, kicking the end of the bed like a sulking child. 'One queen pitted against another, half the country made enemies of the other half and no pity on either side. The winner will take all.'

Any further debate was interrupted by a clatter of hooves in the street below. I glanced through the window to see Phelippes jump down from a horse and unhook a leather bag from its saddle, while a boy emerged from the gates at the side of the house to take its reins. Dawn had barely broken and the cryptographer had already been on the road; I wondered if it was Bessie's coded message from last night that had called him out with such urgency.

Phelippes summoned me to his room almost as soon as he returned.

'The Jesuit was very talkative last night, it seems,' he said, folding his cloak neatly and laying it over a stool. 'Fortunately for you.'

And for him, I thought, though I wondered how much of what a man says under threat of torture could be trusted. If the Jesuit Prado suspected someone was being lined up to impersonate him, might he have slipped some false information into his answers that would trip me up the minute I repeated it? I had to hope that fear had stripped him of the chance to think so clearly, shackled in Walsingham's cellar through the small hours of the night.

'Now listen carefully.' Phelippes straightened his papers and tapped the edge on the desk. 'Padre Xavier Maria Gonzales Prado, born Madrid, third of December 1552, employed as a trusted courier of sensitive messages between Ambassador Mendoza in Paris and the Spanish court for the past two years. Arrived in Southampton the day before yesterday on board a merchant ship, passing himself off as the representative of a textile exporter. Had this on him' – Phelippes waved a rolled-up paper, somewhat creased – 'a bill of goods for bolts of silk, written over invisibly with alum solution. The secret writing is a letter of recommendation from Mendoza, with a copy of his seal as guarantee.' He picked up a square of muslin from the desk and gingerly unwrapped it to reveal a small silver disc the size of a sovereign. I reached out for a closer look but he drew his hand back. 'I wouldn't, if I were you. You don't want to know where he had that hidden. Prado says his instructions were to bring funds' – he patted a small wooden strongbox on the desk – 'in earnest of more Spanish support when the plot was further advanced. Mendoza also asked him to find out how many English Catholic nobles have promised men and arms to support a coup once Mary is freed, with estimated numbers of troops and safe havens to land. As you know, that information was one of the things we hoped Clara would bring us. Obviously it will be your task to secure it instead.'

'Not by the same means, I hope.'

Phelippes frowned, looking me up and down. 'I doubt that would be effective. To the best of my knowledge, they are not sodomites.'

'I was not serious, Thomas.' I should have remembered humour was wasted on him.

'Depending on how long the business takes, I will arrange to have dispatches sent back to Mendoza in Paris. Master Secretary will make sure Prado's writing hand remains unaffected so I can learn his script.'

I winced. 'Jesus, Thomas – spare me the detail.'

He glanced up. 'What?' When I shook my head, he continued, briskly: 'I will need to shave you and cut your hair this afternoon.'

'You?' I ran a hand through my hair in alarm. 'Do you have the skills?'

'I have a razor, if that is what you mean. These are for you.'

From under the desk he brought out a pair of tall riding boots and offered them to me. Even at a glance I could see they were expensive.

'You shouldn't have. It's not even my birthday.'

'Try to concentrate, Bruno. You will need all your wits about you today, so don't waste them on levity. They will not be expecting humour from Father Prado. He's not a very amusing person, by all accounts.'

'Nor would you be, with Walsingham fishing the ambassador's seal out of your arse.' I arranged my face into an expression of perfect seriousness. 'Sorry. Father Prado will be a model of dull sobriety. Should I try them on?'

'They will fit you. They have been made to your measurements. Now look at this.' He manipulated the heel of the left boot until it sprang open to reveal a small compartment. From inside he took out a slim silver penknife and folded it open and shut to demonstrate. 'This is in case you are searched and relieved of your weapon at any point. Useful to have a concealed blade about you.'

I wanted to ask Phelippes when he had had the opportunity to measure my feet. While I was asleep? The thought was oddly disturbing. I pulled off my old boots and tried on the new ones, to find he was right; the fine-grained Spanish leather moulded softly to my leg, and I was pleased to see the adapted heels added a good inch and a half to my height. Phelippes watched me admiring myself.

'There are the clothes from Prado's luggage. You are a similar size, they should fit.' He indicated a chair against the wall, where a doublet and breeches of amber silk had been laid out, together with a ruffled, lace-collared shirt and a matching velvet cap with an extravagant ostrich feather.

'You want me to wear *that*? Is the idea to draw attention wherever I go?'

'The idea is that you look like Prado, who was passing himself off as a merchant's son with a taste for fine clothes. If you go about in your usual black, your face may jog someone's memory, even without your hair and beard.'

I ran my hand across my chin. Archibald Douglas would

not be fooled by a gaudy suit. This would be the moment to mention him, if I were going to. I eyed the clothes on the chair, imagined myself wearing them, walking into a room of strangers, the sheer dazzling audacity of the deception fizzing through my blood, and realised with a jolt that I wanted to see if I could carry this off as much as Walsingham wanted it. If I told him about Douglas, and took the easy way out now, I would never know if I could have succeeded. Phelippes did not miss my hesitation.

'What is it?'

I shook my head. 'Nothing. I will look like one of those birds from the Indies. Or, God forbid, a Parisian.'

'That is the intention. Father Prado has come from Paris, remember.' He indicated a leather travelling bag next to the chair. It looked like the one I had seen him swinging down from the horse earlier. 'Shirts, hose and another suit are packed in there. All made in Paris, in case any of your new companions grow suspicious and decide to look through your belongings. Which they might, so there is a false compartment in the lining for anything you don't want them to see. But I recommend you leave nothing incriminating in your new lodgings. Try to keep it about your person, if possible. Now – communications.' He picked up a small bottle from his desk that looked like a vial of perfume. 'Pay attention. If you must send a written note, use this. You know about alum solution? You reveal the message by—'

'Holding it to a candle flame.' I did not bother to hide my impatience. 'You are teaching your grandmother to spin here.'

'My grandmother is dead.' He frowned, confused.

'It's an expression, Thomas. An English one, I thought. Never mind – do you know who expounded the practice of writing in alum?'

'The natural magician Giambattista della Porta, in his *Magiae Naturalis*, published in Naples in 1558. Now, this solution is strong, so it is best used on linen, and in fact that would be to your advantage, since scraps of cloth are more likely to be overlooked than papers, if anyone is watching for secret communications. There is a supply of linen strips in the hidden compartment. If anyone should wonder about them, you could always cut your thumb and pretend they are to bind the wound. To read the message on linen, you need to—'

'Drop the cloth in water. I knew della Porta in Naples. He was a sort of mentor to me in my youth, for a short time.'

Phelippes paused, nearly impressed. 'Really? He is the author of a learned work on cryptography. It remains one of the most important texts of our age on that art.' He tilted his head and gave me a curious look. 'It is said he formed a secret society for men prepared to carry out experiments challenging the laws of nature.'

I could have told him of my adventures with della Porta's secret society, but I did not fully trust Phelippes, and suspected his interest would be limited to his own sphere, so I merely nodded.

'Whatever I know of code-breaking, I learned from him.'

'Hm. Then perhaps you do know something after all.'

'Thank you for your confidence. How do I convey messages to you?'

'I'm coming to that. I have devised a cipher for you to use. Memorise the key and burn it. I do have faith in your memory skills, at least.' He passed me a folded sheet of paper. As I took it he clicked his fingers and a shadow stirred against the far wall of the chamber, so noiselessly that I almost leapt in the air. A boy of about thirteen years stepped forward into the light, and I realised that I recognised his face from the scabs on his lip; he was the same child who had been outside the house holding Poole's horse before we rode to Southwark. He watched me from under long dark lashes, dipping his head in a brusque nod.

'This is Ben,' Phelippes said. 'He carries messages around our network. He's fast and you can trust him.'

'How can I be sure to find him, if the message is urgent?'

'You and Gilbert will move today to lodgings at Herne's Rents, in Holborn. Babington takes rooms there, you will be close by to keep an eye on him. At the corner of Holborn and Snow Hill there is a tavern called the Saracen's Head. In the yard there is a disused dovecote. Leave your message in one of the cavities for Ben to collect – he will check it at intervals through the day. He will also leave responses there for you, if he can't find you in person.'

'If you need me urgently, I'm usually in the yard at the Saracen's, if I'm not on a job,' the boy said, digging his thumbs into the waist of his breeches. I liked his breezy manner; he carried himself with the self-possession of London street children.

'Will people not notice you hanging about there?' I asked.

'It's my dad's tavern,' he said. 'People know me.'

'The father is one of ours,' Phelippes said. 'Keep that in mind if you need a safe meeting place outside your lodgings.'

'Right.' That was as good as saying that if I were ever to meet anyone at the Saracen's Head, it would be reported to Phelippes before I had picked up my first quart of beer. 'And if I need to see you or Master Secretary in person?'

'That would not be advisable until the business is over. But in extreme circumstances, Ben will arrange a location. You must not be seen here or at Seething Lane for as long as you are Father Prado. Do you have any questions?'

'Yes. If they should suspect me—'

'You stick to your story. You tell them to appeal to Mendoza if they have doubts. That should silence them – they will not wish to offend the Spanish by questioning his judgement, and in the time it would take for a letter to reach Paris we can get you out if need be. I can always provide a response from Mendoza if I must.' He tapped the seal with the penknife.

'But if the matter is more urgent than that? If they suspect me to the point of threatening my life imminently?'

Phelippes rubbed his chin, considering.

'If they attack you in a private room, I'm afraid your only option will be to defend yourself. I was assured you have some skill at that.'

'Yes, but – there are four of them, and Poole and Gifford could not come to my defence without breaking their own cover.' Gifford might even take the opportunity to join in, I thought.

'Then you had better not let anyone suspect you.'

'I can watch out for you, mister,' Ben said, with a breezy swagger. 'People never notice me.'

I smiled, despite myself. 'Well, thank you for the thought. Could you kill a man?'

'What makes you think I haven't?' He rocked back on his heels, and with a flourish pulled a small knife from the waist of his breeches, the kind used at table. So if John Ballard or any of the others put a blade to my throat, my best hope of support was a child with a fruit knife. I almost laughed, but there was something in his insouciance that made me pause. Perhaps it would be wise not to underestimate Ben.

Phelippes tutted. 'Neither of you is to kill any of them, if you can possibly avoid it. That would not serve our purpose at all. They must be kept alive for questioning, and to testify against Mary Stuart.' He slipped the boy a couple of coins and dismissed him; Ben gave me a brief salute, two fingers to his temple, and disappeared as silently as he had arrived. Though I strained for the sound of footsteps on the stairs I heard none. Either he was admirably light-footed, or he was still there listening. Neither would have surprised me.

'I'm sending Gifford this morning to see Babington at Herne's Rents, to advise him of your arrival,' Phelippes continued. 'If he accepts the idea and everything seems straightforward, Gifford will come for you later this afternoon and take you to him. In the meantime, learn the cipher, go over your Father Prado story until you can recite it in your sleep, and remind yourself how to say the Mass.'

'What? Why?' I turned to him, alarmed.

'You're supposed to be a Jesuit priest.' He looked impatient. 'They may expect it of you. You should be prepared, just in case.'

'I am out of practice.' I was not worried about forgetting the words – the formula and the gestures were etched almost as deep in my bones as my mother tongue – but there was the small matter of my excommunication; a lingering superstitious part of me feared my fraud would somehow be evident in my face.

'Then there is your task for the afternoon – repeat it until you have it by heart. Any more questions?'

'Yes. One. Bessie's note, last night. Tell me how you deciphered it so quickly.'

'That has nothing to do with the business in hand.'

'I find that hard to believe. But even so – before I go. Satisfy my curiosity, as one enthusiast to another.'

He flicked an impatient glance to the window, assessing the light to judge how the day was progressing. Eventually he let out a sigh. 'Very well. Then you leave me in peace. You understand the method of a cipher based on a shared text?'

'Of course. The key to the substitution is derived from identifying certain words on certain pages of the book that both the writer and the recipient have in common. So if, say, the key is 25,12, it means the cipher alphabet begins with the first letter of the twelfth word on page twenty-five.'

'Exactly. Or the key might say 25,12,17, meaning the alphabet changes every seventeenth word of the message, so the cipher is almost impossible to decode without a copy of the book.' He set down his penknife, warming to his theme.

'Before Mary Stuart was moved to her current quarters at Chartley, her guard was more lax. She received gifts from her supporters which were not searched as thoroughly as they should have been, most particularly books. She contrived a means of communication whereby certain books were marked with green ribbons, those which contained the keys with her correspondents. But because her library was limited, she tended to fall back on the same books, so it was easy to become familiar with them. After a moment last night, I recognised a pattern as belonging to one of the texts Mary had commonly used – a book that she had with her when she was in the care of the Earl of Shrewsbury, Bessie Pierrepont's step-grandfather. So the connection was there.'

'You think Bessie is writing to *Mary*?' My eyes widened; this would be a new twist to the business.

'Keep your voice down.' He glanced at the door. 'Hard to tell. The note was ambiguous.'

'What did it say? Go on, Thomas – it was I who brought it to you, I am hardly going to divulge to anyone.'

After a pause, he relented. 'It said, "For the love I bear you, it shall be done."'

'That could mean anything.'

'As I said. It could be a love note, either to Gifford, unlikely as it seems, or for him to pass to one of the Babington gang if she is involved with them. Or it could be intended for Mary herself. What we lack is any correspondence to which this might be a reply, and that would make all the difference. We need to know what "it" refers to.'

I exhaled slowly, understanding the import. 'You mean that if she and Mary are writing to one another, then those letters can only be passing via Gifford, and he is double-dealing with you.'

'We have had doubts about Gifford from the beginning – that is usual when someone's loyalty has been coerced with money or threat. But his association with Bessie is more worrying. It means he is passing letters that he is not declaring to us. Even if it turns out that the girl is involved with one of the Babington group rather than directly with Mary Stuart, the idea that she has undertaken to do something for love of someone is a cause for concern – Bessie Pierrepont has access to Queen Elizabeth's most intimate chambers.'

'Can you not move her, if you think she is a danger?'

'I have been discussing this with Master Secretary early this morning. To do so would be to reveal that we suspect her, and as yet we do not know if she represents a separate threat, set on by Mary herself, or if Bessie is part of the Babington conspiracy, or merely a foolish young woman with a lover who happens to know Mary's ciphers. She will be watched closely and not allowed too near the Queen's person. For now, it would be better if she or her correspondent gave themselves away more explicitly. And you will be watching Gifford. If all goes well, you will be at supper this evening with the group when he passes over the letters from his recent trip to Mary. Take good note of what papers he gives to whom. Check his doublet when he is asleep to see if that message is still there.'

I nodded. At the thought of that supper, I had the sudden sensation of the room rushing towards me and time contracting; by the evening, I would be a different person, in a different life, walking a knife-edge among men who would kill me if I mis-spoke one word of the Mass and gave myself away. There was a chance that my intervention could save Queen Elizabeth's life, or bring the Queen of Scots to the block. The enormity of what I was about to undertake rose up before me like a wave, so that I had to steady myself with a hand against the desk, almost overwhelmed by it. I breathed hard, afraid I might involuntarily retch; the feeling was not unlike seasickness.

'Are you all right?' Phelippes asked, briskly.

I nodded; all I could do was wait for the moment to pass.

But behind the fear I could also hear in the hammering of my heart the drumbeat of exhilaration. I would be Father Prado, and not even the prospect of Archibald Douglas would stop me.

PART TWO

TWELVE

I had changed names more than once in my thirty-eight years. It was one thing I had in common with Sophia Underhill; we both understood what it meant to find yourself so tightly tangled in circumstances that the only way out was to step out of your old self like leaving behind dirty clothes, and walk away unburdened as someone else. Except that it never works out like that, of course. My parents had christened me Filippo; when I was admitted to the Dominican order at the age of seventeen, they renamed me Giordano, a new name to signify the start of my new life as a servant of God. Ten years later, when I was forced to run from San Domenico under cover of darkness rather than face the Inquisition, I used my birth name again, and took the family name of my mother's side – Savolino – in case the name Bruno reached the ears of their agents. I had tried out other names on my travels, when it seemed prudent, and Filippo Savolino had served me well on some occasions, but though I had necessarily adapted details of my life story for the curious, I had never really been playing anyone other than myself. Becoming Father Xavier Prado was a different prospect altogether. I was not worried about making obvious mistakes – I had been over the form of the Mass with Phelippes until you would think I'd been saying it daily; my Spanish was fluent, so that only another Spaniard would notice the inflection of a Neapolitan accent, and there were ways to explain that, in the unlikely event that I ran into one – but it would take every ounce of concentration not to slip, like the inn-yard jongleurs who juggled with flaming torches or balanced one on top of the other by only one hand. The moment I stepped out of Phelippes's lodgings that afternoon in the amber silk suit that rustled disconcertingly as I walked, I realised I was already carrying myself differently, and I felt the sudden, sharp thrill of a blank page, the terrifying possibility of a fall.

Herne's Rents was a long, timber-framed building of four storeys at the edge of Lincoln's Inn Fields that looked as if it had once been an inn, but was now divided into apartments and occupied, for the most part, by men of the clerical class and young gentlemen of limited means sharing rooms. It was close enough to the Inns of Court and the City walls to be convenient for professionals, and anonymous enough that no one paid much attention to comings and goings; I could see why Anthony Babington had chosen it as a base, though with his income he could easily have afforded better.

Gifford was uncharacteristically quiet as I put down my bag in the set of rooms Phelippes had taken for us. He sat on the end of his bed, chewing the side of his thumb and watching through the doorway that joined our rooms as I laid out the ruffled shirts on my own bed, smoothing their creases.

'So what else did he say?' I straightened and ran a hand over my newly cropped hair. Phelippes had done a surprisingly professional job – another of his unexpected skills – and the wind felt cold around the back of my neck. I kept reaching to rub a beard that was no longer there.

'As I already told you and Thomas – he was delighted to hear about you.'

'He didn't find it suspicious that the Spanish had responded so quickly?'

'Not a shadow of doubt that I could see. He takes it as proof of his own rightness and God's favour for their enterprise. He was won over by the sight of the Spanish ambassador's seal, though I doubt he could have identified it.'

'I'm pleased it convinced him. It was worth all the trouble.'

He pulled at a loose thread on his sleeve. 'But Babington is trusting, you'll see. He's too open for a conspiracy of this nature. It's Ballard you'll have to get past.' His tone suggested he wouldn't wager much on my chances. 'Are you ready?'

I adjusted the bright silk doublet, took a deep breath and nodded.

'As I'll ever be.'

Gifford passed his hands over his face and let out a shaky sigh. 'Let's go, then. You had better do most of the talking – I'm afraid I'll say something foolish.'

'I'm sure you won't. No more than usual, anyway.'

He gave me a weak smile, glanced around the room, gathered himself and opened the door. 'After you, *Father*.'

We passed along a corridor with uneven boards underfoot and plaster flaking from the walls – Gifford cocking his head with a grin at the sounds of frantic coupling coming from the next apartment to ours – and took the wide staircase down to the next floor, where the ceilings were higher and the rooms larger. He knocked on a door at the end of the first landing. I cut a sidelong glance at him; he was bouncing on the balls of his feet and trying too hard to control his breathing, he could not have looked more edgy if he had been about to fight a duel. I made a calming gesture with my hand; he frowned, not understanding, and mouthed '*What*?' Before I could answer, the door cracked an inch and a voice hissed urgently, 'Inside.'

Almost before it was closed behind us, I found myself drawn into a scented embrace and kissed enthusiastically on both cheeks. I stepped back but my new host clasped me by the shoulders and held me at arm's length, appraising me with a frank gaze and a smile that blazed like the torches on London Bridge. Beneath the perfume, he smelled strongly of wine, though it was not yet five.

'Welcome, friend. We have been praying for a sign, and here you are.'

'*Aquí estoy*. Here I am.' I matched his delighted expression, and played up the accent.

'God be praised.'

Anthony Babington was a handsome young man, no question. Dark blond hair grown long so that it curled over his collar, the way mine had until that morning; neat, straight features and prominent bones, his face all angles and hollows, girlishly full lips and inquisitive hazel eyes that seemed too large for him, giving him the look of a pretty spaniel. A sparse beard emphasised the line of his jaw – he was too fair, or too young, to grow one properly – and he wore a gold ring in his right ear. His shirt was of fine linen, unlaced at the neck to reveal a smooth chest. Clara Poole could not have found it too much of a hardship to coax secrets out of such a well-made boy, I thought; many women had to put up with worse. Immediately I felt a pinch of conscience; I must remember who these men were, and what they were capable of.

'Sit, please.' He indicated a chair by the hearth. Babington's room was large, with two long windows facing the street. 'Gilbert, close the casements, will you, while I fetch our guest a drink. Wine, Father?'

I hesitated. 'Best you call me Prado, friend.' I nodded towards the door. 'How do you say it in English – the walls have ears? I will take a small glass, thank you.' I had no intention of drinking it. Father Prado would have to be abstemious on religious grounds, I decided, so that I could stay sober and keep my wits about me. Babington handed me a glass and pulled up a chair opposite, leaning forward eagerly, elbows resting on his knees.

'So Ballard explained our venture to you in Paris?'

I was ready for this one. 'Alas, I did not have the pleasure of meeting Señor Ballard. Our mutual friend the ambassador dispatched me after their discussion, there was no time to make his acquaintance. It was thought less suspicious if I arrived in England separately.'

'Did they give you any trouble at the port?'

I thought of my two eager interrogators in Rye and made a face. 'The usual insults, a few questions. But I came in on a merchant ship and they took me for what I appeared to be, in the end.'

Babington nodded. 'What about Paget? Did he tell you the details of our enterprise?'

'I have not had the pleasure of meeting him either. My only conversation about this business was with Don Bernadino de Mendoza, who appraised me of your intentions.' I dropped my voice so that I spoke his name barely above a whisper.

He frowned. 'Still, it is strange that you should live in Paris and not know Paget. He knows everyone.'

I kept my expression carefully neutral. 'Naturally, I know him by reputation. But I work much of the time as a courier, you understand – I am constantly on the road between Paris and Madrid with letters. It gives me little time to make friends in either city. Besides,' I added, with another tilt of my head towards the door, 'the ambassador gave me strict instructions that I should not mention him or his associates in relation to this business of yours, until the crucial stages are completed. For everyone's sake.'

He nodded, his expression excessively earnest, and I saw that he was already quite drunk, despite the hour. Not to the degree that his speech or movement was impaired; still, it was telling. He struck me as a man looking to take the edge off his anxiety. 'We proceed well. I have faith that God will bless our enterprise this time. He must, for we do His will.'

'Spain has faith too.'

His face brightened at this, and he grasped my hand. 'Yes.

And we thank you. I know this is not the first such attempt, and it would be understandable if Spain doubted our ability to make good our promises, but you see' – he loosened his grip and lifted his glass with his other hand for a long draught – 'they were too hasty, the last time. They confided in too many people, Throckmorton and his friends, and did not trouble to discover traitors among their number. Whereas we have kept our counsel, and told our plans only to those sworn to uphold our endeavours.' His eyes focused and narrowed. 'Talking of which – do not think me impertinent, but have you some proof of Spain's good faith?'

'Besides the ambassador's seal, you mean, and the considerable risks I have taken as a priest in entering the territories of the heretic Elizabeth?' I aimed for mildly offended; it seemed to work. Babington held up his hands, conciliatory.

'I meant no harm – we deal as men of honour, and brothers in Christ. Only – we cannot be too careful, you understand. Already—' he broke off, a shadow passing briefly over his flushed face. I wondered if he had been going to say something about Clara Poole, but he only gave a brief twitch of his head, as if to dislodge whatever stray thought had troubled him.

'I have this.' I reached inside the ridiculous doublet and brought out the bill of goods with Mendoza's secret letter – or, to be more accurate, a painstakingly rendered forgery that had taken Phelippes the best part of the morning, since alum writing, once revealed by heat, cannot be erased.

Babington broke the seal and glanced at the contents. 'Quantities of silk and linen.'

'That is not the whole of the message.'

'How do I read it?'

'In the usual way.'

He nodded and smiled, as if to convey a shared knowledge of this world of subterfuge, and tucked the letter into the silk purse that hung at his belt; I guessed that the technicalities of deciphering were not something he concerned himself with directly. Someone would examine every pen stroke of that letter, though; I wondered if it would be the infamous Ballard. I found I was looking forward to testing myself against him.

Babington eyed my clothes; I felt myself grow hot under his scrutiny.

'Gilbert here says you bring us money,' he said eventually. There was a gleam in his eye that did not come merely from the wine.

'A gift from Spain. I have it safe. My instructions were to entrust it to the group, for the sake of openness.'

'You mean, so that I can't pocket a few escudos without the others knowing?' He sprawled back in his chair, a lazy smirk at the edges of his lips. 'Fair enough. Don't worry, I have no need to steal your master's coins. It is more for your sake, to assure us that Spain is earnest in her support. And that you are to be trusted.'

I dipped my head modestly. 'I place myself at the mercy of your good judgement, and that of your friends. This is a business of shared trust on both sides, is it not? For my part, I have only your word that you are not a government agent waiting to whisk me off to gaol the moment I give you the information you want.'

Babington laughed, and tilted his glass in my direction. 'Imagine if I were.' Gifford gave a sort of hiccup behind me. 'That kind of thinking will send us all mad. Let us take one another in good faith, and embrace as brothers. For God's sake, sit down, Gilbert, you're making me nervous, hovering like that. You're very quiet today, are you mooning after some girl?'

Some girl. So Gifford's infatuation with Bessie Pierrepont was not common knowledge among his associates. That did not necessarily mean that she had nothing to do with Babington. Gifford approached from the window where he had been hanging back, pulsing with pent-up energy. He cast around for a chair, found none, so took a cushion and sat at

Babington's feet, careful not to catch my eye. 'My mind is on higher things, Anthony. I did not wish to interrupt our honoured visitor.' His voice was subdued, but Babington appeared not to notice. 'Have you read the Queen's letters yet?'

It took me a moment to realise that Gifford meant Mary Stuart – though Phelippes had drummed into me the need to be mindful at all times of how the Catholics reversed the titles of the main players in this drama. For them, Mary was the only true queen, and the present sovereign of England was always 'the heretic', 'the usurper', 'the bastard' or, if they were feeling unusually respectful, merely 'the Tudor'. It was the most obvious shibboleth – one slip of the tongue and I would be betrayed on the instant.

Babington stretched and cast around for the wine bottle. 'Give me a chance, you only brought them this morning. And I am slow at decryption, as you know. I will have them done by tonight, or Titch can help. Are you quick with a cipher, Prado?'

I inclined my head again. 'It is a necessary part of my work. If you would care to show me the message, I would be happy to cast an eye over it.'

Babington mulled this over as he poured. 'Or perhaps we had better wait for Ballard before I go showing you the letters, just to be sure. I mean no offence, Father,' he added, with a flicker of anxiety.

'I take none, sir. We have all learned to be cautious in these times.' I glanced at Gilbert, who was absently fingering the seam of his doublet where Bessie's note was hidden, or had been. I almost wanted to click my tongue at him, the way a nursemaid will with a small boy who won't leave his parts alone. He was so painfully uncomfortable in the presence of me and Babington together, I thought it best to get him away so he had time to gather his wits before supper; a sharper man than Babington – John Ballard, for example – would note Gifford's edginess immediately. 'Perhaps I should not keep you any longer from your letters.' I pushed the chair back in anticipation of leaving.

'Yes, the others will want to hear the news tonight. You will join us for supper, I hope, at The Castle? We are expecting Ballard back – he will want to know everything your master discussed with you about Spain's contribution to the business.'

'I look forward to making his acquaintance, with the rest of your comrades.' I stood then, and effected a little bow; by the relief on Gifford's face, I saw that my instinct to cut the meeting short had been correct. I was almost at the door when Babington jumped abruptly out of his chair and clutched at my sleeve with both hands.

'Wait – not so fast, I pray you.'

My heart lurched; had I given myself away with some word or gesture? Over his shoulder, I saw the colour drain from Gifford's face. Babington dropped his gaze to the floor.

'Give me your blessing, Father, before you go.' He spoke quietly, his speech sober; I reminded myself that Babington might well be cleverer than Robin Poole had given him credit for, and the drunkenness could easily have been a show to put me off my guard. I must not take any one of them at face value. 'May God forgive my weakness,' he said, 'but sometimes when I wake in the night, I find myself wracked with doubts about our chances of success. Not because God is not on our side, only – we are few, there is so much that must come together, and the heretic Tudor has spies everywhere.'

'So I understand,' I murmured.

'And we all remember what happened to Throckmorton.' He glanced up to meet my eye and there was fear in his face, beneath the bravado. 'Is it a sin to want reassurance, Father?'

'Of course not, my son. And you are not few now. You have the might of Spain at your back.'

He smiled at this and squeezed my hand. Gifford, behind him, looked impressed. Babington released me and rummaged in the purse to draw out a silver crucifix, pressing it to his lips as he meekly bowed his head to my hand. I spoke a few words in Latin, a priest's blessing to his flock, harmless pieties. Gifford's mouth twisted in disdain and he turned away; he was a fine one to have scruples about hypocrisy, I thought, but I raised my eyes to the window and imagined, as I had on the boat, what the ledger of my offences against God must look like by now, always supposing He was there to record them.

THIRTEEN

The Castle Tavern, on Cornhill. A private room, upstairs, with a table set for seven. Three branched candlesticks along its length gave out a soft light that seemed to breathe in and out each time the door opened; more at either end of the room kept the shadows in the corners at bay. A bead of sweat trickled down the inside of my collar; I pulled with a finger at the elaborate ruff where it scratched my neck and wished again that Father Prado could have disguised himself as something other than a young gallant of fashion. The air was close and stuffy; though it was still pleasantly light outside, at only eight o'clock, here the casements had been closed and the curtains drawn, the better to conduct the secret business of bringing down a queen and a government.

A serving boy had left a pitcher of wine on a dresser against the far wall, before being sent away; Babington poured it himself for his guests and passed the glasses around. I had walked to the tavern with Gifford, neither of us speaking much; as we climbed the stairs I had braced myself for my first encounter with Ballard, and could not quite disguise the shake in my breath when we pushed open the door to find only three of the conspirators present.

Babington handed me around the room like a rare treasure

he had brought back from his travels: to Robin Poole, who appraised me with a cool glance as if it were truly the first time we had met, then bowed his head and kissed my hand reverently, a nice touch; next, to a young man presented as Chidiock Tichborne, his closest friend, son of a noble Catholic family from Southampton, about Babington's own age or younger. He and 'Titch' had travelled in France together some years earlier, I gathered, in search of disaffected English exiles to share their grievances – an adventure that, I knew from Phelippes, had brought them both to the attention of the authorities, since they had failed to apply for a licence to travel out of the realm. Young men of the old Catholic families heading for France – where secret priests were trained and conspiracies brewed – always attracted interest, as you'd think they would have anticipated. Perhaps not the brightest, then; if they hadn't foreseen that, I wondered how they had ever believed they could manage a plot to assassinate Queen Elizabeth, spring Mary from prison and organise a Catholic uprising in concert with a Spanish invasion, all without the government noticing. But the better for our purposes, if they really were so naïve. This Tichborne was unusually tall, taller even than Sidney, and skinny with it. Unlike Sidney, he did not own his height, but seemed to apologise for it by hunching over like a heron watching for fish. His only other striking feature was a pair of startlingly blue eyes that transformed his boyish, slightly ferrety appearance into a face you would look at twice. His smile as he shook my hand appeared nervous, but I decided this was just his manner, rather than any direct suspicion of me; I could see that he was a youth brought up with an unquestioning reverence for priests, and that he was a follower, not a leader, content to fall in with whatever Babington suggested.

'Titch is a poet,' Babington announced, with a breezy wave of his glass; the boy shook his head, alarmed, and backed away muttering something self-deprecating about scribbles. 'Do you like poetry, Prado?'

I hesitated. Could it be a trick? Did Father Prado enjoy poetry? The matter had not come up in the briefing Phelippes had given me; it had probably not been the first thing they thought to squeeze out of the poor wretch in Walsingham's cellar. I took a breath and let my head clear; it was of no importance, these men were never going to meet Father Prado. His taste in poetry, or anything else, was entirely left to my devising, and I must learn to think on my feet, without second-guessing a trap in every enquiry, or I would be unmasked before the first course arrived.

'Who would not? Poetry is a gift from God,' I said piously.

'Not the way he writes it,' Babington said, punching his friend lightly on the arm, and the others laughed. He reminded me of Sidney in that moment; what was it with these rich English boys, always cuffing and scrapping with their friends to disguise any show of affection – fear of being thought a sodomite?

'We may as well sit,' he said, motioning to the table. 'There's no knowing what time Ballard will be here – he could have been delayed by the tides.' He pulled up a chair at the head.

'And Savage?' Poole asked.

'He will be wherever Ballard is,' Titch muttered.

'No matter – we'll call for bread and more wine while we wait. But we should not discuss the business until Ballard is here.'

'Because he would not like it?' Poole again; his voice was light, but pointed.

'Because we will only have to repeat it all, and I do not want our new friend to find us tedious company,' Babington said, also lightly, though defensive. I remembered what Poole had told me on our ride to Southwark; that Ballard was the de facto leader of the conspirators, though Babington's money was furnishing the plot. Clearly there was tension there. 'Anyway – how does your sister, Robin?'

A sudden silence; I felt Gifford tense beside me as I pulled out a seat.

'I have not seen her this past week,' Poole said, in that same easy tone. 'Her employer keeps her busy, I expect.'

'Yes, that is what I feared. Can't be easy, working for a Walsingham.' Babington let the remark hang in the air. No one spoke. It could have been an innocent observation – that Lady Sidney was a demanding mistress – or something more sinister; was he implying that he knew who really employed Clara Poole? I watched him closely, but his face gave nothing away.

'I suppose we must think of Lady Frances as a Sidney now, though,' Poole said, carrying the jug of wine to the table. I had to admire his composure; he had not exaggerated his skills at dissembling.

'Makes no difference. Both sides of that family are lapdogs to the usurper, running about to do her bidding. I wonder Clara stands living cheek by jowl with such a nest of heretics.'

'She endures it,' Robin said patiently, 'the better to help us. We are fortunate that she is willing to take such a risk – do you ever think what the Sidneys would do if she were discovered to be Catholic?'

All credit to him; his voice did not waver. Babington let that go. 'Talking of which – I had hoped to hear more from Clara about the so-called queen's intended Progress next month. She said she would look among the old man's papers when she had the chance and bring us dates and locations. It is odd that she has not been in touch, do you not think? What say you, Titch?'

'What?' Titch jerked around; he had been standing by the window, peering out through a gap in the curtains.

'Clara – have you heard from her? Come away from there, for God's sake – people will see you.'

'It's not a crime for friends to take supper together – there is no reason for us to skulk about as if we have no right to be here, we only draw more attention. And I haven't seen Clara – why would I?'

'I was merely asking. I don't like it when people go quiet, especially at this stage – it makes me nervous. God knows we have enough at stake here. Sit down and have a drink.'

'You need have no fear on my sister's account, Babington,' Poole said, and there was a flinty note in his voice that made the young men glance sharply at him. He was looking at both of them as if they were something he would like to scrape off his shoe. 'She is a good girl and true to the cause. If you fear betrayal, it will not come from that quarter, I will stake my life on it.'

A complicated look passed between him and Babington.

'I meant only that I worried she had been caught, Robin. You are the one who brought up the subject of betrayal.'

They faced one another down; perhaps only I saw the veins standing up on the back of Poole's hand as it rested at his hip, near his knife, the muscles minutely quivering in his fingers. Walsingham said it had taken all his powers of persuasion to stop Poole running Babington through when he heard of Clara's murder; I suspected the urge had not left him. I felt I should say something, in character, to break the moment.

'You fear betrayal? My master would be alarmed to hear this, I think. One does not invest in a ship that is rumoured to be holed below the waterline.'

'By God, no – you misunderstand.' Babington let out a nervous laugh and clasped my arm. 'Our ship is watertight and seaworthy, Prado, believe me. We are all sworn to this enterprise, no one's love for the Queen or the faith is in doubt. It is just that – we have a young friend to our designs, Robin's sister, who lives in the household of Secretary Walsingham's daughter. She brings us useful information, the better to plan our access to the heretic Elizabeth.'

'And you are sure her loyalties are not compromised? Because I have heard, you know, that such people can have, how do you say it, double faces?'

Robin Poole took a step forward and pointed a finger in

my face. 'Watch yourself. Priest or no priest, if you insult my sister's honesty, I will settle the matter with you as a man.'

I tried to look taken aback, but the ferocity in his eyes seemed unfeigned; this was not quite how I had imagined the conversation unfolding.

'Peace, Robin.' Babington half-rose in his chair, the other hand stretched out, placating. 'No one is impugning Clara's loyalty. I am only concerned that we have not heard from her in several days, it is not like her, and Prado is right to be cautious, when his master is risking so much in our support.' He turned to me. 'Forgive us, Father. A business such as this puts everyone on edge – it is easy to start jumping at shadows. But all will be right when Ballard arrives and you hear what encouragement Gilbert has brought us from Staffordshire.'

The company turned to look at Gifford, still hovering by the door.

'Yes, what news of the Queen, Gilbert?' Poole took his seat on Babington's right and patted the chair beside him. Gifford sat, as if reluctant to commit himself, and refused to meet my eye. I could see how he was feeling his way with every step around me, terrified of putting a foot wrong; I wanted to shake him.

'In good spirits,' he managed, though his mouth was dry and his voice emerged as a croak. 'At least, according to the brewer, who heard it from the kitchen girl.'

'So she should be,' Babington said, lifting his glass as if in a toast. 'Her hour is at hand, and she knows it. Here's to the good brewer. And now that Spain is on board—'

'What brewer?' I asked.

'You have not heard our scheme?' Babington looked delighted; he set his glass down and poured a fresh round of drinks for everyone. 'I am amazed Master Gifford here has not boasted to you already of his ingenuity. Gilbert, tell our friend the system you have devised for getting letters in and out of the prison. You will like this, Prado – it is a fine example of English know-how.' He nudged the wine towards me; I inclined my head in thanks, but did not touch it.

Finally Gifford raised his head and looked across the table at me with an effortful smile. 'Well – you will have heard how Her Majesty is kept close at Chartley Manor. Her keeper, Sir Amias Paulet, is cruelly strict in his dealings. She may not walk outside, and her servants are not permitted to come and go, or associate with the household staff. Even her laundresses are searched when they leave and enter her chambers, right down to their shifts, to make sure they are not carrying any messages.'

'I'll bet Paulet takes charge of that himself, the old lecher,' Babington cut in. 'I'll bet he checks every crevice twice over, with the other hand inside his breeches, for the good of the English Church. Saving your presence, Father. But you see what hypocrites these Puritans are.' The others laughed, except Titch, who continued to scratch splinters from the tabletop with his fingernail; I affected to look amused and shocked at the same time. 'Continue, Gilbert.'

'So, you see our difficulty. How to get letters in and out without discovery? Well – we hit upon an ingenious solution.'

'You need not say "we", Gilbert, when the plan was all of your devising – take credit where it is due.' Babington grinned, but I saw Gifford's eyes flash to mine, stricken; that 'we' was his first slip of the tongue. Though I had not heard the details, I knew that the system of communication with Mary Stuart's household had been carefully worked out by Phelippes, with all risks assessed and accounted for; to suggest the involvement of others was a serious mistake if Gifford was meant to be passing this off as his own idea. Again, I was relieved that Ballard had not arrived; he would have noticed it, I was certain.

'I meant only, myself and the brewer, of course,' Gifford said, flustered.

'Tell me of this brewer, then.' I smiled encouragement, hoping it would calm him.

'Well.' He laid his hands flat on the table as if to steady himself. When he began again, he sounded more in command. 'A household the size of Chartley gets through a good deal of ale, you may imagine. They take deliveries twice a week from a brewer in the town of Burton, an honest man who is a friend to the Queen of Scots' cause. I take him the letters sealed inside a waterproof tube, which fits through the bung-hole of a beer barrel. The cask in question is marked with a chalk cross, very small. Then, when the delivery is unloaded in the kitchen yard at Chartley, one of the serving girls, also a friend to us and glad of a few extra coins, takes out the tube and passes it in secret to Queen Mary's secretary. And once the Queen has written her reply, it returns the same way when the brewer collects the empty barrels, and I wait to receive it from him and ride with all haste to London, as I have this past week.'

'Is it not cleverly done?' Babington looked at me, his eyes dancing, like a child expectant of praise.

'Most ingenious,' I agreed. 'And the letters cannot be tampered with?'

Gilbert's eyes widened, as if to warn that I had strayed from my script; before he could answer, the door flew open, crashing against the inner wall, and an imposing figure filled the space.

'The only person who could tamper with them is the courier,' declared the newcomer, in a cultured voice. 'Gentlemen, be advised your talk carries down the stairs, take better care or half London will know our business.' He crossed the room, trailing a gust of sweat and horses. Close behind him followed a shorter man, wiry and muscled, with a shaved head and a small pointed beard. The one who had spoken ruffled Gifford's hair in passing, unknotting his travelling cloak with the other hand. 'Only sporting with you, Gilbert, son. We know you for an honest man too, am I right?' He swept off his broad-brimmed hat, handed it to his companion, cast around the room, then stopped dead and looked from me to Babington with the face of a man who has found his wife in bed with the neighbour. 'Who the devil is this?'

'Here is Captain Fortescue!' Babington exclaimed, rising as if to embrace the new arrival, then thinking better of it and remaining trapped in a half-crouch. A quiver in his laugh betrayed his nerves, and he gestured to me as if presenting me at court. 'Behold, the fruit of your labours.' He lowered his voice and sat down. 'This is Father Prado, come from Paris on the orders of Ambassador Mendoza, to bring us earnest of Spanish support after your meeting.'

The new arrival kept his black gaze fixed on me without smiling; I stood, bobbed a quick bow, and met his eye, steady and unhurried, to show him I would not be daunted. So here was John Ballard: my own age or thereabouts, but his wiry dark curls and thick brows were already threaded with grey, as was the full beard hiding a small mouth. Ruddy spots bloomed across his cheeks, as if he spent much of his time in strong winds, or strong drink, but he had good teeth. He was taller than me, though less than six foot, running to fat around the middle, but with a slab of a chest, broad shoulders and large hands; I guessed he would still give good account of himself in a fight. He wore an outfit as garish as mine: beneath his travelling cloak a cape edged with gold lace over a green satin doublet slashed to show crimson lining. I recalled Poole saying he passed himself off as a soldier, hence the military alias, though in that get-up he looked more like he should be on stage at The Curtain, embodying the vice of Vanity or Self-Regard.

He continued to eye me as if daring me to look away first; I could see how a man might be afraid of him, even one who had nothing to hide. I drew myself up, determined not to be shaken by his scrutiny. It was to be expected, I told myself; he would have regarded the real Father Prado in the same way.

'Is that so? Mendoza sent you?' One brow arched in a

show of curiosity, or scepticism. I inclined my head in assent. This would be the test; only Ballard knew precisely what had been promised by the Spanish ambassador in their meeting, and I feared that Walsingham had not had time enough to extract from the Jesuit all the necessary information to convince him. Ballard pulled at his beard. 'You must have set off hot-foot the moment the door closed behind me. When did you arrive?'

'Yesterday morning.'

'Did they search you?'

'Of course. Unsuccessfully.' I took my seat again.

'Evidently, or you would not be here. But you had letters, I presume?' He glanced around at the company. 'Even an excitable pup like Babington would not be so trusting as to admit you without proof that you are who you say, I'm sure.'

'I had letters. They were well concealed. I am skilled in this business, *Capitan*, as you are. That is why the ambassador chose me. Here.' I reached into my doublet and passed him Mendoza's seal – now scrubbed thoroughly in boiling water, Phelippes had assured me.

He held it to the nearest bank of candles and made a show of examining it. 'I meant no insult, *hermano*. You understand how much caution must be exercised. The heretic whore has her men everywhere. And women too, I don't doubt.' He left a pause. 'The more people know our business, the greater the chance one of them will sell us out for profit.'

'You came to my master. He sent me direct to London. Who else could know of it?' I wondered if his reference to women was general or specific.

Ballard considered this for a moment and nodded. 'Does Paget know you're here?'

'I have no idea. I take my orders from Don Bernadino.'

'He's brought money, John,' Babington said, eager to redeem himself after the barb about his lack of proper caution.

'Well, that will speak eloquently for him. I should like to

see it.' Ballard walked slowly around the foot of the table to stand at my shoulder. I reached for the leather bag I had stashed under my chair and brought out the strongbox, unlocking it for his examination. I could not tell at a glance how much it contained and I did not suppose Ballard could either, but the amount was clearly significant. Phelippes had shown me the contents – all in Spanish gold pieces. Ballard looked down at the slew of coins in silence for a minute or two. Eventually he raised his head and met my eye.

'This is not the sum agreed.' He made it sound casual, an observation rather than an accusation, but I felt the sweat prickle inside the absurd ruff and my mouth dried.

'It is all I was able to carry without attracting attention.'

'*All*?' The eyebrow shot up again. He waited.

'This is what I was given. If you have a complaint, take it up with my master.'

After a short pause, he let out a bark of laughter.

'I'm not complaining, man. This is far more than Mendoza led me to expect. He plays his cards close to his chest, eh?' He lifted a handful of coins and let them slide through his fingers.

'He wanted to surprise you,' I said, feeling again the racing heart that went with the slippery sense of relief at having dodged a shot. I was glad I had kept my seat so my shaking legs could not betray me, though I had to bite down a smile, picturing Walsingham's irritation at the thought that he could have kept some back.

'Prado, is it?' Ballard leaned a hand casually on the back of my chair and bent down until his mouth was six inches from my ear. 'You're a difficult man to read. I can't tell if you're playing games with me. I suppose that must be a good thing, in this world. Is it your real name?'

I twisted my head to look at him.

'Today it is.'

He laughed again, and lines fanned out from the corners of his eyes; he grasped me by the shoulders and kissed me once on each cheek. 'Very good. *Que Dios le bendiga.* You and your money are welcome. But we will swear you in before the evening is done, to be certain.' He pulled out the chair at the foot of the table and Savage slid into place on his left. 'Now then, my gallant boys, before I tell you of France, I bring sobering news from south of the river. Gilbert – stand by the door, check none of those serving lads is loitering.' When Gifford had confirmed that the staircase was empty, Ballard leaned forward in confidential manner and the others mirrored his pose. 'I stopped off at the Unicorn on my way into London tonight. You know how it is – Captain Fortescue has accounts to settle, messages to collect, questions to ask.'

An uneasy titter rippled around the table. Ballard turned to me. 'Are you familiar with Southwark, my friend?'

'I have not had the pleasure.'

'Ah, we will acquaint you before too long. Southwark is a lawless place, Prado, full of black-hearted rogues, and the Unicorn the most lawless of all. A den of gamesters, conmen and whores, patronised by some of the best men in the city, even a few in government—'

'—the worst conmen of all,' Savage cut in, looking around the table for a laugh. I noticed a strangeness about his eyes as he looked at me; they were different colours, one blue and one brown. I had never seen such a thing before; it made his regard disconcerting.

'Quite so,' Ballard continued, smiling, 'though they pay a good price to pass incognito. Babylon and Sodom would blush to see the goings-on at the Unicorn, believe me. There's not a sin you've heard in confession that isn't for sale there, and plenty no one would ever confess to. Nothing happens in all of London they don't know about, which is why I take my lodgings there when I'm in London.'

I produced an expression of distaste. 'Is it usual for priests in England to frequent brothels?'

Ballard's expression clouded.

'It is *usual* for priests in England to end up with their haunches nailed to a church door in four different wards and their heads on London Bridge, unless they are careful to conceal their identity. There are watchers everywhere, Prado, primed to sniff out the likes of you and me. So we must be cunning as serpents, as Our Lord Himself commanded. And did He not spend His ministry among fallen women and tax collectors? Who would think to look for a priest in a whorehouse?'

'I see you have not spent much time in Paris,' I said. 'That's the first place I would look there.'

Ballard seemed pleased with this; he laughed heartily, slapping his hand on his leg, and the others joined in, as if relieved to have permission. I had observed before that if you want to win the approval of an Englishman, all you have to do is insult the French.

'*Muy bien*. You are not wrong. In any case, I see you understand. My virtue remains unblemished, I assure you, but it's the sort of place my alias Captain Fortescue feels quite at home, and it diverts attention, should anyone be watching me. Fortescue has friends at the Unicorn, who keep him abreast of the latest news.'

'Abreast,' Babington said, making squeezing motions with his hands, casting around for approval. He quickly subsided under Ballard's withering glare.

'And what I learned this evening,' the priest continued, 'is that a body was found in the Cross Bones four days ago, and spirited away north of the river at first light, before anyone could claim it.'

'And what has that to do with us?' Babington asked, at the same time as Titch jerked his head up and said,

'A body?'

'A woman's body. A gentlewoman. Robin' – Ballard turned to Poole – 'craving your pardon, I must ask – when did you last hear from your sister?'

Poole stiffened, and the colour drained from his face. 'What? Anthony asked me the same before you arrived. Why would you think—? Not these past few days, but – what are you trying to say?' He clutched his glass; his hands had begun shaking. 'It's not possible.'

Ballard cast his eyes down at his clasped hands and sat a moment in silence. Eventually he looked up and fixed Poole with his most solemn, priestly expression. 'I know nothing for certain, I only fear – could she have been in Southwark five nights ago? The twenty-seventh, it would have been?'

'I don't know, I am not her keeper.' Poole's voice had grown taut. 'For God's sake, man – say what you mean. You think Clara could be—'

He was good, Poole; again I had to admire him. Everything about his reaction seemed entirely authentic. From the tail of my eye, I watched to see how the others would respond. If Clara's murder was truly news to them, it would surely be written in their faces; likewise their guilt. These were young men – boys, almost – not trained, like Ballard or Poole, in the art of deception.

'Certain items . . .' Ballard hesitated, and cleared his throat. 'You know how it is, when a body is found by people desperate for money, especially one that is well-dressed. Certain items can disappear before the watch is ever alerted. Some of these tend to pass through the hands of the Unicorn people, who know how to find a ready trade. They showed me one such trinket that had been taken from the body in the Cross Bones. I paid them for it – I thought you should see it, Robin.'

Poole's face was rigid and white as a death mask. Ballard reached into his layers of silk and brought out a handkerchief, trimmed with lace, which he smoothed on the tabletop. Washing had not erased the rust-brown blotches of bloodstains. A coat of arms was embroidered in one corner; I recognised it immediately.

'I saw this,' Ballard said, 'and knew it for the Sidney crest. Am I right?'

Poole pulled the scrap of cloth towards him and ran his fingers over the raised thread. Then he buckled at the waist as if he had caught a blow to the gut; Gifford, to his right, laid a tentative hand on his shoulder. Poole shook it off, still doubled over, making incoherent noises.

'I do not say this gives us anything certain,' Ballard said, sitting back with an expression of mild concern. 'It is possible that some servant of the Sidney household, or a distant relative, could have come by such a handkerchief, or it might have been stolen. But the body was a young woman. I think it behoves you, Robin, to take yourself to Seething Lane and enquire after your sister. I urge calm, in case I have jumped to a hasty conclusion – we do not want to alert the Sidney household unduly. Ask after her as if you are merely paying a visit – it may be that you arrive to find Clara peacefully at her needlework, wondering why you have turned up in such a lather. I pray it may be so. Gilbert, perhaps you should go with him.'

Gifford looked taken aback. 'What, *now*?'

'You can be there and back in under an hour.'

Poole pushed out his chair with a vicious scrape. 'You are wrong. I cannot think of any reason why Clara . . .' He paused, gathered himself. 'Did they say, your friends at the Unicorn, what happened to her? The woman in the graveyard?'

I found I was gripping the sides of my chair, trying to keep the tension from my face; don't let Ballard mention the mutilation, I prayed silently.

'No one saw first-hand,' the priest said smoothly. 'Only the old watchman, Goodchild, and he has been taken up for questioning. You know how rumour runs riot – I should not like to speculate on what's true until you have confirmed whether it affects us – affects *you*, I should say.' He smiled, and I was grateful for his tact; perhaps, despite his reputation, there was some kindness in him.

Poole swept up his cap and hurried out of the room; Gifford threw me a last look of desperation – he was out of his depth, playing extempore – before following him.

'Oh, and, Gilbert . . .' Ballard called him back just as the door was closing, and dropped his voice to a whisper. 'Make sure Robin enquires at the servants' door, and gives nothing away if they say she has not been seen, let him not give them cause to think he fears for her. Bring him back here immediately – don't let him do anything hasty.'

'I'm not sure I could stop him—' Gifford began, but Ballard cut him off with a soothing smile.

'We are all relying on you. And on your way out, tell the serving boy we are ready for our first course now. They will keep yours and Robin's warm until you return.'

A difficult silence stretched between us after the latch clicked. I let my gaze travel as unobtrusively as possible around the rest of the company. Jack Savage leaned back in his chair, mismatched eyes fixed on Ballard as if awaiting instruction, his expression alert but unruffled. Babington and Titch were a different story; both were pale as death and looked as if they might vomit. Babington's gaze was wild and staring, his eyes shiny with tears; he lifted his glass and drained what was left in one swallow. Titch had grown very still, and continued to stare at the table as if answers might be written in the grain of the wood.

'It can't be true, can it?' Babington stared at Ballard, his voice wound tight. 'Clara, dead?'

Ballard reached for the wine jug, by now almost empty. 'I must say I fear the worst.'

'But why should you?'

'I could not mention this in front of Robin, so none of you repeat it.' He pointed a finger around the table; we all nodded mutely. 'The woman that was found – she had clearly been tortured.'

'How do you know this?' I asked. He snapped his head to me so sharply I wished I had kept silent.

'The body was seen, before it was taken away, by a servant boy from the Unicorn. Face smashed to pieces, he said, and the ears cut off. Now, ask yourself – who would torture a woman, kill her, and make the body disappear?'

'You are asking me?' I shook my head. 'You told me this Southwark is a lawless place. Everywhere there are men who like to hurt women for pleasure.'

'Yes.' Ballard acknowledged this sad truth with a dip of his head. 'But. There are also, in this city, men who inflict pain to get information. Some of them hold the highest offices in government. Do you understand?'

'I think so. By your reasoning, if the dead girl is this Clara, then you believe she has been tortured and killed by, what? The agents of Elizabeth the heretic?'

'Precisely. Clara Poole was a sort of companion to the daughter of Master Secretary Walsingham – you will know of him, I suppose, from Mendoza?'

I allowed a thin smile. 'There is no love lost there. It was Walsingham who had Ambassador Mendoza thrown out of England for Spain's part in the last plot to free Queen Mary.'

'Quite. Clara had promised to find out and deliver to us certain details concerning a Progress Elizabeth intended to make next month around Surrey and Kent – details that would have allowed us the chance to get close to her person in a way that is almost impossible in London, now she is so carefully guarded.'

'So . . .' I spoke slowly '. . . you think Clara was caught stealing this information from Walsingham's house?'

'If the body is hers, I do not see another explanation. Which means we may all be compromised – if she was suspected of being part of a plot, they will have tortured her to find out details. From what was done to this girl, so I hear, she would have shouted any name under the sun to make it stop.' He pressed his fingertips together and shuddered.

'You think even this government would treat a woman so?'

Ballard's eyes narrowed. 'Don't be naïve, Prado. Many good Catholic women have died horribly in England for their faith, these past years. Pressed, hanged, starved in prison. The heretic Elizabeth shows no tenderness for her own sex.'

'I believe you. But this is grave indeed – you mean, she may have betrayed us all already?'

'It can't be her,' Titch said, sitting up suddenly. He flexed his fingers together and his knuckles cracked loudly in the silence. Everyone turned to look at him.

'Why do you say that?' Ballard leaned in closer, hands clasped prayerfully.

'It makes no sense. Why would she be in the Cross Bones?'

'Whore's graveyard,' Savage remarked, to no one in particular. 'Where better to dump a body than Southwark? I'm amazed the constables came at all. Usually a corpse would be kicked into a ditch or the river once the thieves had stripped it, and no one saw nor heard anything.'

'Exactly. That's why it doesn't make sense,' Titch persisted. His expression was strained, as if he were trying to persuade himself. 'It's said that Master Secretary Walsingham has torture chambers under his own house so he can bypass the law when he catches a priest. If he'd wanted rid of Clara, there's no chance he'd be so careless as to leave the body lying about to be seen and picked up by the watch, in Southwark or anywhere else. She'd have vanished one night and ended up in a hole in the ground far from London, no one any the wiser.'

'He has a point,' Savage conceded.

'You don't think he disposes of corpses with his own hands?' Ballard shot him a scathing look. 'My guess is the men he paid were lazy, dropped her the nearest place they could think of. Perhaps they hoped people would take her for a dead whore. But the minute there was speculation about the body, Walsingham sent his people down there right away to make the evidence disappear.' He turned back to Babington. 'I am disappointed in you, Anthony.'

Babington's tearful eyes widened in dismay. 'Me? How is this my fault?'

'I have been riding about France securing allies for our endeavours.' He gestured to me. 'You were supposed to keep things running smoothly here. Yet none of you even knew about this body until I came home, though it seems Bankside's been talking of nothing else for four days. God's blood, must I take charge of everything? I feel I am dealing with children.'

'Children whose money you're happy to spend,' Babington muttered.

'Must we concern ourselves with every whore that washes up south of the river when your back is turned?' Titch sat forward, fists bunched, his body rigid with anger. I noted that he seemed willing to confront Ballard in a way that Babington was not; that struck me as curious, given the difference in degree. Among the conspirators, only Babington, Titch and Gifford were gentlemen, of established families; it would have been more usual for them to assert their status, yet Ballard seemed to have some hold over Babington, for all his money. I wondered if it was Ballard's natural leadership qualities, or if, perhaps, he was the boy's confessor. Once you have told a man your secrets, he holds you in the palm of his hand, even if he is a priest.

'You should concern yourselves with every scrap of news in London at this point,' Ballard said with cold authority. 'You do not know what it may signify. Holy Mother – do you understand the magnitude of what we are trying to do here?' He stared the younger men down until they both averted their eyes. 'At the very least one of you should have been keeping a closer watch on Clara Poole.'

'How should we have done that, without drawing undue attention?' Babington's cheeks flushed but he kept his temper. 'Hang about in Seething Lane peering in the windows, for Master Secretary himself to spot us? Clara knew how to look after herself, I saw no need to worry.'

'Well, we shall find out in the next hour whether that is true,' Ballard said, still calm, as Babington's colour rose along with his voice.

'It's not my responsibility if something has happened to her, John, you can't blame me. Shouldn't her brother have been looking out for her? She was not my *wife*.'

'No, that's true.' Ballard looked placidly down at his hands. 'How does your wife, Anthony, by the way?' he added pleasantly. 'And your – what is it, a daughter you have?'

Babington glared at him for a long, unreadable moment, then shoved his chair back and stormed out.

'Go after him, Titch,' Ballard said.

'I'm going for a piss, leave me alone,' came Babington's voice from the stairs, before the door slammed behind him.

Ballard gestured sharply with his head; after a brief hesitation, Titch obeyed. 'And give the serving boy a nod while you're down there, in case Gilbert forgot. Jack's bloody starving, aren't you, old friend? He hasn't had meat for at least two hours.'

'I'll eat the serving boy if he leaves it much longer.' Savage grinned, draining his glass. I noticed he was drinking only water.

'I had not expected quite so much spectacle,' I said drily, when the younger men had gone. 'Your boys appear somewhat emotional, Father Ballard.'

It had not escaped my notice that Babington had talked of Clara in the past tense, even as Titch seemed determined to deny that the body could possibly be hers. Ballard I could not read at all. Everything in his words and demeanour suggested that this was the first he had heard about the body in the Cross Bones, and that he was angered by the discovery, but it was entirely possible that this was an act to rattle the younger men, or a double bluff to cover his own tracks. This latter seemed the least plausible explanation; on my brief acquaintance with Ballard, I suspected that if he had seen the need to silence Clara Poole, he would have it done it quickly and unobtrusively, just as Titch had suggested of Walsingham, to cause the least disruption to the plan. What would he have to gain by drawing attention to the murder with a grisly display? He also seemed to have assumed that the mutilations had been an act of torture, rather than being carried out after death, as I believed from seeing the body. One thing I could report back to Phelippes with certainty: the murder of Clara Poole had not been a collective decision. If one of the conspirators were guilty – and how could it be anyone else? – he was keeping it a secret from his comrades, and that meant there were fault-lines in the group that I could try to force, once I was closer with them.

'They are young men, with strong feelings,' Ballard said, though I caught the exasperation in his tone. 'Do not be alarmed – and, I pray you, do not report this yet to your master, until we understand the circumstances better. If the girl is dead, that is not necessarily bad news for our cause.'

'I do not see how it could be *good* news. Tell me – was this Poole girl a friend to the whole group for love of the Catholic Church, or did she have a more *particular* incentive for spying on her employers?'

'God, I wish you Jesuits could speak plain. You're asking if she was fucking one of us?'

I affected shock. 'I was asking how her affections tended, yes.'

'Well, if she was, it wasn't me, and I doubt it was Jack here.'

'Not me, more's the pity,' Savage said. I looked pointedly to the door where Babington and Titch had disappeared, an eyebrow raised expectantly. 'No idea,' he said, taking my meaning. 'Always assumed Titch was still a virgin, from the look of him, and Babington – well. I mean, he's married, *although* . . .' He let the rest of the thought fall away, unspoken.

'Enough, Jack.' Ballard turned back to me with an easy smile. 'I can see why you would feel you had to ask, but her *affections* are not the issue. Clara was a modest girl, from the little I saw of her – she offered her help for love of her brother, Robin, and of Mary the Queen. Robin is a decent man – his family history is good cause to trust him. And if he vouches for his sister's integrity, I believe him.'

'That is assurance enough for me,' I said. Ballard held up a sudden hand to silence me; the sound of several pairs of feet drummed on the stairs outside and a child's voice called out, 'Supper, my masters!'

The serving boys crashed in with their dishes: a steaming pot of mutton stew; a bowl of some root vegetable boiled beyond recognition; loaves of dense bread. Standard fare for a London inn, heavy and bland, but I had tasted worse, and I was hungry. Babington and Titch followed and settled to their places, subdued and silent, a mute glance slipping between them; I wished I could have found a way to follow them outside and catch whatever words had been exchanged. When more wine had been poured and the children dismissed, Ballard leaned back in his chair and speared a lump of meat on the end of his knife.

'Gentlemen, we should set this sad business aside for now while we wait for Gilbert and Robin to return with more news, and let us hear about the letters from Queen Mary.' He looked expectantly at Babington, who forced himself with some effort to sit upright and raise his eyes from his plate.

'Titch and I worked on the cipher all afternoon,' he said. 'It was not easy. Sometimes Her Majesty skips a character in the coded alphabet, I suppose in her haste, and you have to go back to work out where she missed it, because then all those that follow are also wrong, and I spent a good half hour at least misconstruing a sentence that—'

'To the point, Anthony.'

'Very well. She commends our plan.'

'To the letter?'

'Not in so many words. She offers advice as to the number of armed men we should bring when we ride north to her – fifty or three-score, she says, to be assured of overpowering her guards, and she suggests how we might broach her prison.'

'Oh yes?'

Babington smiled. 'She says we should set fire to the stables at night, so that her keeper and his household will run out to deal with the commotion while we come for her unnoticed. She reminds me to make sure all our men are wearing a mark to recognise one another under cover of darkness.'

'Quite the military strategist,' Ballard murmured, amused.

'We must suppose she knows better than us how many men guard her,' Babington said, a little testy. 'Her knowledge of a campaign is greater than that of "Captain Fortescue", at any rate.'

Ballard grinned. 'The good Captain is a veteran of many manoeuvres,' he said. 'You'd be surprised what he knows. But do go on. Does she acknowledge our purpose towards the usurper, and give us her blessing? That's what I told you to secure. Without her assent in writing, there is nothing to protect us once the deed is done and Mary is on the throne, if she should wish to distance herself from it. We need that proof. Do you understand?'

Babington looked doubtful. 'She promises reward for our efforts, and urges us to be wary of false friends. Though there is one thing I thought strange.'

'What is that?'

'She adds a postscript asking me to tell her the names of all the gentlemen involved in our design, and by what means and how we plan to proceed. She can only mean the plan for the execution of Elizabeth, so I suppose that is tantamount to endorsing it?'

I caught a flash of something – fear? recognition? – in Ballard's eyes as he took this in, but his face remained calm.

'She has not demanded such details before,' he mused.

'No, though she has asked what towns and ports we expect to provide safe harbour for Spanish troops, and which English nobles loyal to her cause might let us use their lands to station an army. Which names we will have as soon as Thomas Salisbury returns from his travels, I hope in the next week.'

'That would be most useful to my master too,' I said, smiling.

'Naturally, you will be the first to know,' Ballard said, through a mouthful of stew. 'You still have the letter, Anthony?'

'Of course.' Babington patted his doublet. 'She instructs me to burn it immediately, but—'

'Do no such thing,' Ballard snapped, pointing his knife down the table. 'If she promises us rewards, we need written evidence. What?' He spat a piece of gristle into his hand and shook his head at the expressions of the younger men. 'You want to believe Mary Stuart is a saint. Good for you. But women are capricious, my boys, and royal women most of all. They can become squeamish when it suits them, especially if blood must be shed to get their way. They like to sweep that under the carpet, once it's done, pretend it never happened, and the men who obligingly risked their lives for them can become an awkward reminder.'

Savage laughed, as he wiped sauce from his chin with the back of his hand. 'I'd hardly call Mary Stuart squeamish. She had her second husband blown up once he'd served his purpose by giving her a son.'

'My point exactly. What happened to the man who arranged it for her?'

Savage shrugged, blank.

'I'll tell you this much. He's not living in luxury, enjoying the land and titles she promised. Prison, house arrest, exile, living as a fugitive, another arrest and trial, prison again –

that was his reward, because she preferred not to acknowledge the deed once it was done.'

'But Her Majesty is not currently in a position to do this man good, so your censure is unfair,' Babington said, ever Mary's staunch defender. 'Once she claims her rightful throne she may be able to recall him, whoever he is.'

'His name is Archibald Douglas,' Ballard said, 'and he should serve as a warning to those who trust too readily in the promises of princes.'

I had to fight to avoid any reaction to the name; I watched Ballard carefully, but he too was practised at keeping his countenance and I could not gauge from his tone whether he was acquainted with Douglas or knew him only by reputation. Even so, I saw no flicker of recognition among the rest of the group, and allowed myself to exhale with cautious relief; it appeared from their response that he was not closely involved with the conspirators – at least, not yet. What, then, was his purpose in London, where he ran the risk of arrest?

'If you really think Queen Mary will wash her hands of us the moment she is crowned, I wonder you bother wasting your time with this business,' Babington said, offended again. 'You are welcome to leave, Captain Fortescue.' He stood and stretched a hand towards the door. I saw Savage tense, ready to spring if he was needed.

Ballard sat back and chuckled. 'Peace, Anthony. Easy on the wine, it's clouding your judgement. I mean only to protect our interests. Besides, you would not last five minutes without me. That letter is our insurance, that's all. You had better let me keep it. I would like a closer look at this postscript you mention.'

Babington dropped heavily into his chair, face flushed, a boy reprimanded by his tutor. He fished inside his bag and passed the paper down the table. I would have liked to ask Ballard what more he knew about Archibald Douglas but I could not think of a way to make Father Prado's interest sound plausible.

Before I had a chance to consider it further, the door crashed open again to reveal Gifford, sweating and flustered, his eyes flitting anxiously from Ballard to me. I prayed his acting skills were up to this. He slammed the door, breathing hard; Ballard's glare pinned him against it.

'Well?'

Gifford shook his head. 'At Seething Lane they say Clara Poole has not been seen for four days. They assumed she had gone to visit family, but now, with Robin's visit, they are worried.'

'Family, my arse. Those dissemblers know exactly what's happened to her. And where the devil is Robin?'

'Set off in haste to see if he can talk to the constables and find out where the body was taken.'

'Damn you!' Ballard slammed his fist against the table. 'Did I not tell you to keep him in your sights? Asking questions will only draw attention, he must see that.'

'He borrowed a horse,' Gifford said, looking at me with pleading eyes, as if there were any way I could step in. 'I couldn't keep up.'

'Borrowed a—?' Ballard looked incredulous. 'He's already got my old grey mare, how many does he need?'

'John – you know you can trust Robin.' Savage turned his cup of water between his fingers. 'I've seen him in prison. That's a man can lock his feelings away so deep you'd never think he had any. He won't say an idle word. He'll ask what needs to be asked, without arousing suspicion.'

'This whole business will do nothing but arouse suspicion.' Ballard drummed his fingers on the table, thinking. 'Listen, then. Gilbert, sit, for God's sake, and eat something. Let us assume the body in Southwark was Clara. What must we conclude?'

'That she was found out,' Babington said, his voice wavering again. 'That she was tortured' – he made a small, hiccupping noise as he worked to master his emotion – 'and since she must have given us up, we are sitting in plain sight like fattened deer, waiting for the huntsmen.'

'And yet, here we are,' Titch said, pushing his plate away, the food barely touched.

'Meaning?' Ballard stopped his drumming, laid his palm flat and leaned in for the answer.

'You said the body was found four days ago. That means, if it is her and she talked before she was killed, they've had our names for five days at least. And yet here we are, at liberty, taking our supper. So – either it isn't her, or she didn't give us up.'

'Or they are waiting for a more opportune moment,' Ballard said.

'Why would they do that? If they know who we are, they could have cast a net over all of us at once, if only to have us questioned. Our lodgings are not secret. Anyone could have found out we were meeting here tonight.'

'Perhaps they have been waiting for our friend to join us,' Ballard said, nodding to me. 'That would be an even greater prize – proof of Spain's intent to aid a coup. They'd gladly pull his arms out of their sockets to learn whether that order came from King Philip himself.'

'But Clara didn't know he would be coming – she couldn't have told them that.'

'That means nothing – God knows, there are spies enough in Paris.'

I gave a brief, involuntary shudder and tried not to think of the real Father Prado, locked away at Barn Elms, and how his arms might be holding up. 'Only you, Mendoza and Paget knew I was coming,' I said, affronted. 'I do not like the tenor of this conversation. You assured the ambassador that your plan had no weaknesses like the last one. I did not come here to have my arms pulled out by your government, as you so graciously put it.'

'Nor will you.' Ballard set his mouth in a grim line. 'None

of us will be guests of Master Secretary Walsingham, if I can prevent it. We will see how this evening unfolds. Robin's call at Seething Lane tonight will at least have alerted them that he is looking for his sister. If they know of our design and are holding off to see how we proceed, well then, so much the worse for them. We will wrongfoot them.'

'I don't understand,' Babington said, shaking his head. 'If you seriously think they know about us, surely our only course is to scatter before they pounce?' He glanced at the door as if he were about to launch himself through it. I watched them, each in turn; the three younger men looked shaken and uncertain, while Savage, apparently unconcerned, served himself another helping of stew.

'Perhaps that is what they want – for us to flee in fear and abandon our main intention.'

'I don't see that we have another choice, if you are right.' Babington did not meet the priest's eye.

'What?' Savage jerked forward. 'You would give up everything we have worked for?'

'I do not say give it up,' Babington hissed. 'Only that, with all this, perhaps the time is not right. We could lie low for a while – return to our homes, forget the summer Progress, gather more intelligence about what is known and what is not. They could not watch all of us in separate places. We could regroup in a few weeks, take stock of where we are.' He raised his head, brighter, as if cheered by his own solution. 'It would give the English Catholics time to ready their forces, we could be sure of our support, Spain' – he nodded to me – 'will need notice to put warships to sea. It would be to everyone's advantage to hold the business off until summer is over and come back to it better prepared.'

A long silence unfolded while he awaited Ballard's approval; the candle flames wavered in a draught. Eventually Savage let out a snort of laughter. 'If summer ever starts,' he said, pulling his jacket around him.

'God save us, you are a child, aren't you.' Ballard stared at Babington, unblinking. He spoke softly, and all the more menacing for it. 'Do you honestly think they would forget us if we left town? You think Walsingham's people can't find their way to Derbyshire? You *seriously imagine*' – he jabbed his finger on the table with each word – 'we could slink back at summer's end, unnoticed, and pick up where we left off? Do you? Has Prado come from Spain with a chest of money to sit kicking his heels while you scurry home to hide, because you've suddenly got cold feet?' The volume was gradually rising; I saw Babington flinch.

'He didn't come here to get arrested either, as he said.' He twitched his head towards me.

'Are you really so stupid? If we lose our momentum now, we will all be arrested long before summer's end. They will come to your lovely country house, Anthony, that your father left you, and they will search it from top to bottom, and find illegal books and relics hidden there—'

'—I keep no forbidden books at home—'

'—no matter, they'll provide the books themselves, and they'll drag you out in chains in front of your pretty wife and little daughter, and make you tell them everything.' He exhaled slowly. 'No – if they are holding off, it's because it serves their purpose. Perhaps they think we will give them some greater proof they can use against us, or against the Queen.'

'Then that is every reason to drop the business for now.' Babington's voice had risen to a squeak; his eyes kept flitting to the door.

'Or else we raise the stakes.' Ballard cracked a smile and looked around the company. 'Come now – I know you are all card players. They expect us to fold. So we give them what they least expect.'

'And what is that?' I asked. He turned to me.

'We bring it forward. None of this waiting for a royal Progress that may or may not happen, no hanging about for

Spain to muster warships – with all respect, Spain can come in with reinforcements once the deed is accomplished. The only way we can save ourselves, and give our plan any chance of success, is to execute the usurper as soon as possible and get Mary to safety. In the next week, I say.'

No one spoke. Ballard's face urged encouragement, but the others stared at him in mute disbelief.

It was Savage who broke the silence. 'We can't do this alone, John. Even supposing we could reach the Tudor, if we were to manage it, the assassin would be brought down by her soldiers on the instant, and Mary's guard trebled.'

A flash of anger darkened Ballard's face.

'I have never known you for a naysayer, Jack. Listen.' A wild light kindled in his eyes. 'We fix on a date. Two of us get on the road north two days earlier, to break Mary from her prison before the news comes from London. We take her to a safe house nearby—'

'Where will we find three-score loyal armed men to ride north in under a week?' Babington was openly sceptical now. 'Where do you suggest we lodge them?'

'It would not take so many, the woman exaggerates. A dozen would do it. Gilbert's family estate is in Staffordshire – your father must have twelve strong men you could fit out with weapons, Gilbert? Pitchforks if it came to it. It needs only the element of surprise. Think of it – Mary at liberty, Elizabeth dead, the country would be in uproar.' He leaned forward so far in his enthusiasm I thought he might climb on the table. 'Meanwhile Prado here will send word to Mendoza, who sends word to King Philip, who readies his warships to support us. As the news spreads, the old Catholic families will raise private armies to escort the rightful Queen to London, and people all along the way, those who have prayed for the return of the true Church, will join them with makeshift arms, once they hear the Pretender is dead, and a great glorious army of the righteous will march on Parliament.' He ended on a note of triumph that demanded applause, but none came. I watched him, revising my opinion. When Poole had said Ballard was ruthless, I had pictured a calculating sort of man, one untroubled by finer feeling, who would proceed by reason and single-mindedness, weigh up the odds, unpick my every utterance in search of inconsistencies and see through me at a glance if I made one slip, while Babington was the impetuous, idealistic youth with delusions of redressing the world's wrongs. But I had seen the look on Ballard's face before, and knew it for pure fanaticism; his belief in the cause had warped into obsession, and his ruthlessness was the kind that would drag his comrades to the gallows rather than listen to reason.

Babington cleared his throat. 'Jack is right about one thing,' he said, when it became clear that no one knew how to respond. 'The Tudor is so tightly guarded in London, it would be almost impossible to get close enough. She doesn't even walk to chapel on Sundays to show herself to the public like she used to – her councillors have her behind her palace walls at all times. If we won't wait for a summer Progress, I don't see how we get near her.'

'With a good musket I could do it from twenty feet away.' Savage made a gun of his fingers and mimed taking aim.

'You won't come within twenty feet of her, especially not with a musket. You'd be taken down before you had it loaded.'

'I am prepared for that,' he said, solemnly. 'We would none of us be here if we weren't prepared to sacrifice ourselves.'

'You are more use to us and to God alive, Jack,' Ballard said, laying a hand on his friend's arm. 'Besides, Anthony is talking sense for once. It's impossible for any of us to do the deed. We need someone who can get close to her without suspicion.'

'Who do you propose?' Titch shifted in his seat and lifted his head briefly to show Ballard his sarcastic look. 'Shall we bribe one of her bodyguards, or do you suggest converting a member of the Privy Council?'

Ballard ignored his tone. 'Neither, my friend. Who surrounds the Tudor at all times, when even her guards are left outside the chamber? Who passes her a cup of spiced wine before she sleeps, and attends her at her close stool, and combs out her hair in the morning?'

'Wig,' Babington muttered bitchily.

'Her women.' Titch was staring at him now, the sarcasm forgotten. 'You mean to recruit one of her women? How?'

'We already have the perfect candidate, do we not?' Ballard looked expectantly at Babington, who stared back with a blank shake of the head. 'Come on, Anthony – what of that girl you mentioned? The one who used to share the Queen's bed as a child, who still receives presents from her?'

'Bessie Pierrepont?' Babington frowned.

Gifford gave a small yelp; I kicked him under the table. 'Sorry. I banged my knee,' he muttered, when the others turned to him; I was sure I was not alone in noticing the fierce colour that had flushed his cheeks, but Ballard's attention was all on Babington.

'You know this girl. You said she keeps her affection for Queen Mary.'

'Yes, but—' Babington shook his head, uneasy. 'She would like to see the Queen at liberty, that is true. I'm not sure she would murder the Tudor with her own hands to achieve it.'

'Sound her out. She doesn't need to use her hands – poison would do it. No one would even know it was her.'

'Oh, do you think so?' Titch flared up again. 'And what if she dislikes the idea, and runs straight to the Tudor, Your Majesty, there is a young man of my acquaintance has asked me to poison your wine, shall I tell you where to find him?'

'I would suggest Anthony has more skill in diplomacy than you give him credit for,' Ballard said, keeping his voice pleasant. 'By his account, this girl might be open to his persuasion.'

Gifford stifled another exclamation; Babington assumed a modest expression.

'I don't know, John. It was some years ago. And I understand she has now set her sights elsewhere.'

For the love I bear you, it shall be done. To whom had she written those words? Not Babington, evidently. And what was she promising? I watched Gifford's eyes widen as he struggled to interpret this, and wondered if I ought to kick him again. I decided to intervene another way.

'Forgive me, but you are thinking of involving another *woman* now?' I allowed my lip to curl in scorn. 'When you fear one has already given you away?' I did not think this would be out of character; I had met enough Spanish Jesuits to know their view of women.

'We don't know yet that Clara gave us away,' Titch said, rounding on me. 'It's not for you to impugn a woman you never met.'

'I am thinking aloud,' Ballard said, reaching a pacifying hand to me. 'This girl Anthony mentions, Bessie Pierrepont, formed an attachment to the Queen of Scots as a child. She also took a fancy to Anthony here, when he served as a page to her grandfather, the Earl of Shrewsbury.'

'I'm sure she has forgotten such foolishness now,' Babington said, preening. 'She set her cap at me, it's true, but I was eighteen, and she barely thirteen. I did not encourage it, you know how girls can be. Their affections flit one way and another as the weather changes.'

'The point is, she is now a lady-in-waiting to Elizabeth Tudor, with better opportunity than any of us to come near her person.' Ballard would not be dissuaded.

'I am not sure my master would have offered Spain's support so readily if he had known you planned to put the business into the hands of a woman.' I sniffed, doing my best to look like a haughty Spaniard.

'We did not plan it this way. But we must be flexible as the situation changes – your master would understand that, I think? Listen, Prado.' He patted my arm again. 'Say nothing to Mendoza yet, I pray you. I will think on everything we have heard tonight, and we can meet again tomorrow, before we approach the girl or reply to Mary. In the meantime, let us renew our oath to the Queen, and to one another.'

'Must we?' Titch slumped in his chair. 'How many times have we sworn it now?'

'Father Prado has not sworn it with us. I should like to hear him pledge faith to our cause.'

'The money was not pledge enough?' I said.

'Surely you have no objection, Father? Your oath, before God?'

'Why should I?'

'Well, then.' Ballard smiled, but it did not reach his eyes. 'Anthony – you lead us.'

Babington stood and took a deep breath. A bank of candles at his back cast a gold disc of light on the wall behind him, gilding his hair like a prayer book illumination of Christ at the Last Supper. The wine glowed, and from the way the crimson reflection wavered on the table, I could see how his hand was shaking. He raised his glass, and looked around. 'So we are of one mind, gentlemen? Perform or die?'

FOURTEEN

'Walk with me,' Ballard said, as we left The Castle through the back door, into a smoky alleyway that ran behind the building. '*Paseemos*.'

'Where to?' I glanced at Gifford, who hovered beside us. 'I go with Master Gilbert to Herne's Rents, are you headed that way?'

'Gilbert can find his own way home, I'm sure.' Ballard rested a hand on my shoulder as we emerged into Cornhill. 'I would like to talk to you alone. Let's take a stroll. Ho there, boy!'

Out of the shadows, a slight figure appeared, obscured by rippling torchlight. As he stepped closer, I saw that it was the child Ben, though he gave no sign of recognition. Link-boys could always be found loitering outside taverns with their lanterns and torches, ready to guide unsteady drinkers home after dark, but Ben's presence made me feel unexpectedly looked-after, as if Walsingham and Phelippes had not simply left me to fend for myself.

'Where to, masters?' Ben spat on the ground and touched a finger to his felt cap by way of deference. 'I don't go south of the river this time of night.'

Ballard turned to me, amused. 'The *cojones* on this one.'

Ben glanced up and for a fleeting moment caught my eye with a glint of mischief. He understood *cojones*, anyway. Ballard said, 'You'll go where I pay you to go, lad. My friend and I are taking the air.'

'You're not from London, then. People pay good money to get away from the air here.' Ben sniffed and spat again.

'A wit too.' Ballard chuckled. 'You walk ahead and light the way, and keep your mouth shut. Down Cheapside, towards Paul's.' His voice had become subtly bigger, deeper, and his chest seemed broader; he was assuming the persona of Captain Fortescue that he wore in public. He had sent Savage off to stash the chest of money I had brought; all Ballard carried was a plain leather bag that he seemed to have acquired at some point before leaving the tavern.

I looked over my shoulder at Gifford and noted the alarm on his face. 'Bugger off home to your bed then, Gilbert,' Ballard said, 'there's a good boy. You'll be on the road soon enough, get your sleep.'

Gifford hesitated a moment, cut me an anxious glance, then bade us goodnight and walked off southwards, calling out for a link-boy as he went.

Ballard left his hand resting gently on my shoulder, as if to make sure I didn't try and run. I fell into casual step beside him, waiting for him to voice whatever was on his mind. The further we walked from the lights of The Castle, the more uneasy I became; one skinny boy with a small knife would not be much by way of back-up if the priest had already seen through me. Ballard let Ben put a few yards between us as we passed the Royal Exchange, so that we were almost out of the circle of his torch-light, before beginning again in Spanish.

'I don't think you told us the whole truth back there, did you, Prado – or whoever you are?'

My pulse jarred; I felt my throat tighten, but I forced myself to keep the same pace, aware that that fingertip touch on my shoulder would register any tension immediately. 'You can call me Xavier if you prefer, my friend. I find the English have trouble with the pronunciation, at the back of the throat – though perhaps you won't, your Spanish is very good.'

'So is yours.' His tone was smooth and pleasant; he was giving nothing away.

'Thank you, I've been practising all my life, but it's good to have the approval of an Englishman. You have travelled in Spain, I take it?'

'Here and there. I've travelled all over.' His teeth gleamed in the distant light of the torch. 'Where is your accent from? I don't recognise it.'

'Here and there,' I said. 'I too have been all over.' He laughed, and gave my shoulder a brief squeeze before lifting his hand.

'Fair enough. We are wary of each other – that's to be expected. I was not even warned that you would be at the supper tonight. I'd have liked to have been told, so that I could be prepared.'

'I am sorry for that. I was instructed only to seek out Master Gifford and he would direct me to your group. I had the impression the others were not sure when you would return from France. But you only arrived today, is that right?'

'Of course. Why would I pretend otherwise?'

'I did not suggest you had. But you say you think I have deceived you in some way?'

It seemed best to address the accusation head-on. I tried to run my mind back over the conversation as it had unfolded, desperate to identify the slip that had given me away so that I could come up with a rebuttal, but my thoughts were racing so fast I could put my finger on nothing. He slowed, and walked for a few moments in silence, pulling at his beard, his eyes on the ground.

'It is not true to say no one except me knew you were in London. As you know.'

I waited, my heart skidding. He stopped dead and turned to face me.

'I'm talking about the French.'

'Ah,' I said, to buy myself some time while he expanded on this.

'I mean to say, if you are to send your dispatches back to Mendoza in Paris through the French embassy, they must know of your arrival. Paget told me he would write ahead and tell them to expect you. But my question is this: how much of your business here do they know?'

'That is a question for Paget, surely,' I said, breathing carefully while I tried to process a number of reactions: relief, that he did not suspect me of not being Prado, combined with panic about what Paget might have told Ballard regarding the French, that I was supposed to know. The opportunities to give myself away seemed to multiply at every turn. 'I don't know how much he has told them.'

'Are you serious?'

I couldn't tell if he was angry or amazed, or both. I was feeling my way blind; why hadn't Walsingham found out about Prado's communication arrangements with the French? That would have been far more use than his birthday. 'Why – you don't trust them?'

'Well, there's the question. Does one ever trust the French? Things are better now, I suppose, than under the last ambassador, but that's not saying much. You'll know about him from Mendoza, of course – Michel de Castelnau. It was his fault the Throckmorton business failed in '83 – letters to Mary being leaked to Walsingham through the embassy.'

I nodded soberly, waiting for him to go on.

'But did you know this – ' his voice rose in indignation – 'they say he kept a known heretic lodging with him at the embassy. A Dominican from Naples, excommunicate, wanted by the Inquisition. The King of France sent this man to London to keep him out of trouble, because he was going to get himself killed in Paris. Paget reckons he was the one intercepting the letters.'

'Disgusting,' I said, swallowing hard. 'But this man is long gone, I presume?' I hoped he would not see me wiping the sweat from my palms on my breeches.

'Oh yes. At least the new ambassador, Chateauneuf, is a true Catholic – he wouldn't have someone like that under his roof, and told King Henri so.'

'But still you doubt the French?'

He lifted a shoulder, non-committal. 'Even without the Italian, that embassy is leaky. I know Paget and the rest of Mary's friends in France use the diplomatic packet to send their letters to her, and Gifford collects them when he rides to Staffordshire, but we have never thought it wise to involve the French directly in this plan. I can see that it's the quickest way for you to get letters to Paris, though. I just wanted to know if Chateauneuf had any idea about' – he jerked his head back towards The Castle – 'what we spoke of in there.'

'Not to my knowledge,' I said carefully.

Ben had stopped, a few yards away, at the junction with Cheapside. Now he ambled back towards us, torch balanced in the crook of his arm, one thumb tucked into the waistband of his breeches.

'Not my business, masters, but if you're going to stand around in the street gabbling away in foreign, that's a good way to get rocks thrown at your head, or worse. If there's any trouble, I'm off. Just saying.'

Ballard clicked his tongue, impatient. 'All right, go on ahead. We're behind you.' He resumed his pace again, sunk in thought.

Glimmers of candlelight filtered through the shuttered windows of the grand houses along Cheapside. The street was cobbled here, and for a while the only sound was the click of our boot heels on the stones.

'What happened to him?' I asked, in English, to prevent another question I might not be able to answer – and also because, with unforgivable vanity, I wanted to know what was being said of me in Paris. 'The Italian, I mean.'

'King Henri's heretic? Giordano Bruno. He went back to Paris when Castelnau was recalled,' Ballard said. 'Got himself into some trouble at court and the King kicked him out on his arse, according to Paget. I understand he's still hanging around the university there. He writes *philosophy books*, apparently.' He reserved more disgust for this than for any of the deviant practices to be found at the Unicorn.

'Oh yes. I've heard they're good,' I said, even as the voice of reason urged me to drop the subject. 'Well written, I mean.'

Ballard shot me a curious sidelong glance. 'They're heretical. Paget says he wants to abolish the church as we know it – not just the Catholic faith, he wants to remake the whole Christian religion. This Italian writes that the universe is infinite and man can become like God through his intellect.'

I stifled a laugh. 'I would imagine his argument is more sophisticated than that—' I broke off, seeing the look on his face. 'I mean to say – I would suppose he argues his heresies like a sophist. Though he sounds like a fool.'

He grunted. 'He sounds like an atheist. Paget's clearly got some sort of vendetta against him. Says he'll burn eventually, if he – Paget – doesn't get him first. One thing's for sure – this Bruno won't be coming back to England in a hurry.'

'That's good to hear,' I said, and meant it. 'Enough about him. What do you make of Paget?'

'Don't you know him?'

'Only by reputation,' I said, glad he could not see my face in the shadows. I had no idea if Prado was supposed to know Paget; all I could do was stay consistent with my version, and I had already told Babington that we hadn't met. I had time to wonder, fleetingly, if Ballard was trying to trip me into contradicting myself. 'I am interested to hear your view.'

'Huh. Well, I hope you won't report back if I say I don't entirely trust him.'

'You don't trust anyone,' I said.

He glanced at me, and let out a bark of a laugh. 'You have me there. Would you, in my position? Men like Paget, though . . .' He let the sentence trail away. 'You know the kind. Entitled. His father was a baron. I'm not convinced he cares about the souls of ordinary English folk – the Catholic faith for him is a question of reasserting his family's status. Or perhaps you sympathise. What's your background?'

'My father was a soldier, my mother a midwife.'

'But you were educated? How did they afford that?'

I shrugged. 'I was a bright boy. The Jesuits saw something in me and took me in.'

He nodded thoughtfully. The details belonged to my life, not Prado's, except that it was the Dominicans and not the Jesuits who had considered me worth the investment, but it seemed to make Ballard warm to me.

'My father was a master carpenter,' he said.

'Like Our Lord.'

He laughed again. 'Yes, except in Putney. He sent me to the grammar school, but really he wanted me to follow him into the guild. I never had that skill with my hands, though, nor his patience. I was a great disappointment to him, I'm sure. When I was a boy, I wanted to be a soldier.'

'So you became a priest, to play at one?' I said, returning to Spanish.

'Do the scriptures not speak of spiritual warfare?' He grinned, but it quickly faded. 'I have a temper, Prado. It's a terrible thing. Flares up in an instant. As a youth I could have stabbed a man easy as that' – he snapped his fingers – 'for spilling my beer or looking at me wrong. Not something I'm proud of. I pray daily for the grace to govern it, instead of allowing it to govern me as it did in my youth. This life I have chosen gives me the chance to direct my rage to a fight I know to be just.'

'So killing does not trouble your conscience now?'

'Killing the innocent would, naturally. But I have no qualms about dispatching the enemies of Christ. Why should I? They have none. You heard what was done to that girl, Clara. These people are merciless.'

'You truly think she was murdered by agents of the Tudor's government?' Though we were still speaking Spanish, and I was sure Ben could not understand, I dropped my voice to an urgent whisper.

'I do not see another explanation.' He let out a long sigh. 'I knew nothing of this business until I returned to London tonight. I would have preferred to discuss it with the others before you arrived, to have a clearer picture of where we stood. But I was not given the choice.'

'Better that I know the situation.' I paused. 'If your group has been betrayed, there must be nothing to connect Spain with it – the diplomatic consequences are unthinkable. I should take my master's money and leave quietly.'

He fastened his hand around my wrist. 'No need to be hasty, my friend. You have sworn your oath as one of us, remember? Besides, we don't yet know all the facts.'

'You mean, you could be mistaken? It might have been a jilted lover, perhaps?'

'I did not know the girl well. I concede she may have had other lovers. I count it unlikely, though – she seemed a good, modest girl, devout in her faith, from what I saw.'

'*Other* lovers? You mean, besides whatever attachment she had in your group?'

He glanced at me; I caught the shine of his eyes and teeth in the dark. 'As I have already said, Prado, that is speculation. Look, you must understand it. You and I have taken our vows, we are practised at mastering our urges.'

'I suppose you could not spend so much time in a brothel if not.'

He did not smile. 'Those boys, you saw them, Babington and Titch. They are young pups, eager for adventure. They do not have the vocation. If they are sometimes distracted by the promptings of the flesh, I try not to condemn.'

'They might take their money elsewhere if you did.'

'God sees the heart, and I do not think their commitment to our cause any the less for a youthful indiscretion.'

'Do they confess their sins to you?'

He gave me a reproving look. 'You know I cannot speak of the confessional. Of course,' he added, in a brisker tone, 'your friend Weston would not agree with me on this matter. He thinks any sin is a conduit for the Devil.' This was said with a knowing chuckle, as if expecting agreement. 'He would have them exorcised on the spot for even glancing sidelong at a woman. Tell me, are you all so severe?'

I laughed with him, to cover my anxiety, but my pulse was running again. Who was Weston? 'You all' made me guess that he must be another Jesuit – or possibly another Spaniard? – but the friend part worried me more; if Prado had friends in London, that was surely something Walsingham should have ascertained before he sent me into the fray. My biggest fear had been that I would run into someone – Archibald Douglas, for example – who would recognise me as Bruno. It had not occurred to me that I might encounter anyone who knew the real Prado.

'Are you all right?' Ballard asked, releasing his grip on my arm. 'You seem tense.'

'I thought I heard someone behind us.' I looked back and pulled my cloak closer around my face. It was not entirely untrue; all along Cheapside I had sensed shadows stirring in our wake, and my neck prickled with the familiar uneasy sense of being watched. It was a feeling I had known for years, the legacy of running from the Inquisition. You never knew who might creep up on you in a crowd, or a dark street.

Cheapside was a sea of bobbing lights as men in pairs or small groups passed us east and west, coming from the taverns. Snatches of song and laughter trailed behind them, peppered with an occasional curse as someone trod in horseshit or worse. We had drawn level with the row of goldsmiths' shops at the west end of the street, their painted signs creaking in an eerie chorus. Ahead, behind the Cheapside Cross, the vast bulk of St Paul's church reared up like a beached ship, dwarfing even the five-storey townhouses on either side.

'You're right to be on your guard,' Ballard murmured. 'London is not a safe place at night, though no worse than any other city and better than some. But we need not jump at shadows, eh, you and I? We do God's work, and we must trust that He will protect us. I suppose you will see Weston while you are here?'

He would not let the Weston business drop. I decided it was time for Father Prado to become cagey. If I had learned anything from court politics in France and England, it was that the best defence is to meet a question with another question. 'Is that important?'

He took a moment before answering. 'We have kept our plan very close, as I told you. We have not involved Weston because – it pains me to say this, but there has not always been perfect accord in the English mission, between the secular priests like myself and your brethren in the Jesuit order. They like to – how can I put this – *manage* things.'

I bowed my head, to show that I understood. 'Then perhaps it is best if Weston does not know I am here, for the moment,' I said. He looked relieved, though not as relieved as I felt. I made a mental note to find out from Phelippes if this Weston was really a friend of Prado; I could hardly ask Ballard if he had been using the term literally. The last thing I needed was a Jesuit turning up to reminisce about the good old days.

We approached the precincts of St Paul's. Beyond the walls, the darkness thickened, broken by points of lights from braziers or torches. I could not help another look behind me; I wondered how it must be to walk the streets with Ballard's delusional confidence in God's protection. You ran a risk visiting the churchyard here even in daylight. The place was a notorious haunt of thieves and cut-purses, newsmongers, handbill sellers, vagrants and fraudsters; in the north-east yard, at the foot of the walls, lean-to wooden structures with canvas awnings had become permanent fixtures where London's less reputable booksellers and printers laid out their wares for the crowds who gathered to hear preachers in the elevated outdoor pulpit they called Paul's Cross. Hostel agents touted rooms to rent; while they explained their prices with a friendly arm around the shoulders of newcomers to the city, their associates would relieve these poor dupes of their luggage and valuables. From wooden booths around the walls, card-sharps competed for the attention of the crowds with foolproof tricks that always left the volunteers marvelling at the loss of their coins. If you could walk from one side of Paul's church-yard to the other without your pocket picked, without being arrested for reading illegal pamphlets or drawn into a brawl, you could count yourself blessed. At night, you would be lucky to come out alive.

As if following my thoughts, Ben faltered at the gates to the churchyard. 'You're going in there?' he asked, in disbelief.

'You can go now, boy.' Ballard fished a penny out from somewhere inside his doublet.

Ben darted a questioning look at me for the space of a heartbeat, but I could make no signal. He bit down on Ballard's coin, nodded to us and slipped away into the dark, his torch burning low. I watched with regret as he disappeared.

Ballard laid his hand between my shoulder blades and steered me into the churchyard. Without Ben's light I was walking blind at first, but as my eyes began to adjust I made out the hexagonal outline of Paul's Cross ahead, at the same time as I became aware of the many shapes slipping invisibly through the shadows around us, into drifts of woodsmoke from the braziers. As we passed huddles of men, some bare-foot, all in patched and ragged clothes, I caught the glint of watchful eyes following us. These were the people who went unseen by day in the streets of London; the vagrants, the workless men, the lame and those who begged or stole food, but I was in their domain now, the kingdom of the invisible. I saw how the anonymous eyes boldly appraised my boots, my hat, my jacket, weighing up how much they would fetch; I tensed inside the unfamiliar suit and wished again that Prado's chosen disguise had been something less flamboyant. As we moved further into the churchyard, they began slowly to draw closer; I realised, belatedly, that we were surrounded by a circle of men: silent, holding back, but clearly waiting for some signal. My nerves grew taut as I tried to keep a focus on all the figures at once, my hand near enough to the knife at my belt for a quick draw, though not so close as to provoke them.

Ballard – whose attire was even more ludicrously extravagant and expensive – seemed untroubled; I had the impression that he was known here. He stopped, glanced around at the men who had gathered, then reached into his leather bag and pulled out loaves of bread, legs of chicken, dried apples – all leftovers from our supper that he must have collected from the kitchen after the plates had been cleared. He distributed what he had brought and the men passed it around wordlessly, until the bag was empty. There was no shoving, no complaint that one had more than another – they took care that no one was missed out. The business was done in no more than five minutes and, without speaking, the men melted back into the shadows. Ballard took out a kerchief to wipe his hands and ushered me towards the church, into a space between two of the booksellers' kiosks.

'Can't stand to see food thrown away while people are going hungry,' he said brusquely, as if I had demanded an explanation.

'Couldn't you ask Babington to buy those men bread?'

'I have. He says he gives out alms on his estate at home,

and that's enough. He's afraid I'll end by asking him to feed all the beggars in London.'

'He has the money to spare, as I understand.'

'Not so much glory, is there, in using your money to put bread in poor men's mouths, when you could spend it on an army to overthrow the Tudor?'

I murmured my understanding and we stood in silence for a few minutes. All around us, the darkness crackled with unseen footsteps, the low mutter of voices, the pop and hiss of damp wood in the braziers. Ballard continued to peer into the blackness, as if expecting someone.

'What do we do now?' I asked, trying to keep my voice even.

'We wait.' His eyes flitted to mine with the relish of one who knows a secret, and a hint of a smile touched the corners of his mouth. In that moment, I realised my folly in allowing him to corner me here. He had seen through me the instant he walked into The Castle, I was sure of it; he had been toying with me all night, and now he had brought me here to kill me. All I had was the knife at my belt; whatever the priest tried, and however many of these masterless men he could command to set on me, I would not go down without doing some damage.

Before I could ask what we were waiting for, it all happened faster than the speed of thought: I became aware, unmistakably, of a silent presence at my back in the dark; I sensed rather than saw the lift of the man's arm; before he could bring it down I had ducked and wheeled around; I stood in one sudden movement, smashing the top of my head into his chin before he could step back. As he reeled from the impact, I drove a fist into his stomach – it was like punching a wall, but he was knocked off balance enough for me to slip a foot between his ankles and trip him so that he fell heavily on to his back; almost before he had hit the ground I was astride him, sitting on his chest with the point of my dagger at his throat.

My would-be assailant raised his hands in surrender, turning his head to the side and spitting blood. In the scrap his hat had fallen, and I found myself looking into the blue and brown eyes of Jack Savage.

'Jesus Christ,' he said, with feeling, and spat again; he had bitten his tongue when I headbutted him. I kept the blade at his throat; I could not seem to make my shaking hands understand the need to move it. My breath came in jagged gasps and the top of my head throbbed. Behind me, Ballard laughed. He sounded impressed.

'My God. Which seminary did you learn that in?' When I did not answer, he laid a gentle hand on my shoulder and coaxed the knife from me. 'Don't kill Jack on your first day, Prado, we should be hard put to find a replacement for him at such short notice. You can let him up now,' he added, more firmly. 'He's not going to hurt you.'

'Not tonight, anyway,' Savage muttered. I allowed Ballard to take my elbow and lift me to my feet. Savage stood, rubbing a trail of blood from his mouth.

'There was me thinking I was the one with the temper,' Ballard remarked mildly.

'Forgive me . . .' My voice sounded strangled. 'He came up behind me so suddenly, I didn't realise—'

'No harm done,' Ballard said, though Savage's eyes told me I could expect to be paid back some time. 'Useful to know you have such skills,' he added. 'Mendoza did not mention that you were a fighter.'

'I spend a lot of time on the road, as you know.' I turned away as I brushed myself down, hoping they would not see how I was trembling. 'I have had to defend myself more than once.' When I trusted my expression, I faced them again. 'Your pardon, Master. It was an instinctive reaction. Nothing personal.'

Ballard was still watching me with the same intent look, somewhere between admiration and suspicion. 'There's not many men could get the better of Jack,' he said.

'He caught me off-guard,' Savage said, glaring. 'In a fair fight, I'd crush the fucker.'

I acknowledged the truth of this with a bow of my head.

'Peace, Jack. We are all friends here.' Ballard tilted his head towards me. 'Except that you clearly thought I had led you here to have you attacked?'

'I am a foreigner in a strange city.' I offered him an apologetic shrug. 'Experience has taught me to be alert.'

'Of course. Though it is not always an asset to have a man so jumpy. We'll say no more of it for now. Here.' He handed my knife back. 'You'd better put that away. We shall be careful not to upset you.' His eyes gleamed in the dark. 'Perhaps I should have explained our business here. Do you have anything for us, Jack?'

Savage grunted, and spat again. 'One up at Shoe Lane, another St Laurence's Hill.'

'What nature?'

'Dying, I think. The first, anyway. St Laurence, it was garbled. Childbed – could go either way.'

'Right.' Ballard thought for a moment. 'Take Prado to Shoe Lane, I'll do the other.'

'What's happening?' I asked.

'We have a night's work ahead of us, my friend. Here – this is for you.' He reached inside his doublet and drew out a black silk purse. 'Open it.'

I unknotted the strings to find a miniature glass bottle with a silver stopper, and a silver pyx. I understood then what was being asked of me. 'Holy oil?'

He nodded. 'Catholic priests are not so plentiful in England that we can afford to let one sit around idle. The faithful go on dying and giving birth and getting sick, and we are needed, whether our greater plans come off or no.'

'But . . .' I turned the pyx in my hand, running my thumbnail over the elaborate tracery on the lid. 'This is dangerous, is it not? I mean to say – if we should be caught, what happens to the plan? I was not told this would be expected of me.' I thought of Robin Poole's boast that he had been imprisoned alongside Catholic suspects without giving away that he was Walsingham's man, and the limp he had as a result. The pursuivants were vigilant in London; I knew they watched Catholic houses. If I should be taken giving someone extreme unction, would I be permitted to reveal my identity? Would they even believe me?

Ballard regarded me with a cold eye. 'It was expected of you the day you were ordained,' he said. 'I know you Jesuits prefer to sit around disputing footnotes to codices rather than waste your intellectual gifts on the poor and the sick, but there are hundreds of people in this city who have need of a priest, and that is what we are. So hold your nose and get your hands dirty. You have a duty.' Without another word, he turned and walked away into the night.

Savage grinned at me. 'Shall we?' He gestured to the gate. Reluctantly, I began walking, forcing myself not to glance over my shoulder, knowing he was deliberately keeping behind me. 'And keep your hands where I can see them,' he added, as we emerged into the street. 'You might have fooled the rest, but I know exactly what you are, *Prado*.' He said this in a low voice, so close to my ear that his hot breath made me flinch. I did not respond. Instead, I turned my thoughts inward, searching my memory for the rites for extreme unction, hoping I could remember all the words I had not said for a decade before we reached Shoe Lane.

If my conscience had troubled me over the idea of befriending Babington and his fellows in order to betray them to Walsingham, you may imagine how I felt deceiving the simple faith of people who were risking imprisonment or worse to bring the old rites to their dying grandmother or sick child. I hoped the rituals I managed to perform without too many obvious errors would bring some comfort, and that they would never have cause to find out that the gentle Spanish priest whose hands they clasped with tears in their eyes was in fact an excommunicate heretic spy. Before I had even completed my novitiate I had abandoned any belief that there was magic in the host or the sanctity of the person intoning the prayers – God knows I had met enough priests and friars with worse sins on their souls than the people they were shriving – but the business made me uneasy all the same. It was not helped by Savage at my shoulder, his odd eyes fixed intently on my lips, as if recording my every word for a report. The families who had begged for a secret priest might not notice if I stumbled over the Latin form of the Viaticum, but I had a feeling Savage would, and that any slip would be noted as evidence.

After the old woman at Shoe Lane, there was an infant with a fever off Cowcross Street and a family in Hosier Lane who thought their mute daughter might be possessed. I had neither the energy nor the confidence to go through the charade of casting out demons, so I assured them she was not and left the poor girl with a blessing. The parents were evidently disappointed not to have the drama of a full exorcism, and I thought of Ballard's words about this mysterious Weston, who was apparently eager to cast out spirits wherever he went. I sincerely hoped I would never run into him.

Savage said little as he led me between appointments. It was past two when I had finished with the last one; when he took me back to Holborn Bridge, handed me a lantern with a feeble stub of candle and pointed me in the direction of Herne's Rents, muttering that I was free to go, I almost kissed him with gratitude born of exhaustion. My fear of being left alone with him had abated; for that night it seemed he was committed to his duty of shepherding me safely to the flock, but I was certain he had not forgiven me for humiliating him in front of Ballard, and that payment for that incident would be exacted at some point, when I was least expecting it. His veiled threat about knowing what I was still rang in my ears;

it took all my determination not to ask him what he meant by it, lest that give away my fear of being unmasked. My head ached brutally from the effort of concentration and the impact of his chin earlier; by the time he left me, I could think only of falling into my bed and closing my eyes. Unfortunately I first had to write my report for Phelippes before the evening's events faded.

I was perhaps thirty yards from the door of my building, feeling my way by the thin light of a crescent moon, when the minute click of a scuffed pebble on stone caused me to whip around again, hand to my knife; someone had followed me, and I was so bone-tired and sunk in my thoughts, I had let them.

'Show yourself, or I'll run you through,' I hissed, pointing the blade out randomly to either side. I could see nothing beyond the pale circle of light in my hand.

A patch of shadow detached itself from the greater darkness and solidified into the shape of a boy.

'Ben?'

He pressed his finger to his lips. I sank back against the wall.

'Christ's blood – I thought you had come to kill me on my doorstep.'

'I've been following you all night. Didn't like the look of that bloke with the funny eyes.'

'I appreciate your concern.' I didn't know whether to laugh or hug him. Instead I flipped him a penny, which he caught in one fist, quick as a blink, and slid inside his jerkin.

'Any messages?'

'Tell Master Phelippes it all went off well, they don't suspect me so far, and they know about Clara. Say I'll have a full report ready by tomorrow morning. I'll leave it at the dovecote for you.'

'I'll be there at first light.'

'Do you never sleep?'

'No money to be made sleeping. Besides, all the interesting stuff happens at night.' He grinned, gave me a mock salute and turned to go.

'One more job for you,' I said, lowering my voice. 'Can you find out something else for me?'

He gave me a condescending look, as if the question were hardly worth asking. 'If anyone in London knows it, I can find it out.'

'Good. I want you to track down a boy for me. South of the river. Try the Unicorn first.'

Ben raised an eyebrow. 'I know where to get you a boy cheaper, if that's what you like. Unicorn'll charge through the nose.' He rubbed his thumb and forefinger together in the universal sign for greed. 'Anything you want that's off the main menu there, they'll make you pay extra to keep it quiet. I know this lad up at Smithfield, definitely doesn't have the pox and he'll do most things for half—'

'*Jesus*, Ben. I don't mean like that, God forbid. It's a particular boy, I need to speak to him. That's all.' I gave him a stern look.

He lifted a skinny shoulder. 'Not for me to judge, master. Plenty do, that's why places like the Unicorn make money. What's his name, then, this boy?'

'I don't know, but he stands out in a crowd – he's dark, like me – his skin even darker. A bit younger than you, ten or eleven, maybe. Small. Runs fast.'

'Yeah, you'd learn that at the Unicorn. That where he works?'

'I believe so. Or you might find him hanging about the Cross Bones burial ground. He steals horses on the side. I'm sure you can ask around.'

Ben nodded, calculating. 'And if I track him down – should I fetch him to you?'

'No. He won't speak to me willingly. Find out where I can corner him uninterrupted, and don't let him know anyone's looking for him – I need to ask him some questions. I'll pay you when you bring news.'

'All right. I'll have something for you by tomorrow, and I'll pick up your letter first thing. Give you good night, master.'

He sauntered away and dissolved back into the shadows, my skinny guardian angel, before I could thank him for his vigil.

I opened the door to our rooms as quietly as I could, expecting to tiptoe around Gilbert snoring. Instead I found the place ablaze with candles, and Robin Poole lolling on my bed with his boots off, while Gilbert paced, a glass in his hand. He leapt at me before the latch had even clicked shut.

'God's blood, where have you *been*? We thought Ballard had killed you.' A dark crust of wine stained his lips. He grasped my shoulder and tried to fix a bleary gaze on me. 'We thought you'd given yourself away and we were all dead.'

I stepped back from the fumes on his breath. 'Thank you for your confidence. You may sleep easy – no one has tried to kill me yet. Ballard has had me ministering to the faithful.'

'You?' Gifford swayed a little, frowning. 'But you can't give the sacraments, you're excommunicate.'

'Damn, you're right – I should have thought to tell him that.' I sat heavily on the end of my bed and pulled off my boots, slapping Poole's feet out of the way. He shifted obligingly to make room. 'I'm going to need to sleep soon,' I said. 'Ideally not with you.'

He swung his legs around to the floor and sat with his elbows on his knees, hands in his hair. 'I waited for you so we could make sure we were all straight with our stories. And to keep an eye on him.' He jerked his head towards Gifford, who was pouring himself more wine.

'Did you go to Seething Lane tonight?' I asked.

'Of course not. We sat in a tavern until it seemed like a reasonable time for him to return. With hindsight, a tavern was probably not the best idea, as you see.' He gestured again to Gifford with a knowing tilt of his eyebrow. 'Tell me what they said of Clara while we were out.'

I filled him in on the conversation he had missed. As I spoke he continued to stare at the floor between his feet, nodding occasionally, while Gifford paced and huffed and glared at his reflection in the window, drinking loudly.

'Interesting,' Poole said, when I had finished. He left a long pause, rubbing at the stubble on his cheeks with the flat of his hands. 'Can Ballard really think it was Walsingham? Is he feigning, do you reckon?'

'I only met him for the first time tonight. But he strikes me as a man who thinks on his feet, and I could see all his thoughts bent on how he could save the plan. He was not panicked, but he was rattled. I'm almost willing to swear he had no knowledge of your sister's death until tonight. Unless he is a greater actor than any I have seen – excepting yourself.'

He glanced up at that, and I saw how hollow he looked. 'Your meaning?'

'Only that I was impressed this evening. You played your part to perfection. I could have believed you had learned the news for the first time too. I was on the verge of tears at your grief.'

'Oh, my grief is not an act, Bruno.'

'No – I didn't mean – forgive me.'

He brushed the apology away and returned his attention to the floor. 'I told you – I can wear a mask when I need to, so close it moulds to my face. But then so can you, evidently. The only one we need worry about is –' he jerked a thumb to the window, where Gifford stood with his back to us. 'So, if you really think Ballard had no part in her death – then which of them? Not Savage, I'd wager – he would not act without Ballard's knowledge.'

'That only leaves the young men.' I shook my head.

'Babington and Titch. But if she was killed because they suspected her of betraying the plot, surely neither one of them would have acted alone on something so significant. Especially not without Ballard's approval.'

'Babington is increasingly at odds with Ballard about how to proceed, you saw it yourself,' he said. 'Maybe he has decided to assert his leadership by making his own decisions.'

'Even so, he must have realised that a murder would only draw more attention. And did you not think they too seemed shocked to hear of her death?'

'I grant they did,' he said wearily. 'But they are not without skill at deception. Babington especially.'

'The manner of it still makes no sense to me. Titch's point about Walsingham holds good for them too – if any of them wanted rid of her, surely they would have made certain the body was not found?' I recalled my initial reaction on seeing the girl's mutilated face: that this was a statement about betrayal that was intended to be seen. But by whom? Naturally, I could not ask Poole.

'I've told you my theory about that,' he said. 'She fought back and hurt him, so that he had to flee before he had time to bury her.'

'Of course.' I thought it best to change the subject. 'So – I'm sorry to ask this, but – was it Babington that she was . . .' I stopped, searching my tired brain for a suitable euphemism.

'Was fucking?' Poole said morosely. He left a long silence while I wondered if I should apologise. Eventually he shook his head. 'You know, she never told me the detail of her dealings with them.'

'I suppose you wouldn't, with your brother.'

'It was not mere modesty. She liked the idea of doing this work for herself, independent of me. She said I should bring Master Secretary such information as I found out in my way and leave her to do the same. I didn't press her after that. I didn't really want to think of it, if I'm honest. Which of them she was—' He leaned back against the wall and chewed at his thumbnail.

'Babington has a wife, though, I thought?' I stretched my legs and heard my knees crack. If I fell back on the mattress now and closed my eyes, I would be out before he could reply.

Poole gave a dry laugh. 'Oh yes, and Titch is betrothed to some heiress from Southampton, and Ballard is an ordained priest, and Savage has no interest in women, but I saw the way they all looked at my sister – there's not a one of them would have resisted if she'd returned that look. She was a girl who could make a man forget his own name, never mind his scruples.' He broke off and turned his face away.

He had spoken with evident feeling, but something in his tone made me sit up and look at him; I recalled Walsingham's remark that there was no doubt Robin Poole loved his sister, in a tone heavy with meaning that I could not grasp. Had he been implying that Poole's affection went beyond the usual brotherly limits? They were only half-siblings, after all; such things were not unheard of. Could he have been jealous of Clara's affair with another of the conspirators? But surely that would not have been grounds enough to kill her – especially at this crucial stage of the proceedings, when he knew that if all went according to Walsingham's plan, these men would soon be rotting meat on London Bridge. And would a man like Robin – who seemed, from what I knew of him, dedicated to Walsingham's service and willing to make sacrifices – be capable of jeopardising the operation and killing his own sister so cruelly out of jealousy? Perhaps, at a stretch, if one of them had got her with child, but Walsingham's physician had checked that this was not the case. I pinched the bridge of my nose and allowed my eyes to fall shut for a moment. God, I was tired; I felt like a man who had wandered into a labyrinth on a sunny afternoon, thinking it good sport for half an hour, and found himself still turning the same dead-ends as night fell and a cold fog set in.

'To answer your question,' Poole said, standing abruptly and looking around for his boots, 'I could not say for certain which of them she won over with her favours. Perhaps none, and everything she learned was done chastely. But if I had to wager, I would assume Babington. Wouldn't you try him first, if you were a young woman?'

'I'd take him over Savage, that's for sure,' I said, half-smiling, hauling myself to my feet to see him out. But as I spoke, I realised it was not true: in Clara's place, I would have chosen a less obvious target. A shyer, less swaggering sort of man, not so used to female attention, and therefore more responsive to it. Chidiock Tichborne alone among the conspirators had repeatedly insisted that the body in the Cross Bones could not be Clara: was that because he wanted to deflect attention, or because he was in love with her and did not want to believe she was dead? Either way, I decided I needed further conversation with him, when the opportunity arose.

'I must sleep,' Poole said. 'And tomorrow put on the mask again. At first light I will go to Phelippes and ask him how we should proceed in the matter of her death. I suppose it can be made public now that the conspirators know – Walsingham will want to decide on an official story. Perhaps I shall finally be allowed to bury her.'

I wish you luck with that, I thought. Well, it was Walsingham's problem, not mine, to tell him his sister was already underground in an unmarked grave. I squeezed his shoulder. 'You may arrive at Leadenhall Street before my letter – tell Phelippes to expect it. And to prepare for the plot moving forward sooner than he expected. I will set it out in more detail and send it to him in the morning.'

At this, Gifford turned from the window to point a finger at him. 'Say nothing about Bessie yet,' he said, so sternly he sounded almost sober. So he had been paying attention.

Poole cast a glance at me, brow quirked in a question. 'You're asking me *not* to tell Phelippes that the conspirators plan to use a young woman in the Queen's service to murder her? What, should we tell him *after* her wine has been poisoned? Whose side are you on, Gilbert?'

'I am with you, of course,' he said, swaying slightly as he let go of the window frame. 'But she has not yet been approached by Babington, much less agreed to help them. It would be unfair to place her under suspicion when her loyalties may be beyond reproach. In any case' – the finger pointed unsteadily again – 'if she does not agree, she will be the first to tell the Queen herself.'

'And then Walsingham will wonder how three of his trusted espials managed to let that development pass them by,' Poole said, gesturing between us, his mouth twisted with scorn. '*Unfair!* Christ, do you think this is a game of bowls, Gilbert, where everyone must be given a sporting chance? It is the Queen's *life* we are talking about. The security of the realm. Why are you so keen to keep Bessie Pierrepont out of it?'

'Because she has done nothing wrong,' Gifford said, blushing scarlet to his ears.

'Yet,' I said pointedly.

'Wait at least until tomorrow, can't you? Till we learn how Ballard thinks we should proceed, and whether she is willing.'

Poole cut me a fast glance again; I responded with a minute nod. Let Gifford think we were giving Bessie the benefit of the doubt; if he feared she was being watched, he might not risk any more private meetings with her. From the discussion at The Castle, it seemed evident that Bessie was not, so far, part of the conspiracy, and yet she was handing over cryptic notes to Gifford in a code used by Mary Stuart; who, then, was she writing to?

'Very well,' Poole said, buttoning his doublet. 'We will leave her name out for now.'

Gifford visibly relaxed; I followed Poole to the door.

'He's getting spooked,' he whispered, darting a look over

my shoulder at Gifford, who had emptied the wine bottle and was scouring the room in search of more. 'He's convinced Ballard is on to all of us, and playing us along.'

'Do you think he could be right? You know these people.'

'I see no sign of it. Ballard was wary of you, but I would expect nothing less. If he sent you out to give the sacraments tonight, I'd say you've convinced him.' He pulled on his cap. 'Listen, you need to talk Gilbert round, because I have tried. If he goes on drinking like that, he will give himself away sooner or later, and us with him. Should I say something to Phelippes?'

I shook my head. 'Let's see where we are tomorrow. Once Ballard has decided how to proceed, Gilbert will be put on the road with a letter to Mary keeping her up to date. He'll be less of a liability once he's out of London.'

Poole grimaced, in a way that implied solidarity. 'You'll mention Bessie in your report?'

'Of course. But he doesn't need to know that.'

He nodded, and promised to let me know any messages from Phelippes the next day. When the door had closed behind him, I bolted it and turned to Gifford.

'Did you bring anything to drink?' he asked, holding up the empty bottle.

'No. Not even the consecrated wine from the Eucharist. I need to write a report, and you should sleep – you need your wits about you for tomorrow.'

I rummaged for the linen strips and alum solution in the pack I had brought from Leadenhall Street; only hours before, though it felt like days ago. A headache pounded bluntly behind my eyes. I pulled up a chair at the small table beside my bed and pressed the heels of my hands against my eyelids, as if that might clear my head.

'Ballard is going to kill us, you know,' Gifford said, in a matter-of-fact tone. 'If we left tonight, we could be twenty miles clear of London by first light, with good horses.'

'What?' I swivelled in my chair to look at him. 'Why would you think that? Ballard had me giving extreme unction to a grandmother tonight – would he have allowed that if he doubted me?'

'The postscript.' He shifted position and tried to focus on me. 'On Mary's letter. It's a forgery. Babington was fooled, because he's an idiot, but Ballard will see through it in an instant.'

I recalled the journey to see Clara's body; Phelippes's voice in the dark of the carriage, saying that evidence could be made more convincing. 'How do you know it's a forgery?'

He rolled his eyes at my slowness. 'Because I was there when Phelippes opened the letter. There was no postscript. Phelippes must have added it afterwards, to entrap them. And Ballard will know that immediately.'

'You're panicking for nothing. Phelippes will have made sure the hand is undetectable.'

'It's not the hand. It's the very question. Mary Stuart would never ask Babington to name his fellow conspirators, nor put details of Elizabeth's execution in writing – she knows that would condemn her as well as them. As soon as Ballard reads it – which he is probably doing at this moment' – he jolted upright and stared at the door, as if Ballard might be about to kick it in – 'he will know the correspondence has been tampered with, and he will have Savage torture me until I tell him everything.' He appeared to be on the verge of tears, his hands trembling as he twisted them together.

Sweet Jesus. I pushed the chair back and perched on the edge of the bed beside him.

'There'll be no running anywhere tonight,' I said, firmly, like a mother reprimanding a child with night-terrors. 'That's the drink making you fear the worst. One more day, and you will be taking Phelippes a letter for Mary setting out all their plans so clearly they may as well deliver themselves to the hangman. After that, it will be over.'

'That's why they must not name Bessie, don't you see?' He clutched at my sleeve. 'If her name goes in that list along with the others, she'll be arrested and questioned.' His eyes flitted again to the door. 'Do you think Robin will say anything to Phelippes?'

'He said he would not. You know him better than I.'

'Do you think I should warn her?' He sat forward as if he were about to leave on the spot, his face so earnest I wanted to laugh.

'Warn her of what? As you said yourself, if she is loyal to Elizabeth, she will want no part of the conspiracy. And if you think she might be swayed by Babington's pretty smile—'

'She has no love for Babington,' he snapped, so fiercely my sleeve was flecked with spittle. 'That is his vanity, to think all women want him. Bessie's affections are not so shallow. She may have liked him once, but she was little more than a child.'

'You have an understanding with her, then?' I asked, taking care not to look him in the eye; I did not want him to think it was an interrogation.

'She knows my heart,' he said, too indignant to be on his guard.

'And do you know hers? Has she declared that she loves you?'

His grip tightened on my sleeve. 'Not as such. She is too modest to state her affection so boldly. But she knows the extent of my devotion, I have proved it, and she will look kindly on me, she has promised, when I am in a position to offer her—' He broke off, and his eyes narrowed.

'Offer her what?' I said, encouraging. 'Marriage?'

His face closed up, as if a shutter had come down. 'I don't know why I am telling you any of this,' he muttered, pulling himself unsteadily to his feet.

'Because you have no one else to talk to, Gilbert,' I said, trying to sound reassuring. 'Your fear of Ballard will become a self-fulfilling prophecy, especially if you keep drinking like you did tonight – you'll have no hope of keeping up your pretence. So take my advice – confide in me and I may be able to help you. If you're hiding something about Bessie, it's best that—'

'Oh, fuck off, Bruno,' he said, with surprisingly precise enunciation, and launched himself off the wall towards his own room. 'You are not my master. I'm going to bed.'

I stood and blocked his path, snatching up his shirt-front in my fist. '*Prado.* My name is Prado. Remember that. I hear you call me anything else and it won't be Savage you have to worry about.' I released him with a little push. He swayed on the spot, opened his mouth as if to consider arguing, then decided against it.

'Give you good night.' I returned to my writing, smiling to myself. In the next room I heard him pissing into the pot, followed by the thud of a stool as he knocked it over, a deal of rustling and shuffling, and within ten minutes he was determinedly snoring. I pushed the chair back as silently as I could and crept in. His doublet lay on the floor by his bed; a quick feel of the lining confirmed that Bessie's note was still concealed there. So it had not been meant for any of the conspirators and, by Gifford's own admission, the letter could not be for him. He must be intending to carry it to Staffordshire with him, and there was only one obvious correspondent there; it was Mary Stuart's cipher, after all. What was Bessie promising Mary for love? Could it be that she and the conspirators had the same aims? If so, she would surely welcome Babington's approach, and Walsingham would need to get her away from Queen Elizabeth as quickly as possible. I wondered how much Gifford knew about the content of the letters he was carrying for his beloved, and whether he posed a greater danger than Walsingham and Phelippes realised.

FIFTEEN

I slept three hours at most, and not well, waking at every creak of the floorboards overhead and every grunt from Gifford's room. As soon as the first slants of dawn light poked through the cracks in the shutters I was up and dressed, folding inside my doublet the sealed report I had spent half the night writing and encrypting for Phelippes. I hesitated at the threshold, wondering if I should wake Gifford and let him know where I was going. His wild words about fleeing London had alarmed me, but now, in daylight, I doubted he would act on them; he would not want to leave Bessie Pierrepont to the conspirators, and his fear of Phelippes and Walsingham was equal to his terror of Ballard. Besides, I could not make myself his nursemaid if I was to continue with my own investigation. I decided to leave him sleeping it off and take my letter to the Saracen's Head for Ben to deliver. If the tap-room was open, I could break my fast while I waited for him to bring me news from Southwark. When Ballard mentioned at supper that a boy had seen Clara's body in the Cross Bones, my thoughts had jumped straight to the dark-haired child who had silently watched Poole and me from the wall before stealing the horse; I was willing to bet all the Spanish gold in Prado's chest that he was the one. He could have taken Clara's sleeves and shoes, if he was so light-fingered; there was a chance he might have seen someone leaving the graveyard, or even witnessed what happened. A thief would not talk willingly, but the child was young, and might be persuaded by the prospect of a reward, if I could find a way to question him.

The sky over Holborn was grey and heavy as wet wool. A fine rain drifted like mist and I pulled my cloak tight to keep it out; the street smelled of damp leaves and horseshit, and the air felt more like March than August. God, this island! I skirted puddles in the ruts left by cartwheels, wondering why I had been so eager to return here. The idea of freedom, I supposed. It had been easier to publish my books in England than in any Catholic country, where few printers wanted the risk of being associated with my name, but that freedom was only an idea, after all. In practice, Elizabeth's kingdom was as barbaric to those who wanted to think or believe freely as anywhere still under the authority of Rome, for all she promised not to make windows into men's souls. But you could not be truly free anywhere in Europe; every country I had lived in was busy tearing itself apart over the meaning of a piece of bread and a sip of wine, or whether God insisted on speaking only in Latin. If you dared to raise your head and measure the heavens, as the Pole Copernicus had done, and I had tried to do after him, and suggest that we were not the centre of Creation but one world among many, they would threaten to burn you. I thought of the dying woman in Shoe Lane the night before. She had not cared how much ink had been spilled by theologians over the matter of transubstantiation, nor how many had gone to their deaths defending it one way or the other. In her fear and pain she wanted, from a priest's hand, a piece of bread she believed was her Saviour, and it had brought some small relief in her last hours. For that, if we had been caught by the pursuivants, her family would have been imprisoned and I would have been racked and likely disembowelled, at least if I were a real priest. I was so weary of it, all that bloodshed, over so little; I felt it pressing down on my neck that morning like a lead cloak. All it would take – so I believed – was one ruler willing to allow people of different faiths to live alongside one another without persecution, and surely they would begin to recognise that their common humanity superseded the divisions they had been taught to fear? This was the philosophy I had attempted to propose in my books. But King Henri had tried it in France, to a degree, and the extremists of the Catholic League threatened to depose him for it. Tolerance did not win public support as easily as telling the unlettered that half the country was their enemy, especially when the harvest was bad and the price of bread raised, and it was easy to cry that God was punishing the land for allowing heresy to flourish—

I whipped around, snapped out of my gloomy musing by a movement at my back; I had thought I caught the flick of a cloak at the edge of my vision, but when I turned the street was empty. I rubbed my hands over my face and breathed in. Since my fight with Savage the night before, I had been edgy, leaping at shadows, waiting for a strike to come out of nowhere, and Gifford had begun to infect me with his fears of Ballard seeing through us. I had to relax or I would give myself away. But despite the empty street, the feeling of being watched did not leave me as I approached the Saracen's Head.

The yard was already milling with people, though it was not much past seven; all the activity settled any worries about how I was to leave my letter without being noticed. Boys led horses from the stables and saddled them for travellers making an early start; broad-shouldered men hefted barrels from a cart, shouting to one another, while others rolled them across to an outbuilding; a youth shovelled stained straw from corners into a barrow while a girl tipped pails of water over the stones beneath, washing away the stale piss of last night's drinkers. Amid all the bustle I wandered casually across to the dovecote and slipped the rolled-up linen into the hole on the lower left side. To my surprise, there was already a paper inside; I tucked it into my doublet and made my way to the tap-room.

The Saracen's Head was a comfortable old inn, cleanly kept, smelling of beer and woodsmoke, its bricks and beams soot-blackened. Small leaded windows of warped glass allowed little light; in the dimness of the main room, men were breaking their fasts with grunted early-morning conversation, thoughts turned inward to the business of the day ahead. Two at a bench near the serving-hatch raised their heads and gave me a look that was not friendly; they exchanged a couple of words, watching me. I looked away. I had grown used to those looks in England, with my appearance, and learned to ignore them, but in my present state of heightened alertness, anxiety flickered under my breastbone. I would have felt better protected in my own clothes; my black wool doublets and breeches and leather jacket made me less noticeable. Now, in the gaudy amber silks and pearl buttons of Father Prado's wardrobe, I looked like a reveller from the Venice carnival washed up in a London tavern of working men in brown and grey patched worsted, asking to be robbed.

I pulled up a stool at a table under the window and ordered hot milk, bread and cheese from a serving girl, making sure not to catch the eye of the two men who I sensed were still staring at me. I was desperate to read the note from the dovecote, but knew better than to take it out while I had attracted unwelcome attention. It didn't take them long.

'Fuck the Pope.' One leaned across, his hands flat on the table before me. I flinched at the reek of his breath even from a couple of feet away and kept my eyes down.

'Did you not hear me?' He slapped the table. I glanced up to see a broad red face, a mouth twisted in fury, teeth missing. 'I said, fuck the Pope.'

'In his arsehole,' his short friend added, for clarification.

'Yes, good,' I said pleasantly. 'You may fuck him wherever you like, he is no concern of mine.'

They exchanged a glance, wrong-footed. 'We broke from Rome to keep people like you out,' said the first one, falling back on the favourite old refrain.

'Gentlemen, I do not look for trouble. I wish to eat my breakfast and go about my business, as I'm sure you do.'

'People like you have no business in England.' He reached across the table and pinched my sleeve between his finger and thumb. 'Nice. Worth a bit, eh? You might want to take it off before I beat the shit out of you. My mate here will look after it.'

The second man grinned. 'Wipe my arse on it, more like.'

'You have a great interest in arses, my stunted friend. What is that about?'

I should have left it, but I couldn't help myself. The man's face darkened.

'Come outside, you Spanish cunt. I'll kick your Papist arse back to . . .' he struggled to think of a location.

'Madrid? Vigo? Sevilla? Or have you not heard of a world beyond Dover?' I flexed my fists, resigned; I hardly had the energy to fight again, but it seemed to go along with being Father Prado. I met the stare of the one leaning over the table and knew before I stood up that they would have the better of me; there were two of them, I was exhausted, and the manic light in his eyes told me that his blood was up, that despite the early hour he would find nothing more stimulating than beating a foreigner to a pulp. But I could not let them take the letter in my doublet, so I had no choice. He knew he had already won, and his mouth curved into a sarcastic smile. Suddenly, he jerked backwards with a cry of surprise and lost his footing, landing on his back in the sawdust.

'Get out. Chrissakes! And you. Yapping at my customers like a couple of street dogs.'

I looked up to see a solid man in a canvas apron, with greying cropped hair and a face so familiar it was like rushing through time to see young Ben in thirty years. I couldn't place his accent, but it was not London.

'Ah, come on, Dan.' The fuck-the-pope man struggled to his feet, brushing himself down, his bravado somewhat dented. 'You don't want the likes of him in here. Stinking the place up, dressed like a fucking sodomite.'

'He smells a sight better than you.' This Dan set down a bowl of hot milk and a trencher of fresh wheat bread in front of me. 'On the house, son. Sorry for the disturbance.' He turned back to my new acquaintances. 'Thought I told you to go?'

'We haven't finished eating,' the man with the missing teeth protested.

'You have now. And if you don't fuck off out of it, you won't be eating here again.' He tilted his head towards the door and glared until they deflated and began to slink away.

'Your kind always stick together,' the smaller one threw out over his shoulder, as they left. Dan made as if to take a step towards them; the door banged shut as they left in a hurry.

'Our kind?' I asked. He was still watching the door, his lips pressed tight.

'Outsiders, he means.' He turned back to me with a grimace that might have been an attempt at a smile. 'Don't take it personally. Little men.'

'Oh, I don't. They're not the first. You're not English, then?'

'I'm Cornish, son. Londoners don't like us any better than they like you. Daniel Hammett.' I opened my mouth, wondering how I should introduce myself, but he held up a hand to stop me. 'I know who you are. We'll be seeing a lot more of you here, no doubt. Well, you're welcome. Let me know if you get any more grief from them, or any like them.'

I thanked him, though I couldn't help bristling at the suggestion that I needed him to watch out for me. But then his son was already doing so; perhaps I had become a ward of the family. I glanced around the tap-room.

'Is Ben . . . ?'

'He's gone out. Don't look for him, he'll find you if he needs to. He has a knack for that. I'll bring you cheese and honey. Do you want more bread?'

'Thank you, this is fine. Don't you worry about him?' I asked. He laughed, as if I had purposely made a joke; there was a warmth in his face I liked instinctively.

'If I let myself stop to worry, I'd never sleep,' he said. 'Can't afford to fuss over him. I'm only glad the boy has honest work – he knows how to look after himself. Oh – he said you might want to borrow a horse. Ask the stable lad out the back – tell him I sent you.' He turned to leave, then paused to cast a glance over my clothes. 'Like I said, you're welcome here any time. But you might want to wear something a bit less – you know. Girly.'

I acknowledged the wisdom of this, wondering how I should revise Father Prado's dress to avoid looking like either myself, or the kind of foreign dandy who is asking for patriotic Londoners to kick his head in. When I could be sure no one else was paying me any attention, I fished out the note from the dovecote and smoothed it flat on the table with one hand while I drank the milk.

I had assumed it would be a word from Phelippes, in response to whatever Poole had reported back from the night before; instead I found a few lines written laboriously in a child's hand, with a good deal of crossing out and inkblots, but clearly legible:

His name is Joe. Works in the stables at the Unicorn in the day. Also theef. For a shiling I'll tell you another secret about him when I see you.

I balled the paper in my fist and lobbed it into the fire, smiling. Daniel Hammett was right that his son knew how to look after himself. Honest work. I presumed that Phelippes was paying Ben for running back and forth with messages, but the boy had found a way to make extra profit. I didn't begrudge him – I had not expected an answer so soon, he must have been abroad half the night – but decided I would hold on to my money until I had found this Joe and sounded him out on the matter of Clara Poole's body; he would no doubt exact a price for any information too.

Church bells rang the hour of eight as I crossed the river. Most of the traffic was heading north over London Bridge into the city this early, so that the journey to Southwark was much quicker than the last time I had made it with Poole. Hammett's stable hand had loaned me a piebald mare, not young but serviceable; I was determined not to let her out of my sight in Southwark, especially if I managed to find the boy Joe.

South of the river, the streets were littered with the last dregs of a Southwark night: men and women sprawled in the gutters, puddles of vomit and empty bottles beside them; others stumbled grey-faced through the streets as if they had just now risen from their graves. Between them, the bustle of a borough coming to life for the working day: men with dray carts and hand barrows delivering provisions to the inns; boatmen mending their oars along the river-front by the stairs, or calling out for customers; the endless syncopated hammering of building work; drovers herding their flocks towards the bridge for butchering at Smithfield; women in the drab smocks of servants hoisting baskets, exchanging greetings, and others in the gaudy of Winchester geese, looking bedraggled as the sheep.

The yard of the Unicorn was as busy as the Saracen's Head had been. I dismounted, casting my eyes around for the dark-skinned boy among the delivery men and serving girls. A gangly youth with an unfortunate skin condition approached, a rope halter in his hands.

'Help you, sir?'

'Thank you, I was just looking . . .' I scanned the yard;

there must have been a dozen boys at work, though none the right one. 'For a boy.'

The young man pressed a finger to his lips. 'You ask for that inside,' he said in a low voice, nodding to the white-fronted inn. 'You're a bit early though, mate – everyone's still abed. Getting their beauty sleep.' He gave me a leery wink. 'Just arrived in London, is it? I'm sure they can accommodate you – the food's good enough while you wait. Want me to look after this old girl for you?' He slapped the mare on the side of her neck; she barely bothered to look at him.

'How much?'

'Two pence for the day.'

I hesitated, uncertain about entering the Unicorn. Ballard took a room here, and was evidently on good terms with the women who ran the place; someone of my appearance would attract curiosity, and he was bound to hear of my visit. It would be hard to explain that away without arousing suspicion that Father Prado was spying on him. I was reaching into my doublet for spare coins – I knew better than to carry a purse at my belt in Southwark – when a slight figure emerged from the back of the building balancing a wooden pail of water in each hand. I stepped forward for a better look; at the same time, the child raised his head, his dark eyes met mine, recognition and panic flared in the same instant, he dropped the buckets and raced to the far end of the yard, where he began scrambling up the boundary wall.

I thrust the mare's harness into the youth's hand. 'Pay you when I return,' I shouted over my shoulder, following the boy. He was nimble and light, and had disappeared before I could find the first foothold, but determination drove me on; ignoring the cries from the yard, I shinned over the wall and dropped into a filthy alley in time to see the boy Joe whisk around the corner at the end. I raced after him, skidding on muddy ground, brown water and God knows what else spattering my boots and my hose as I chased him along the next street, down another alley, over a fence at the end, across a yard piled high with broken furniture and cartwheels, over the wall at the other side and into a lane between tenements where the stink of human waste made me gag so hard I struggled to catch my breath. The child Joe was fleet and agile as a cat, but I was not prepared to let the one chance of finding a possible witness slip through my fingers. At the end of the foul lane, the boy disappeared without a backward glance as if he had melted through the fence.

When I reached the place where he had vanished, I saw that there was a loose plank covered by an old piece of sailcloth, the gap narrow and low enough for a child Joe's size but not for a grown man, even a Neapolitan. I looked up at the fence. It was eight feet high at least, with nails studded along the top to deter anyone thinking of climbing over. I glanced behind me; this was not an alley to be trapped in. No one had followed us, though I couldn't escape the sensation that there were suspicious eyes behind the broken and empty windows of the tenements on either side. I took a deep breath, crouched and sprang upwards, catching the top of the fence between nails, hauling myself up with only the strength in my arms as I scrabbled for footholds, to the point where I could drag myself over. The nails tore at my clothes and skin, but I clenched my teeth against the pain as I dropped to the other side, landing clumsily on my hands and knees in the dirt of a yard behind a brick building with shuttered windows. Though small, this yard was cared for: swept clean, the midden heap in one corner enclosed behind boards, and the three sides lined with an array of earthenware pots planted with a variety of unusual herbs. I brushed myself down as best I could and squatted to examine the leaves of a plant I thought I recognised from the time I spent as a youth assisting the infirmarian at San Domenico Maggiore. Solomon's seal; I had not thought it grew in England, nor expected to find anyone who knew how to use it. When I turned my attention to the other shrubs – the child Joe almost forgotten – I saw that they held similar surprises; this was a medicinal herb garden, no question, and a sophisticated one, planted by someone who had travelled outside this damp island.

'Don't move. Put your hands on your head and turn around slowly.'

The voice was a woman's, her English heavily inflected with a foreign accent. I cursed myself for allowing my attention to wander. I did as I was told and found myself facing a figure as striking as any from the tales of the Greeks. She was tall, with skin the colour of teak and a mass of black curls that hung down her back, tied up in a red scarf; her hands and the front of her dress were splashed with fresh blood as though she had come straight from a battlefield, her eyes flashed like obsidian and she held a crossbow at her shoulder, primed and pointed at my face.

'Get out.' She jerked her head at the back fence. 'Same way you came. Do it fast and I won't need to put this through your eye.'

'Is this your garden?'

'Yes. So get out of it.'

'You have a fine collection of plants,' I said, aiming to sound unthreatening.

'I know. Don't make me tell you a third time.'

'A good number of these are poisonous.'

A flicker of something crossed her face; perhaps she was impressed that I recognised them. 'I know that too. I'm serious – if you don't move, I'll send you out of here with a bolt through your knee, at the very least. There's not a plant in this garden will save your leg if I do.'

'There is, actually,' I said, pointing. 'You have yarrow there, otherwise known as soldier's wort – most effective in staunching blood from wounds. Achilles himself was said to carry it into battle.'

I thought I saw the twitch of a smile at the corner of her mouth. She lowered the crossbow an inch.

'Very good, so you know plants. That is not a reason not to kill you. I don't have time for this.' She darted a quick glance back towards the house, as if afraid of leaving it for too long.

'Look, I mean no harm. I just want to see Joe. Is he your son?'

Her face hardened and she raised the weapon again. 'Last warning.'

'I can pay you.' I lowered a hand to my doublet; on the instant she stepped forward, eyes blazing, and spat on the ground.

'He is not for sale. You people disgust me. I see you anywhere near him, I'll cut off your miserable pizzle with a kitchen knife.'

'Is that what happened to the last person who asked to speak to him?' I nodded to the blood covering her hands.

'You don't want to find out.'

'I need to ask him a question. That's all.'

She muttered something guttural under her breath and spat again, but I had met enough Moors in Naples to have picked up a little useful Arabic and I understood the gist of it.

'My mother would be very upset by that suggestion,' I said. Her eyes widened in surprise – she had clearly not expected to be understood – but before she could speak, the silence was broken by a cry from the building behind her; a howl of pain so intense it sounded ripped from the guts, barely human. The woman started, cast me a look of contempt, and lowered the weapon.

'Just get out,' she said, and ran into the house. After a moment's hesitation, I followed her.

Inside I found a large room lit by tallow candles, and in the centre a table where a girl lay emitting those animal howls, smock around her waist over a domed belly and her knees pointing to the ceiling, blood pouring out of her to collect in a basin on the floor, already overflowing. The boy Joe, in his shirtsleeves, was valiantly trying to staunch the flow with strips of cloth, but the rupture was too severe. The dark-haired woman barked out a series of commands in Arabic, squeezing the girl's hand before taking the drenched cloth from Joe and pressing it hard between her legs. The cries grew weaker, though no less heart-rending.

'It won't stop, Mama,' the boy said, panic in his voice.

'Bring me a fresh bowl of hot water. And get the opium.'

'Which first?'

'I'll get the water,' I said. I could see a pot of it boiling over a well-stoked fire in the hearth. 'She's haemorrhaging, you need to stop it quickly. Pressure on the wound should do it, though if she is bleeding internally—'

The dark-haired woman snapped around, her face clouded briefly with fury, then she appeared to revise the situation.

'Are you a physician?' she asked.

'No. But I have worked in an infirmary.'

'You know plants. Can you administer tincture of opium?'

'I've seen it done.'

'Fine.' She took a key on a silver chain from around her neck and passed it to the child. 'Joe will get some for you. Give her a dose that will send her into a good sleep, but not permanently. Shut your mouth, Joe, and show the man.'

The child was staring at me, his face rigid with alarm. He darted to a wooden cupboard against the back wall, unlocked it, and pressed a dark green bottle into my hand.

'It's not about the horse,' I mouthed to him, when his mother's back was turned.

'She has not expelled the whole of the afterbirth,' the Arabic woman said briskly. 'I'll have to get it out. Without that tincture, the pain might kill her. It might anyway.'

'But she'll die if you don't try,' I said. 'Have you tried massaging the abdomen?'

She cut me a quick, impatient look. 'Yes, I had thought of that. I was trying it when you trespassed in my yard. Stop telling me my job and give her the medicine, fast.' She took out a long, curved metal implement and plunged it into the bowl of boiling water that the boy held out. I would have been curious to watch the operation – at San Domenico, we had only ever worked on male patients, for obvious reasons – but there was no time to stand around. I poured a measure of the tincture into a cup and gently pulled the girl's hair back from her face so that she could swallow it. At the sight, I jumped back, and could not help a gasp: half her nose was missing, leaving a gaping hole and scarred flesh.

The midwife glanced up. 'What, you never saw the French pox before?' she said, with a note of scorn. 'That's why the baby . . .' She left the sentence unfinished, only gestured beneath the table. The light did not reach into the shadows there; I could make out a basin full of blood, the pale shape of tiny, twisted limbs within, unmoving.

'Dear God.' I could not think of anything more useful to say.

'What women suffer, eh? Now hold her steady until it takes effect.'

I did as I was told. Joe brought a fresh supply of cloths and hot water, and massaged the girl's stomach when his mother instructed him; I made myself useful carrying bowls of blood to the yard, where I tipped them on to the midden heap, to be filled again faster than they could be emptied. The business took perhaps half an hour, but eventually the girl's bleeding slowed and she lay inert on the table, her skin white as marble, the rise and fall of her chest so shallow as to be barely noticeable, but still breathing, against all odds.

After the three of us had washed our hands we pulled up stools and sat, watching the patient, blood-spattered and exhausted like three survivors of a violent skirmish. Only the crackle of the fire and the soft scrape of the girl's breathing broke the silence.

'Will she live?' I asked, after a few minutes.

The woman shrugged. 'For now. Not that she has much to live for. Poor child, perhaps it would be a kindness if she didn't wake.' She reached up and pulled the scarf from her hair, wiped her forehead with it, combed the wild curls back from her face with her long fingers and tied it again.

She was very beautiful, I realised; about my age or perhaps older, her skin smooth and clear over high cheekbones and a strong jaw. But it was her hands that intrigued me. When she had first washed the blood away, I had thought she had some kind of skin disease, but now I could see that her hands and forearms were decorated with elaborate tracery and patterns in what looked like red-brown ink.

'What is that?'

She gave a weary smile. 'Henna. You've never seen it?' She held out her hands, palms down, for me to take a closer look. 'How do you know my language and not know this? It's something women do for special occasions, where I come from.' She twisted her mouth. 'I suppose I should thank you for your help, but I know men well enough to think you'll expect something in return.'

'I want only to ask Joe some questions,' I said, folding my hands between my knees. 'But I'm glad I had the chance to assist you. I have never seen such a procedure.'

'But you knew to massage the stomach. How?'

'My mother was a midwife. In—' I stopped myself; I had been about to say Nola, my birthplace. I must remember not to give anything of myself away. 'Is she a Winchester goose?' I nodded to the girl on the table. She clicked her tongue at the phrase.

'She's a street whore, call her what she is. Unlicensed. I'd wager she got the pox before she even arrived in London. Picked it up on the road or whatever village she ran from. Sixteen at most, I'd guess. I've seen plenty die younger.'

'You care for the street women? Is there a living in that?'

'I attend to the girls at one of the licensed houses, that's how I put food on the table. The madam values my skills. No male doctor could do what I do, or would care to. I treat their complaints, keep them clean and fit to work. Clear up any unwanted consequences.'

'Like that?' I indicated the infant corpse under the table. She looked away.

'Girls like this one I treat because what else can I do – let them die?'

'I suppose you would be arrested, if it was known?'

She gave a dry laugh, and her eyes flashed in the firelight. 'Burned before I could open my mouth to defend myself. There are those who call me witch even among the women I tend, for the knowledge I have, and the herbs – but mostly because of *this*, let's not pretend.' She pointed to her dark face. 'Why – are you planning to report me?'

'Knowing you have that crossbow behind the door?' I smiled. 'Of course not. I have some experience of how the English treat those who look different.'

She made the clicking noise again. 'But you are a man, and not so unlike them. What are you, Spanish?' When I did not reply, she curled her lip and nodded, as if she had expected no better. 'Well, ask the boy what you must. But he is not bound to answer you.'

'He left her there unguarded,' Joe blurted, squeakily defensive.

'Who? Who left her?'

'Your friend. The tall one.' He frowned, as if it were a stupid question. 'She was old anyway, it wasn't like she was worth much. She's better off out of her misery.'

'How can you speak that way about – wait, *old*?' I had assumed he was talking of Clara Poole, since that was where my thoughts were bent. Belatedly, I caught up with his meaning. 'I'm not here about the horse,' I said.

His mother snapped her head to him.

'What horse? Damn you, child, what have I told you?'

'Never mind,' I cut in quickly. 'I wanted to ask you about

the Cross Bones though.' I saw a warning glance dart between mother and son. 'A woman's body was found there, five days past. I heard a boy saw her before the constables came. Was it you?'

'Are you from the constables?' he asked, assessing me with the same sharp, black eyes as his mother.

'Do I look like a London official?' I tried to make it sound like a joke, but the woman's eyes narrowed.

'Informers come in all shades these days,' she said. 'You're dressed like a gentleman, for all your foreign looks. Or at least, you were.' I followed her gaze to my clothes, now bloodstained, torn and filthy.

'I am not from the authorities. My interest is – personal.' Seeing this drew only more suspicion, I added, 'I knew the girl's family.'

'You *knew* her,' the woman said, slowly and with a degree of incredulity, as if I had claimed the Virgin appeared to me at my close-stool.

'Look, I am trying to find out what I can about her death. The body was taken away quickly, I understand, and the business hushed up – whoever saw her may have vital information. I will be discreet. I will not pass on who told me, if you know anything.'

Joe looked to his mother for instruction. She pursed her lips. 'You said you had money to offer? How much?'

'Depends how much he knows.'

She rattled off a few sentences in Arabic, so fast my limited knowledge could catch only one or two words; the boy shook his head and glanced at me.

'We will name our price when he has told you all he has to tell,' she said, folding her arms.

'That hardly seems fair.'

'You're the one who wants the goods. I set the price.'

'But you would give me what I ask before I hand over payment?'

'Consider it a gesture of good faith.' Her lips curved into a half-smile; I acknowledged the compliment and motioned for the boy to go ahead.

Joe looked at the floor between his feet. 'I go to the Cross Bones some nights. The watchman there is my grandfather Goodchild. I take him hot food and keep watch with him so he can sleep – he's old now and his legs hurt if he stands too long.'

'He doesn't need the family history,' his mother said. 'Get to the meat of it.'

'People come in sometimes, especially in summer. Men and women, you know. They go to it under the trees, we let them be.' He shifted on his stool and picked at his fingernails. 'When they've gone, I go and look around in the grass. Things fall out their clothes when they're rolling about, you never know. Or they lose an earring in the tumble, a brooch. If they're drunk, they might even fall asleep after, so I check if—' He broke off and a secret smile crept over his face. 'If they're all right.'

'If they have anything worth lifting, you mean.'

'He didn't say that,' the woman cut in.

'I'm not an idiot. I'm not interested in what you do with them. Tell me about the girl.'

'I thought she was asleep,' he said, his voice growing tight; the memory clearly upset him. 'She was sitting up against the back wall, under the tree, with her head forward, like this.' He demonstrated. 'She had fine shoes, that was the first thing I saw. Leather with glass beads on them. I touched her leg and she didn't do anything, so I—' He bit his lip.

'You took them. Then what?'

'She didn't even twitch, so I thought I'd see what else she wouldn't miss. But suddenly she moved.' He flinched, as if it had just happened, and a shudder racked his thin body. 'She slid sideways. I jumped back, but then I realised she had just fallen over, passed out. I had no lantern, I don't when I creep up on them – I see well enough in the dark, but there was not much moon that night. I went to feel if she had any jewellery on, earrings or necklace or the like, and my fingers came away sticky. So I ran to grandfather for a lantern and then we saw. What he had done to her.' His face creased and his gaze returned to his shoes.

'Did you see him? The man?'

The boy shook his head, mute, but he would not raise his head and look at me. I wondered if he was lying out of fear.

'I reckon he went up the tree, over the wall. By the time I looked, there was only her.'

'Did she have any jewellery? A necklace, perhaps?'

'No. I swear it. No earrings, neither – well, she didn't have any ears. They'd been cut off. And her hair, and her nose all smashed. She looked like someone with the pox, like her' – he pointed to the girl on the table – 'only worse.'

'Did you hear them go to it,' I asked, 'before you went to see what they might have left behind? Or did you hear any sound of a struggle?'

'Nothing like that.' Joe sniffed. 'They were quiet. I only listen to know when they're done, but grandfather makes a joke of it sometimes – "Ooh, that was a bit quick," he'll say, "didn't get his tuppence-worth there," or "She's having a fine old time, this one, good fellow." But I didn't catch a sound that night after we heard them come in, not even a scream. So she must have been dead when he cut her, right?' He lifted his eyes to me then in a question.

'I already told you that,' the woman said, with a trace of impatience. 'She won't have felt a thing.'

'I know, but he's a doctor.' His eyes were imploring; he looked as if he might cry. Unusual, I thought, for a child of a Southwark midwife, used to gore and premature death and disfigured faces, to be so visibly distressed by the memory, but then he was so young. The woman's words made my eyes stray to the inert girl on the table. *She won't have felt a thing.* Not if she had been drugged.

'I'm not a doctor. And your mother is right. She wouldn't have known. So what did you do then?'

'Grandfather said I should run home. He was afraid they might think we did it, he didn't want me in trouble. He said I should wash the blood off and at first light he would send for the constables.'

'So you didn't stay and search for any more valuables?'

He shook his head again. 'I only took her sleeves and her shoes, I swear it. I was going to leave the sleeves, but I knew Mama has a mixture that can get blood out of cloth, and they were good silk – *ow*—'

The woman leaned forward and cuffed him around the back of the head. 'Sometimes I think you were born with no wits. That's your English blood.' She turned to me. 'He has no more to tell.' To the boy she said, 'Go and change your shirt before you get back to work, you look like you've been in a battle.'

'I don't care about her sleeves,' I said. 'I want to find out who killed her.'

'Did you love her?' She sounded genuinely curious. I hesitated.

'A friend of mine did.'

'Ah.' She gave me a knowing look. 'Well, I am sorry for your *friend's* loss. But my son can't help you any further, so you can be on your way.'

I stood, looking down at the sorry state of my clothes in the candlelight. In the penumbra of the room I had almost forgotten it was morning outside, though I understood why the windows needed to be kept boarded up.

'How much, then?'

'I don't want your money.' She stood and smoothed down her blood-drenched dress. 'The old watchman. Abraham Goodchild, my father-in-law – he was arrested when he reported the body, and they've kept him locked up since, on some invented charge. He's done nothing wrong. You're a gentleman, or you're pretending to be one. Speak to the City authorities, tell them to let him go.'

'Mistress, I am a foreigner here, as I said. I have no influence with the authorities.'

'You could at least make enquiries. They're more likely to answer a man. I can't even find out which gaol he is in.'

I bowed. 'I will do my best.'

'I'll hold you to it.' She gave me a long look up and down, appraising me, and I saw that something in her expression had changed; I almost fancied I saw a spark of interest. 'What is your name?'

After a long pause I said, 'Xavier.'

'Spanish, then. As I thought.' Her lip curled in magnificent contempt.

'You have something against the Spanish?'

'Do you think so?' Her face suggested she would like to cuff me around the head too. Too late, I realised my ignorance. She pointed a finger at my face with the same intent that she had levelled the crossbow. 'Your parents drove my family out of Granada.'

'I'm sorry for that. My mother can be unreasonable when she's had a drink. But after what you said about her privates—'

She glared at me for a moment before bursting into laughter. 'And where will I find you, Xavier, if I should need your assistance again?'

'You can ask for me at the Saracen's Head in Holborn.'

'How appropriate.' She led me back to the yard, this time unlocking a gate set in the fence. With a hand on the latch, she turned and lowered her voice. 'I'm no fool, Xavier. I can make an educated guess about what you are, and why you don't want to draw attention to yourself with the authorities.' She shrugged. 'Not my business. You keep my secrets and I'll keep yours. But if I am right, you will know men of influence. If you can find news of where my father-in-law is being held, or plead his case, I would be grateful.'

'What about your husband?' I glanced around, in case he might come charging out from behind the plant pots at any moment.

'Dead,' she said bluntly. 'Let me go and fetch that child.'

She disappeared into the house and a few moments later Joe scampered out behind her, wearing a clean jerkin.

'See this gentleman safely back to the river,' she said. 'And don't say another word about the Cross Bones till he's paid what he promised.' She stepped closer and laid the flat of her hand over the buttons of my doublet. 'And you – if you care about your *friend*, tell him he would be wise to leave this business, however much he loved her.'

'Why?' My skin prickled; I had sensed from the first mention of Clara that both Joe and his mother knew more than they were telling.

She left her hand there, and her voice softened. 'Because they don't lock up an innocent man for finding a dead girl in Southwark. You get more fuss over a dead horse around here. They don't spirit a body away as if it was never there and hush up everyone who saw it. There's something more to this murder, trust me – the old man was right to keep Joe out of it, and I don't want him dragged in now. We have enough trouble of our own already, just for being who we are.'

I met her eye and nodded. 'I still don't know your name.'

She hesitated, then appeared to relent. 'Leila. Leila Humeya. Wait.' She licked her thumb and rubbed at a spot on my brow. Her breath was hot on my cheek. 'Blood,' she said, by way of explanation, before turning abruptly and disappearing into the house.

SIXTEEN

Joe led me back through a maze of streets towards the river. Along the way I attempted to ask him further questions about finding Clara, but he had clammed up, evidently more afraid of his mother than of me, for which I couldn't blame him.

'It must have been a terrible thing to witness,' I said, as we neared the inn. He darted a wary glance sidelong at me.

'I'm not afraid of the dead,' he said, in a voice that was small but firm. 'Grandfather says they can't touch us. It's the living you got to look out for. Especially men.'

'He sounds like a wise fellow.'

'Will he go straight to Hell?'

'Your grandfather?'

'*No.*' He clicked his tongue in a way that reminded me of his mother. 'The man who killed that girl.'

'Well . . .' I was not sure how to answer this; too much had happened on too little sleep for me to debate judgement and salvation with a child. 'I'm sure you know your commandments, Joe.'

He nodded, uncertain.

'Then you know what God says about killing. I don't think anyone who does that to a woman should go unpunished, do you? By God or the law. So if you know who he is . . .'

I left the question hanging. He appeared to consider it for a few paces. 'Would someone go to Hell if they did something that they didn't think was bad, but a person got hurt because of it?'

I slowed my pace and kept my eyes fixed ahead, aware that a misstep now could frighten him into silence.

'No. I think God sees our intentions. If this person never meant anyone to be harmed by what he did, I don't believe God would make him suffer. But I don't see why you think I am an expert.'

'Mama said you are probably a priest.'

I laughed. 'Your mama has plenty of imagination. Don't repeat that to anyone, will you?'

He shot me a look of pure scorn that was so exactly like Leila that I laughed. 'We know how to keep secrets in our family.'

'I don't doubt it.' We turned a corner and the river appeared ahead, at the end of the street. To our right was the wide double gate leading to the Unicorn's yard. 'But listen – if you ever want to talk about any of your secrets, or this friend of yours who did something he's worried about – I'm good at listening. I can keep secrets too.'

A small, nervous smile creased his face. 'I don't doubt it,' he said, in a fair mimic of my accent.

We passed under the arch to find the yard even busier than we had left it. I slipped Joe a couple of coins. 'Will you fetch my horse? The piebald mare.'

But as we rounded the corner to the stables, I froze. A few paces away, chatting easily with one of the ostlers, stood John Ballard, decked out in full Captain Fortescue fashion, all gold-trimmed satin and starched lace, an ostrich feather bobbing in his hat, jaunty despite the damp. He took in my appearance with one swooping glance, patted the stable lad on the arm and sauntered towards us, eyebrows raised in mock surprise. Joe stopped dead too; his face turned ashen and he whisked around Ballard and ran to the stables without a word. I watched him disappear; evidently this was not his first encounter with the priest, and I wondered what could have caused that reaction in the boy.

'Well!' Ballard said heartily, gesturing to my clothes. I looked down and properly took in the state of myself. There was a gash in the breeches from climbing Leila's fence; the fine leather boots were caked in mud, horseshit and probably worse; the silk hose had rips down both legs, but all those were nothing compared to the quantities of fresh blood covering me from head to foot.

'Southwark is renowned for fights, but I hadn't thought they started at this time of the morning. What the devil happened to you?'

'I—' I blinked at him. There was no convincing explanation for the way I looked. I willed my mind to work faster. 'I – wanted to continue God's work.'

'*What?*' The bonhomie evaporated.

'After the visits last night – when I woke this morning, I felt the hand of God urging me to do more for his flock.' I laid my palm flat on my breast, warming to my invention. 'I recalled what you said about the streets south of the river, so I made my way here thinking there might be poor souls in need of help.'

'And were you set upon?' His expression was a tussle between concern and suspicion.

I hung my head. 'I'm afraid so. I was too confident – I thought God would protect me, as you said. But a gang of apprentices on their way to work – I think they did not like my face. I fought back as well as I could, but—'

'I'm sure. I remember what you did at Paul's. Never seen a man take Savage down, in all the years I've known him.' He looked at my front. 'But dear God, the blood! One would think they knifed you – did they? – but then surely you could not be walking.'

'They didn't. Only their fists. The blood is not mine – I caught one of them in the nose. He pushed me to the ground, and this happened.' I gestured to my clothes.

'He must have had enough blood for ten men,' he said, with a sceptical tone that warned me he did not necessarily take me at face value. 'Are you sure you didn't knife him? That would have been very unwise.'

'No one was knifed.' I drew my dagger from its sheath at my belt to prove it was clean.

'And the Moorish child – what were you doing with him?'

'He found me in the street. I asked him if he could point me to the Unicorn – it was the only name I could think of, because you spoke of it. I thought I might ask for some water.'

Ballard gave me a long look, weighing me up. I suspected he found the story as implausible as I did, but he was not willing to make an outright accusation. He moved as if to lay a hand on my shoulder, took account of the state of my doublet and thought better of it.

'Listen, *hermano*. This is important. What you did was extremely foolish. I have no doubt you meant well, but you have to understand how our business works. We do not call on people at random – there is a delicate network of communication, so that I can receive word of those who need my offices. Savage coordinates it so we stay a step ahead of the pursuivants. Someone like you cannot take it upon yourself to wander the streets of Southwark on the off-chance anyone needs the sacraments.' His face constricted in alarm. 'Are you carrying the Host on your person?'

'I am not entirely a fool, John. I did not come looking to minister as a priest.' I dropped my voice to a whisper. 'I thought only of more practical help, in case I found anyone destitute in the street. Like the Good Samaritan.'

He laughed, and I heard the condescension in it. 'That is admirable. But instead, it is you who needed to be rescued. It's funny . . .' he put his head on one side and regarded me

'. . . Mendoza did not lead me to believe you were an impetuous fellow. Quite the reverse. He assured me you were extremely cautious.'

'Sometimes the Spirit can move us to act without thought for ourselves.' God, I was making Prado an insufferably pious arsehole.

'Within reason,' he replied. 'But it would be better if you could temper your zeal with consideration for your comrades, while you are in London. Especially now that we fear we may be watched. Come . . .' he began walking towards the main entrance of the inn. 'Let's get you a drink and a wash. You'll have to hand your knife in at the door.'

I followed him, glancing over my shoulder to see Joe leading out the piebald horse. The boy gave me a questioning look; behind Ballard's back, I shooed him back to the stables. I would have to wait before I could ask him why the sight of the priest had made him so alarmed.

The Unicorn was a handsome building – two centuries old, at my estimate, three storeys, double-fronted, with a garden to the rear. If not for the whitewashed façade with the sign of the mythical horned beast painted above the entrance, you might have taken it for an upmarket coaching inn. We had barely set foot in the grand entrance hall, with its linenfold panelling and polished floor tiles, before a maid appeared in pristine white apron, greeted Ballard with familiarity and recoiled at my appearance. He explained what we needed; she took my knife in its sheath and told us to wait.

'Do you always lodge here?' I asked Ballard, to pass the time.

'I find it convenient,' he said, with a knowing smile. 'For all the reasons I told you. There's no gossip in London that the madam here doesn't find out first – she's a trove of knowledge. And she's sympathetic too, if you take my meaning.' He tapped the side of his nose.

'She knows who you really are?'

'She knows a number of people in the network. This old building is full of hiding places. She sometimes takes consignments of banned books and other items from the continent when they come in by boat. The pursuivants wouldn't think to look for Catholic relics in a place like this.'

'Ingenious,' I said, filing that information away for later as a plump woman in an emerald-green gown came bustling down the corridor, throwing up her hands in a show of horror.

'Oh, Captain Fortescue, what has happened here? Has your poor friend been attacked? God save us, good Christians are not safe on the streets of this borough, it's time the bishop took things in hand.'

She was a remarkable-looking creature; I guessed her to be in her mid-fifties, though her face was so caked in white ceruse that it was hard to tell. Fine hairline cracks appeared in the make-up when she spoke; she had a wide, animated mouth painted red, and merry, dancing eyes that took in everything and assessed it in an instant. Most striking was her hair; a confection of auburn curls piled precariously on top of her head like sugar sculptures on a cake, clearly intended to imitate the wigs Queen Elizabeth wore. She grabbed my hands between hers and wrung them with vigour. 'Are you all right, my love? Any friend of the Captain's is welcome here.' To Ballard, with a broad wink: 'Isn't he handsome? You didn't tell me you had another such comely friend, Captain.'

He gave me a worldly smile. 'Don't be too flattered – Madame Rosa thinks every man handsome who brings a full purse.' He turned to the madam and swept off his hat with a great flourish. 'Now listen – my friend needs hot water, some salve for his bruises, and a change of clothes. Do you have anything that might fit?'

Madame Rosa tilted her head and sized me up as if she could take a man's measurements by sight alone. 'I can find something. Will you want those laundered, my love?'

I looked down at my clothes. 'I fear they are beyond salvation.'

She let out a cheerful giggle. 'Aren't we all, south of the river? You leave them with me, we've got a marvellous girl who works here, woman really, she makes up a mixture can get stains out of anything.'

'I imagine that would be very useful in this business,' I said.

'You're not wrong. You wouldn't believe some of the things I've seen. She's a Moor, but she's very skilled.' She whispered this in confidence. 'All right, my darling – I'll get them to heat you a tub and sort out clothes for you.' Her look sharpened as it flitted from me to Ballard. 'Will he want a room tonight? I'm not sure I have any vacant, I'd have to check the ledger—'

'Don't trouble yourself,' Ballard said. 'A bath will suffice, and my friend will be on his way to his own lodgings.'

'Who's paying?' she asked.

I reached into my doublet, but Ballard waved the gesture aside.

'Put it on my account. May I say, Rosa, your hair is looking magnificent today,' he added, with exaggerated gallantry.

'Do you think? I should bloody hope so, it cost me a fortune.' She reached up and patted the monstrosity on her head, simpering. 'But a girl's got to keep up appearances, eh, Captain? Look.' With both hands, she lifted the entire construction on its supporting frame away from her head. Without it, she looked like an old man; her own pale scalp was almost bald, sprouted with tufts of grey, and sore-looking blisters where the wire chafed the skin. 'Do you think it makes me look like Her Maj?'

'The very likeness,' Ballard said. 'Only more regal.'

'Ah, you're a charmer. Don't think you're getting a discount.' She spluttered out another laugh and swiped at him flirtatiously with the back of her hand, settled the wig into place – a little lopsided – and hurried off to make arrangements.

'Dear Lord, one tries to be charitable, but did you ever see such a sight?' Ballard turned to me with amusement. 'Whichever poor desperate girl sold her hair won't have seen a fraction of what our Madame Rosa laid out for that awful thing.'

'Women sell their hair?'

He frowned. 'You Jesuits do live a rarefied life, don't you? The poor will sell anything they own to buy bread, and often all they have are their bodies. They sell those whole or piecemeal – hair, teeth, anything the rich will pay for. I dare say if they could take out their healthy offal there's some would sell it. Girls can get a good price for hair these days, now that the Tudor has made wigs so fashionable, though it's the wig-makers seeing the profit.' He leaned across and whispered close to my ear. 'What a different world it will be, when the true Queen takes her throne and England is restored to the Church again. The poor will not suffer as they do now.'

If I had been speaking as myself, I might have replied that I had lived in Catholic countries and they were not noticeably models of egalitarian Christian commonwealth, where no one had to sell themselves or beg for bread; he would know that if he had ever set foot in the Papal states. But Ballard clearly believed his own fantasy that the ascent of Mary Stuart would bring about God's kingdom on Earth, and as Father Prado it seemed best to avoid further argument, so I merely murmured, 'God be praised.'

'May I ask you something, Prado, in confidence?' When I nodded, he leaned closer. 'What do you make of young Gifford?'

'Gifford?' I tried to keep my face pleasant, open; behind it, my thoughts were racing. 'A nervous disposition, but perhaps to be expected. He is inexperienced. From the little I know, I find him sincere.'

'You really think so?'

'Why – you do not?' I could feel sweat prickling between my shoulder blades; if Ballard suspected Gifford, we were both sunk. In his present state of nerves, Gilbert would not last five minutes with the priest without bleating everything.

'Something bothers me about this new letter from Mary,' he said, dropping his voice to a whisper. 'Perhaps I should not burden you with my misgivings, but I do not want to say anything to Babington yet, and as you are rooming with Gilbert . . . How did that come about, by the way?'

'I was told to make contact with him when I arrived,' I said blandly. 'Mendoza said only that Paget used him as a courier, and that he was reliable.'

'I hope he is right. And you haven't noticed anything suspicious about his behaviour?'

I shook my head. 'He strikes me as a devout young man. What is wrong with the letter?'

Ballard sucked in his cheeks. 'This postscript, where she asks the names of the gentlemen who will carry out the deed, and the means. It's most unlike Mary – she understands the dangers of committing too much detail to paper, in a way that Babington does not. And I think – though I can't be entirely sure – that it has been added after.'

'That is the nature of a postscript, is it not? Perhaps she thought of it at the last minute.'

'I meant, after the original letter was written. I think the ink is different.'

'That does not necessarily mean anything. If it was added some time after she finished the letter, she might have mixed new ink. The paper was sealed when it came to Babington?'

'True, but . . .' He pulled at his beard. 'Gifford was picked up by the authorities when he first arrived in England. Babington doesn't know, but I have my sources at the ports. They released him without charge, yet . . .' He pursed his lips.

'Then they must have had no reason to suspect him. It's not unusual for them to question young men coming out of France, I understand? I was certainly given a hard time by the searchers.'

'You're right. The unusual part is that his father was released from prison two days later. He'd been there a year for recusancy. Does that not seem a coincidence?'

'What does Gilbert say about it?'

'He says that his father's friends managed to raise the money to pay his fines. I don't know, Prado – perhaps I am seeing treachery everywhere. I had thought everything was unfolding beautifully, in God's ordained time, but that girl's death has thrown it all into disarray. If Gifford has been turned, then all our letters . . .' He stroked the plume of his hat between his fingers, his eyes to the floor, and for one absurd moment I genuinely wanted to reassure him.

'Forgive me for speaking bluntly, but from a limited acquaintance, I do not think young Gifford has the mettle to carry out such double-dealing. He would be too intimidated to lie to you.'

Ballard looked gratified. 'Yes, perhaps you're right. Thank you, brother. Listen – I have business to be getting on with – you don't mind if I leave you in the care of these women? You can get back across the river without any more trouble?'

'I'll do my best. And please forgive my foolishness – I can repay you—'

He waved this away again. 'Nonsense. And do not think I don't admire your dedication to God's work. But we must bend our minds to our true purpose now, and it will help no one if you draw attention to yourself. We will meet again tonight – I have a surprise for everyone.' He gave a broad wink and left me, less assured than I had been; in my present situation, surprises were not something to be relished.

I bathed and put on a clean shirt and a doublet and breeches of more modest grey wool that had been left for me by the maid. They had provided me with a tub of hot water in a chamber on the ground floor; when I emerged into the corridor, it was empty, though I caught the murmur of voices from behind closed doors. I found my way back to the main entrance and was about to leave when an idea struck me. As I was considering how best to put it into action, the maid appeared from the opposite passageway, carrying a bundle of linen.

'You done?' she asked.

'Yes – thank you.'

'Anything else?'

'I only wondered where I might find your Madam Rosa, to express my gratitude?'

She nodded back the way she had come. 'In her parlour, usually. But she's upstairs at the minute. You can wait outside if you want.'

I thanked her, and followed the direction of her gesture into another corridor, to find a door on my right with a rose painted on it. I tried the door and was surprised to find it opened easily into a small room with a desk, wooden chairs around a fireplace and a surfeit of embroidered cushions. A large, leather-bound book lay open on the desk and I made a discreet fist of victory; this was what I had hoped for. If Madam Rosa kept a ledger of when her rooms were occupied, it might provide the answer to one of the questions that had been niggling at me as I tried to imagine who could have lured Clara Poole to the Cross Bones in the first place. Ballard had seemed defensive the previous night when I asked him if he had landed in England that same day. There was only his word that he had not come back sooner, and though Walsingham had his watchers at the ports, it was all too easy for someone to slip ashore unobserved – an inlet or a creek on private land, a remote beach unseen by the boats that patrolled the coast.

Madam Rosa, for all her theatrical manner, was clearly a shrewd businesswoman: the ledger was set out neatly and clearly, with every transaction recorded, down to the last ha'penny of a tip. I flipped back through the pages, my eyes scanning rows of names – all of them false, I was sure – with the corresponding room numbers and precisely what services they had purchased. If I had had longer I might have stopped to marvel at activities I had not even considered people doing for pleasure, but time was pressing. I skipped back to the night of July 27th, and found what I was looking for: *Cap. Fort., Rm 9*. The only charges to his room were for supper – a guinea fowl, almond tart, cheese – and a pitcher of wine. It seemed he had at least told the truth about his vow of chastity. But not about his arrival in England; he must have caught the boat directly after his meeting with Paget and Mendoza in Paris. He had not only lied to his friends about his return, he had been in London – specifically in Southwark – the night Clara was killed.

I slammed the book shut and ducked out from behind the desk just as Madam Rosa sailed into the room and stopped short at the sight of me. Her eyes narrowed, but she quickly assumed her usual manner.

'Look at you, handsome, all lovely and clean – I bet you smell delicious.' She leaned into my neck and inhaled as if checking whether a joint of meat was done. 'Ooh, dear, I'll get myself in a lather. Did you want something?'

'My knife,' I said, 'and to offer you my thanks.' I bowed low and slipped a shilling into her hand as I raised it to my lips.

'Don't be daft,' she said, simpering, though she tucked away the shilling and told me as she returned my knife that I was welcome back there any time, with my lovely manners. But her sharp eyes stayed on me to the door.

SEVENTEEN

The stable boy at the Saracen's Head told me when I returned the horse that there was someone to see me inside. Among all the possibilities my mind had run through on the few yards to the tap-room, I had not expected Gifford; he sat at a table alone nursing a quart of small beer, his hands twined together and his eyes stricken.

'What's happened?' I asked, sliding on the bench opposite.

'You can't go back to Herne's Rents. There's a man waiting for you.'

A vision of Douglas flashed across my mind's eye, and my chest squeezed tight, even though I knew it was impossible he could have known I was in London. 'Who?'

'Not *you*. Prado, I mean. He's English, but he says you studied together at the seminary in Seville.'

I cursed softly in Italian, and then realised I must get into the habit of doing so in Spanish. 'Is he called Weston?'

Gifford's almost-invisible eyebrows shot up. 'Yes, that's it. William Weston. Do you know him?'

'No, obviously. But Prado does. *Mierda*.' I banged my fist against the table, not hard, but it made Gifford jump back and spill his beer. 'You didn't leave him in the room?' I thought with a jolt of panic about the instruments of my secret writing hidden in my bag.

'Of course not. I told him I had to go out. But he said he would wait outside the building for you. He seemed very excited about it. Can't wait to catch up, he says.'

'This is a complication we could have done without.'

'It's not the only one,' he said, trying to mop his shirt front with his sleeve. 'Babington came by earlier with a message from Ballard. We are all to meet tonight at the bear garden to discuss what happens next. He told me I should prepare to be on the road tomorrow with a letter to Mary. But he also said Ballard wants a word with me tonight. Why would he want that?' His voice rose to an unhappy squeak. 'He suspects me, I am sure of it.'

After my conversation with Ballard, I did not feel confident in contradicting him.

'Phelippes may have gone too far this time with his damned postscript,' I said. I pushed my hands through my hair, only to find most of it gone; I was still not used to this cropped appearance. 'He could have slipped that past Babington, but not Ballard. God, I hate the bear-baiting.'

'Me too. But it's a good place to hide in plain sight. Crowds of men, no one listening. There are always fights after, when people have lost money.' He exhaled hard through his nose and laid his hands flat on the table. 'We are going to be killed, Bruno, I know it. He has seen through us. We'll be knifed in the back and left in an alley, and everyone will think it was a brawl over a bet.'

'For God's sake!' I kicked him hard under the bench. 'Speak my name again in public and I'll knife you myself. If he has suspicions about that postscript, that's all they are. He has no evidence. Stay calm, and stick to your story. Get through tonight without doing anything stupid, and you'll be on your way to Staffordshire, out of his reach. You can leave the rest to me.'

Relief and anxiety struggled for mastery of his expression. 'What about this Weston?'

'Can't you tell him I'll call on him later?'

'I tried that, but he wouldn't say where he was lodging. Stands to reason, if he's a priest.'

'Then tell him to try again in a few days. Jesus, Gilbert – start thinking on your feet once in a while. I can't write your whole script for you.'

Gifford was about to protest when Dan Hammett passed our table and set down a pot of beer in front of me.

'That's more like it,' he said, nodding to my clothes. 'You should get some air when you've finished that,' he added casually, on his way to the kitchen, jerking a thumb in the direction of the yard. I guessed there must be a new message to collect.

'What happened to your fancy suit?' Gifford asked, only now noticing my appearance.

'I left them at the Unicorn.'

He blinked, taking this in. 'Why were you—?'

'Long story. Did you know, they've acquired a chest full of men's clothes there because sometimes customers behave with so little courtesy they get thrown out in the street before they've had a chance to get dressed, and they don't have the nerve to ask for their breeches back? Imagine.' I sat back and drained my cup. 'Now please get rid of this Weston, I have letters to write and I want to lie down on my bed. It's been a long day already and it's not even noon.'

Outside, the sun had broken through the lingering clouds and the yard was almost warm; beneath the dovecote on the far wall, a tabby cat stretched itself in a patch of light as if determined to make the most of England's feeble efforts at summer. Ben passed me, whistling, barely visible behind a saddle that was twice his width.

'Back in a tick,' he said, lumbering with his burden towards the stables. I strolled to the dovecote as if casually taking the air, bent to fuss over the cat, retrieved the paper hidden in the hole, and leaned against the wall to wait for Ben.

'You find that boy all right?' he asked, when he returned. 'Did you make him talk?'

'You make me sound like the Inquisition.'

'The what?'

'Never mind. I got some answers out of him, thank you.'

'That's got to be worth something?' He cocked his head to one side and grinned.

'God's blood, boy. I've already paid you for finding him.'

'But I found more than that.' When I didn't respond, he gave a theatrical shrug and made a show of walking away. 'Guess you don't want to know the secret, then.'

I called his bluff and left it until he had almost reached the corner of the building, waited for his expectant look, and beckoned him back. 'All right. Go on.'

He held out his grubby palm. 'A shilling.'

I laughed. 'Ben – even if you told me that boy is the bastard son of the Queen herself, it wouldn't be worth a shilling.'

'Sixpence, then. It's a good one, promise.' He kept his hand out, offering an impish smile. He didn't care about the price; the game was all in the bargaining. I fished in my doublet.

'You can have a groat.' I flicked it in the air and he dived forward and caught it with one deft hand, making it vanish somewhere in his clothes. 'This had better be worth it.'

He drew himself up as if about to make an important speech. 'That boy Joe, yeah? I asked around. Then I followed him.'

'You must have been up at the crack of dawn.'

'So was he. He runs errands for his mother. He takes herbs round the poor houses in all them streets round the back of the stews. She's a witch,' he added with relish.

'No she isn't. Was that the secret? I'll have my groat back if it was.'

He took a step back in case I was serious. 'No. That's

common knowledge. She makes potions for the whores to get rid of a baby, and another for the men to make their cock-stand last all night and if that's not witchery, you tell me what is.' He waited, defiant, for a contradiction. 'The secret is that while I was following that Joe, he stopped for a piss.'

'So?'

'He went down this alley to hide, right? And I followed because I didn't know that's what he was going to do, I wanted to see where he went. And he pulled down his breeches, so I thought he was going to take a shit, I almost left, didn't need to see that, *but* . . .' He paused for effect, his eyes wide.

'Yes?' I put enough impatience in my voice to let him know his groat was in jeopardy.

'He didn't. He has to piss squatting because he hasn't got a prick.'

'What?' I had not expected that.

'Yeah. I reckon he's one of them, you know – like the Turk has, to look after all his wives. They have their balls cut off so they can't do it. My dad told me about them.'

'A eunuch?'

'That's the one.' He examined his nails, a man of the world. Suddenly I saw it: Joe's slightness, his quick, delicate hands, Leila's angry remarks about the dangers of men.

'Right. Although the more likely explanation, Ben, is that Joe is a girl.'

He stared at me, as though something so mundane had not crossed his mind. 'Oh *yeah*. Don't blame her, in that case. I wouldn't want to be a girl, if I could choose. You just die having babies, like my ma.'

'Southwark,' I said wearily. 'His mother takes care of the women in the stews. They put girls to work there at eleven or younger – about the age Joe would be. No wonder she wanted to keep a daughter hidden.'

'She won't be able to do that forever,' he said, with a

knowing nod. 'Not once . . .' he made a gesture with both hands to indicate a generous pair of breasts.

'True. But don't you say anything. It's not your secret to sell. Except to me.'

The hand shot out. 'Give me sixpence and I'll consider the information sold to you in its entirety, no longer in my possession to profit from. I'll forget I ever knew it.'

I sighed and drew out another groat. 'I'm serious, Ben. This isn't a game, it's a child's safety at stake.'

He bit the coin ostentatiously to show me that we were two businessmen doing a deal, with no room for sentiment. 'She'll have to learn to look to her own safety, sooner or later,' he said as he left. 'Everyone else does in London.'

While I waited for Gifford to return, I borrowed a candle from Dan, found a spot around the back of the stable block on an upturned crate, away from prying eyes, heated the paper with the flame and read the new message from Phelippes. I had memorised the cipher by now, and though I could not read the encryption as quickly as Phelippes would have done, I was able to do it without needing to write the characters down. The cryptographer was no less curt in writing than in person:

To answer your questions in order, we have learned from XP:

1) He was instructed to send dispatches to Mendoza through the French embassy. They are expecting him, but will probably not make contact first. Even if they come looking for you, they have not met him before so you should be able to keep your cover.
2) William Weston is the superior of the Jesuits in England. He and Prado studied together for a time at the seminary in Seville. This is a problem we did not foresee. As far as we know, Weston is not involved in the conspiracy

and considers the order above such actions; but if he sees you, he may feel obliged to warn the conspirators that you are an imposter. In fact, it could work in our favour. We have been trying to catch Weston for two years, so you may be the lure to draw him out. If you learn his whereabouts, convey them immediately. Nota bene: He sees demons everywhere.

3) It may interest you to know that the remains of the wine in the bottle you found at the Cross Bones, from the Unicorn, contained a strong quantity of opium. Whether that was used to subdue CP prior to death cannot be established, but it would be reasonable to speculate. Do not mention this detail to RP – let him continue in his belief that the blood came from CP fighting off her attacker.
4) Information regarding Bess P very useful. We have someone watching her. We await further details.
5) No success yet with locket note. W wants your thoughts. Characters copied below.

I tore off the part of the paper where Phelippes had copied the four symbols from Clara's message, and held the candle flame to the rest of the letter until it caught, and his neat, cramped characters blackened and curled to a handful of ash in the air. Opium. There would be plenty of people who sold it in London, of course, but only one with such an obvious connection to the Unicorn. My mind jolted back to my conversation with Joe on our walk earlier: when the child had asked if someone would go to Hell for a deed they did not intend to cause harm, had he meant something connected to Clara Poole's death? Joe had told me they knew how to keep secrets in his family; I understood better now what he meant. I made myself go on thinking of Joe as 'he' to avoid slipping up. I wondered if he could have stolen or sold his mother's opium to make a few pennies, not knowing it would lead to a murder.

If that was his meaning, then he must know for certain that Clara had been drugged, which meant he must know her killer. I recalled his reaction that morning when he saw Ballard. Joe was scared of the priest, that much was clear, but did it have anything to do with the child's fear of going to Hell for this unnamed deed?

I rubbed my hands across my face. My head was swimming with too many questions, and lack of sleep to consider them with any clarity. For answers, I would have to return to Southwark. Leila would not willingly tell me if she or Joe were selling opium, but at least now I had some leverage I could use on her; I knew the truth about Joe, though I would not endear myself to her by using it as a threat. I needed to ask Phelippes where they had imprisoned her father-in-law, Goodchild, the old watchman; I sensed that favours would work better than pressure with a woman like Leila. She would laugh at any attempt to coerce her, and then aim her crossbow at my balls. I found I was intrigued by the prospect of seeing her again, though I could picture the scorn in her dark eyes if I tried to persuade her to say anything that would put her or her child in danger. It was my curse, I thought, to be interested only in fierce, difficult women, and Leila had a fire in her belly that I guessed was kindled from struggle, like my Sophia.

Ridiculous: she was not mine. I wondered where she was at that moment, how she was bearing the tedium of Lady Grace Cavendish's company, and a thought struck me. Phelippes's note said they had someone watching Bessie Pierrepont – could he have meant Sophia? Had Walsingham recruited her already? There was no way for me to find out; I doubted Phelippes would tell me anything if I enquired, and it would be difficult to arrange a meeting in my guise as Father Prado. But thinking of her consumed me with a longing to see her that I felt sharp as a cramp in my gut, and I decided I would ask Ben to take a message to her. He would barter with me, but I thought he could be trusted. I closed my eyes and leaned my head against the wall, allowing the sun to warm my face, recalling the way she had looked at me during that encounter in the street outside the playhouse, and how quickly she had retreated when she thought I was brushing her off.

I must have dozed; in what seemed like only a heartbeat I found myself shaken by the shoulder and opened my eyes to see Robin Poole looming over me.

'Nice that someone has time for dreaming,' he said.

'I was *thinking*. How did you know I was here?'

'Gilbert said you'd be skulking around the Saracen's somewhere. I've just come from your rooms – Weston's gone for now, but he's left you a note. I thought you and I should catch up. Will you walk with me?'

We strolled back westwards over the Holborn bridge, away from the City, towards the Inns of Court. The clouds had almost dispersed and a volley of birdsong burst from the trees; the usual surliness and head-down jostling I had come to expect of Londoners in the street appeared temporarily replaced by a common goodwill, people bidding one another good day as they passed, a number of them actually smiling.

'So my sister's death is now public,' Poole said, looking straight ahead, his voice expressionless. 'The official story given out is that she was distributing alms to the poor women of Southwark when she was set upon and robbed. If anyone asks, they will say they are holding a man in custody on suspicion of killing her.'

'Which man?'

'That watchman who found her. Walsingham can kill two birds with one stone that way – stop the old man spreading gossip about what he saw, and keep the public quiet with news of an arrest.'

'But they know he didn't do it. Surely Walsingham wouldn't let him go to the gallows?'

'They reason that if they hold him until the next assizes, they'll have Babington's lot rounded up by then and the rest of London will have forgotten about Clara. It's not like she was anyone important,' he added with venom. 'There'll be a dozen more dead girls in Southwark for people to talk about by the time he's due for trial.'

'At least now you'll be able to bury her,' I said, trying to sound reassuring.

'Oh, he's already dealt with that.' His voice shook with quiet anger. 'Put her in a nice little plot way out of the city, in Canonbury. He'll pay for a handsome memorial, he says, once this is all over, as if that will be recompense.' He broke off and shook his head, mastering himself. I pitied him again for having to hide his sorrow.

'Do you know where the old watchman is being held?' I asked.

'In the Tower. I suppose they want to stop him talking to anyone. Why?'

'He has a family who are worrying about him. Remember that boy who stole your horse?'

'Ballard's horse.' He made a face. 'I still haven't told him she was stolen. I'd like to get my hands on that little fucker. What about him?'

'He's the watchman's grandson. And listen – I think he might know something about the murder. He was in the Cross Bones that night.'

'Really?' He stopped walking and turned to me, his face more animated than I had seen him. 'You think he saw who she was meeting? Where can I find him?'

I held up a hand in restraint. 'Let me see if I can get him to tell me. He's scared, obviously. It needs to be handled delicately.'

'I wasn't planning to beat it out of him.'

'No, but you're . . .' Desperate, I wanted to say. There was a blaze in his eyes; for all his skilled dissembling, I feared his suppressed grief and rage was close to the surface. 'I think I have a means to persuade him.'

'Huh. Persuade him to give that fucking horse back while you're there. And whatever else he stole from my sister's body.'

'What will you do if we find out which of them killed her?' I asked, curious.

He looked away. 'Nothing I can do for the moment,' he said, after a long pause. 'The operation comes first, you know that. I must bide my time. Can you begin to imagine what it's been like for me, to sit around a table with them, catching the eye of each one in turn, wondering which of them could have—' He broke off and we continued walking in silence. 'When I know who it was,' he said with quiet determination, as we approached the junction with Chancery Lane, 'I don't want to kill him. He'll die the cruellest death anyway, once the Privy Council's finished with him, they all will, and I won't even go and watch. It wouldn't bring her back. All I want is for him to understand what he's taken from me.'

It struck me as a brave sentiment. I wanted to make some gesture of sympathy – a squeeze of the shoulder, a touch of his arm – but I didn't know him well enough and I sensed that pity wouldn't be welcome.

'And you definitely don't think it could have been Ballard?' I said, instead.

He gave me a sharp look. 'Why – do you have reason to think otherwise?'

'I've found out that he was in London the night she died, and he's lied to the rest of you about it. And the boy from the Cross Bones evidently knows him, and is afraid of him.'

'The boy told you that?'

'I witnessed it for myself. This morning he came face to face with Ballard and turned tail as if he'd seen the Devil.'

'I don't blame him. Ballard makes me want to turn and run most of the time. What – you think the boy might have seen him in the graveyard that night, and fear Ballard knows it?'

'I can't work it out. Ballard knew the boy had been in the Cross Bones and seen her body. But if Ballard killed Clara and feared there was a witness, I don't think that boy would be walking around freely. There's clearly some connection between them, though, and not a happy one.'

'What were you doing in Southwark this morning, anyway?' he asked.

'Just nosing around.'

'So Walsingham has asked you to look into her death.' His mouth pressed into a grim line. When I didn't answer, he merely nodded. 'Good of him to tell me. I wonder what he thinks you could bring that I could not.'

'Distance, I suppose.'

'Huh.' He glanced away, as if to restrain himself from any unguarded comment. 'You'll tell me, won't you, if you discover anything? I can't shake this feeling that he's keeping something from me. Him and Phelippes.'

'I'll let you know anything that might be useful.'

He gave a thin smile. 'But you still get to decide what would be useful for me to know about my own sister's death.' I saw him bite back a further comment. 'Well – I will be in your debt for any information. But forgive me if I continue to pursue it in my own way.'

I could say nothing to that; it was not for me to tell him I was in charge of finding his sister's murderer. It surprised me that the gossip of the Southwark stews about what had been done to her had not reached him; perhaps, now that she was buried, it could be dismissed as gruesome speculation. I would continue to deny any knowledge of the details if he ever asked.

'We could look around together later,' he suggested. 'Babington sent word to say we are meeting tonight at the bear garden, at seven. It seems Ballard has some new plan in mind.'

'I suppose this could all be over soon,' I said. 'Our job is to learn the means and the time when they intend to assassinate the Queen, so she can be forewarned, and have it set in writing to bring in evidence against them. If Ballard decides that tonight and Babington puts it explicitly in a letter to Mary, surely Walsingham can move to arrest them as soon as Gilbert hands it to him?' The thought that I might only have to play Prado for another day or so filled me with relief, and at the same time a melancholy sense of anticlimax; if it was all over so quickly, would my contribution be significant enough to have earned the reward of the Queen's patronage?

'I don't know.' Poole shrugged. 'Walsingham may want to wait until there is an unequivocal reply in Mary's hand giving the new plan her blessing. That could take another couple of weeks, for Gifford to ride to Staffordshire and back.'

'Ballard will not wait two weeks,' I said. 'He's champing at the bit – the fear of arrest has made him abandon caution. He reasons if he is to be caught, he will take the Queen down with him.'

'You may be right. Well, we shall learn more tonight. One thing is certain,' he added, as he turned towards Chancery Lane, 'it will never be over for me. I didn't even get to see her.'

As I watched him walk briskly away, I couldn't help thinking how wise Walsingham had been to keep him away from Clara's body; I doubted his restraint would have survived if he had seen that face. I made my way back to Herne's Rents turning over in my mind what her killer had done, and why; I felt sure there must be something I was not seeing. I considered again that it would have taken an unusual degree of emotion, or its absence, to stave in a woman's face so thoroughly, even if she were already dead or sedated. Either way, it would have taken time to butcher her like that; if the man knew the Cross Bones well enough to have chosen it for murder, he would likely have known that the old watchman would be about, and perhaps Joe too, and yet he had risked being caught by staying to cut off the girl's hair, as well as mutilate her face. This was not a killing of necessity; it was a statement, or an act of vengeance, or love warped into hatred. And what of the parts he had severed? Easy enough to throw gristle to a street dog. But the hair: I thought of Madam Rosa and her terrible wig. Robin had told me Clara had long, auburn curls – exactly the kind of hair most valuable to wig-makers wanting to imitate the Queen's look. I could try enquiring at wig shops to see if a man had brought in that kind of hair to sell in the past couple of days, but that could take weeks, and the killer might have had the sense to wait until any fuss about the dead girl had died down before approaching buyers.

One thing was certain: I needed to visit Leila and Joe again to ask about the opium. Perhaps I could slip away from the conspirators after the bear-baiting, before I was pressed into visiting the sick for another night. I wondered if I could persuade Ben to come; not that I was afraid of walking the streets of Southwark alone, but it might be useful to have someone looking out for me, even if it was only a boy with a fruit knife.

EIGHTEEN

The sky was clear as we approached the arena from Falcon Stairs, while the bells of nearby St Mary Overy rang the hour of seven. Evening light softened the curved whitewashed wall of the bear pit at Paris Garden. This was not my first visit; three years ago I had ended up here during my involvement with what had become known at the English court as the Throckmorton Plot, after the last young Catholic gentleman who believed he and his friends could replace Elizabeth Tudor with Mary Stuart and bring England back to Rome. On that occasion, I had found myself hunting someone through the bear pit late at night, the stands dark and empty and the animals all locked away. Now, despite the chattering crowds and the exuberance of a summer evening, the sharp stink of blood and animal excrement brought that memory rushing back – the stumbling pursuit in the dark, the heart-racing fear for my life. My skin prickled and I worked to suppress a shudder, hoping Babington and Gifford would not notice. One sideways glance at Gifford as we approached the gates told me that was the least of my concerns; the boy was in no state to worry about anyone else's behaviour. This was partly my fault. I had returned to Herne's Rents intending to write again to Phelippes; though I only meant to close my eyes for a few moments, sleep had landed on me like a hammer blow and I had lost two hours, during which Gifford had taken himself to a tavern. Furious with him – but more with myself – I had made him eat some bread and cold beef before we met Babington to head south, but the boy was still shaky and the boatman had almost refused to take us across the river, seeing his green face. Now I would have to make sure I watched him all evening, and as far as possible keep him from being alone with Ballard in his present state, or we were both sunk.

The atmosphere at Paris Garden reminded me of the theatre, but with a greater edge of menace. Though the gentry came in their finery to see the spectacle, crossing the churned-up ground outside the building on wooden walkways laid down to keep their soft leather shoes from the mud, the majority of the crowd were working men in shirtsleeves, loud and full of beer, jingling their coins for the bookmakers who gathered around the entrance, taking bets and handing out tokens. I saw fathers with young sons hoisted on their shoulders, and groups of apprentices egging each other on to catcall the Winchester geese who inevitably flocked to the bear ring; there was a raw male energy on show here, good-natured enough for the moment, but ready to tip into a fight if more drink was taken and fortune didn't smile on their wagers. Gifford was right: there would be brawls later, and it would be easy for someone to end up with a knife in the ribs. I recalled the gleam in Ballard's eye earlier when he had spoken of having a surprise for us this evening; I sincerely hoped Gifford had been wrong about the nature of it.

We hovered around the jostling queue at the gates, waiting for the others, watching as the wealthier patrons were allowed to pass the crowd and enter separately through a private door. A woman in a green silk gown and pearl-studded hood, lifting the hem of her skirts with one hand, glanced nervously up at the wooden stands where people were already taking their seats. She had cause to look anxious; only three years earlier, a bank of seats at the bear ring had collapsed, killing a number of spectators. The more puritanical among the city's aldermen had suggested it was God's punishment for putting on the entertainment on a Sunday, but Queen Elizabeth had vetoed any change to the law – she was a great lover of the bear-baiting. The arena had been rebuilt, but for some time afterwards people kept away from the tiered seating out of superstition. I hoped that Ballard would keep us on the ground to discuss business – though how he hoped to convey secret plans above the roars from the crowd and the volley of barking from the mastiffs was anyone's guess.

Babington had been unusually quiet on the walk from Herne's Rents, and now stood with his hands on his hips, casting his eyes around uncertainly as if fearful of seeing an unwelcome face in the crowd. Gifford kept his gaze on his shoes, arms wrapped around his shoulders, trying to hold himself together. Ballard may have thought it a good ruse to hide in plain sight, but a sense of unease had infected the group since the announcement of Clara's murder. It was left to me to keep the conversation going.

'Did you hear any more news about the girl?' I asked. With some effort, Babington pulled his attention back.

'Ballard says it is Clara Poole, for certain. It's being given out that she was attacked by thieves while distributing alms among the destitute in Southwark, and they have a man arrested for her murder.'

'Who?'

'No one we know. The old man who found her. Which as good as confirms that her death is being covered up by the authorities—' he broke off and bit the side of his thumb, his eyes flitting from side to side. 'And yet Ballard thinks it a good idea for us to meet in the most public place in London, where we might be apprehended all together, without warning.'

'You do not agree with Ballard's judgement, then?' I asked. Gifford raised his head and looked from me to

Babington, roused from his self-absorption by the turn of the conversation.

'Ballard has nothing to lose,' Babington muttered. 'He has no name, no family, no estate or dependants to think about. Easy for someone like him to hurl himself headlong at martyrdom.' He glanced sideways at me. 'Saving your presence – I know you came to help us at his urging, but now that Clara is dead, that changes everything.'

'You think the plan should be abandoned?'

'You heard what I think last night. Postponed, at the very least, until we learn how much is known. I think Ballard will not be persuaded to caution. He will say there are too many wheels in motion to change course now. But what he proposes – to rush to execution of the Tudor, with no back-up in place – it's madness.'

'And yet you all do as he says, even if it will end on the scaffold. Why?'

He turned and looked at me directly. 'You've met him. There is a force about him, a conviction – I can't explain it. When he talks of bringing England back to God, and righting the country's ills – he makes you believe it. He carries you with him, like a prophet.'

'And I thought you English were so cold and reasonable,' I said. I smiled, to show the remark was meant in good humour, but Babington's frown hardened.

'Most of us are better at talking than action, it's true. I've been in Paris among the exiles, I've sat in alehouses and listened while angry young men rail against the Tudor and her government. I've been one of them. But that is *all* they do. You know what I mean, Gilbert.' Gifford nodded miserably. 'It's what the English do best,' Babington continued, 'sitting over a pot of beer complaining about all that is wrong with the country. Ballard is one who truly wants to *do* something. When I first met him, he made me ashamed for my apathy. That's why I threw my lot in with him, gave my father's money. But now I fear his passion outweighs his reason.'

I thought of Ballard the night before, handing out food to the men in Paul's churchyard, risking his life to take the sacraments to the poor. I did not doubt the priest's sincerity, or his desire to do good, but Babington was right: he was willing to burn everything down around him to achieve his vision of a better England.

'So the English are capable of passion,' I said.

'Contrary to popular belief,' he replied, still not smiling. 'Most of us learn to keep it battened down.' He left a pause, in which I thought he might elaborate, but he turned away and scanned the milling spectators again.

'Well, I am sorry for the girl's death, God rest her soul,' I said, 'and not just because of what it will mean for your plans. It is hard to lose a comrade. Especially hard for her brother, poor man.'

At that, he turned to look me in the eye with an expression of such tenderness that I revised my earlier opinion of him; he was clearly struggling to hold back genuine grief. 'Yes,' he said, nodding vigorously and laying a hand on my arm, 'thank you. I don't think I have fully grasped the import of her loss. And Robin – what he must be feeling. To live through this again.' He shook his head briskly and I saw the shine of tears in his eyes. 'We always knew that one of us might be taken, and what it would mean to be questioned. We never supposed it would be Clara.'

'What do you mean, again?' I asked. Before he could answer, Gifford dug me in the ribs.

'Here they come. And Ballard has brought a couple of – oh my God.' His mouth hung open. I followed the direction of his gaze and saw Ballard, dressed in an assemblage of fruit-coloured silks under his gold lace cape, with what appeared to be a courtesan on each arm; two young women in long cloaks and low-cut dresses, their hair piled high on their heads with scarves and combs, cheap gaudy jewellery clinking between their breasts. They wore so much make-up that it took me a moment to realise what Gifford had seen as soon as they appeared – under the face paint and the whore's disguise, it was Bessie Pierrepont and Sophia Underhill, or Mary Gifford, as I must remember to call her. Behind them came Jack Savage, his jacket open to reveal the knife at his belt to anyone who cared to look, and at his side, Robin Poole, his face drawn and pale.

Ballard appeared to be enjoying the charade a little too much; I had to fight to keep my countenance as he slipped a hand around Sophia's waist and squeezed her, making her squeal playfully, and Gifford looked ready to explode with fury when he did the same to Bessie. I trod firmly on his foot as a warning, but he barely noticed.

'Gentlemen!' Ballard was in full Captain Fortescue mode. 'I told you I had a surprise for you, and am I not as good as my word?' When no one spoke, he patted the girls on their behinds and pushed them forwards, beckoning the rest of us closer into a huddle. 'These lovely ladies may look like Winchester geese, but nothing could be further from the truth – they are chaste and pious gentlewomen and friends to the Queen's cause.'

Bessie Pierrepont darted a coy look at Babington from beneath her lashes and bobbed a curtsy. 'Hello, Anthony. I was delighted to hear from you after all this time. I thought you had quite forgotten me now that you're a married man.'

Babington smiled, and for an instant I caught something in his expression that looked almost like disgust, before his good breeding smoothed over it and he bowed low.

'Bessie – I knew we could count on your discretion and your wits. I will forbear from observing that you have grown into a handsome woman, since I imagine you hear that from every man you meet.'

The girl acknowledged this with a self-satisfied smile. 'But since I was old enough to receive compliments from men, there was only one whose opinion ever mattered,' she said, batting her lashes at him as if her living really did depend on it. Beside me, Gifford made a small noise of indignation in the back of his throat; I pressed on his toes with my boot heel again. 'And this is my friend Mary, whose loyalty I vouch for with my life.'

Sophia gave a graceful curtsy and looked around the company; her gaze locked with mine for the fleetest moment before sliding away as if we had never met. 'I will serve your cause, gentlemen, however I may.'

Babington regarded her coldly. 'I could not have been clearer in my message, Bessie, that you must speak to no one of this.'

'Yes, but you are asking me a favour, Anthony, and quite a dangerous one, not giving me orders, so you must let me decide how best to help you.' Bessie flicked a lock of hair over her shoulder as if there were no more to argue. 'Now – are you going to introduce me to your friends? Captain Fortescue I know, and these good gentlemen I have just met' – she indicated Poole and Savage – 'but who are these? I wish to know who I am trusting myself to with such an undertaking.' She turned the full dazzle of her smile on me and Gifford in turn, affecting not to notice that he had turned puce and was opening and closing his mouth like a fish. So she was not acknowledging her acquaintance with Gifford in public. Their furtive manner at the playhouse had suggested as much.

'Master Gilbert Gifford, of Staffordshire,' Ballard said, pointing; Bessie's gaze skimmed over him with a polite nod and came to rest on me. 'And Señor Xavier Prado, a cloth merchant from Spain.' He gave an extravagant wink as he said this.

I bowed low and kissed her hand; she giggled. 'Cloth merchant, is it? Perhaps I shall have to buy some of your wares to have a new dress made – there seems to be hardly anything of this one. I'm amazed they don't freeze to death, these Winchester girls.' She tugged at her bodice, which had inched even lower. I looked away as primly as I could and caught Sophia's eye again; at her infinitesimally raised eyebrow it was all I could do not to laugh.

'Where is Titch?' Babington asked.

Ballard looked around as if he might have misplaced him along the way. 'I thought he was coming with you?'

'No. His lodgings are nearer yours – I thought you would call for him.'

'There must have been a misunderstanding. No matter, he knows where to find us. Now . . .' he dropped his voice to a whisper and we all gathered closer to hear him, 'I have spent this afternoon sounding out young Mistress Pierrepont here on our proposal, and for the sake of the true Queen and true religion, she is persuaded to be God's instrument.'

No one spoke. Bessie allowed her gaze to travel around the company; the twist of her mouth suggested she had expected a more enthusiastic reception.

'It is no small thing you ask of me, gentlemen,' she said, a little ruffled. 'I would like to feel that I have your full confidence.'

'How will you do it?' Savage asked, evidently put out that he had been displaced as assassin.

'It would have to be untraceable,' Bessie said, affecting an expert air, as if she dealt with such matters all the time. 'Something slipped into her drink at night, I think, so that by morning it will be thought she took a seizure or some such sudden illness.'

'And you are in a position to administer this without being caught?' Savage sounded sceptical.

'This week I have been off duty and staying with my aunt, Lady Cavendish, at her house on the Strand, but on Sunday I return to Whitehall, to the Tudor's Privy Chambers. I am confident I can find the opportunity. I am trusted by Elizabeth, for the sake of my family name, and for my good service.'

'Where would you get such a poison?' Savage demanded. He seemed determined to find a weakness in this new plan.

'I will take care of that,' Ballard said. 'There is a woman at the Unicorn here on Bankside who has a skill with herbal preparations unrivalled by anything I have seen on my travels. For the right price I'm sure she could make something that fits our purpose.'

'And this woman would not ask questions about why you wanted to buy a deadly potion?' I said.

Ballard let out a hearty guffaw and slapped me on the back. 'My dear friend, we are talking of the Unicorn. People know better than to ask impertinent questions. Besides, this woman is in my debt – she will keep her mouth shut.'

I nodded. It was clear he meant Leila; I wondered what debt she could owe Ballard, and whether it had anything to do with Joe's reaction to seeing the priest that morning.

'So there is the how. The bigger question is, why?' I said.

Bessie fixed me with a look that would turn milk. 'Excuse me?'

I glimpsed the displeasure in Ballard's expression, as I felt the others' eyes on me.

'Out of nowhere, these men approach you with such an extraordinary request – one which, as you say, will put you in significant danger. Why would you agree?'

Her gaze narrowed; she was used to flattery from men, not scrutiny.

'I'm sorry – who are you, again?'

Ballard laid a hand on her arm and softened his voice. 'You may trust him, for all his blunt ways. He is only being careful of his interests.'

'Huh.' She tilted her chin at me with disdain. 'It's a little thing called loyalty. Anthony knows my affection for the Queen of Scots goes back many years. I knew her as a child, and loved her then. She sewed a gown for me when I was four years old, and to this day I keep it in a chest.' She smiled around the company, and appeared to realise that this did not mean much to a group of men. 'I would not have dared take such a risk on my own, naturally, but to learn that such gentlemen as yourselves have plans so advanced, and to think I might play my part . . .' She laid a palm flat on her breast and paused, as if overcome. 'Of course, I was unprepared, and the idea frightened me at first. But I have prayed on the matter since talking to Ballard, and I am sure of God's hand in the enterprise – for the love I bear the Queen, how could I refuse to serve?'

Ballard nodded approval. I could not work Bessie out; there was such artifice in her manner that if I had been a genuine conspirator, I would have wanted better proof of her allegiance. But perhaps she always came across as if she were overacting, and her intentions were entirely sincere. Ballard was clearly so desperate to hasten the assassination that he was willing to accept her ready agreement without further questions, and the others – though they looked uneasy – seemed to believe that his judgement was good enough. I would have to ask Sophia what she thought, if I found a chance to speak to her alone.

'And your friend?' I pressed, stealing a glance at Sophia.

'I have made Mistress Gifford my confidante because she is also a true believer – aren't you, Mary? She lived among the exiles in Paris. And because her life is so dull, poor Mary.' Bessie patted Sophia's arm in sympathy. 'Besides, I shall need someone to carry messages to you once I am back on duty – I cannot be seen to be meeting men when I am out of this disguise.'

Sophia cast her eyes down sadly, as if acknowledging the tedium of her life and her gratitude to her friend. I had to admit she was playing her part well – as if I didn't already know her skill at dissembling.

'I had not thought we were in the business of providing entertainment for bored girls,' Savage said, not bothering to disguise his contempt.

'Do not condescend to us, Master Savage,' Bessie said, drawing herself up, her expression making clear what she thought of men like him. 'We are not silly girls. Mary here speaks three languages, including Latin and Greek.'

'Oh, well then,' Savage said, 'I can't think how we have managed without her.'

'Come now, Jack,' Ballard turned to him with his most reassuring expression. 'We serve a common purpose here, let us not bicker among ourselves. When the Almighty closes one door, he opens another. Without Mistress Pierrepont we have no hope of getting close to our target in the immediate future, and all will have been in vain. She is the answer to our prayers.'

I glanced at Gifford, knowing his prayers with regard to Bessie; he looked as if he might be sick at any moment.

'And have you decided when the deed shall be done?' I asked Ballard.

'We will discuss this further inside.' He glanced up at the sky. 'I think we should not wait for Titch – he can find us when he arrives. The first bear is due any minute and we will be more noticeable as a group if we have to walk through the spectators to take our seats once it has started. Come, ladies – you are playing your roles admirably, I must say.'

He held out an arm to Bessie and Sophia and set off towards the entrance, where the queue had dwindled; the others made to follow him. Gifford glanced over his shoulder and shot me a look of pure panic. Perhaps his fear transmitted to me; I watched Ballard's back with the sudden sensation that my doublet was too tight, that my chest was constricted and I couldn't breathe in enough air. I babbled an excuse of relieving myself and told them to go on without me, then stumbled around to the far side of the arena, where a patch of grass faced the river, separated from the bank by a low wooden fence. Away from the crowd I leaned on the rail to steady myself and breathed deeply, inhaling dank river air. I had experienced again that feeling of the ground rushing up to meet me, as I had looked around the group and thought of all the cross-currents of deception at play: Gifford and Bessie pretending not to know one another; likewise Gifford and Sophia; me and Sophia, affecting to have met for the first time (and I the only one there who knew her real name); Bessie's motives unknown, and Gifford, Poole and I, all working to convince the conspirators that we were loyal comrades, while each of us watched the others for any hint of a slip that might lead all three of us to our deaths. I had felt like one of those jongleurs who string a rope tight between two trees in the marketplace and walk its length; I asked one once in Paris how he did it, and he said the trick was to keep moving and not look down. I had been in danger of looking down a moment ago, and for the space of a heartbeat the sensation had terrified me.

I was trying to calm my breathing when a pair of hands clamped over my eyes. With the speed of reflex, I whipped out the knife from my belt and spun to thrust its point at the belly of my assailant before I even had time to process what I was doing. She let out a small yelp and jumped back, checking to see if I had stabbed her.

'Jesus, Sophia!' My blood was drumming in my ears. 'You can't sneak up on people like that, I could have run you through. That would take some explaining to your new friends.'

'Good to know that would be your greatest concern.' She smiled, but I could see I had frightened her. 'Sorry. I forgot how jumpy you are. Though I suppose it makes sense in the circumstances. *Señor Prado*.'

'You should stay alert too, *Mary*, since you are about to become an accessory to regicide.'

'Ah, but that's what I came to tell you.' She clutched at my sleeve, her face lit up with an excitement I had not seen in a long time. 'I have a new job.'

'So I see.' I indicated the low-cut dress and the jewellery. 'Have you made much profit so far?'

She slapped my arm with the back of her hand. 'Isn't it awful? I feel naked – all those men staring and making comments. But Bessie said we could not go to the bear garden and meet Babington's group as ourselves, people would talk. I think she just wanted to dress up – she's having the time of her life.' She smiled. 'A dozen men have asked her how much, and each time she says "More than you make in a year, sweetheart" in this terrible accent, and doubles over laughing. It's a pity she was born to the nobility, she'd have made an excellent living. Alas, I don't have her assets.' She glanced down ruefully at her small breasts. 'I'd probably starve if I had to rely on these.'

'Your assets are beyond price,' I said, and realised, from the way she looked at me, that I had spoken with too much feeling. I quickly changed my tone. 'So what is your new job, if not the one you are dressed for?'

She drew me with her into the shadow of the wall and bent to whisper; I felt all my muscles tense as she leaned against me. 'Same as yours.'

'So you're a priest?'

'No. Spy.' She spoke so close that her cheek brushed mine and her lips touched my ear. My mouth had dried. She took a step back and looked at me to see the effect. 'A man came to find me. Sandy hair, pock-marked face. I thought he was so strange at first, he talked as if he had learned how to speak from a book, but not how to put expression into his words.'

'I know him.'

'I know you do – he told me. And he explained all this—' she waved a hand in the direction of the bear pit, to indicate Babington and the others. 'He said they needed a trusted person to watch Bessie, and that the Queen's life could depend on it.'

Her eyes widened with the thrill of it; I recalled how important I had felt when Walsingham had first asked me to join the Queen's service. Somehow her excitement provoked a cold jealousy in me.

'That was an exaggeration. They have plenty of people

watching this plot – he wouldn't leave you responsible for the Queen's safety.'

'Oh.' She looked briefly disappointed. 'Well, anyway – I was glad to be of use. They want me to search Bessie's room, make copies of any letters I find, win her confidence and report back anything she says about Mary Stuart, or any lover. Beats sewing cushion covers with Lady Grace.' She mimed putting a noose around her own neck and I laughed, feeling ashamed of my desire to belittle her. 'He said they will try to find me a place in the Queen's household so I can continue to report on Bessie next week – can you imagine? Me, in the palace of Whitehall!'

I felt obscurely cheated; if she was absorbed into the Queen's entourage, it would be impossible for me to see her. And beneath that, a petulant, childish objection: I had shown my service to Queen Elizabeth several times now, at great risk to my life – where was my place at court, if Walsingham could hand them out so easily when it suited him? I reminded myself that Sophia's elevation to royal servant would only be a temporary measure, until the conspiracy was fully uncovered and dealt with.

'Is that why you agreed? Because you are tired of sewing cushions?'

'No – though if you think that would not be reason enough, I can only suppose you have never embroidered a cushion in the company of the most boring woman in England. But you will not guess what else he said.' She grasped my hands in hers this time, barely able to keep the smile from her face.

'I'm sure I won't – tell me,' I said, knowing exactly what she was going to say.

'He promised they would find my son,' she whispered, her voice cracking with emotion. 'They know everything, these people, you'd be amazed. Though I suppose you know already. But this man, Thomas, told me they had started making enquiries. If I help them, they will help me.'

'That is wonderful news,' I said, squeezing her hand. It was not for me to point out that she had little prospect of gaining access to the boy, even if they found him; she looked so happy and hopeful. 'But – be careful, Sophia.'

Her face fell. 'You think they are false?'

'I think they're good at making promises when they want something.' I was considering how much more to say – conscious, too, that I was doing this to demonstrate my greater knowledge and experience in Walsingham's service – when I glanced over her shoulder and saw, unmistakably, weaving through the last remaining stragglers on this side of the building, the figure of Archibald Douglas. 'Kiss me,' I hissed.

Sophia frowned. 'God's sake, Bruno – I thought we had moved beyond that—'

'I need to hide my face. Now.'

Before she could protest, I pushed her urgently against the wall of the bear pit and kissed her; she resisted at first, and then I felt her subside and give in to it. Her mouth yielded and she began to respond with her tongue, one hand hooked around the back of my neck, the other at my hip, pulling me into her, and there was no pretence in it; I forgot Douglas as she arched against me and I ran a hand over her breast and slipped my thumb inside her bodice, feeling her nipple harden. She moaned into my mouth and moved her hand down to my breeches; God knows how we would have proceeded if we hadn't been interrupted by a sudden outburst of barking from inside the ring, followed by a loud cheer from the crowd. The show had started. She pulled back and we stared at one another, breathing hard, half-amazed by the sudden force of our desire.

'Has he gone?' she whispered.

'Who?'

'Whoever you were hiding from.'

'No idea.' I couldn't take my eyes from hers for long enough to look around; it no longer seemed important.

She ran her hand down the side of my face, brushed her thumb over my lips, gave me a soft smile and said,

'That'll be five shillings.'

She told me, laughing, that I could pay her next time; I said she could send word to me at the Saracen's Head. Even the suggestion that it could happen again was enough to lift my spirits. Despite the dance she had led me these past three years, she wanted me, I was sure; you don't kiss someone that way if you're indifferent. All my earlier anxieties about Ballard and the rest struck me as trivial now; I felt invincible. I stood facing the wall after she had gone, leaning on one hand, adjusting my breeches with the other, trying to bend my thoughts back to the evening's business. I could not return to the others until I could be sure it was not obvious what I had been doing; it would hardly inspire confidence if Father Prado looked as if he had been grappling with a woman round the back of the bear pit. I closed my eyes, picturing again Sophia's upturned face, her parted lips, and what I would have liked to have done, when the cold edge of a blade pressed against the soft skin beneath my ear and my whole body shrank from it.

'Hello, old pal,' said a Scots voice, still familiar after three years. 'Fancy running into you. Seems only yesterday we were last here.'

'Douglas.' I didn't bother to open my eyes. All I could do was wait.

'Didn't like to interrupt you just now,' he said conversationally. 'Seems unsporting to cut a man's throat while all his blood has rushed to his breeches. Perhaps I should wait for your cockstand to go down.'

'Oh, it's gone,' I said through my teeth.

'Aye, I have that effect. That was a tasty little whore you had there – why didn't you stay and finish the job? Maybe I'll give her a try later on – she looked like she'd be dirty enough for anything.'

At that I brought the arm leaning against the wall sharply back in a fist; I would have caught a less practised fighter on the jaw, but Douglas was quick enough to dodge. I turned and felt a warm trickle on the side of my neck where the movement had caused the tip of his knife to nick my skin.

'Now see what you've done,' he said, as if he was disappointed in me. He tucked the blade close to my ribs, just below my heart. 'I wasn't going to hurt you if you were a good boy. So she's your special whore. That's useful to know.'

'She's not a whore,' I said, before I realised I should have kept my mouth shut.

'Oh, I know that. She was with the Pierrepont girl at The Curtain the other night, the first time I saw you, before you got your smart haircut and shave. Come on, Bruno – you should know better than to underestimate me.'

'Have you been *following* me?'

'Obviously. You're terribly careless – it's lucky I didn't want to kill you. I could have done,' he added, off-hand.

'I thought that was exactly what you wanted.'

He laughed. 'Of course not. Revenge is for petty men. You and I are bigger than that. I knew there would be something interesting afoot if you were back in town, and I wasn't wrong.' But he kept the knife where it was. 'I'm curious about your new friends, though. You can't keep away from Mary Stuart's admirers, can you? Wherever there's a plot to break the old girl out of prison, there you are in the middle of it.'

'So you know them.'

'I know *of* them. Your pal Walsingham's not the only one with informers in France.'

'Who are you working for these days?'

'My own advantage, as always. Just like you. Tell me, do your new friends know who pays you? Do they know what you did to Throckmorton and the last lot of eager boys who wanted the Queen of Scots on the throne?' When I did not reply, a wolfish smile curved across his face. 'Thought not. Would you like to keep it that way?'

'What do you want, Douglas? They'll come looking for me in a moment.'

'That would be awkward, wouldn't it? We'd have to explain how we knew each other. All right, listen – this is what's going to happen. You're going to keep me informed of those gentlemen's plans at every step.'

'Then – you have nothing to do with the conspiracy?'

'Me? I'm offended you would even think it.' He chuckled. 'Mary Stuart is last year's cause, Bruno. No one with an ounce of political nous believes she'll rule anywhere, not even her – only naïve boys and fanatics still rally to her banner. I watch which way the wind is blowing.'

'So why are you in London? Aren't you a wanted man here?'

'Oh, they want me everywhere. Let's just say I'm on a most sensitive mission, and it's very much not in my interest for those lads to succeed in whatever they're plotting – I assume some new hare-brained scheme to get rid of Elizabeth. And since you're obviously monitoring them for your friends in high places, you can pass whatever you find on to me at the same time.'

'Why would I do that?'

'Because' – he brought his face an inch from mine – 'if you don't, I'll tell your new friends who you are. And then I'll find your pretty little slut and ruin her face.'

'What?' I stared at him. Douglas was the kind of man who could throw out a comment like that without thinking, but he was also entirely capable of doing it.

'You heard. You can find me at the Unicorn. It's where all the best people stay – but then you know that. We'll take a drink together – I know you've missed me.' He puckered his lips in a kiss. I turned my face away in case he actually tried. He laughed again, enjoying himself.

'How long have you been in London?' I asked, my thoughts scrambling to catch up.

'A week. Why?'

'Did you know Clara Poole?' It was a stupid question; he was hardly going to admit it if he had.

'I know so many women – you can't expect me to remember all their names. Who is Clara Poole? Oh . . .' he nodded as understanding dawned. 'Is that the servant of Lady Sidney who was found murdered along the way here the other day? I heard talk of that. Tragic business. Nice girls should know better than to hang around Southwark after dark.'

'She had her face ruined.'

'No! Why would someone do that to a woman, I wonder.'

'You tell me. You're the one who just threatened it.'

'Figure of speech. My ancient warrior blood, Bruno – what can I say?' Another roar rose up from the wall behind us. He shook his head with a wince. 'Listen to that. I can't abide it. People paying money to watch an old blind bear ripped to pieces by dogs kept starving, women and bairns laughing and cheering when the poor creatures lose another chunk of flesh? Fucking monstrous. Makes you lose faith in humanity, Bruno, it really does.' He lowered the knife and sheathed it. He knew I would not try anything now.

'My name is Prado,' I said.

He grinned. 'Course it is. I'll be seeing you, Prado. Mind I do.'

I took my seat alongside the others in the stands; no one seemed to have noticed my long absence, with the exception of Robin Poole, who gave me a quizzical frown and pointed to the trail of blood down the side of my neck; I brushed it away quickly and shook my head. I sat down next to Babington, whose attention was all on Bessie to his left. It was hard to know where to look: not at Sophia, seated next to Ballard and affecting rapt attention to his every word; even the line of her profile caused the heat to surge through my blood again, and I could not afford to have my responses clouded by lust. Not at the exhausted, blood-soaked animals in the ring; I agreed with Douglas on that spectacle, though it struck me as odd that he should be so vehement in his objection, knowing the brutality he was capable of with people who inconvenienced him. It made me think of a Dominican Inquisitor I had known in Naples, who was rumoured to eat his supper with one hand while crushing a man's knees in a spiked vice with the other, but wept like a child when his dog was trampled by a horse. Gifford and Ballard were discussing in low voices how long it would take to get men up-country to Staffordshire, who should go and whether they should leave this weekend, if the execution – as they still referred to it – was to happen in the next week, once Bessie returned to Elizabeth's service. None of them seemed to have questioned Bessie's immediate and enthusiastic agreement to their proposal. Babington was right about Ballard abandoning all caution; he appeared ready to seize on any means to get his way now, regardless of consequences. And unless Sophia could find a copy of the letter to which Bessie had replied with her promise that *it will be done*, the girl's true loyalties remained unknown.

I leaned in to give the appearance of interest in the conversation, but my mind snagged on other, unanswered questions. That sudden flash of emotion Babington had shown when I spoke of Clara's death earlier; there was real feeling there, despite his efforts to hide it. Perhaps he had been in love with her after all, though it did not follow that he had killed her. In fact, the more I saw of the conspirators, the clearer it seemed that Clara's death had thrown them into disarray; Babington appeared genuinely fearful that the murder meant the plot was now discovered, and he seemed to be losing his appetite for it, even as Ballard's had been sharpened by the threat of arrest. Chidiock Tichborne's absence was odd too; he might simply have forgotten the meeting, which struck me as unlikely, or he could have taken the chance to flee, as Gifford had proposed last night – either because he feared discovery as her killer, or because he thought the conspiracy was blown. But I had not seen any convincing evidence so far that any one of them had reason to think that murdering Clara served their purpose. Finally, there was my bizarre conversation with Douglas. Mary Stuart is last year's cause, he had said. It was true enough that in his time he had taken great risks for Mary, as Ballard had reminded us, and seen little reward for it except imprisonment and exile; it made sense that he would look for better prospects elsewhere. Given what I knew of him, I could guess his new allegiance: Mary Stuart's only son, twenty-year-old King James of Scotland. Now that it was certain Elizabeth would not produce an heir of her own, it was widely believed that young James would be named as her successor, as the nearest suitable heir by blood and religion, but so far the Queen had refused any public commitment to him. Could Douglas's *sensitive mission* have something to do with ensuring James's place as the next king of England? If Douglas was working for James, it made sense that he would not want a conspiracy on behalf of Mary Stuart to succeed, and he was quite capable of committing murder to prevent it. Could he have killed Clara in cold blood and left her body in a public place to draw attention to the Babington plot, and thereby thwart it? He had been in London at the time, and staying at the Unicorn. But if he knew enough to target Clara, he must already have an informer within the Babington group, which made no sense of his threats to me.

Whatever his involvement, I knew I should tell Phelippes and Walsingham immediately that Douglas was in town. If they knew that I had seen him, they would almost certainly want to pull me out of the conspiracy, knowing my identity was compromised. A couple of days ago, that might have come as a relief; now I felt I was too deeply enmeshed. Call it pride, stubbornness, curiosity; I could not simply give up now without untangling all the threads. Though there were moments – like the one earlier that had driven me to seek respite behind the bear pit – when I felt overwhelmed by the demands of being Prado, Walsingham had been right from the beginning, damn him: I was feeling more alive than I had in months, and the thought of returning to the daily grind of my life in Paris before Clara's death was resolved filled me with dread.

When the baiting was over and the torn corpses dragged out of the ring, we pushed through the crowds and gathered again outside the entrance; I was relieved to escape the smell of blood and meat. Sophia studiously avoided my eye and I had to force myself not to keep stealing glances at her. As a distraction, I cast around for Douglas in the crowds leaving the arena, but he seemed to have vanished, for the time being.

'Prado?'

I jerked my attention back to my companions; Ballard was looking at me expectantly.

'I said – you will send word to Mendoza urgently that we mean to proceed in the next few days. Anthony will write to Mary tonight telling her that our plans have changed and the hour is at hand, but saying nothing of why – we must not alarm her at all costs, since she will need a clear head and steady nerve in the next few days. Gilbert will ride with the letter tomorrow, with all haste, and should be with her by Saturday. I will procure the necessary means and by Monday, when Mistress Pierrepont is back on duty, she will look for an opportunity to dispatch the usurper. In the meantime, Anthony and Titch will ride north to liberate the Queen, and meet Gilbert in Staffordshire.'

'If we ever find Titch,' Babington said, chewing his thumb again.

'He'll turn up,' Ballard said. He seemed galvanised by the evening's entertainment. 'Is that clear enough, Prado? You can code all that into a dispatch to send tomorrow? Tell Mendoza to ready troops and we will send the list of landing places as soon as we have it. And make sure you don't alert the French.'

'I will put all this into a dispatch the moment I get back to my chamber,' I said. That, at least, was true. 'In fact, perhaps I should go now, to make a start.'

I looked up at the sky; the light had almost faded behind drifts of cloud touched with lilac and orange. The river gleamed like beaten silver. I had not been paying attention to the bells, but I guessed it must be near half past nine. I hoped that if I could be excused from priestly duties that night, I might make some excuse to slip away from the group now into the back streets of Southwark and find Leila, to ask her about the opium, and quiz Joe about whatever he had done that made him fear the fires of Hell.

'Not yet.' Ballard took me by the elbow and steered me a few feet away from the others; Savage followed. 'Listen, Prado – I've decided it's best if you don't come with me to the faithful tonight. You are quite conspicuous, and I don't want to draw unwelcome attention from the pursuivants. Besides . . .' he paused, seeming uncomfortable, 'some people have said they don't want a foreigner ministering to them, even if you are a priest.'

I did my best to look disappointed.

'I'm sorry,' he said, a hand on my arm. 'I know from this morning how keen you are to continue God's work.'

I met his eye; it was impossible to tell whether he was being sarcastic. 'God has other purposes for me, I'm sure,' I said.

'Well, I do, certainly. I want you to go with Jack to see if you can find Titch.'

I glanced at Savage. 'You think something has happened to him?'

'I don't like his absence. I played it down in front of the others because I fear Babington is losing heart, and I don't want to make him more skittish. But Chidiock has been a faithful member of our group – it's unlike him not to turn up with no explanation. Go to his lodgings and make discreet enquiries. If Clara Poole gave names under interrogation, they may be picking us up one by one, starting with those they think will be easiest to break.'

'Then – the authorities may be waiting for us?' I asked. It seemed that Ballard still believed Clara was murdered by Walsingham's agents. Unless it was an elaborate trap, and he intended Savage to kill me on the way and throw me in the river. I darted a quick glance around; there were link-boys milling around the yard outside the bear garden, waiting to escort the wealthier patrons home, but no sign of Ben among them.

'That's why I'm sending my best fighters,' Ballard said with a smile, though his eyes looked tired. I wondered how much he had slept the previous night. 'If anyone can get the better of the pursuivants and escape, it's the two of you. Titch lodges at the sign of the Blue Boar in Crooked Lane, off New Fish Street. I'm going to dine at the Unicorn now with Anthony and Robin. They both need encouragement, in their different ways. You can bring me word there when you have news. And no punching each other – save that for our enemies.' He looked from me to Savage with something like affection, as if he were a benevolent father reprimanding squabbling brothers.

Savage began walking without looking back. I hastened after him, when I felt a hand catch at my sleeve.

'Father.' Babington sidled up to me, his voice low. As always, there was a moment – the space of a heartbeat – when the title jarred, and I almost found myself looking around for a priest.

'What is it, son?' I asked. His face was agitated.

'Tonight, when you return to Herne's Rents. Will you come to my room? I need to speak to you alone.' He flicked a glance over his shoulder as he spoke, as if afraid one of the others might hear.

'Is everything all right?'

'Yes.' He lowered his gaze. 'I want to make my confession. Will you hear it?'

'Of course. But – I thought Father Ballard was your confessor?'

'He has been. But there are things I have not told him. This time I would rather speak to you. Don't mention it to him, he wouldn't like it.'

'I won't say a word. But I don't know what time I'll be back tonight.'

'Doesn't matter. Come whenever. I don't sleep well these days.'

'I'll be there.' I patted him reassuringly on the arm, though my heart was pounding: was it going to be this easy? There was clearly something weighing on his mind and I wondered if it was about Clara; the thought that he might simply deliver it up to me was too good to be true.

'Gentlemen, I will meet you at the Unicorn shortly,' Ballard was saying. 'Ladies, alas, I cannot take you there – Madam Rosa is territorial. But we shall meet again as soon as I have the means to proceed.' He bowed low and kissed Bessie's hand. 'You will find your way home safely? Southwark is no place for nice young ladies.'

'Oh, but we are not nice young ladies,' she said, giggling, with a toss of her hair. Sophia caught my eye and flashed me a secret smile.

'I can escort the ladies home,' Gifford piped up, eager as a puppy.

'No, I don't think so, Gilbert.' Ballard hooked an arm around his shoulder. 'You and I need to have a little talk. In private. Walk with me along the river a while. Robin, you can see the girls home. Perhaps you could put them on my grey mare, if you can remember where you left her.'

Poole blanched. 'About the mare—' he began. Ballard held a hand up with an indulgent laugh.

'Don't worry, my friend – I know you have a great deal on your mind at present. We can discuss the horse some other time. Look to the ladies, now.'

Poole gave him a curt nod and bobbed a brief bow to the women, who set off with him along the bank.

Gifford wrenched his head around as he was led away eastwards along the bank, to shoot me a look of pure terror over Ballard's shoulder. I stared back at him, helpless; I could hardly volunteer to accompany them. As I watched them walk away, a terrible foreboding gripped me; I had been a fool to underestimate Ballard. Gifford was right; he had seen through us, and was separating us to dispatch us. Even if all he had were suspicions, the present state of Gifford – half-drunk and panicked – would be enough to confirm them, and we were both dead men. Further along the bank, Savage had slowed his pace, but I would have to run to catch up with him; he was not going to make any concessions to me. As Robin Poole offered her his arm, Sophia threw a quick glance back at me and winked.

NINETEEN

'When this is all over,' Savage said, speculatively, looking up as we passed under the Drawbridge Gate on London Bridge, 'I'm going to beat seven shades of shit out of you.'

'Fair enough.'

He seemed disappointed. 'Aren't you going to ask me why?'

'Because you don't like me, I assume,' I said. 'No great mystery. Because I made you look weak in front of Ballard. So, if beating me helps you prove something, go ahead. But I don't think it will make him admire you more, if that's your aim.'

'That's not it,' he said, though I could see I had needled him.

'Because I'm foreign, then.'

He continued walking in silence, purposefully not looking at me. I would have taken it as bluster, except for his words the previous night, which continued to trouble me.

'Yesterday,' I said, my hand straying to the knife at my belt, 'you said you knew what I was. What did you mean by that?'

He gave a mirthless laugh. 'You might have fooled Ballard, but you haven't fooled me. You can let go of that dagger – what are you going to do, run me through in the middle of the bridge?'

I let my hand fall to my side. There were plenty of people crossing the river at this hour, mostly groups of young gallants, already drunk, arms slung around one another's shoulders and singing bawdy catches, heading south for the stews of Southwark.

'I've met your kind before,' he said, in a low voice, from the side of his mouth. I felt my throat tighten; if he had seen through me, had he told any of the others? He was right that we couldn't fight here on the bridge without drawing attention, but could I outrun him if he turned on me? I kept an eye on his hands; they were bunched at his sides, nowhere near his weapon, but I knew his reflexes were fast.

'You don't care about our cause. I see the way you look at us,' he continued. 'You think you're cleverer than us. Because you can argue in Latin and Greek, you think God put you above us.'

'I'm a priest,' I said mildly. 'I think God sent me to serve.'

'You don't really believe that, though, do you? I saw you last night. You didn't want to be there, ministering to those people, it was written all over your face. I'd wager it's a while since you've given anyone the sacraments, you sounded like you were struggling to remember them half the time. You'd rather have been in some seminary debating chamber arguing about Aristotle.'

My arms and legs turned cold at the mention of Aristotle; he knew me, for certain.

'Why do you say that?'

'That's what you Jesuits like, isn't it?'

'If that were the case, I would not have risked my life coming to England undercover,' I said, a little haughty, to disguise my relief at the fact that he apparently still thought I was a Jesuit.

'I know exactly why you're here. So Spain can swoop in and take all the spoils once we've done the dirty work. I never wanted John to go to France, so you know.' He stole a look at me, his mouth set hard. 'I said this was English business and we should not involve foreign powers, or they would end up taking everything, but the others felt we could not manage without. They imagine your King Philip will respect English sovereignty, when the Tudor is dead, but they are fantasists.' He shook his head with a bitter laugh. 'You may be a priest, but that's nothing to me. I don't think it gives you magical powers.'

'I wonder why *you* are here, if you hold the Catholic Church in such contempt.'

'Not for love of the Pope or Mary Stuart, put it that way.'

'Then why? Why risk your life if you don't believe it's God's will?'

He snorted. '*God's will.* I marvel at the arrogance of any man who claims to know that. I'm here for John, that's all.'

'You must think very highly of him.'

'I owe him,' he said simply. 'He saved my life, and I pledged him my loyalty. I'm a man of my word.'

We walked on in silence. He had retreated into his thoughts; I sensed he disliked talking about himself.

'How did he save your life?' I asked, after a while.

'None of your fucking business, Jesuit.'

The sentiment didn't matter; when I heard him call me Jesuit, even as an insult, I wanted to embrace him. As long as he believed that's what I was, I could put up with any amount of resentment. But as we approached the end of the bridge, he seemed to relent.

'My daughter died,' he said, in a different tone. 'Four years back.'

'I'm sorry.' A priest should probably commend her soul to God, but I didn't think Savage would appreciate that.

He shrugged, as if to say that my condolences were meaningless. 'Sweating sickness. It took a lot of people that summer. She was nine. Our only child. My wife lost her wits with the grief of it. She had her faith in the old Church – she went looking to priests for comfort, much good it did her. They were happy to take her offerings though. Then one day she disappeared.'

'Where?'

'No idea. Just – pfft.' He mimed a puff of smoke with his fingers. 'I walk around London looking in the face of every beggar woman I see. When I go around those houses at night with John, in the poor neighbourhoods, I hope every time for a sight of her.' He shook his head. 'Even though I know in my heart she's at the bottom of the river or in a common pit by now. After she left, I drank.'

We passed under the wide gatehouse on the north bank. He turned to look at me, gauging my response, and in the light from the torches, his mismatched eyes were strange and sad.

'I'd worked as a legal clerk, but I couldn't keep my job. So I fought for money – I always had a talent for that. Illegal fistfights in the Southwark inn yards, with crowds egging us on as if we were cocks or dogs. I beat men for money, and when I got paid I drank it. I kept that up for a few months – I was good, people made a profit on me. But the drink took the edge off. One night I drank before the fight instead of after, I lost badly, and so did the men who'd expected me to win. I was told not to come back. So I found myself on the riverbank, just back there.' He indicated with his thumb as we began to walk up New Fish Street. 'I knew if you went in right by the bridge, the current between the arches would pull you under before anyone could try to drag you out. I was standing there, screwing up my nerve, and I felt a hand on my shoulder.'

'Ballard.'

'Yup. He said, "Come on, son – you're a fighter, aren't you? Then fight."' He broke off, a catch in his voice. 'So that's the story,' he said briskly, when he had recovered himself.

'Do the others know your history?' I asked.

'No. Only John. So don't you say anything.'

'I wouldn't. Why did you tell me?'

'I don't know. I suppose because I see that you look down on John, and I wanted you to understand what kind of man he is. Why people are drawn to him.'

I nodded. We walked on in silence for a while.

'What was her name?' I asked. 'Your daughter.'

'Lucy,' he said, without hesitation, his face softening. 'My wife was Sarah.'

'Ballard was right,' I murmured, 'you are a fighter. I don't know that I could have suffered so much, and go on putting one foot in front of the other.'

'Sometimes I think it would have been better to have chosen your life, be a priest and have no family, to have avoided the pain of it.'

'But then you would have missed the rest too. I have never held a child of my own. I could envy you that.'

He slowed his pace and turned to me, and in that look something frank was exchanged, because in that moment I was not lying.

'True. I had nine years with her. I would not have missed that for anything.'

'You must feel for Robin Poole, in his grief,' I said carefully.

'I don't know if murder is better or worse,' he said, after some thought. 'At least you'd have someone to blame, you could look for vengeance. But then you'd always feel it could have turned out different. With sickness, all you can do is blame God, and He doesn't listen. I do feel for Robin – it's a hard hand to be dealt.'

'Babington said it was especially cruel for him to go through this again. What did he mean?'

He gave me a sidelong glance. 'He means his father. Robin's father, George Poole. He was killed by government agents too. Years ago, this was.'

'Really? I heard he drowned.'

Savage let out a brief, hard laugh. 'You think a man can't be pushed?'

'Why was he killed?'

He checked over his shoulder, and drew closer to me. 'All right, but you mustn't let Robin know I've told you. He doesn't like people talking about his family. His father was supposedly an informer.'

I feigned shock. 'For the government?'

He nodded. 'George Poole was trusted among the Catholics. He used to help organise safe passage and lodgings for priests coming into the country from the French seminaries.'

'And all the time he was in the pay of the Tudor?'

'Exactly. Passing on information about his brothers and sisters in the faith, who trusted him with their lives. Except that – *he wasn't*.'

'Wasn't what? Forgive me, perhaps my English is not so good, but I'm confused.'

'He wasn't really working for the Tudor. Oh, he was taking government money all right, but only to keep his family safe. He'd agreed to inform because he'd been caught with forbidden books, and Sir Francis Walsingham – you know who I mean?'

'Naturally. Everyone has heard of him.'

'He threatened George. It was gaol or worse if he didn't agree to work for the government. But George was never truly turned. The information he passed to Walsingham's people was always false, or wrong in some particular. He tried to protect everyone – his family and his friends. You can't keep that up for ever.'

'So Walsingham found out this George was playing him false, you think?'

'For certain. And had him killed for it, so it looked like an accident. Then he gave George's children, Robin and Clara, positions in his household, to show his generosity.'

'How do you know all this?' I asked.

'After I first started helping John, I was picked up and

thrown in prison for a couple of months, on suspicion of spreading propaganda,' he said. 'In the Wood Street Counter. There's a lot of Catholics in there, locked up for nothing much. I met an old man who'd known George Poole, told me the whole story. He swore George never gave true testimony to the Tudor's agents, so they got rid of him when they realised he couldn't be trusted.'

'And did Robin and Clara know this too?'

'Of course. Why do you think they were part of this plot? They wanted revenge. But now Clara is dead too, almost certainly by the same hand, and for the same reason as her father. I fear it may tip Robin into recklessness. John will have his work cut out talking him round.'

'That is an extraordinary story,' I said, my mind whirling with the implications. I felt as if I had been looking at a painting that had suddenly been flipped upside down to reveal an entirely different picture. If both Robin and Clara Poole believed that their father had been killed on Walsingham's orders, what did that mean for their involvement in Babington's conspiracy? How long had they known – had Walsingham been mistaken all this time about their loyalties? But it still didn't make sense – if Clara had been killed by Walsingham's people, he would never have asked me to investigate it. Unless I was being used, so that he could give the appearance of doing something to appease his daughter.

'Hey.' Savage flicked me on the arm and I jolted back to him; I was so wrong-footed by this revelation that I had stopped listening.

'I said, we must keep our wits about us,' he said, as we turned up Crooked Lane. 'If Titch has been taken, they may be waiting.' His hand slipped to the hilt of his long knife as the sign of the Blue Boar came into view on a tall building ahead.

'He went out at about six, as soon as the boy came with the note.' Tichborne's landlady folded her arms and blocked the threshold. 'He didn't say where, but he set off as if the Devil were at his heels.'

'What boy?' Savage asked. The woman – tall and angular, in her late fifties, a widow by her dress – scowled at him.

'I didn't ask his name. Just a regular messenger boy, with a letter for Master Tichborne.'

'And no one else has been here looking for him?'

'Not to my knowledge, though I was out for an hour earlier. What is this about – is Master Tichborne in trouble?'

'Not at all. Please don't be alarmed, madam.' I gave her my most charming smile, but she didn't seem reassured.

'I suggest you come back tomorrow, *gentlemen*.' From the way she looked at us, I suspected the last word was not meant sincerely.

'We'll wait for him,' Savage said, and made to push past her.

'You will not,' she said, standing her ground. 'This is a respectable house. Do you want me to shout for the watch?'

'No need for that, good madam.' I produced a half-crown from my purse. 'We are friends of Master Tichborne and promised we would meet him here when he returned. We will make no disturbance.' I bowed low and she appeared somewhat placated, though she turned the coin over in her hand with an astute eye.

'You'd better not. And if he's not back in an hour, you leave. I won't have strangers in the house late at night.'

The house was a handsome old building with a wide wooden staircase. Titch rented two rooms on the top floor. The door to his lodgings was locked, as I had expected.

'Not a problem.' Savage bent to examine the lock, and pulled out a long thin metal implement from the sheath of his knife, looking up at me with a quick, knowing grin.

I feigned admiration as he worked the mechanism of the lock, trying not to wince as I heard it scrape repeatedly, pressing my nails into my palms to stop myself offering to help, knowing I could have done the job in five minutes; he was enjoying showing off a skill he supposed the intellectually arrogant Jesuit could not compete with.

Eventually the lock yielded and we found ourselves inside a narrow pair of adjoining rooms below the roof, with a low slanting ceiling rising to a point in the centre – an odd choice for a man of Titch's size, who must have found it impossible to stand upright except under the highest point. It was almost dark now; I found a tinderbox on the windowsill and lit a couple of candles.

'It didn't sound like he'd been arrested,' I said tentatively, looking around. I knew, as Ballard and Savage could not, that Walsingham had no intention of picking up any of the conspirators yet, but I was curious to hear what other explanations Savage might put forward, since he knew Titch better than I did. The rooms were barely furnished, with a bed, desk and washstand, and a large wooden chest standing open, a jumble of shirts, doublets and hose strewn around the floor.

'All we know is the pursuivants didn't come to the house,' Savage said, lifting some of the clothes and peering in the chest. 'This messenger boy could have been a decoy, to lure him somewhere they could pick him up more easily. But if he's been taken by the authorities, I'd expect this place to have been searched. She says she was out this evening – they could have waited for her to leave.'

'The lock had not been forced.'

'They wouldn't need to use force, government men – they would do what I did. The state of this.' He picked up a red silk doublet from the floor, dusted it down and began folding it. 'This would cost more than some men make in a year, and look how he treats it. Hard to tell if searchers have been through the room, the way he leaves his things.'

I almost laughed; he sounded like the boy's mother. 'Did you fold your clothes, at his age?'

He gave a reluctant smile and rapped on the bottom of the

chest with his knuckles, at each end and in the middle. 'Probably not. We should take a look at his papers, see if anything's missing. Try the desk.'

'How would we know what's missing? Surely he wouldn't have left letters lying around. Listen, do you think he could have run?'

'Lost his nerve, you mean?' He crouched by the chest, considering. 'I suppose it's possible. But if I'd had to bet on any of them bolting, I'd have said Gifford. He's the nervy one. Jumps like a startled hare if you so much as look at him.'

'Everyone does that when you look at them.'

Madonna porca, Gifford; even now he would be on his walk with Ballard along the riverbank, bleating out God only knew what in his panic. I had to hope he could keep his mouth shut for one more evening; once he was on the road to Staffordshire, he was no longer my responsibility.

Savage acknowledged the truth of my words with a dry laugh. 'I wouldn't have thought Titch had it in him to take off – not without Babington's permission. They've been friends since they were boys, apparently – Titch follows him everywhere. From what I can see, he's never made a decision of his own in his life.'

And yet, I thought – Titch had been the one vehemently refusing last night to believe that Clara could have been murdered. He and Babington had appeared visibly shocked and upset by the news, but they had responded to it in different ways; that argued some independence of thought on Titch's part, or perhaps some knowledge that his friend was not privy to.

'He seems a quiet sort of boy,' I said, picking up the books on the desk one by one and shaking them for loose papers. There were no letters that I could see. I wondered what message this boy could have brought to Titch that had sent him running in such a hurry, willing to miss his meeting with his friends at the bear pit without even waiting to send an explanation. I crossed to the bed and checked under it, to find a large leather travelling bag, pressed flat. At first glance, it did not appear that Titch could have fled for good – unless something had scared him so much that he had run with only the clothes on his back.

'He keeps his thoughts to himself,' Savage said. He had emptied the chest and was feeling his way around the inside, pressing the corners with his fingertips; I could guess what he was looking for. 'You want to talk about motives for being part of this business – I couldn't begin to fathom his. I've seen no sign of fervent faith in the months I've known him, though he takes the Mass soberly enough with the rest of us, and I know he resents his family's losses under the Tudor. But I've never heard him hold forth about justice or true religion or Mary Stuart's sufferings, or any of the stuff that gives young Babington such a cockstand. I'd have said Titch is only with us for the same reason he went off to France with Babington – he was bored and his friend wanted an adventure. Except that – *ah*.'

Whatever he had been about to add, it seemed he had found something in the chest that distracted him. While I waited for him to share it, I checked under the mattress and pressed my fingers along its seams in search of hiding places but could see nothing. Either Titch had no secrets to hide, or he had concealed them so well they were defeating us. I stood and stretched my back. As I did so, my gaze alighted on a twist of paper in the empty grate. In a room so conspicuously devoid of any papers, notes or letters, it stood out. I sidled across to the hearth, hoping that Savage would not notice, but he was bent deep inside the chest, his attention all focused on whatever was within. I heard a smooth click; in the same instant I bent and retrieved the scrap of paper and slipped it into the lining of my doublet.

'Here, look at this.' Savage lifted out the false bottom of

the chest to reveal a secret compartment. Inside were several bundles of papers and a number of fat cloth bags; he picked one up and tossed it in his palm, with the unmistakable chink of coins. 'He hasn't run anywhere, not without his money. And there are letters here – any government searcher worth his salt would have found these.' He lifted a sheaf of papers tied with red ribbon.

'Then what?' My mind raced through the possibilities. The answer was all in the message the boy had brought to Titch earlier. I had a feeling it might be written on the paper I had just hidden away; I had noticed that a corner was singed, as if someone had tried to burn it with a candle flame in haste and tossed it into the grate without checking to see it had caught. But I did not want to read it in front of Savage, in case it contained information that would give me an advantage.

Before he had a chance to voice another theory, we were interrupted by the sound of footsteps on the stairs, galloping up two at a time. Savage motioned me behind the door; we blew out the candles and drew our knives, breath held, as the steps drew closer. The door crashed open, admitting a long shadow and the wavering light of a lantern catching on the edge of a sword—

'Fuck me!' Titch jumped back, almost dropping his weapon, his eyes darting from me to Savage. 'She said there were men waiting, I thought they had come to arrest me.' His gaze darted to the open chest with its false compartment removed, and his expression hardened. 'But this is near as bad – what are you doing, going through my letters? Did Ballard send you to *spy* on me?' He held out the sword and levelled its point from me to Savage, hurt and fury etched on his face.

'Peace, brother.' Savage raised a hand to placate him. 'We also thought you had been taken, when you failed to show up at the bear pit.'

Titch waved this away, as if it were an unimportant detail.

'I had to be elsewhere at short notice.' I could have sworn then that his eyes flitted to the hearth, but if he noticed the paper was missing, he gave no sign of it. 'That's not a reason to break into my rooms, God's *death*.'

'We were afraid that if you had been arrested, they might have made a search of your lodgings,' I offered.

'Even if they had, you have no need to fear – I am not a fool. I keep nothing here that would incriminate the rest of you. And who are you to go through my belongings, master Spaniard? Until last night I didn't know you from Adam.' But his gaze returned to the chest; he had not expressed any concern about his money, though there was plenty there for the taking – only that we might have looked at his letters. I could not help wishing he had come back later and given us a chance to read them.

'You should have sent word to say you weren't coming.' Savage sheathed his knife decisively and held out his empty hands to show he meant no harm. 'After what happened to Clara, we feared for you, and for ourselves. As for the intrusion' – he gestured to the chest – 'we have taken nothing, nor read a word. Count the money if you want. You have no cause for anger. John asks that we have no secrets among ourselves.'

Titch let out a bitter snort of laughter, but he put his sword away. '*John asks*. John Ballard is not my master as he is yours,' he said, leaning down to speak close to Savage's face with a sneer. 'The bear-baiting is an entertainment for fools, and if I have no appetite for it I do not need his permission to stay away.'

'Whereas whoring is a pastime of honourable gentlemen,' Savage said, stepping back with an expression of distaste. 'Don't look so surprised – it doesn't take a great wit to work out where you've been. Your doublet's buttoned wrong and you smell of cunt. Wash yourself after, next time.'

Titch sat heavily on the bed and stared at me, shocked by Savage's bluntness.

'It's true,' I said, sounding apologetic. It was only now that I noticed his flushed, sated face and hooded eyes, and the smell of sex on his clothes and hands.

'So must I make my confession to you now, Father?' he said, scathing.

'Only if you wish to.'

'I don't. I have done nothing wrong.' The belligerent look fell from his face and for a moment I glimpsed a glazed, dreamy expression in his eyes that might just have been the afterglow of his passion.

Savage snorted. 'Listen, boy – I don't care how many whores you tup, that's between you and your wife, but—'

'I have no wife,' Titch protested. 'I am betrothed only, and it is not adultery if no marriage vows have been exchanged, isn't that right, Father?'

I spread my hands in equivocation, uncertain of the theological niceties, but I was spared the need to answer by Savage cutting in.

'Not interested. I care only that your thoughtlessness causes the rest of us to fear for our lives, and dash across town in case you've been taken. Who was your message from?'

'My what?' Titch pressed himself back against the wall, instantly defensive.

'Your landlady said a boy sent a message this evening and you went racing off. So who summoned you?'

'It was . . .' he lowered his eyes, blushing, and tugged at the hem of his doublet. 'You're right. It was from a – a girl.'

Savage moved around the side of the bed and leaned in close; I watched as Titch shrank from him. 'First I've heard of a whorehouse that sends out for the customers. You had better not be playing false with us, Tichborne. Prado here will be able to smell if you're lying, it's an old Jesuit trick.'

Titch flicked his eyes sideways to me; he could not tell if he was being played for a fool. 'I'm not lying,' he said, barely audible. 'But she's not a whore, you're the one who assumed that. She's a barmaid. She sends to let me know – her husband is out.'

Savage reared up, rolling his eyes like a spooked horse. 'God save us. Well, I hope whatever she does to your skinny cock was worth it. Next time you find quim more pressing than your oath to your comrades, give us warning so you don't waste any more of my fucking time. Got it?'

Titch nodded, deflated, and sank back against his pillows.

'Come on, Prado.' Without waiting, Savage stamped away down the stairs. I glanced at Titch.

'You know, I would be happy to hear your confession if you wish it,' I said, from the doorway. It had not occurred to me that my role as a priest might invite confidences with minimal effort; I was beginning to like the idea.

'No thank you, Prado.' He looked up at me with tired eyes. 'I have nothing to confess. Shut the door behind you.'

I bowed my head in deference and left him. I didn't need to be a Jesuit to smell when someone was lying.

'Arrogant little bastard.' Savage was still fuming when I caught up with him in the street.

'Not as virginal as you thought.'

'Seems not. He needs to learn to keep it in his breeches. Barmaid, for Christ's sake.'

'It could have been worse,' I said. 'At least we know he is not arrested or on the run.'

'Left us worrying half the night for nothing, though. I don't like people wasting my time. God's teeth, these rich boys – they think they can do what they want, without a care for anyone else.'

'He's young. Wouldn't you have rushed across town for a hot barmaid, at his age?'

'Probably. Seems a long time ago,' Savage said. 'Since Sarah left, I find I don't look at women like that. I'm only forty.' His face twisted, as if the memory of being young and carefree pained him. 'And you're soft-hearted, for a Jesuit. Can you get home from here? I must go back to the Unicorn and let John know he can stop worrying about Titch.'

'I'll be fine. Give you good night.'

We looked at one another, uncertain of how to take our leave after the unexpected confidences that had been shared. A long pause stretched between us; eventually he reached out a hand, shook mine with an awkward formality and walked away. I slipped back into the shadows, listening for his footsteps to die away; I too was heading back to Southwark, and wanted to avoid any possibility of catching up with him.

At the end of Crooked Lane I passed a tavern with a flaming torch fixed to a wall bracket over the door. Moving in as close to the light as I could, I took out the scrap of paper from Titch's fireplace that I had tucked inside my doublet and unfolded it. Whatever I had expected to find written there, it was not this: the four symbols I knew by heart from the paper inside Clara's locket. Half-moon, seashore, ploughed furrow, rose. The drawings were identical, and I was certain they were by the same hand, though I could not compare them to the original. I leaned against the doorpost, staring at the note, trying to work out what this could signify. Without asking Titch directly, there was no way of knowing if this was the same note that had been delivered to him this evening, but I would have bet good money it was. Could it be that the person who had given Clara the message was also writing to Titch? Evidently it meant something significant to both of them; Clara had thrown her locket into the bushes to keep her killer from getting his hands on it, and Titch had rushed out, forgetting his friends, in response to it, after trying to burn his copy. It was clear that he had lied about the barmaid; though the evidence suggested he had been with a woman at some point during the evening, I wondered if that was just a cover, and what else he might have been doing before or after.

I replaced the paper inside my doublet to send to Phelippes when I had the chance; perhaps he had had an epiphany about the meaning of the symbols by now. Titch had made clear that he had no desire to confide in Father Prado, and I could not ask him anything about the note without arousing suspicion, but at least I had evidence of a link between him and Clara Poole – one that they had both been at pains to hide. He would have to be watched closely. I wished we had had time to read those letters in his trunk – he had been so defensive over them that I was sure their contents were worth a look. Perhaps Poole and I between us could contrive a means to keep him away from his rooms long enough for one of us to examine them – but of course he would have found an alternative hiding place, and he would be on his guard now for any sign of intrusion. I would have to leave that with Phelippes. In the meantime, I needed answers that could only be found in Southwark.

TWENTY

Leila's house was impossible to find in the dark. I tried to work my way back from the Unicorn, taking care to keep to the shadows in case any of the conspirators had stepped outside for a walk; I could not easily explain my presence in Southwark to Ballard a second time. That morning I had ended up in Leila's yard via the back streets, propelled by the urgency of catching up with Joe; now, with the feeble torch I had bought from a link-boy on the bridge already burning low, I did not like my chances of finding my way there by the same means. I suspected the residents of Southwark would not welcome a stranger climbing over their back fences at night, and I wondered how many more of them had crossbows. But after half an hour of wandering in what had seemed like the right direction, I had to concede that I was lost, and this was not a desirable situation. If Ben had been with me, he would have found the place in no time, but in his absence I was obliged to ask a young woman lolling in a doorway, eyes clouded with drink and her face already showing early signs of the pox.

'The Moorish witch, you mean?' She looked me up and down unsympathetically. 'What do you want her for? You got cockrot?'

'No.' I drew myself up.

'You will have by morning, you keep hanging around these streets.' She cackled at her own wit. 'Suppose your woman needs rid of a bastard, then, if you're looking for the witch. What's it worth?'

I gave her tuppence and she tucked it somewhere in her skirts before issuing garbled directions that led me a few streets away, where I eventually recognised the filthy lane that led to Leila's yard. I briefly considered knocking at the front of the house, but guessed she would be unlikely to open it this time of night. Fortunately, I was better prepared than I had been that morning; I stuck the torch upright into the mud, then took off the borrowed doublet, folded it and placed it over the nails along the top of the fence, so that when I jumped and pulled myself up and over, it kept them from tearing my clothes. I dropped down silently into the yard and felt my way between the plant pots to the back door. Lamplight shone through cracks in the shutters, and from within I could hear the sound of a woman crying.

I knocked softly, but there was no reply. I caught a low murmur of voices and renewed sobbing. For a moment I considered leaving the way I had come; it was clear that Leila was treating a woman in some distress, and I felt guilty for intruding. But I reminded myself that she had almost certainly supplied the opium that had been used to sedate Clara Poole before she was killed, and if she or Joe could say who had bought or stolen it, I would have the murderer. I pushed open the door and stepped inside the wide ground-floor room.

Leila sat on a low stool by the fire, clasping the hands of another woman whose dark hair hung around her face. When they started and snapped their heads up to look at me, I saw that both were crying. A shadow of absolute fury passed across Leila's face as she recognised me, but fortunately her crossbow was leaning against the wall beside the door, too far for her to reach.

'You,' she said quietly, dropping her gaze to the floor.

'Is this him?' asked the other woman, staring at me with naked hostility. She seemed familiar; as I looked back, I realised she was the girl with the spotted hair scarf who had propositioned me and Poole on our first visit to Southwark. Her hair was loose now, and the scarf bunched in her lap; she raised it in a fist to wipe her eyes.

'I'm sorry if this is a bad time,' I began, 'but I needed to speak to you and it couldn't wait.'

'Just a moment,' Leila said, not looking at me, her voice subdued. She stood and poked the fire in the hearth, where her pot of water was simmering. The logs cracked and sparked as the flames leapt up with renewed vigour. In my view the fire did not need stoking; the room was already unbearably hot. She remained there unmoving, crouched over the fire for a few moments with the poker in her hand, until I began to wonder if she had forgotten me. I cleared my throat to speak, and with one swift movement she spun round, took two strides across the floor and held the glowing orange tip of the poker half an inch from my eye.

'You piece of shit.' Her voice was shaking with fury. I thought it best not to move. 'Where is he?'

'What?' I held up my hands in surrender, but she only pulled her lips back in a snarl; I could see the muscles working in her jaw as she spoke through her teeth.

'Tell me what you've done to him or I'll burn both your eyes out and you can listen to them sizzling and popping. Where is my son?'

'You don't have a son,' I said. It was a gamble, in the light of her graphic threat, but I thought it was worth a try.

There was a brief silence; I heard the other woman draw in a sharp breath. Leila stared at me and then let out a bloodcurdling roar.

'Oh, you filthy, sick bastard – if you've laid a finger on Joe—' The words collapsed into a sob; she fought to master herself, but for a moment the arm holding the poker wobbled, long enough for me to grasp her by the wrist and force her hand up until we were battling to hold it vertical over our heads. I tightened my grip and she let it fall to the ground with a clatter.

'I haven't touched Joe,' I said, releasing her and stepping back.

She rubbed her wrist. 'Then how would you know he – she – if you haven't—'

'I sent a boy I know to find Joe this morning. He happened to see her stop for a piss.'

She cursed softly in Arabic. 'Stupid child. I told her to be more careful about that.' Her eyes snapped up to meet mine. 'Who have you told?'

'No one.'

'And this boy of yours?'

'He won't say anything.'

She did not look convinced. 'I don't trust you. Do you blame me? Have you seen what they do to girls Josefina's age in Southwark? And with what she sees at close quarters in here' – she gestured to the table where she had operated on the young woman that morning – 'do you wonder she doesn't want to become a woman?'

'They do it to boys too, as I understand.'

'True. But it's easier to protect a boy for longer, so as far as you're concerned, if my Joe wants to be a boy, that's what he is. Now tell me what you've done with him.'

'I haven't seen him, I swear. I was hoping to speak to both of you. Is he not at the Unicorn?'

'Hasn't been there since this afternoon. Hasn't been home. Hell of a coincidence – you turn up asking questions about what he's seen in the Cross Bones, and a few hours later he vanishes.'

'Could he have run away?'

She shook her head. 'He wouldn't. Not unless he was really afraid for his life. More likely someone thought he might have seen them with the dead girl and wanted to stop him talking. That leaves you, or whoever you told.'

'I think Joe was afraid,' I said. 'Listen – I need to ask you something, it might be connected.'

She put a hand on her hip, swiped fiercely at her eyes with the knuckles of the other and nodded for me to continue.

'It's – private,' I said, looking at the dark-haired woman, who had remained silent, watching us intently.

'Don't mind her.' Leila tossed a glance over her shoulder. 'This is my neighbour, Anneke. She's lost her friend too.'

'I'm sorry,' I said, not knowing what else to offer. 'God rest her.'

Anneke balled her scarf between her fingers. 'She's not dead. At least, I don't know for sure. She's missing, like little Joe. But she—' She broke off and fresh tears sprang to her eyes. I looked back to Leila in time to see the warning in her eyes.

'Sit,' she said to me, indicating the empty stool by the fire. She crossed to a cabinet in the corner and brought out a bottle filled with a clear liquid, and three small glasses. She handed one to me and Anneke and filled them. I sniffed at it suspiciously.

'What is this?'

She gave me a long look. '*Aguardiente*. I'd have thought a Spaniard would recognise that.' I didn't reply. After a pause, she said: 'If you know anything that will help find Joe, let's hear it. Don't look at it like that, drink it – do you think I'm going to drug you?' She knocked back her own glass and gestured to Anneke to do the same. I hesitated, then drank it off, though I still did not entirely trust her. A sharp heat spread through my veins and I felt beads of sweat stand out on my brow, so close to the fire.

'Do you sell your opium?' I asked, when the burning had passed.

She made a noise of contempt through her teeth. 'That's your question? No. I keep it to relieve pain, for when I treat patients.'

'Where do you get it?'

'Not your business.' She glared at me, then sighed. 'A man I know works on cargo ships from Morocco, he brings it in with the spices and silks. But I never know when he's coming, so what I have has to go a long way. Besides, you need to know how to mix the tincture in the right proportion. It's powerful stuff, and I've seen what it can do in the wrong hands. I would not just hand it out for profit.' She curled her lip; I had offended her.

'Could someone have stolen some from you?'

'Impossible. I keep it locked in that cupboard with all my dangerous herbs, as you saw, and the key around my neck. No one could have got in here without my knowing. I know how to defend myself.'

'Yes, I've seen,' I said. 'Could Joe have stolen it? He knew where the key was.'

She shook her head. 'I'd have noticed if any were missing. Anyway, Joe wouldn't touch it, why would you think that?'

'He told me he was worried about going to Hell for something he'd done.'

She cursed again under her breath. 'That's Captain Fortescue putting that in his head again, I'll bet. Did Joe say what it was, this sin of his?'

'No. Only that he didn't intend any harm, but harm had come of it. And I believe the dead girl in the Cross Bones was drugged with opium before she was killed.'

At that, Leila's eyes widened, and she exchanged a glance with Anneke.

'It's funny you should ask about Joe stealing,' she said slowly. 'I'd swear my opium has not been touched, but I did notice something missing a few days ago.' She held out her hands, palms down, so I could see the reddish-brown tracery painted on the backs. 'It's fading, see. I thought I should refresh it, but when I went to mix my henna paste, it wasn't there. I asked Joe if he'd seen it and he said I'd run out. But

I was sure I hadn't. I don't know what that has to do with anything.'

'Is henna a drug?'

'No. That's why I don't keep it locked up.'

'Then I can't see that it's relevant. Can you think of anyone else around here who might be able to get hold of opium? It's important – if I can find out who drugged the murdered girl, then I believe I have her killer, and they can let your father-in-law go free.'

Her expression brightened briefly at this, before a shadow fell again. She glanced at Anneke, who shrugged as if to say it was not her decision.

'I shouldn't be telling you this. I'll do it if it will get the old man out,' Leila said, her voice tight with anger. 'Everyone knows Abe Goodchild wouldn't harm a mouse. But there will be consequences for me if it's known I told you.'

'I will protect you from any repercussions,' I said solemnly. It was an absurd claim, and I realised the emptiness of it as soon as the words were out. So did Leila.

'Oh will you, my handsome Spanish saviour, who is probably not even Spanish?' She let out a scornful laugh. 'How lucky I am, to have your protection. You know, I could have killed you twice over today, if I were less generous.'

I acknowledged this with a rueful smile.

'Well, then,' she said. 'Your friend, Captain Fortescue. I know you know him – Joe told me he saw you greet each other this morning at the Unicorn. He is the only other person I know in Southwark who has a ready supply of opium.'

'Fortescue?' I tried to temper my amazement. 'Where does he get it?'

She looked at the floor. 'From me.'

'So you *are* selling it?'

'There is no money exchanged, and no profit to me, believe me. He halves my supply.' She twisted her mouth in anger.

'Then – why?'

'Call it a quid pro quo. He helped me once, and that was his price.'

'Seems steep. It must have been quite a favour.'

'I believe I have paid back the original debt several times over. But he does not see it that way.'

I pressed my hands together between my knees and stared into the fire. So Ballard had a ready supply of opium, *and* he was in London when Clara was killed.

'What does he do with it?' I asked. 'Does he take it himself?'

'I couldn't say. He says he wants it for the same purposes as I – to relieve the pain of those who suffer. But he is not a physician, as far as I know, so I'm sure he is doing more harm than good, even if he means well. I know what he is, mind you.' She gave me a direct look. 'What kind of man would spend all his time at the Unicorn and never touch the girls, except one who has taken a vow? And perhaps the same is true of you, since you are his associate.' I began to speak but she held up a hand. 'Your secrets are no concern of mine, as mine are none of yours. So there is your answer.' She poured each of us another shot of aguardiente. 'I must suppose it will not help me, nor my father-in-law, since you will not want to believe your friend a killer.'

'He is not exactly my friend,' I said, drinking the liquor down. 'Joe is afraid of him. I saw that this morning.'

She tossed her hair. Anneke gave a contemptuous snort.

'He fills Joe's head with hellfire. I don't care if he is a priest – you don't preach to a child like that, put them in fear of eternal punishment.' Her face pinched in anger. 'He's told Joe we are destined for Hell because of my religion, and because I am a murderess.'

'*Are* you?'

'I've killed better men than you,' she said, straight-faced. She left a beat, then she and Anneke burst out laughing at my expression; I laughed too, in a slightly forced way, since I suspected it might well be true. 'He means the girls,' she continued, her face serious again. 'The service I do for them. He calls it murdering babies in the womb. We have argued about it – I tell him often the women would die if I did not get the child out, and in most cases it is nothing you would recognise as an infant, just a clot of flesh. Don't make that squeamish face – you are not a woman, you will never have to see it. But Fortescue calls it murder, and says it is against God's law, and now I have Joe asking me every night, Mama, shall the Devil come for you because you kill unborn babies?' She shook her head, her lips tight. 'He may be a good man, but to fill a child's head with that—'

'*Is* he a good man?'

She looked at me sharply. 'What, you don't think so? I thought he was one of yours.'

'I hardly know what to make of him. I think he's a man with an unshakeable sense of right and wrong.'

'They're the most dangerous.' She swallowed her drink. 'He does some good, I can't deny that. He takes seriously his duty to care for the poor and the outcasts, which is more than many so-called men of God bother with. But I wish he would leave off his mission to terrify my child into the arms of Christ because he's afraid I'm raising him as a secret Mohammedan. Joe even gave me back—' She stopped, biting down her words, as if afraid of saying too much.

'Show him,' Anneke urged, leaning forward to pour herself another shot. 'He might be able to help.'

Leila rose reluctantly and took the key from around her neck to unlock the cupboard where she kept the opium. She returned with what looked like a silver necklace glinting between her fingers. When she dropped it into my lap, I recognised it immediately.

'A misbaha,' I said, turning the beads over between my fingers. The craftsmanship was exquisite, the silver worn smooth in places from years of use.

Leila nodded approvingly. 'Ignorant English people think it

is a rosary. I suppose it would be as dangerous to be caught with either. These were my father's prayer beads. They were one of the few precious things I was able to bring from Spain with me when I was taken to England. I gave them to Joe to wear in secret, to honour my parents, who he never knew. When he told me a few weeks ago he didn't want them any more because Captain Fortescue said all the Mohammedans were burning in Hell, including his grandfather, I swear, I almost went after your friend and tore his throat out. Instead I lost my temper at Joe.' She took the beads from me and caressed them under the pad of her thumb. 'Joe cried and said he was sorry. He promised to wear them for my sake. But he knew to keep them secret – he would not have lost them or let them be stolen. This is how I am certain he hasn't run away, and I fear for him. Anneke found these this evening, on the riverbank.'

'I was out there earlier,' she said, pulling her stool closer to me. 'I went with a customer – there's an abandoned boat on the mudbank there where you can get some privacy and not have to lie on the wet ground. The tide was out, so after he'd gone, I walked along the edge to see what had washed up, especially by the stairs. There was a bear-baiting tonight too, that always brings well to-do people across the river, you'd be amazed what they drop as they're getting in and out of boats.'

I nodded, thinking of Joe combing the graveyard for lost valuables, embarrassed that I had not thought before of how many people lived by scavenging in this city.

'There's a little jetty between Goat Stairs and Falcon Stairs,' Anneke continued. 'The boatmen don't use it for passengers because it's mostly rotten, they just tie up there if they're having a break. But as I was walking past, I saw something glinting. I climbed out along it and found the beads on a post at the end. I knew they were Joe's, so I came straight to Leila.'

'What time was this?' I asked.

'Not long after eight,' she said immediately. 'I can be sure because my client finished his business just as the bells at St Mary Overy struck eight. I said to him, "That's good timing." He didn't think so – he said his wife was expecting him home at seven.'

I turned to Leila. 'When did you last see Joe?'

'I passed him at the Unicorn around three this afternoon,' she said. 'I was on my way out, I'd had a message to go down to the Cardinal's Hat, there was a girl there needed treatment for a nasty – well, you don't need to know. Joe was in the yard, brushing down a horse – he said he'd see me at home if not before. He usually finishes work around seven but he'll stay to earn extra if it's busy, so I wasn't worried when he didn't come back by eight. Until Anneke turned up with the misbaha.' Her face drew tight and I saw how afraid she was, and how hard she was trying to hide it. 'Joe would not have been parted from this willingly. So I can only think that he must have been taken, and dropped it on the jetty as a sign.'

'Taken somewhere by boat, you mean? But in broad daylight – that means he must have gone willingly, otherwise people would have noticed a scuffle, surely?'

'You'd be surprised. People turn a blind eye to anything in Southwark.'

'He's right, though,' Anneke said. 'It's busy out on the riverfront, someone would have remarked on a child being bundled into a boat against his will. Maybe Joe knew the person.'

'Leila – I know Joe didn't tell me the whole truth this morning. Did he say anything more about what he had seen in the Cross Bones the night the girl was killed? If we're to find him, any detail might help.' I didn't say, if we're to find him alive. She knew what I meant.

'No detail. But he did say' – the beads clicked rapidly between her fingers – 'he was going to get his grandfather out of prison. He knew that Abe hadn't touched the girl – we all knew that – but Joe said he could tell the constables something that would mean they had to let the old man go.'

'Because he knew who the real killer was, do you think? And did he speak to anyone?'

She let out a weary sigh. 'Look, I know you're a foreigner, but even you must have realised by now – people round here don't talk willingly to the authorities. See what happened to Abe when he tried to do the right thing and reported that girl's death. I told Joe to forget whatever he thought he'd seen. The old man went to gaol to keep Joe out of it, I told him, and it would do no good for the child to go about Southwark shouting that he knew what really happened, with the killer still out there.'

'So he didn't tell you any names?'

'I didn't want to hear them. I told him never to speak of it again, to me or anyone else. But someone knows, don't they?' She looked at me and her dark eyes were bright with fear. 'Someone thinks Joe saw them that night.'

'Did anyone else see Joe this evening, after you? It might give us an idea of when he disappeared.' If it was one of the conspirators, I thought, it would have to have been before the bear-baiting began at seven.

'I went round to the Unicorn to ask the stable boys – no one recalls seeing him much after I did,' Leila said. 'In fact, the head ostler was annoyed because it was busy and he thought Joe had given himself the afternoon off. That lad with the scabby face said he saw Joe talking to a man at the entrance to the yard sometime in the afternoon, but that could have been anyone, and the boy was too useless to remember a description, except that the person was tall.'

Ballard was quite tall, I thought. But then so were Titch and Babington, and even Douglas had a way of carrying himself that made his stature seem greater. Any one of them could have got Joe across the river by boat and been back in Southwark in time for the bear-baiting. The mystery was why they would bother taking him north to the City; if you wanted to be rid of someone quietly, Southwark was the obvious place to do it.

'This jetty – is it near the bear garden?' I asked.

'Quite near. I would take you to the place, only . . .' her eyes slid sideways to the door, 'I want to be here in case Joe comes back.'

'I could show him,' Anneke said, a little too eagerly.

Leila gave her a tired smile. 'Steady, girl. I'm not sure he's allowed what you've got to show.'

Anneke put her head on one side and looked me up and down, appraising. 'What a waste.'

'I know.' Leila laughed. I began to feel slightly uncomfortable, with the two of them assessing me as if I were the one for sale.

'Ladies, let us concentrate on the matter in hand,' I said, rising from the stool and feeling the effects of the liquor in the hot room. 'And leave off speculating about what I am allowed. I answer to no one but myself, and idle talk can be dangerous.' I met Leila's eye. 'As you should know better than most.'

She nodded, looking briefly chastened as she opened the door; a welcome blast of night air rushed in to cool our faces. 'Let me know if you find anything. I'll owe you.'

Anneke hooked her arm through mine as she led me on a shortcut through the alleys towards the river, pressing closer than she needed to; she said I made her feel safe. I held up the lantern Leila had given us and tried to ignore the soft pressure of the girl's breast against my arm. Anneke was not pretty, but there was a liveliness about her that seemed especially admirable given the life she must lead, and her warmth was making me think too much of my earlier encounter with Sophia.

'Don't mind Leila,' she said, after a while. 'She is fierce because she worries about Joe.'

'I get the impression she has a low opinion of men.'

'So would you, if you had to see the things she sees. Southwark women get the worst of what men can do, and Leila has to clean them up after. It's no wonder she fights to protect that child like a mother bear.'

We emerged on to Bankside. The sky was clear and a wash of moonlight gleamed silver on the river and the mudflats alongside. Points of light from wherries bobbed up and down further out on the water, and to our right I could see the lights from torches burning at the entrances to the brothels. I hoped I would not run into any of the conspirators on their way home from the Unicorn; Father Prado would have a hard time explaining what he was doing combing the riverbank in the company of a street whore.

'Over here,' Anneke said, pulling me towards the shore. Ahead, a long dark shape stood out against the movement of the water.

'Is that your abandoned boat?' I asked.

'Yes. Do you want to go there quickly? It's dry, better than lying on the ground.' She gave me the appraising look again from the tail of her eye. 'A shilling, for you?'

'No – thank you.' I tried to soften the rejection. 'Bit cold. You don't work at the Unicorn, then?'

She let out a bright burst of laughter. 'Are you joking? They can afford to be picky at the Unicorn, people pay a lot of money, they want girls who look like well-bred virgins. When Lotte and I came off the boat, we were already much too old for any of the licensed houses. I'm twenty-six, and Lotte twenty-four. Old nags now, both of us. But there are always men whose purses don't stretch to the licensed houses, so we keep food on the table. Just about.'

'The boat from where?'

'What you would call the Low Countries. There are a lot of Flemish girls in Southwark. The Dutch and Flemish merchants know this – when they're in town on business, they like to be able to relax and speak their own language. I know a little of your language too, if you want that.'

'English is fine. Is Lotte your friend who has disappeared?'

She nodded. 'I am worried for her.'

'Have you told the constables she's missing?'

She turned and stared at me, then laughed again. 'Don't you listen to anything? This is Southwark. Girls go missing every day here, and no one cares about a foreign whore. The only reason they have poor Abe Goodchild in gaol over that girl in the Cross Bones is because they think she was a gentlewoman and they have to make a show of doing something. No one is going to help me look for Lotte. I just hope she hasn't done anything stupid.' She bit her lip.

'Why would she?'

'She's been very down lately. She thought she had early signs of the pox. But that's Lotte – a headache and she's convinced it's the plague, a little rash and she's dying of the French pox. I told her she should let Leila examine her, then she would know for certain, and Leila has treatments, but I think Lotte was afraid of having it confirmed. When she is melancholy, she can sometimes do reckless things. Anyway, you don't want to hear about her – we're supposed to be looking for Joe. This is the jetty, here.'

She let go of my arm so that I could walk out to the wooden posts, just visible in the moonlight against the gleam of the river. I could see when I held up the lantern that the boards were half rotted away, and some of the slats were missing. Careful not to lose my footing, I walked the length of the short jetty, watching the black water swirl beneath me in the gaps, testing each plank before I put my weight on it. At the end, I crouched and examined the posts where Anneke said she had found the prayer beads, but I could see no sign of torn fabric or anything that might indicate a struggle. Across the river, a few scattered lights showed the landing stage at Paul's Wharf; beside it I could make out the façade of Baynard's Castle. A little further west, though invisible in the dark, was Water Lane, and Salisbury Court, the residence of the French ambassador, where I had lived for two years, and where I had first met Archibald Douglas. He was right; in some ways it did feel as if hardly any time had passed since those days. Here we both were, tangled in yet another plot to put Mary Stuart on the throne – except that my role was to help bring her to the block. I wished I knew what Douglas's interest was.

I looked back towards Bankside; there would have been plenty of people passing in the afternoon, and boats on the river. Joe could not have been abducted against his will without someone noticing. I picked my way back to Anneke and suggested we walk west towards Paris Garden, the opposite direction to the Unicorn.

'Why would Joe get in a boat with someone when he was supposed to be at work?' I asked.

She shrugged. 'Threats or promises, what else, with a child? Joe would do anything for his family – if someone told him they would help get his grandfather out of gaol, or said they would hurt his mother, he'd go wherever he was told.'

'Don't you find it strange, talking of Joe as *he*?'

She made a rueful face. 'My old woman put me to work on my back at twelve. Josefina is lucky to have a mother like Leila, who will do anything to keep her from that. I'll call her whatever they want if it helps her stay safe. That's why Leila puts up with that pompous arse Captain Fortescue – because he protected Joe once.'

'Then Balla— Fortescue knows Joe is a girl?'

'I don't know about that. But a few months ago he caught a customer at the Unicorn trying it on with Joe. The man was drunk, he'd pushed the child inside an empty stall in the yard and got his old pizzle out, there was no one else about. Suppose he thought a little brown-skinned stable boy was worth nothing, he'd get away with it.' Her jaw tightened with anger. 'But the Captain went in after them before anything could happen, and he dragged this man out to the yard and beat him black and blue. The bully boys from the Unicorn had to pull him away before there was murder done. Leila said the fellow was barely breathing when he'd finished. Fortescue has a devil of a temper. So you see why she does what he asks – you keep men like that on your side.'

I nodded. We had reached Falcon Stairs, where a couple of wherries were tethered with tired, cold-looking boatmen huddled inside, no doubt waiting for a fare from those stumbling out of the brothels.

'I should go home,' I said.

'Sure you don't want company?'

'I'm tired. Sorry.'

'Shame. You have a lovely face.' She reached up a cold hand and stroked my cheek. I flinched in surprise. 'Well, if you won't have me, I'd better go and earn an honest living elsewhere. A girl's got to eat.'

'I hope you find your friend,' I said, as she turned to go. 'And if you think of anything else that might help Joe, you can get word to me at the Saracen's Head in Holborn.'

'Why are you doing this for Joe?' she asked, her eyes narrowing. 'Or is it for Leila? It wouldn't surprise me. Most men are scared of her, but you have more . . .' she thrust her hips forward and mimed grasping a pair of balls.

'Because I want to find out who killed the girl in the Cross Bones. I think Joe knows, and I fear that my questions might have made things worse for him. The least I can do is try to help him, if that's the case.'

She nodded. 'Must be nice to be the kind of girl who has beautiful men to care when you get killed,' she said, with an edge of resentment.

I thought of the ravaged face I had seen on the table in the leper chapel. 'I don't think *nice* describes her situation,' I replied, a little curtly, and turned to the boatmen, calling 'Oars, ho!'

TWENTY-ONE

I walked home to Herne's Rents dragging my feet as my mind turned over the day's events. Anneke had let me take Leila's lantern – she said she could find her way around Southwark in the dark – but the candle was almost burned out by the time I reached Holborn, and I felt obscurely disappointed that there had been no sign of Ben this evening. Once or twice, on the walk up from the river, I had thought I heard a tell-tale clatter of a stone kicked accidentally, or the swish of fabric as someone walked behind me, and whipped around expecting to find him at my back as I had the previous night, but there was no one. His absence made me feel oddly exposed; I had liked the idea that he was keeping an eye on me. I hoped nothing had happened to him; I was already too preoccupied with Joe's disappearance.

No matter which way I looked at it, everything led back to Ballard. Ballard, who had his own supply of opium; who had lied about being in France when Clara was killed; who had seen Joe talking to me that morning, and whose appearance had frightened Joe so much that he ran off; whose devotion to the plot was so all-consuming I could easily believe him capable of murdering anyone he believed to have betrayed or sabotaged it. Christ, I thought, climbing the stairs to our rooms – I hope Gifford survived their little tête-à-tête.

I had wondered more than once what had persuaded Clara Poole to go to the Cross Bones in the middle of the night; I now realised that Ballard could have convinced her. She was eager to ingratiate herself with the conspirators; if he had said he needed her to pick up an important message there, she would have obeyed without question, to prove her worth. But Ballard had told me he would not take an innocent life, and didn't Joe count as exactly that – a child who had happened to see something they should not? Poole had called Ballard ruthless – but the priest was also a man who risked his life to bring the sacraments to the sick and dying, who took food to the poor, who had stopped lonely, grieving Savage from throwing himself into the river, and beaten a man almost to death for trying to abuse a child. I had to hope that, having saved Joe once, Ballard would have enough conscience not to hurt him, even if he meant to frighten the child into keeping quiet.

I found Gifford picking up the piles of shirts he had strewn around the floor of his room and folding them. I smiled, thinking of Savage's impatience with Titch's untidiness earlier.

'There you are,' he said, peevish. 'Where have you been this time?'

'In the company of women,' I said. 'Glad to see you're not at the bottom of the Thames. You managed not to give us away, then?'

'Don't even joke about it,' he said, sitting heavily on the edge of my bed. 'It was awful, I was shaking like I had the palsy the whole time we were walking, I had to tell him it was because I was nervous about the pursuivants.'

'What did he want?'

'He was asking about my father again.'

'About his release from prison? Does Ballard suspect?'

'No, not that. He's demanding to know how many men

my father could spare to help free the Queen of Scots. Now that there's no time for Babington and Titch to raise an army of a hundred, or whatever they boasted. Ballard seems to think that if my father has ten strong men in his household with farm implements, we can take Chartley Manor.' He let out a bitter little laugh. 'I won't have my father dragged into this, the idea of it would make his heart stop. But Ballard is determined that the success of the plot depends on my family's willingness to make sacrifices.'

'Gilbert,' I sat beside him and laid a hand on his shoulder. 'You do know this isn't going to happen, don't you?'

'What?' He jerked his head to me, eyes wide as if I had confused him.

'The plot isn't going to succeed – that's the whole point of us being here, remember? Babington won't get anywhere near Staffordshire, any more than your Bessie will get close enough to the Queen to poison her bedtime posset. It's all being monitored.'

'She's not mine yet,' he said gloomily.

'Do you think she would really do it? Kill Elizabeth for Babington, I mean?'

'Not for Babington.' He scowled. 'For Mary, though. She loved her as a child.'

'But there's a world of difference between a remembered fondness for someone who was kind to you when you were four, and committing regicide for them. Doesn't it strike you as odd?'

He hunched his shoulders, defensive. 'How do you mean?'

'Out of nowhere, she gets a message from Babington, who she hasn't seen for seven or more years, and by the end of the day she's agreed to assassinate Queen Elizabeth. She didn't seem to need much persuading.'

'Mary Stuart inspires strong loyalties.'

'If you say so. I only wondered if Bessie might have another motive.'

'Such as?'

I shrugged. 'You tell me – you know her. Does she write to Mary Stuart?'

'How would I know?' he snapped, rising abruptly and returning to his shirts.

'Because you are the only person who can get letters in and out of Chartley Manor,' I said, fixing him with a deliberate look. He turned his back to me.

'You're accusing me of carrying letters that I don't show to Walsingham?'

'Not accusing. Asking.'

'I don't answer to you. I saw you looking at the Gifford girl tonight,' he added, with a malicious curl to his voice.

'A man can look.'

'I wonder now that I ever thought her attractive.' He picked up his green cloak from the floor and slapped the dust from it as if it were a personal enemy. 'She has no tits to speak of, and her face is too thin.'

'To each his own,' I said mildly.

'She's taller than you,' he added spitefully.

'Doesn't matter when you're lying down,' I snapped back, and regretted it; I should know better than to rise to his needling. I was about to take off my boots and fall into bed, when I suddenly remembered Babington's request for confession. 'Has Babington written his letter to Mary yet, do you know?'

He left a petulant pause before he answered. 'I should think he's down there writing it now. The supper broke up early – Ballard said he wanted an early night.'

'Just think, Gilbert,' I said, forcing a note of cheerfulness into my voice, 'as soon as that letter is written, you can take it to Phelippes and this business will be all but over. You'll have no need to go to Staffordshire at all, except to visit your father, who will never know how close he came to raising a pitchfork army. Listen – I need a quick word with Babington. Leave the door on the latch, I won't be long.'

He turned at that. 'Find out if he means to mention Bessie in the letter,' he said. 'Advise him not to, if you can.'

'That might look suspicious, if I start interfering.'

'If he sets her name down in writing, she will be arrested for treason.' He twisted the cloak in his hands, giving me a pleading look.

'As far as we know, she's planning to poison the Queen, Gilbert. That makes her a traitor.'

'They would burn her. Does she deserve that?'

'Not for me to say. Or you. We just intercept the letters.'

'I don't believe you are really so callous. Please. Try to convince Babington to keep her name out. Otherwise—'

Otherwise you will destroy that letter before it reaches Walsingham, I thought. I picked up a candle from the table. 'Don't wait up,' I said, and closed the door on his agonised expression, thinking how straightforward all our plans would be, if sex did not cloud our judgement.

I hesitated outside Babington's door and took a deep breath, willing myself into a priestly frame of mind. It was many years since I had heard confession; I must not slip up over the phrases with Babington so keen to unburden himself. My task as Father Prado was to relieve him of whatever was weighing on his conscience, ease it gently from him with promises of God's mercy, and hope that it was something of use to Walsingham. I wished there could have been some way to bring another witness with me, Robin Poole or even Gifford at a pinch, since a verbal confession could always be denied, but if it touched on Clara's murder, it would be a start.

I knocked gently, but there was no reply. To knock louder risked disturbing the neighbours, and it was almost midnight now; instead, I turned the latch as quietly as I could and opened the door a couple of inches.

Inside, by the low light of a lamp, I saw Babington stretched out naked on his bed, head to toe with another man, each of them with the other's cock in his mouth. In the instant it took to process what I was seeing, I thought of the old Gnostic symbol of the ouroboros, the serpent eating its own tail. As I pulled the door shut, Babington's companion raised his head sharply and met my eye. It was Robin Poole.

I took the stairs up to my own floor two at a time, so fast that my candle snuffed itself out and I had to feel my way along the corridor to my room by counting the doors. Well, I thought, that was a confession of sorts. I wondered if Babington had intended for me to walk in on them, or if he had forgotten he had asked me to visit. My room was dark; I fumbled my way to the tinderbox I kept by my bed and managed to relight the candle by the time Poole opened the door and stood on the threshold in only his breeches, breathing heavily. We stared at one another for a moment, until I motioned for him to come in. I was relieved to see that the partition door to Gifford's room was closed.

'You told me you could not get close enough to the conspirators to find out anything useful,' I whispered, trying to keep my voice even while I set the candle in a holder and lit another from it. 'That looked quite close to me.'

'I do what I must to get information,' he said through his teeth. 'Don't you?'

'Not that,' I said.

He made a contemptuous noise. 'Well, you are without sin, congratulations. Judge me if you wish.'

'I'm not judging you. I don't care where you put it. I am only trying to understand what it means for our situation. Does Walsingham know?'

At that, he grabbed me around the throat and pushed me up against the door.

'No,' he hissed, his face an inch from mine. 'Nor is he going to.'

Tired as I was, I mustered the energy to draw my fist back and punch him in the stomach. He rocked on his heels and let go of me; we watched one another warily, but neither of us had the appetite for a fight.

'Phelippes suspected,' he said in a whisper, his shoulders slumping. 'I don't know how. He called me in to see him and asked, in his usual way. "Robin Poole, are you a sodomite?"' His impression of Phelippes's flat monotone and severe expression made me smile.

'I didn't think he would care about that kind of thing,' I said.

'It wasn't a moral objection. He was afraid it would leave me open to blackmail, or that Ballard would kick me out of the group if he knew. That priest has very strong views about sin.'

'I know.'

'So I denied it, and to strengthen my case I thought it would be clever if—' He stopped, passing his hands over his face.

'If you introduced your sister to the conspirators, so that everyone would think she was the one having an affair with Babington.'

He nodded. 'Anthony thought it a good idea too. He feared Savage and Ballard suspected.'

I thought of Savage's remark about Babington's marriage at the Castle dinner, and the way he had left that insinuating *although* hanging.

'He might be right. So what happened – she did not play her part?'

'She complicated things,' he said, through his fingers.

'By falling in love with him?'

At that, he raised his head and laughed. 'God, no. She disliked Anthony from the start, though she was willing to pretend, for my sake.'

'Then what?'

'She—' He broke off and glanced at the partition door. 'Wait – is Gilbert in?'

I turned to follow his gaze. I motioned to him to be silent, and slid the latch open to check. When I heard no sound from within, I pushed the door wider, to see that Gifford's bed was empty and all the neatly folded clothes vanished.

'*Merda.*' I whipped around and stared at Robin. 'He was here five minutes ago, I left him tidying his clothes.'

'Packing, you mean.' He brought a candle and shone it around Gifford's room. 'You fool. Looks like he's run out on us.'

'He must have taken the other staircase, while I was on the landing. He can't have got far, come on.'

I raced down the stairs and into the street, to find it empty; with only the light of one small candle it was impossible to see which direction Gifford could have taken. He may even have been a few feet away, hiding in a gap between houses until he was sure no one was looking for him. Damn him; I realised he must have planned to wait until I was asleep before leaving, to give himself enough of a head start, but decided to take the chance while I was downstairs with Babington. A moment later the street door clattered and Poole joined me, after picking up his shirt and boots on the way.

'No sign,' I said. 'I should have guessed he might do this. He doesn't want to take that letter to Walsingham if it incriminates Bessie. And Babington won't hand it over except to his trusted courier. Would he give you a copy?'

Poole looked at his feet. 'Uh – I don't think he's had time to write it yet.'

I rolled my eyes. 'Oh yes – he's been otherwise occupied. Look – Phelippes needs to know Gifford's bolted. You'd better get to Leadenhall Street right now and tell him.'

He glanced back up at Herne's Rents, where lights still burned in some of the windows – including, presumably, Babington's. 'Can't you go?'

'No,' I said bluntly. 'That's the price of me forgetting what I just saw.' I ran a hand through my hair. 'How in God's name would Gifford get away at this time of night? Where would he find a horse?' Then a thought struck me. 'Tell Phelippes to try the house of Lady Grace Cavendish on the Strand – Bessie might be helping Gifford escape.'

'Wouldn't it be quicker if you went directly there to look for him? If she's giving him a horse he'll be long gone by the time I get to Leadenhall and Phelippes manages to organise men in pursuit.'

I was forced to concede the logic of this, though I too cast a wistful glance up at the window where my bed waited for me. I regretted my enthusiasm for hearing Babington's confession; I could have been asleep by now, and blissfully ignorant of all this.

'I'll be back here as soon as I can. Leave a note under my door if you find anything.' I gestured back to Herne's Rents. 'Better tell your *inamorato* to hurry up with his letter. Say Father Prado has sent you home to pray and repent.'

Poole shot me a withering glare, but he nodded and limped back inside the building. I returned to my room to fetch a lantern and tinderbox and stood for a moment, buttoning my doublet with one hand, looking at Gifford's empty bed and cursing all of them.

TWENTY-TWO

I took the path across Lincoln's Inn Fields with my knife drawn; I could not shake the sense that I was being followed, and in that lonely stretch of countryside, at this time of night, I was making myself an obvious target. Was it Douglas tailing me still? I couldn't see why he would have need, now that he had revealed himself and made his threats, unless to show that he didn't trust me. Though more than once I found myself whipping around for some noise at my back, or starting like a frightened deer when an owl glided low and silent past my face, I saw no one until I came out into Little Drury Lane on the far side of the fields. Here I found one or two late drinkers weaving their way home; at the junction with the Strand I ducked into the shadow of a building to avoid a pair of watchmen, their lanterns held high on a wooden pole, calling to stragglers to get themselves off the streets or face a night in gaol for vagrancy. The Strand was lined with some of the grandest houses in London, belonging to the wealthiest families, so the area was well patrolled, and anyone found loitering immediately suspected of intent to rob. I sincerely wished I had not volunteered for this task; not only did I not know which was the Cavendish house, I was only now realising that these residences would be bristling with guards, and I could hardly knock on the front gate and enquire whether Gifford had called in for a horse.

When the watch had passed, I started westwards along the street, keeping to the shadows on the opposite side to the ornate gatehouses and high walls that separated the palatial façades from the road. At the back, these houses had elaborate gardens that stretched down to the river. I reflected that if I had known the right house, it might have been easier to hire a boat and try to get in that way – but then a wherryman would know my business, and would likely remember the Spanish-looking foreigner seeking to slip over a back wall. As I continued along the street, I recognised the entrance to Arundel House, London residence of Philip Howard, Earl of Arundel; I had been invited to a dinner here three years earlier, during my involvement in the Throckmorton business, and had been lucky to escape with my life. The sight of the gatehouse tower sent an involuntary shudder down my neck. As I paused outside, peering as far up the street as the light from my feeble lantern would allow, a man passed me, weaving from side to side and singing. I took a chance and asked if he knew the Cavendish house; he muttered something about lions and pointed vaguely towards the Charing Cross.

I carried on towards the end of the street and came to a large house with stone lions crouching sentinel on the pillars flanking the front gates. I hoped the drunk was right; it was going to be difficult enough to get into one of these mansions and I didn't want to end up arrested for breaking into the wrong one.

Gifford had not had so much of a head start; if Bessie Pierrepont was fitting him out with a horse to help him flee, I would have expected to see or hear some activity, but the place was sunk in silent darkness. But then the stable yard would surely be at the back, and Gifford was unlikely to have knocked at the main entrance at this time of night if he wanted to slip away unseen. To the left of the boundary wall I noticed the mouth of an alleyway running down towards the river. I followed it alongside the grounds until I had passed the main buildings; on the other side of the wall I could make out only the tops of trees. The wall must have been at least ten feet high, but it was clad in trailing ivy. I set the lantern down, removed the candle and snuffed it, tucking it into the bag at my belt, congratulating myself on remembering to bring the tinderbox. After a moment of waiting for my eyes to adjust to the dark, I grasped the plants with both hands and pulled myself up to the top of the wall, rolled over and dropped to the other side in blind faith, landing awkwardly in a shrubbery, though thankfully not a bed of nettles or rose bushes.

I crouched, listening for the sound of any guard dog or night watchman; when I was certain that no one was coming, I brushed myself down and tried to make out my position by the thin moonlight alone. I could see the shapes of low box hedges, and the pale lines of symmetrical paths where they had been laid in white gravel. I walked out a little way into the gardens until I had a clear view of the back of the house; a light burned in one window on an upper floor, but the rest of the household appeared to have retired for the night. There were a series of low outbuildings to the side of the house which were likely to be stables, but I heard nothing stirring. I turned and strained my eyes to see in the other direction, towards the river, when my eye was caught by a small light further down the garden. I began walking towards it, keeping to the path that ran along the inside of the boundary wall. As I drew closer, the light appeared doubled, and I realised that it was reflected in glass; to judge by the shadow ahead, I was looking at a small pavilion or summer house in the grounds, with a lamp burning inside. Could Gifford be taking shelter here overnight while he made further plans? I crept closer, across grass now silvered with dew, until I was able to crouch and peer into the window. To my surprise, I saw Sophia, wrapped in a heavy embroidered gown, propped up against cushions on a day bed with a wooden tray on her lap that held an inkpot and a sheaf of papers. She had washed all the garish make-up off her face and her hair hung in a loose twist over one shoulder. She twirled a quill between her fingers and her brow creased in a frown of concentration. An oil lamp burned on a small table beside her. My heart clenched with a potent mix of love and desire; I watched her, mesmerised, as she scribbled briefly and returned to stroking the plume of the quill along her cheekbone while she thought. God, I wanted her; it barely occurred to me to wonder what she was doing there, in the middle of the night. The summer house was lavishly furnished; Turkey carpets on the floor, and cushions in the corners, as well as the bed. I straightened up to ease my legs; the movement must have caught her eye because she snapped her head up and froze, like an animal scenting a predator. Her gaze met mine through the window and she gave a little scream, stifling it immediately with her fist as she jumped up, knocking her tray to the floor. She stared at me a moment longer before darting forward to pick up the spilled ink; when she looked up, her face was furious, but she gestured towards the door at the side.

I closed it behind me and stood, watching her.

'I'm going to kill you,' she muttered. 'There's ink all over the carpet – they'll know I've been in here now.'

'Here.' I unbuttoned my doublet, pulled my shirt over my head and pressed it to the stain on the carpet. I was not sure what I had wanted to prove, but I saw her relent; a smile hovered at her lips.

'Always the master of the extravagant gesture, Bruno.' Her gaze travelled over my naked chest. 'I see you've been looking after yourself in London. What in God's name are you doing here?'

'Who are you writing to secretly in the middle of the night?' I had wanted to make it sound like a joke, but it came out accusatory and demanding.

'Why, are you jealous?' She lifted her chin as if in challenge, laughing. I laughed too, to cover the truth that I had been seized by a sudden horrible image of some lover she had left behind in Paris. 'I'm writing to our mutual friend,' she said, lowering her voice, though there was no one for miles to hear. 'It takes me so long, though, to put it into cipher. I suppose you can do it easy as blinking.' She bent and picked up the paper from the floor. 'At least you didn't make me spill ink on my poor efforts. I'll never get it done by the time the boy comes in the morning, and I have important news for Thomas, about Bessie.'

'Oh yes? That she has agreed to the conspirators' plan?'

'Not just that.' Her eyes shone in the lamplight. 'She took a bath this evening after we returned from the bear garden. I knew she'd be at least an hour, so while she was soaking, I went through her room and found some letters. It turns out she does have a lover.'

'Not Gifford?'

'I doubt it. I don't like the girl, but credit her with some taste. I don't know his name, he's too sharp to sign it, but from the context it's obvious that he has some connection with Mary Stuart or her family.'

'That could be any number of men,' I said, though my first thought was: Douglas. 'Did you manage to read his letters to her?'

'I could only find a couple. They're in cipher so you may imagine how long it took me – your friend Phelippes gave me a code to try, and it worked, but it still took me forever. They're quite ambiguous – but in one this man is asking her to deliver an urgent message to Queen Elizabeth. It was dated ten days ago.'

Ten days; that would fit with Gifford's last visit to Staffordshire. 'Is that his word – a "message"? That could cover all manner of things, from a letter to a dose of poison.'

'I thought that. I could not see any sign that Bessie had

started on a reply, though. Maybe she has given it to Gifford already.'

For the love I bear you, it shall be done. Not Mary, then, but a man close to her – someone Gifford was supposed to deliver the letter to. Bessie must have concealed the truth about the correspondence; he would not willingly have agreed to carry love notes to a rival. But until we found Gifford, the man's identity would remain a mystery.

'Have you seen Gilbert here tonight?' I asked.

'Is that why you're creeping around the garden? Why would he be here?'

'He's disappeared. I thought he might have come to borrow a horse.'

'Why would he want a horse?'

'To run away.'

'Ah. But I wouldn't have seen him if he did. I sneak out of the back door, I don't go near the stables. Though I probably would have heard some commotion if they'd been getting horses ready, and it's been quiet all night.' She gestured around the summer house. 'This place is where Sir Henry brings his mistresses when he's at home. Lady Grace put her foot down about having them in the house. He's in Derbyshire at the moment, thank God, so I knew this would be empty.'

She glanced over her shoulder, and I felt the atmosphere in the room shift; we were both suddenly very aware of the bed behind us. I shivered, regretting my gallantry in offering up my shirt.

'Tonight, at the bear pit,' she said softly, taking a step towards me. 'Were you really hiding from someone, or was that just an excuse?'

I smiled. 'No, he was real.'

'Is he dangerous?'

I thought of Douglas's threat to ruin Sophia's face. 'Only if you're married to Mary Stuart.'

She frowned slightly as she tried to puzzle this out. 'But her husbands are dead.'

'Exactly.'

'So, you would not have kissed me if he had not been after you?'

'I would have thought you were beyond my purse.'

She laughed. Then she took another step forward and placed her hand flat on my chest, over my heart.

'Once again, I think you have come looking for me and it turns out you are really in search of Gilbert Gifford.'

'It's becoming a habit.'

'It's almost as if you're obsessed with him.'

'I can assure you it's not him I think about when I'm lying in my cold empty bed at night.'

She looked at me aslant from under her lashes. '*Is* your bed empty, Bruno? I find that hard to believe.'

'What would you care?'

She curled her fingers and scraped her nails lightly through the hair on my chest; a white-hot bolt of desire flashed through me. 'Of course I care. I just—'

'I don't know what you want from me, Sophia.' I had not meant it to sound as frustrated and full of blame as it came out.

She sighed and let her hand fall to her side. 'This is what you always do, Bruno. You can never just be with me. You must always be asking what happens next. You want promises I can't make.'

'Because I love you!' I pushed my hands through my hair and turned away, furious with her and with myself. 'Because every time you walk away from me I never know if it will be the last time I see you. I feel there is no solid ground under my feet.'

She gave a soft, sad laugh. 'What is it you think you want from me? Do you want a wife in a white apron, a little cottage with roses, a couple of pretty children playing around your feet when you come home from delivering your latest book to the Queen?'

'You can mock. I've lived in exile for ten years, often in fear of my life. Don't you think the idea of a home like that sounds like a dream to me?'

'That's all it is. You would tire of that life in a matter of months. You're obsessed with your work, Bruno. I've seen how you light up when you talk of it, these books that are going to change Christendom's understanding of the cosmos, the way Copernicus did. That's the life you want, not the demands of a family.'

'Could I not wish for both?'

She laughed again then, and not pleasantly. 'Yes, I suppose a man can always expect both, because he imagines there will be a woman there making the meals and washing the clothes and caring for the children while he is off doing his great work.'

'That's not what I expect of you—'

She shook her head. 'In any case, I can't have another child.'

I looked at her. 'I'm sorry – I didn't realise – was it the birth?'

'I don't mean that. I mean that I could not. How could I love another child when I know my son is out there somewhere, without me? Until I find him, there is no prospect of happiness for me.'

I did not reply, because what she was saying was that she could never love or want a child of mine. She was right that I was holding on to a fantasy, but it was one that sustained me in my darkest moments – the idea that I might not always be alone. If I had wanted to hurt her in return, I could have told her that she too was chasing a chimera – wherever her son was now, she had little hope of bringing him to live with her and raising him. Estranged from her family, cut off from her friends, Sophia was as alone in her way as I was, and she was clinging to the pursuit of her lost child as a reason to keep going.

She came close to me again and put her arms around my waist, her face against the side of my neck. 'You're cold. Here.' She untied the gown she was wearing and tried to fold me into it. I could feel the heat of her body on my skin through the thin linen shift she wore underneath. 'Why must we always fight?'

'Because you can't decide if you want me or not. You like to keep me in your orbit just in case.'

'If you really loved me, you would not want to own me,' she whispered, and she sounded sad again.

I could not reply, because she pulled me closer until I could feel the pressure of her breasts against my chest. I heard my own ragged breathing loud in the silence of the room and hers quickening against my ear. She let the gown fall from her shoulders and loosened the ties of her shift; I bent my head to lick her nipples as she wrapped her hand in my hair and arched her throat back, making small animal noises. Eventually she led me across to the bed; I made to ease her down on to it but she shook her head and instead pushed me down on my back, pulling up her shift so that she could sit astride me as I unlaced my breeches. I remembered how she liked it like this; I lifted my hips so that she could grind against me while I was inside her, her hair falling over my face and her mouth at my ear, whispering incoherent commands or threats or promises. She brought herself to her climax in barely more than a minute, and even as I enjoyed her pleasure I found myself wondering if it was me, or if she would have been so fast and eager with anyone, and then hated myself for thinking it. When she rolled breathlessly on to her back for me to finish – though she insisted I pull out at the last moment – I knew she had already gone from me, her thoughts were elsewhere, and I thrust hard, half-wanting to hurt her, to make her acknowledge me. After it was over she smiled fondly, distractedly, pressed the palm of her hand to the side of my face and told me that I could leave by a side gate into the lane that was kept unlocked.

'I must finish this letter,' she said, reaching for her gown while I dressed and tried to fight the hollowed-out feeling gnawing at my insides.

'The boy who collects your messages,' I said, my voice deliberately cold, 'does he have a scab on his lip?'

'Ben? Yes, that's him.' She knelt to pick up the tray and the quill. 'Sorry about your shirt,' she said, passing it to me.

'I know Ben. He could bring a message to me, if you ever wanted . . .' I let the sentence die and slipped the shirt over my head.

'If I want to get a message to you, I'll ask him.' She smiled again, but it was brisk now; our encounter was done, and she was impatient for me to leave.

'Or at the Saracen's Head,' I said, shrugging on my doublet. I knew I was outstaying my welcome, she wanted to get back to her dispatch for Phelippes, and I found myself irrationally jealous of him, of all people. I felt a sudden rush of anger with her, for having this power over me and being so careless with it.

'I'll remember. You'd better take a candle,' she said, dipping the quill in what remained of her ink. 'Bruno—'

I turned at the door.

'Don't think it means nothing,' she said. 'This is how it is, with us.'

'It's not enough,' I said, hearing my voice choked with anger again. 'It's not what I want.'

'And must it always be what *you* want?'

She did not speak unkindly, but I turned my back on her and closed the door, stepping out into the night scents of the garden, not trusting myself to answer. I walked towards the gate, my steps deliberately slow in case she decided to come after me with some word or gesture of affection, but she didn't, as I had known she would not, and I stepped into the streets of London alone.

* * *

I arrived at Herne's Rents more furious and frustrated than when I had left, cursing all of them with the most imaginative and colourful oaths I could think of in all the languages I knew. Any encounter with Sophia always left me feeling dissatisfied and rejected, I should know that by now, and yet I kept going back, thinking each time that it might be different. I should never have gone to the Strand. Why should I care if Gifford had run? He was not my problem. This whole charade was pointless; Walsingham knew the names of the conspirators, he knew where they lived, he could have arrested them all long before now, but instead we were playing out this game, Robin and Gifford and I all risking our lives so that he could entrap Mary Stuart. Clara Poole had already died for it; little Joe might be next, and all the time Phelippes had been willing to forge a postscript to use against her; why could he not fabricate an entire letter?

I knew, of course, that I should worry about Gifford; if he had fled because he could not cope with his conflicted loyalties any longer and had come down on the side of the Catholic cause, he might easily have run straight to Ballard and betrayed me and Poole. Even now, I thought, climbing the stairs wearily to my floor, the priest could be waiting inside the room to cut my throat. I drew my knife before kicking the door open and braced myself on the threshold for an ambush, but the room was empty. I lit a candle and had barely taken off my boots when there came a quiet but unmistakable knock. I sat upright, every muscle tensed. For a heartbeat I considered ignoring it, but guessed the light would be visible through the gap under the door. It could be Babington, wanting to know how many Hail Marys would cover his earlier sin, or Ballard intending to kill me. I waited; the knock came again, soft and timid. There was always the chance that it could be Robin Poole or another messenger from Phelippes, with news of Gifford's flight; if so, I needed to know whether my identity had been exposed. I picked up my knife and held it at waist height as I opened the door a couple of inches.

Outside was a man of about my own age, with light brown hair and beard and dark clothes. I had never seen him before.

'Hello,' he said, offering a tentative smile.

'Yes?'

'I'm looking for Father Prado.'

Ah. I opened the door a little further in relief; I guessed Ballard must have sent him, another secret Catholic wanting the last rites for his dying mother, no doubt. I was beyond exhausted, but I assumed a benign, priestly expression, hoped I didn't smell too much of sex, and returned his smile.

'I am Father Prado,' I whispered. 'How can I help you?'

There was a long pause. His round, pleasant face crumpled in consternation and he gave an embarrassed little laugh, as if he might have missed a joke.

'No you're not,' he said.

We stared at each other.

'Oh, God. You're Weston,' I said, remembering at the same moment that his eyes fell on the knife I held, point towards him; in an instant, he had turned and hurled himself towards the stairs. I had to stop and put my boots on again; by the time I reached the street he had disappeared. I listened for the sound of running feet, but heard nothing; he must be hiding nearby.

'Weston,' I hissed, hoping he might be close enough to hear. 'Come out and talk to me, I can explain.'

But there was no reply, and no sign of anyone in the dark street. I waited a few minutes longer, keeping my knife at the ready, but I knew Weston would not come to me willingly; he probably thought I had killed Prado. By rights I ought to go straight to Phelippes and tell him there was now another person in London who knew I was not Xavier Prado; between Weston, Douglas and Gifford on the loose, it was too dangerous for me to continue trying to cling on to that identity. I kicked at a stone in frustration; that bloody Jesuit must have been out here waiting for me half the night, or else he was the one following me. From what Ballard had said, there was no great fellow-feeling between the Babington group and the English Jesuits, but it was highly likely that this Weston would feel obliged to let them know there was an imposter in their midst. I glanced down the street. The prospect of walking to Leadenhall now filled me with dread; Phelippes was probably out organising the search for Gifford, and in any case, I would be less safe alone in the streets at three o'clock than locked into my chamber. One way or another, the morning would bring some kind of clarity. I returned to my room, bolted the door behind me and lay down on the bed, fully clothed, so that I wouldn't be caught unprepared by any more unexpected visitors. I placed my knife on the mattress beside me and had time to notice, as I drifted into sleep, that my skin still carried faint traces of Sophia.

TWENTY-THREE

I woke early after a fitful night, and in the liminal moments between sleep and waking I became aware of a creeping sense of unease – the knowledge that something had gone terribly wrong – before the details took shape. When I finally opened my eyes into stark morning light, the night's events came rushing back: Gifford had fled, Joe had disappeared, William Weston was out there somewhere knowing I was an imposter, Sophia had let me in briefly and then pushed me away, as always, and Robin Poole was Babington's lover. On the plus side, at least no one had come to kill me in the night. Through the open door into the adjoining room I could see Gifford's empty bed, neatly made up. Where was he now, I wondered, and why had he run – blind panic, or desertion to the Catholics? I fell back on the pillow and considered the matter of Poole and Babington. I could not see that what I had discovered about them last night meant much in the bigger picture. Such things had never bothered me; if you spend your youth as a novice friar in a convent full of men sworn not to touch women, you can't help but know it goes on. I had never been convinced by the Church's case against it – I had infuriated my novice master by asking him more than once to cite where in the Scriptures Christ forbids a man to lie with another man, Christ who surrounded himself with men he loved, which had led the novice master to mark me as a potential sodomite as well as a heretic. But I asked because I had seen the shame and guilt bred by the Church's disgust; a young novice of my age at San Domenico died by his own hand rather than live with the knowledge of damnation for feelings he could not avoid, and that struck me as the real sin. I could understand why Poole might have thought that bringing in his sister to pretend a decoy affair with Babington would distract the others from the truth, but Ballard had sharp eyes and I had no doubt that the priest would have strong views about a relationship between two men in his holy campaign. Even so, I couldn't see how it could have contributed to Clara's death. She had 'complicated things', Poole had said, without further detail. But for whom? I found myself wondering again if he could have done it. I had seen how skilled he was at dissembling; a man who could take a beating from prison guards for being Catholic without breaking his cover was perfectly capable of feigning grief over a half-sister he had killed with his own hands. But since Savage's revelation, Poole's loyalties were not necessarily as clear as I had thought – or perhaps as Walsingham believed. If Robin and Clara's father had really been killed on Master Secretary's orders, might one of them have wanted the conspirators to succeed, as revenge? Could they have argued over it, and Robin felt he had no choice but to silence her, either because she wanted to betray the conspiracy or he did? Or had Clara been true to Walsingham, and suspected that her brother's involvement with Babington had compromised his loyalties? Had she threatened to expose them?

I rubbed my eyes; the lack of sleep was sending me mad, clutching at any straws. It still seemed far more probable that Ballard had killed Clara on suspicion of being a spy, been seen by Joe, and taken the child somewhere so he could not talk. However ruthless the priest was in pursuit of a Catholic

England, I refused to believe he would kill a child. If I achieved nothing else that day, I was determined to find Joe alive.

I heaved myself out of bed, washed away the traces of last night's encounter and put on a clean shirt. I wondered if Sophia had lain awake thinking about me, and laughed aloud, with some bitterness, at the idea; even before I had closed the door, her thoughts had returned to her report for Phelippes, and the information it might buy her about her son. I realised that part of my ill temper was hunger; I decided to walk up to the Saracen's Head, break my fast and borrow Dan's horse to return to Southwark. I could visit the Unicorn on the pretext of getting my Father Prado clothes back, and take the opportunity to look around; it occurred to me that Ballard might more easily have locked Joe away somewhere at the Unicorn – he was the one who had told me about the inn's secret hiding places. The prayer beads could have been left on the jetty as a false trail. In the meantime, I would ask Ben to deliver a note to Phelippes, outlining my suspicions about Ballard and my fears for Joe. Though the cryptographer would likely be preoccupied with Gifford's flight, if they had not already caught him, I would suggest that leaving Ballard at large any longer would put more lives at risk, and that the time had come to arrest him. I was aware that this was not for me to decide, but if Robin had secured a copy of the letter from Babington to Mary detailing the new plan against Elizabeth, that would be evidence enough to take in all the conspirators, and I was sure at least one of them would be willing to answer questions once they were locked in the Tower. I did not fancy Titch or Babington's chances of holding out against interrogation once they saw some of the devices Walsingham had at his disposal. The thought was a disquieting one, and I turned away from it.

I was looking out a fresh sheet of linen to write to Phelippes when I heard a sharp knock at the door. I froze, fear tightening my spine; for a few moments I had forgotten the immediate danger I was in, now that Weston could have told any of the conspirators that I was not the real Prado. I snatched up my knife from the bed and waited. The knock came again, louder, and a boy's voice said imperiously:

'I haven't got all bloody day, you know.'

I exhaled with relief before pulling the door open.

'You don't know how happy I am to see you, Ben,' I said, clasping him by the shoulders.

He wrinkled his nose. 'Yeah, all right, don't get soft. You can put that knife down and all. I came to say there's a woman up at the Saracen's wants to talk to you.'

My heart leapt. I had thought this was an expression, but I swear I felt it bounce in my chest; so she had thought of me after all, and regretted her haste in dismissing me the night before. I had hoped she would send Ben with a message, but could not have dreamed it would happen so quickly.

'Walk with me, Ben – I could use your sharp eyes and ears.'

'Why, someone after you?' He looked interested.

'All the time.' I locked the room and we walked down the stairs together.

'Don't worry, mate,' Ben said, patting the waistband of his trousers where he tucked his pocket knife. 'I've got your back.'

'Did she give you any other message?' I asked, as we walked along Holborn, Ben trotting alert as a hunting dog at my side.

'Just said it was urgent.' He wiped his nose on his sleeve. 'Who wants to kill you?' This was evidently much more exciting to the boy than any tryst with a woman.

'About three different people at the last count, and that's just in London. Keep your eyes peeled.'

A weak sun was trying to push through the high veil of cloud overhead, though the previous day's warmth had vanished, the morning was chilly and the people we passed on their way into the City were wrapped in cloaks and hats, making it easier for someone in disguise to catch me unawares. But we reached the Saracen's Head without incident, and all my nerves felt alight as my eyes raked the tap-room for Sophia, anticipating her shy, knowing smile when she saw me. Not finding her, I turned to Ben, confused.

He jerked his head – 'Corner table' – and disappeared through a side door. I followed the direction of his gaze and saw a woman with her back to me, a dirty shawl pulled around her hair, dressed in the drab worsted of a serving girl. My spirits sank; not Sophia, after all. But it might be important, none the less; news of Joe? I approached the table apprehensively and sat down opposite the stranger; when she raised her head I almost exclaimed aloud, but she pressed a finger to her lips.

'What are *you* doing here?'

It was not the correct form of address to a titled lady, but Frances Sidney grinned, her brown eyes bright. 'I needed to speak to you. I could hardly ask you to call at the house, so I thought I'd come to you.'

'Are you not worried, walking the streets of London alone?'

'I'm not an ornamental bird,' she said, a little testy. 'I've done it plenty of times, when Father and Philip are away – I bought these clothes from one of the maids. I like wandering the streets and observing – so much goes on that a respectable lady is not supposed to know about.'

'Does no one recognise you?'

'Of course not. People see what they expect to see, and in these clothes I'm just another servant on her way to market. Anyway, I'm not alone – Alice is over there.' She gestured, and I saw her maid sitting at a table on the other side of the room, looking out of the window. Frances lowered her voice. 'I wanted to know what progress you have made with finding Clara's killer, and I knew Thomas would not tell me, so I thought I should hear it from the horse's mouth.'

I shook my head. 'Not as much as I would have liked. I have a strong suspicion, but I can't prove it yet, and I fear another life may be in danger. But I can tell you that the conspiracy gathers pace, and I think your father will be ready to close in soon, so he will have them all under lock and key. I suppose he can find out the details when he questions them.'

Neither of us spoke for a moment; we both knew what that entailed. A movement at the edge of my vision made me jump; I snapped round to see Dan Hammett holding a plate of soft bread and a bowl of clear honey.

'My lady,' he murmured, setting it down in front of her.

'Thank you, Dan.' She smiled up. 'But it's just Frances in here, remember. And bring the same for my friend, please.'

He gave a slight bow and disappeared.

'You come here a lot?' I asked, amused.

'Dan works for my father,' she said. 'I've known him since I was a child. But listen,' she sighed and twisted her fingers together, 'I owe you an apology. I have not been entirely honest with you.'

'How so?'

She picked at her breakfast. 'I've known all along who killed Clara.'

I reared back and stared at her. '*What?*'

She nodded unhappily. 'At least, I thought I did. But I wanted you to reach the same conclusion by yourself, without any prompt from me, and if possible with evidence that would prove it. I hoped you'd have worked it out by now.' She sounded reproachful, as if the fault were mine.

'I don't understand.' I struggled not to raise my voice in anger. 'If you know, for God's sake why did you not just tell your father? Why drag me into it?'

There was a long pause. She pulled her bread into tiny shreds.

'Because it *is* my father,' she said eventually.

I had thought I possessed some skill at hiding my emotions, but I sat there gaping at her like a child shown a sleight of hand trick. 'Are you *mad*?' I hissed. 'You think Sir Francis murdered Clara Poole? Why would he ever—' Even as I geared up to protest the impossibility of her absurd accusation, a feeling of unease prickled at the back of my neck. I thought of Savage's story about George Poole.

'Listen.' She pulled out a cloth bag from her lap. 'Now that Clara's death has been officially declared, we've been allowed to pack up her belongings for her brother. It was not considered proper to let a man go through her personal things, so Alice and I have been doing it. And I found these.' She reached into the bag and pulled out a pair of well-made ladies' gloves in pale blue satin. 'I gave them to her as a New Year gift, two years ago.'

I looked at them with a questioning shrug, *So?*

She dropped her voice further. 'After her body was found, Sir Francis swept into her room stony-faced, the way he does, and took away all the papers he could find, any notes or letters. Presumably he and Thomas wanted to see if there was anything in her correspondence that would be useful to them – or damaging. But they didn't find these.' She reached into one of the gloves and pulled out a rolled-up slip of paper, then did the same with the other. 'Two notes he didn't get his hands on. I wanted you to see them.'

She unfurled the first one and pushed it across to me. It was a set of four pictograms, like the one in the locket and the copy in Titch's room. But though the layout was similar, the symbols were different, the style less assured. There was a four-legged creature that might have been a dog or a bear; a horse's hoof with an iron shoe and a hammer; a square bordered by trees and hedges that might have been a field or a garden, and a document with the word 'Testament' written in tiny letters on the top.

'Do you know what this means?' I asked, amazed.

'No idea. I hoped you might.'

'I've seen something like it, connected to Clara. But I can't work out what it says. Evidently she communicated with someone who understands these pictures, but I don't know who.' Titch? I wondered. Or someone else, who sends these messages to both Titch and Clara? 'May I take it, to examine further?'

Frances looked disappointed, but she nodded, and I tucked the note into my pocket. 'Well – that one remains a mystery, for now. But there was also this.' She smoothed out the second paper and its provenance was immediately clear, if not its content. It was written in cipher, but the neat, compressed handwriting was as familiar to me by now as my own.

'This is from Thomas Phelippes,' I said.

'Exactly. Do you know what it says?'

I held up the paper and squinted at the characters. 'I don't recognise this code. But I'm sure I could work it out, if you give me some time to study it.'

'No need.' She flashed me a triumphant smile. 'You know that my father keeps his study at Seething Lane. Well, I thought I would have a look for the cipher in his cabinet.'

'He doesn't lock the room?'

'Of course he does. But one evening last year I was taking him in a glass of wine and found him asleep at his desk. So I thought it politic to make an impression of the key in wax. Alice had a copy made from it. No doubt you think me devious.'

'I think you are extremely resourceful.'

She inclined her head, a terse little pout at her lips. 'My father is not a well man, as you have seen. I have been acquainting myself with his files. Someone needs to know where things are in that study, in case the day comes when he is no longer able to – well, you understand.'

'I pray that day is far distant.'

'We all do. But it will take more than prayer to make him slow down.' She made a flicking motion with her hand, as if to brush that aside. 'I know that Thomas Phelippes keeps a copy of every separate cipher he uses for every informer who works for my father, and because there is not enough space at Leadenhall Street, many of them are filed in my father's study at Seething Lane instead.'

'But there must be dozens, if not hundreds. How could you locate the right one?'

She smiled. 'Every agent has a code name. I had only to look under Clara's, which was Juturna.'

'The Roman goddess of – water, is it?'

'Very good – wells and springs, to be precise. Because of her name, you see. Clara Poole. The code names are usually some kind of joke between Thomas and Sir Francis.'

'I didn't think Thomas understood the concept of jokes. Do I have a code name?' I asked, trying to sound casual. I hoped – pathetically – that it would be something suitably heroic.

'Of course.' She looked down at the paper and pressed it flat against the table. 'But I don't think it would be proper to—'

'For God's sake, Frances – you've come here and accused your own father of murdering your friend, and now you're being coy about my nickname?'

'All right. It's Argos.'

'Argos?' I sat back and looked at her. 'As in – Odysseus's dog?'

'That's right. So, I found the cipher—'

'Hold on – when Odysseus returns to Ithaca,' I said, affronted, 'he finds old Argos lying on a pile of shit, infested with fleas and worn out to the point of death. Is that your father's view of me?'

She made an impatient noise through her nose. 'I think it's meant to be a pun. Because you used to be a Dominican. God's dogs – isn't that what they call you?'

Domini canes; she was right, it was an old nickname for my former order. I had been hoping for something like 'Hercules'.

'In any case,' she said, patting my hand briefly in consolation, 'doesn't Homer say that in his prime, Argos was the greatest hunting dog ever known? And he is celebrated for his fidelity – he waits to die until he has seen his master for the last time.'

'Perhaps your father thinks that's why I came back to England.'

Fidelity, I thought. Or else just obstinacy; I do not like to give up. Walsingham knew that, and had certainly used it to his advantage over the years. Frances tapped her finger smartly on the paper to bring my attention back, and I thought how like him she looked in that moment.

'To come to the point – I found the cipher Phelippes used with Clara and translated this note. I brought a copy.'

'How long did it take you?' I asked, curious, as she rummaged again in her bag.

'Half an hour? It's not a long note, and I have a good eye for ciphers. I've been practising since I was a child.'

'That doesn't surprise me. When your father is no longer able to run the Service, they are sure to appoint you his successor,' I said. My admiration was not feigned.

She pulled a face. 'If they had any sense. I could do it, too. But they would never think of a woman. Instead they will appoint Lord Burghley's hunchback son Robert, I would wager on it, who is only out for his own advantage. Now – look at what Phelippes sent to Clara.'

She handed me a paper; in a sloping, feminine hand she had written:

Cross Bones, Southwark. 27 July. midnight. Wait north-east corner. He will wear hat with white feather.

I looked up at Frances. Her small mouth was set in a grim line.

'That is it, word for word?'

'To the letter. That's all it says. But it's clear, isn't it? It was

Thomas Phelippes who sent Clara to the Cross Bones the night she was killed, to meet a man with a white feather in his hat.'

'Who would that be?'

'I don't know – my father has any number of men in his pay who would do that kind of job.' She was battling not to raise her voice in frustration. 'But it confirms my theory, don't you think? They sent her to her death.'

I shook my head, not in denial but in bewilderment. 'It was the one thing I couldn't understand – why she would have gone there in the first place, so late at night. I thought Ballard might have persuaded her to go – I was sure it was him.'

'She was so proud of working for my father, she took her responsibilities very seriously. She'd have gone anywhere if Phelippes had ordered her and said it was for the Queen and the good of England.'

I thought of Sophia and my gut twisted. 'But it makes no sense. Sir Francis made Clara his ward. She grew up with you. Why should he want her dead?'

Frances took a deep breath. 'Perhaps he suspected her loyalties.'

'Ah. Because of her father?'

She frowned at that. 'What about him?'

I leaned forward. 'I heard a story from one of the Babington group that George Poole was loyal to the Catholics all along, and was giving your father misinformation. They believe Sir Francis had him killed as punishment.'

She nodded, understanding. 'Clara told me she'd heard that too. But she didn't believe it.'

'Why not?'

'Clara loved my father. She wouldn't hear a bad word about him, she said, after everything he had done for her and Robin.' She paused; her voice had cracked a little and I looked away discreetly while she took a lace handkerchief from her sleeve and dabbed at the corners of her eyes.

'What do you think?'

She spread her hands. 'I know my father better than Clara did. He's not a vindictive man, but he is entirely capable of having someone pushed in a river if he thinks the security of the state depends on it. I honestly don't know what happened to George Poole, and I don't much care. I'm sure Father had Clara killed, though. You need to find this man with the white feather.'

'Wait, go back – what did you mean about Sir Francis suspecting her loyalties, if you were not talking about avenging her father?'

'Well, because—' she broke off and glanced up at me from beneath her lashes, and for the first time in the conversation she looked embarrassed. 'Because she was pregnant.'

I shook my head and smiled. 'There at least I can confidently put you right. She wasn't. I suggested the possibility, but they had the body opened by a physician, and there was no sign of a child.'

Now it was Frances's turn to look perplexed. 'Oh. Then she must have gone to the woman in Southwark after all. Though I thought I would have known . . .'

'What woman in Southwark?' I asked, a little too sharply.

'She wouldn't talk to me about it. I guessed early on – it's not long since I was with child myself, I recognised the signs. Clara denied it vehemently to me for a good three weeks, until one night she had a slight bleed and I found her crying, terrified she was losing it – though it was fine, I had the same.' She glanced up and met my eye. 'You don't mind me speaking of such things? Philip would have started talking loudly about hunting and found an excuse to leave the table by now.' She smiled, a little sadly. I motioned for her to continue. 'Clara wouldn't say who the father was. But she told me she had heard about a woman in Southwark who could give you a potion to flush the child out from the womb. She knew she ought really to go there, but she thought it sounded a wicked thing to do. I could tell how much she wanted to keep the child, despite the circumstances. I saw it in her face. Her useless dead husband never gave her a baby.'

'You think it was by one of the conspirators?'

'Who else would it be? She never left Seething Lane except to see them. I tried to talk to her about it, but she clammed up again. She said it was better for me not to know – which hurt me, but I tried to respect her wishes. I thought she would tell me in her own time. So I never asked whether she did go to the Southwark woman, because less than a week later, she was dead. I suppose she must have done, if what you say is true.'

'So – your hypothesis is that somehow your father learned she was pregnant by one of the conspirators, believed that would swing her loyalties to them, and therefore he had Phelippes send her to the Cross Bones on the twenty-seventh of July, where she was killed by a hired assassin with a white feather in his hat, on your father's orders?'

'That's it exactly.' She took in my expression and huffed impatiently. 'Look, I know it sounds far-fetched, but you have no idea – my father has come up with more complex scenarios than this to protect his operations, I assure you.'

'I can believe that,' I said. 'Did Clara say anything to make you think she had transferred her loyalty to the plotters now that she was expecting a child with one of them? Did she speak of being in love?' I asked. Frances was right; her theory, outlandish though it was, made sense according to the logic by which Walsingham and Phelippes operated: if Clara had fallen in love with her child's father, how could she willingly cooperate in a plan to bring him to a traitor's death? They would have feared she was much more likely to warn him. One way or another, Walsingham would have had to get her away from the Babington group, and keep her quiet. All the same, I found it hard to believe that he would have condoned such a grotesque display of the body, when she could have been made to disappear discreetly.

'Not directly,' Frances said, picking off a corner of bread and rolling it into a ball between her thumb and forefinger. 'But there was a look that came across her face when she admitted the truth to me about the baby, and a note in her voice – dreamy and girlish. I recognised it – it's how I sound when I talk of Philip. I could tell how distressed she was, thinking about whether to go to the Southwark woman. I always knew when Clara was upset, because she had this habit – it used to drive me mad.' She paused, and let out a little trembling laugh. 'She would bite her nails down so far she would make her fingers bleed and even then she'd carry on, ripping at them with her teeth, I winced to see it. That's why I bought her the gloves' – she indicated the pair on the table between us. 'But it never stopped her. And she was biting her nails all the time, those last few days, before she went to the Cross Bones. Robin has the habit too, isn't that strange? I wonder if Clara copied it from him as a child – what is it?'

She had seen the change in my expression as the extent of my blindness dawned on me. I pushed the table away and stood up as if in a daze.

'It's not her.'

'What?'

'*Dio merda*,' I breathed, staring at her, unfocused, forgetting I was supposed to be Spanish. 'It's not her. I'm an idiot. Absolute *idiot*.' The poor dead girl in the leper chapel; I remembered noting how carefully she had kept her nails. Walsingham should have let his daughter identify the body; Frances would have spotted that detail in an instant. I turned and almost crashed into Dan, who stepped expertly back with his plates before I sent them crashing to the floor.

'It's all right, mate, we've had worse idiots in here,' he said. I grabbed him by the shoulder.

'Where's Ben?'

'Out the back, with the horses.'

'Can you spare him?'

He narrowed his eyes. 'Long as he's earning.'

'Wait!' Frances clutched at my sleeve. 'At least have something to eat and tell me what's going on. What do you mean, it's not her?'

I paused, snatched a mouthful of bread and honey and gestured to her to follow me.

'The body in the Cross Bones. It wasn't Clara,' I said, my mouth full, as we emerged into the yard. 'That business with disfiguring the face – I thought it must be some kind of symbolism. All the time it was to conceal her identity. I can't believe I didn't think of it before. But your father said he was sure – oh. Of *course*. The henna.'

'You are making no sense at all. If it wasn't her, then – where *is* Clara? Is she still alive?' she asked, in a whisper, as if she hardly dared hope.

'I would guess so. Why else would anyone fake her death, except to let her run? Do you have any idea where she would go? Does she have family somewhere?'

She shook her head. 'I don't know – I think a cousin of her father's lives in Essex, somewhere that way – you really think she is alive?'

I nodded, and the expression of stunned relief on her face hardened to one of anger. 'I'll bloody kill her myself, putting us through all that. Why would she do it?'

'She must have thought she was in danger, for exactly the reasons you suggested. Perhaps she worried that letter from Phelippes was a trap.'

'Then you think she's in hiding from my father?' Her grip tightened around my arm. 'Don't tell him. At least let's try and find out where she is before he learns she's still alive. Will you do that?'

I hesitated. 'I won't tell anyone yet – and don't you. Whoever murdered that girl in the Cross Bones to pass her off as Clara may yet kill someone else to protect his secret – and it wouldn't be wise for you to let on that you know it.'

'Who was she?' Frances asked quietly, letting go of my sleeve.

'I think I know. But I must go straight to Southwark now, to make enquiries.'

I found Ben lounging on an upturned barrel by the stables, polishing a harness, the cat curled around his feet. I nodded at the dovecote. 'Anything?'

'Not yet.'

'I need you to come to Southwark with me,' I said. He dropped the harness and considered.

'It'll cost you.'

'The only sure thing in this uncertain world, Ben, is that any help you ever give will cost money.' I turned to Frances. 'I'll send you word at Seething Lane the moment I hear anything about where she might be. Ben will bring a message. But don't tell anyone about Clara. Not even Alice.'

She nodded and squeezed my hand briefly. As she turned to leave, I saw the shine of tears in her eyes, and I remembered how young she was.

'Don't be sad, my lady. Surely this is better news than you had hoped for?'

'She didn't confide in me,' Frances said softly, looking down. 'I thought she was my dearest friend, but she would rather let me think her dead than trust me. What kind of friendship is that?'

I was not sure if she expected an answer, but she swiped at her eyes savagely with the edge of her hand and disappeared back inside the inn.

'Are we looking for that boy again?' Ben said, cheerfully, 'the one who's a girl?'

'Yes, we're definitely looking for him. And another girl. But listen – it might be dangerous.' His face lit up. 'No, Ben – it's not a game. You must promise me that if I tell you to run, you do as I say. No heroics with your little knife. Agreed?' He puffed himself up, offended, but I waited until he gave a sulky nod.

'You'll be glad of my knife one of these days.'

'I'm sure I will. Let's walk down and get a boat across from Water Lane, it'll be quicker. But you'll have to be quiet on the way – I need to think.'

'You sound like my old man,' he said, rolling his eyes and starting up a loud whistling as we turned out of the yard and headed down Fleet Lane towards the river.

So one question at least was answered: the matter of why the body had been left where it would so obviously be found. This had made little sense to me when I was trying to work out who might have wanted to kill Clara Poole, but made perfect sense if the killer's aim was to make people believe Clara had been killed; leaving a dead woman dressed as her in a public place was essential to the charade. I could not believe I had been so stupid. But I had not been the only one – and I thought I understood now why the killer needed to keep Joe silent. Men like Walsingham and Phelippes might not have noticed the detail of a woman's nails, but even they were aware that Clara had a birthmark on her neck, and would have checked the corpse. If you wanted to fake such a mark, in a way that would not wash off, what better to use than the reddish-brown stain of Leila's henna paste? She thought that Joe had stolen the henna; clearly someone had asked the child to do that, for the express purpose of disguising another young woman as Clara. If Joe knew why it was wanted, and who wanted it, he knew the real identity of the killer and the victim. In Joe's absence, the only other person who might have the answers was Leila's friend Anneke.

A stiff breeze blew across the river, whipping the water into yellow-crested peaks. Ben leaned over the side of the wherry to watch the fish jumping, while I thought further about the murder. Every theory I had was turned upside down; I needed to stop thinking in terms of *Clara's* killer and reverse the picture. Whoever had killed the girl in the Cross Bones had done it not because Clara was a threat, but because she needed protecting. I could think of only three people who would feel strongly enough about her to commit murder for her sake: her lover, her brother, or Sir Francis Walsingham. And if one of them had been prepared to go to such lengths, he must have believed that her life was in danger – but from whom? I surmised that her pregnancy had changed things, but that only raised more questions. It did not take great genius to work out – by process of elimination – that Titch must be the father of Clara's baby, but it did not necessarily follow that he was the murderer. On my first night with the conspirators at The Castle, he had been the one loudly denying the possibility that the body in the Cross Bones could have been her; if he had perpetrated the deception, surely he would have been falling over himself to agree with Ballard's conclusion? A double bluff, perhaps. Titch had undeniably been with a woman last night – was it a secret meeting with Clara? If I could decipher those damned pictograms, perhaps they would give me a clue – though that was further complicated by the new note in Clara's glove, similar but different.

It was possible, too, that Walsingham could have learned of Clara's pregnancy and spirited her out of London if he felt it put her in danger from the conspirators, faking her death as a means of preventing them looking for her. But there was too much that did not add up with that theory; I could not see that he would have gone to the trouble of drawing me into the deception, showing me the corpse and asking me to find the killer, nor that he was ruthless enough – whatever his daughter thought – to drug a street girl with opium before killing her as a substitute, or kidnap a child to keep him quiet. That left Robin Poole. If Robin believed that his father had been murdered on Walsingham's orders, for his secret loyalty to the Catholics, did he fear that his sister might meet the same fate, now that she was pregnant by one of the conspirators? Robin was so inscrutable, so evidently skilled at feigning emotion, that he could easily have dissembled well enough to convince even Walsingham that he was contorted with rage and grief for his dead sister. The obvious solution there was to question him – after all, I now had the leverage of knowing a secret that he did not want Walsingham to find out, and might demand answers in return. But it seemed best to eliminate the other possibilities first, and to make certain of my evidence; if he was not behind the murder, it would be quite a shock to Robin to discover that his sister was alive after all, and it was always possible that he was the danger she was trying to escape.

'We're here,' Ben said, elbowing me in the side as the boat pulled in to Paris Garden Stairs; he had jumped out and skipped nimbly up to the quay before the boatman had tied up. The bells had not yet rung nine and it was quiet on Bankside, the usual few stragglers making their way home past the carts coming in with the new day's deliveries for the taverns and brothels along the riverfront. A couple of girls stumbled past us from the pleasure gardens, their make-up smeared as if they had not slept; they gave me the eye as they drew level.

'Excuse me,' I called, as an afterthought, 'I'm looking for a Dutch girl—'

'I'll be a Dutch girl for you, darling,' said one, in a flat London accent. The offer sounded half-hearted.

'Anneke, she wears a spotted scarf, dark hair—'

'I'll do your son half price,' said the other, cackling, as they walked on.

'I wouldn't do you if it was free,' Ben shot back. 'And he's not my pa.'

'Ben,' I said, reprovingly. 'That's not a nice way to talk to ladies.'

'She's not a lady, she's a poxy goose.'

'You think she does that work by choice?'

I waited for the flippant response, but he considered this and fell silent.

'Where we going?' he asked after a while, as we walked towards the row of white-fronted taverns facing the river.

'I need to find this Dutch girl and talk to her. You can come with me, keep your eyes peeled for anyone following us. Then we're going to the Unicorn, to see what else we can learn. That's where I'll need your help.'

'Who am I looking out for, following us?' He spun round in a circle and trotted along backwards for a few paces, as if daring anyone to approach from behind.

'I don't know. Just tell me if you notice anyone acting strangely.'

He sighed. 'That's everyone in Southwark.'

'Then you're going to be busy, aren't you?'

I had fixed particular landmarks in my memory during my walk with Anneke the night before, so that I did at least remember the way to Leila's house this time without getting too far lost. Her shutters were drawn; I knocked on the front door but there was no reply. I wondered if she was out working or looking for Joe. Anneke had said they were neighbours; I tried the house next door, and an older woman answered, responding suspiciously to my enquiries about Anneke by asking who had sent me. I recalled Leila telling Joe that people in Southwark regarded any kind of curiosity about their business as a potential threat. I explained that I knew Leila, that I had met Anneke the night before and wanted to see her again; I offered a penny as an incentive. The woman sniffed, and folded her arms across the shelf of her bosom, glancing up and down the street before deciding to answer.

'She does live upstairs, but she didn't come back last night.'

'Is that usual?' Already I felt a flicker of alarm.

The woman lifted a shoulder, indifferent. 'They come and go all hours. I usually hear them come in though, never occurs to them that some of us might be sleeping. Haven't seen the other one for a few days either, mind. Her next door might know, they're friendly.' She nodded towards Leila's house.

I thanked her, and dragged Ben off up the lane towards the river. When I left Anneke last night, she had said she was going to look for work. If she hadn't returned home, it was possible that someone might have intercepted her – someone who, like me, suspected that her friend Lotte might have told her something that would shed light on her disappearance.

I hurried up New Rents towards Bankside at a half-run, Ben jogging alongside to keep up. When I saw the roofs of the bull and bear rings ahead, I slowed my pace, following a path between them that brought us on to the dock where I had walked with Anneke the night before. Below the quay wall, the tide had risen, the river was higher now, and the abandoned boat she had tried to entice me into was half-floating, its back end sunk on the bank while the prow lifted gently as the water ebbed and flowed. I walked out across the mud, apprehension curdling in my stomach. The sides of the boat were high enough that a person – or even two people – lying in the bottom could not be seen from the shoreline; presumably that was what Anneke liked about it. But I could see gulls and crows circling above it, diving and screeching at one another. I waved my arms as I approached, my boots sinking into the water; a couple of gulls perched on the boat's rail tilted their heads and regarded me with mean yellow eyes for a moment, before flapping a few feet away. I saw the material of her dress, dark with river water, before I saw the face. Her spotted scarf was pulled around her neck; the killer had not even bothered to hide the fact that he had used it to strangle her. I reached over and prodded the freezing skin of her bare forearm. By the stiffness in her limbs, I guessed she had been dead a good few hours.

'Is it her?' Ben asked, craning to see past me.

'Get back – don't look.' I held up a hand to ward him off.

'I've seen dead people before,' he scoffed, straining at my arm. 'Seen my ma dead, and my baby brother.'

'Not like this, I hope.' The crows had already pecked her

eyes out. At least, I hoped it was the crows. 'We need to fetch someone, as quickly as possible. You go – run for the nearest constable. I'll wait with her.'

The boy shook his head. 'No, sir. We need to get away from here, right now.'

I snapped my head up; it was the 'sir' that told me he was serious.

'What are you talking about? A woman has been murdered.'

'Let someone else find her and report it. What do you think will happen if a person like you is found with her body?'

'A person like me?'

He sighed, impatient. 'Foreign. They'll say you did it.'

'That's ridiculous. I'm not going to be arrested, Ben. I know people,' I added, in a confidential tone.

'You think that'll matter?' He glanced anxiously back at the quay. 'Anyway, they find you here sitting beside a dead woman, you'd be torn apart long before I got back with a constable. There's Londoners would love any excuse to beat the shit out of a Spaniard.'

'I thought Southwark was full of foreigners?'

'That's why the locals want any chance to give them a kicking. Come on, let's go.' He took me firmly by the wrist and pulled. As I straightened up, he leaned past me for a look into the boat. 'Eurgh, that's horrible,' he said with relish. I hauled him away.

He was right, I knew, it would do me no good to report Anneke's murder, but I hated the thought of leaving her alone and cold at the edge of the water, irrational though it was. I recalled the warm pressure of her breast against my arm as she huddled into me on our walk, and her anxiety about her missing friend. It had never occurred to me then that she might have been in danger – because I had not been quick enough to guess that it was not Clara in the Cross Bones, though I cursed myself for not seeing it sooner. The only person who might know anything now was Leila. A knot of dread lodged in my throat; if the killer could dispatch Anneke so casually, could there be any hope left for Joe?

'Let's get to the Unicorn,' I said. If Leila was there, I could at least tell her about Anneke. Ben was still holding my wrist, and I sensed that it was not just to make sure I accompanied him; for all his bravado, his narrow face had turned pale, and he was unusually quiet. 'This is where you earn your money,' I told him. 'We're trying to find out what happened to the boy Joe, who worked here. He was last seen in the yard yesterday afternoon, talking to a tall man. Get chatting to the stable lads, find out what they saw, or if Joe said anything to them about someone he was worried about, following him, maybe.' If Ben could learn any more detail about who had approached Joe, it would be worth the risk of running into Ballard. 'And it's an old building with lots of hiding places, apparently – find out if any of them know anything about secret doors, cellars, anything of that sort. They're more likely to talk to you. Go in ahead of me – you can pretend you're looking for work.'

'What are you going to do?'

'I'm going to talk to Joe's mother, if I can find her. Tell her about that poor girl back there. She'll know what to do. Wait for me outside the main gate.'

'Mind she doesn't witch you,' he said darkly. I sighed, wondering if the English would ever get over their fear of anyone who looked different.

Ben scampered off ahead through the main gates. After a few minutes I followed him into the yard, making directly for the main entrance and watching to either side for any sign of Ballard. I was certain of one thing: my encounter last night with William Weston was the spark that had lit the fuse to a barrel of gunpowder. I had no way of knowing how long it would take to burn down, but sooner or later it was going to explode in my face. I only hoped I would be able to find Joe before Ballard and the rest of the conspirators learned that I was not Father Prado. I recalled Anneke's story about him beating the man who had threatened Joe almost to death, and the priest's own admission of his violent temper; I did not want to find myself on the wrong side of it. In my haste to get to the Saracen's Head earlier I had not had time to write my note to Phelippes urging him to arrest Ballard as soon as possible, but I hoped that the knowledge of Gifford's flight would make Walsingham see that he needed to swoop on the conspirators before any more of them realised the plot was blown. I knew it was madness to walk into the very place I was most likely to run into Ballard, but I needed to speak to Leila; if she knew the truth about the girl in the Cross Bones, she might have some idea of who could have approached Joe for the henna, or perhaps Anneke might have mentioned some detail about her friend Lotte's disappearance that would help us.

A distant church bell struck the hour of nine as the maid opened the door, stifling a yawn. It was early to be visiting a brothel, and her surprise when I asked for Madam Rosa reflected this, but she took my knife and slipped away, leaving me jittery in the wide entrance hall, glancing between the stairs and passageways for any sign of Ballard. Fortunately, it took only a few moments for the madam to bustle into view from one of the corridors, her wig seeming to move independently of her head as she walked.

'Hello, my darling, didn't expect you back so soon! You're bright and early, have you come for your clothes? I'll send Dorothy to fetch them.' She called the maid back and barked a few instructions. 'I'm sorry to say you've missed Captain Fortescue – he had a visitor and they popped out together at the crack of dawn – he's such a busy man, isn't he? Do you want to wait for him, love?' She leaned in with a knowing look, and I recalled Ballard saying that she was sympathetic to the Catholic cause. I wondered if she knew his real identity, and guessed me to be another priest, as Leila had.

'He certainly is. Please don't trouble yourself, I'll catch up with him another time.' I tried not to let my relief show, though the news of his early visitor set off another ripple of anxiety. 'How much do I owe you?'

'Oh, don't worry about that – the Captain has taken care of it. But if there's anything else I can offer while you're waiting, Master – I'm sorry, I don't think the Captain told me your name?'

'Prado. Oh – no, thank you. It's a bit early.' I smiled politely; she nodded, as if to say she understood.

'No, the Captain said you wouldn't partake, but I thought I should offer. A man has needs, after all, even when he has his mind on higher things.'

'This is a beautiful old building,' I said, to break the awkward silence. She followed my gaze up to the carved wooden ceiling.

'Two hundred years, at least,' she said proudly. 'It was built as a coaching inn, but it's full of secrets, this old place – the first owner used it to bring in contraband, up the river, and it's said they hid soldiers and escaped prisoners too.'

'A fascinating history,' I said. 'There must be all kinds of secret nooks and crannies, then – I imagine that comes in useful.'

'Very useful indeed. They're downright ingenious, some of them. Why, on the top landing, there's a—' she broke off and gave me a naughty, reproachful simper, as if I were the one who had been indiscreet. 'Well – I mustn't give away all our secrets, even if you are a friend of Captain Fortescue. Suffice to say, we know how to look after people here, in every sense.' She punctuated this with a broad wink, as the maid returned with Prado's clothes, neatly folded in a pile.

'There you go.' Madam Rosa lifted the doublet from her arms and held it up for my inspection. 'She's done a lovely job – you can hardly see it. Told you she was a wonder, our

Moorish girl. She's stitched the tear for you too, look – you'd never notice.'

'Like magic,' I said, laying on the admiration.

'She's not a witch,' Madam Rosa said, immediately defensive. 'Whatever you've heard. I wouldn't have her under my roof if I didn't think she was a good Christian.'

'No, I didn't mean – of course you wouldn't. Who could think otherwise?' She looked mollified. 'In fact,' I said casually, 'is she here? I would like to thank her in person. Show my appreciation.'

Madam Rose eyed the purse at my belt. 'I suppose so. She's with one of the girls at the moment, but Dorothy can fetch her while you change. Show the gentleman a spare room where he can have some privacy,' she snapped to the maid, 'and send Leila to him.'

I was shown to a small parlour at the rear of the building, where, with some reluctance, I changed the grey wool doublet and breeches for Father Prado's amber silk; I had preferred walking around London in clothes that did not demand attention. I was still fastening the doublet when there was a sharp knock at the door and Leila entered without waiting for a reply. Her hair was tied back and her face looked hollow, as if she had not slept; her bronzed complexion seemed ashy in the morning light.

'I hoped you would come. Have you found Joe?'

I shook my head. 'I looked for you at your house.'

'I'm always here early, to check the girls. Occasionally they get roughed up during the night.' A muscle in her jaw tensed. 'Something has happened, I can see it in your face – for God's sake, tell me.'

I glanced at the door and lowered my voice. 'I'm sorry to bring bad news—'

She stumbled before I could finish, as if her legs could no longer hold her, fingers pressed to her mouth; I reached out and led her to the window-seat.

'Not Joe. It's – your friend, Anneke.'

Her eyes widened and she straightened, shaking my hand away as she recovered from her initial shock.

'What about her?'

'She's dead. Murdered. I found her this morning, in that abandoned boat she sometimes used, on the shore by the bear ring. She'd been there a few hours, I'd say – I haven't reported it. I came straight here to tell you. I'm sorry.'

She blinked hard, her eyes turned down, her jaw set hard; I sensed that Leila was a woman who had learned not to let her emotions show. When she raised her head, her gaze was stony. 'Why haven't you reported it?'

'I didn't want to be taken for the perpetrator. After what happened to your father-in-law.'

She tilted her chin, as if she half-believed me. 'You were out there with her last night.'

'I left her at midnight, by Falcon Stairs. I didn't . . . buy her services. I went home and she said she was going to look for work. But listen – I think the killer is the same person who took Joe.'

'Why?' Her expression remained accusatory. 'Who could want to harm Anneke? What has that to do with Joe?'

I sat down beside her.

'They both knew something. The girl found in the Cross Bones was not who I thought she was.'

'Not your friend's sweetheart?' she said, sceptical.

'No. The body had been made to look like that woman – her name is Clara – dressed in her clothes, and the face beaten so that it would be hard to tell the difference. But I think the dead girl was Anneke's friend, Lotte.'

She nodded slowly. 'Poor Lotte. I did not hold out much hope for her when I heard she was missing. So they are both dead, to save a rich girl. But why?'

'I believe someone thought Clara was in danger, so they staged her death in order to allow her to escape from London, and so that the people who wanted to harm her would give up looking for her. But Clara had a distinctive birthmark on her neck and collarbone. The only way to reproduce that convincingly would be to stain the skin with something like—'

'Oh, God. Henna.' She touched her fingers to her lips again. 'You think Joe stole my henna to help someone make Lotte look like this Clara girl. But Joe would never have done that if he'd had any idea she would be killed – he loved Lotte, she used to look after him when he was small, if I had to go out – *oh*,' she said, as if sudden understanding had dawned.

'What? Did Anneke tell you anything about the night Lotte disappeared? Did she go with someone?'

'Yes. It all makes a strange kind of sense.' She rubbed at her eyes with the heels of her hands. 'Lotte had cut her hair off, the day before.'

'She cut her own hair off?'

'Anneke said Lotte was afraid she had caught the pox, and she wanted to sell it while it was still worth something, before it started to fall out. She had lovely hair, Lotte – just an ordinary brown, but long and thick, all down her back. She asked Anneke to cut it for her and they planned to take it to the wig-makers on Silver Street, up by the Cripplegate, to see if they could get a good price. And then, that same day, when she was walking along Tooley Street, a man approached and said she was just what he was looking for, and he'd pay her good money if she'd spend the evening with him the following day. Anneke told me that Lotte was excited about it, because it was such an unusual request.'

'What did he ask her to do?'

'According to Anneke . . .' she paused, and a shadow passed across her face, as if she had just remembered that the girl who had told this story only the night before was lying in a rotten boat out on the Thames shoreline. 'This man wanted Lotte to pretend to be his wife for the evening.'

'His *wife*?'

'He told her he must have dinner with an elderly relative who was going to leave him a large inheritance. This old uncle or whatever wanted him to bring his wife. The man told Lotte he had left his wife some months before, but if the uncle knew this, he would not bequeath him the money, as the uncle was very proper about marriage. So this man proposed to pay Lotte a good deal if she would dress as his wife and pretend to be her for the evening, to secure the will. The old uncle hadn't seen the wife in years and would never know the difference. Anneke told me Lotte couldn't believe her luck and said, imagine being paid to put clothes *on* instead of take them off. He offered her five shillings, too, just to have dinner. Lotte said she wouldn't have cut her hair off if she'd known that was around the corner.'

'I'd guess that's precisely why he thought she would be suitable – it was easier to disguise the body. And the henna?'

'Anneke said the only thing this man asked, apart from putting on a wig, was that she let him draw a birthmark on her neck, because the wife had one. I can't believe I didn't think sooner that Lotte might have wanted my henna for that, and asked Joe.'

'How would this man have known about henna? Are Englishmen familiar with it?'

She gave a wry smile. 'Hardly. I don't know anyone else who uses it. Which makes me think this man must have been acquainted with the Unicorn. Some of the girls here used to ask me to paint henna designs on their hands and feet, they thought it looked pretty, but Madam Rosa asked me to stop because she said it was too – *exotic*. Some of the clients didn't like that.' She made a face.

'So this mysterious stranger with the wife story could well have seen henna paintings on the girls at the Unicorn, and known that it would not wash off the skin. He must have known where to get hold of it, too.'

'You mean – he's someone who knows me?' She frowned;

I could almost see her thoughts chasing one another behind her eyes. 'Lotte must have asked Joe to lend her the henna,' Leila said. 'Joe would gladly have done her a favour – he probably meant to put it back before I noticed.'

'That must have been what Joe meant when he asked me if he would go to Hell for something he did, even if he hadn't meant anything bad to happen. He must have known the body was Lotte as soon as he saw her. Did Lotte tell Anneke anything that would help identify this man?'

She twisted her mouth, trying to recall. 'Only that he was English, quite handsome, and not too old. Lotte said it was a shame – one of the few she wouldn't have minded bedding, and he didn't even want that.' Her expression hardened again. 'You must have some idea who he is, if you know this Clara?'

'There are several possibilities. Nothing definite. I'm trying to find evidence that will narrow it down.'

'I'll tell you how we'll narrow it down.' She placed a hand on my thigh and leaned in so that her face was inches from mine, her wide dark eyes boring into me. My pulse quickened, but with apprehension, not excitement. Fast as blinking, she whipped out from somewhere in the folds of her skirt a slender pocket knife, like the one Ben carried, and held it with the tip to the soft hollow at the base of my throat. 'You bring these possibilities to me. Or you take me to them. I'll make the bastards answer questions – by the time I've finished they'll have told me everything they've ever done in their sorry lives and be crying for their mothers.'

'I'd let you at them in a heartbeat if I could,' I said, trying not to move a muscle. 'But it's not as simple as that.'

'Why not?'

I swallowed carefully. 'It's about more than finding Joe.'

'Not for me. You think I give a shit about anything else?' She burned me with her stare for a moment longer, then reluctantly lowered the knife. 'Joe's gone because you started poking around asking questions.'

I breathed out slowly. 'No. Joe's missing because he knew about the henna, and he probably saw the killer in the Cross Bones that night.' But she was right; if Walsingham had not asked me to look into Clara's death, the killer would have believed he'd got away with it, and Joe might have been safe.

'Who *are* you?' she asked, softly.

'I've told you.'

She sucked her teeth. 'You've told me nothing. I thought you were a secret priest, but now I'm not so sure. Are you working for the authorities?' When I didn't reply, she tilted her head back and gave me an appraising nod. 'I see. Then why don't you arrest these people you think might be possibilities? Put them in your prison instead of my father-in-law, make them tell you where Joe is?'

I looked down; her fingers were still clamped tight around the knife in her lap. 'Because it's bigger than these murders.'

'Two innocent girls dead for this Clara woman. Abe Goodchild in prison. Maybe my Joe dead too. But when you say there's something more important than all that, you mean rich people's lives, right?' Her voice was cold as flint.

'Listen.' I could not fault her logic. 'As far as I know, the person who killed Lotte doesn't yet know that anyone has discovered his deception. He thinks the world believes it was Clara's body. While he thinks that, he'll imagine he's safe.'

'As long as he's silenced everyone who could tell the world otherwise,' she said. 'Starting with Anneke and Joe.'

'And you,' I said quietly, as the realisation dawned. 'He might think Joe or Anneke had told you about the business with the henna and pretending to be his wife. You need to take care. Is there a friend who could stay with you for a while, until this killer is no longer at liberty?'

She held up the knife with a dry laugh. 'You don't need to worry about me, Spanish boy. I was a prisoner of war, and a slave at twenty-four. It was your soldiers taught me how to defend myself against men.' The blazing fury was back in her eyes; if I were a superstitious man, I might have been afraid. I wanted more than anything to tell her I was not in fact Spanish, to deflect that anger and contempt, but I was still a man, so I doubted it would get me off the hook.

'Promise me one thing,' she said, her voice calmer. 'When you find this person, tell me he'll be properly punished for what he's done to those girls.'

'I can promise you that when this man is arrested, he's going to suffer.'

'Good. It will be nothing to what I would do to him if he's touched a hair on Joe's head. He should count his blessings.' She stood abruptly, tucking the knife away invisibly in her skirts. 'I must go and see about Anneke, have her body brought in. The parish will put her in the Cross Bones, I suppose. There's an irony.'

I reached into the pocket of my doublet and drew out a half-sovereign. I was running out of money with all these bribes, but in some obscure way I felt Walsingham owed the dead girl, who would in all likelihood be alive now if he had not insisted on leaving the conspirators at liberty so that he could lure Mary Stuart to the block. She turned the coin over in her palm and raised an eyebrow.

'Blood money?'

'For the funeral expenses.'

She snorted, but she tucked the coin away.

'One more question,' I said, as she reached the door. 'Did a young woman come to you in the past couple of weeks, asking to be rid of a child? A gentlewoman, mid-twenties, long auburn hair?'

She shook her head immediately. 'No one like that. I get asked to see gentlewomen sometimes, but they don't come here, they send their servants to bring me to them. Mostly I say no, despite the money. It wouldn't be worth the consequences if anything went wrong.' Her eyes narrowed. 'Why, is that your Clara? She'd got herself in trouble, that's why someone faked her death?'

'It's one theory.'

'So two street girls had to end up in the Cross Bones to get her out of trouble.' She clicked her tongue. 'Lucky for some. And where is she now?'

'I'm trying to find her.'

'Spit in her face for me when you do.'

'Leila—' I said, as she opened the door. 'Take care of yourself. I'm serious – as far as this man knows, you're the only one left who might know the truth about Lotte.'

She rolled her eyes, and patted the side of her skirts where she kept the knife hidden. I did not doubt her willingness to fight – nor her boast that she had killed a man – but I felt an uneasy sense of responsibility for her, as well as her child.

TWENTY-FOUR

I found a stone bollard by the quayside where the boatmen tied up and sat down to wait for Ben, my face tilted up to thin morning sunlight. The story Lotte had told Anneke, about her mysterious customer, was so absurd as to be almost unbelievable, yet it made a strange kind of sense. The killer had been logical; perhaps he and Clara had been discussing her escape, and on seeing a young woman of similar appearance and build, with her hair already shaved, he had formed a plan that was guaranteed to put Clara beyond the reach of whoever wanted to harm her. How he had persuaded Lotte to climb the wall of the Cross Bones with him I had no idea – perhaps he had suggested that he wanted a tumble after all – but at least I knew why he had chosen the place. Nothing to do with the symbolism of being a harlot; Clara was supposed to be at the Cross Bones that night. Phelippes had sent her there, and she must have shared that note with the killer. That argued against Titch – would she have risked his trust by telling him that she had actually been working for Her Majesty's spymaster? I couldn't see it. But it also argued convincingly against Walsingham; to make Clara appear to turn up dead in the very place where Phelippes had sent her suggested that the deception was intended to fool them too. The only person

I could imagine her confiding in about everything was her brother. He was tall and good-looking, with a supreme talent for dissembling.

I drew out the note Frances Sidney had given me earlier, and looked again at the pictures. The four-legged animal – unfortunately the artist's skill was not sufficient to distinguish it, which didn't help; the horseshoe and hammer; the field or garden; the document that read 'Testament'. That last could be a will; the man who lured Lotte to her death had pretended he needed help to secure an inheritance. Could that be connected?

'Is it a puzzle?' a voice said, brightly, as Ben's tousled head popped up over my arm. I jumped a foot in the air, and cursed myself for my lack of awareness; next time someone snuck up on me like that, they could be holding a knife.

'It is, Ben – it's a secret message that means something to someone, but I'm damned if I can read it. Go ahead, if you want to try. Just don't let it blow away.'

He took the paper and frowned at it, the tip of his tongue poking between his lips in concentration.

'Smithfield,' he said, after less than a minute.

'What?'

He pointed to the middle two images. 'It's like, say what you see, isn't it? That's a horse being shod – smith – and that's a field.' He gave me a look as if embarrassed on my behalf, for my stupidity. I remembered Phelippes making a sarcastic joke about a place called Beechfield, when we were studying the first note; perhaps he had not been so far off the mark.

'All right,' I said, not quite convinced, 'but what about the rest?'

'Something about the Lion, I reckon. That's a lion, there—'

'I thought it was a dog.'

'Nah, that's meant to be its mane, look. It's not a very good lion, granted. Maybe this person is saying to meet at the Lion in Smithfield.'

'That's a real place?'

'It's an inn.'

'And the testament?'

He grinned. 'You got me there. Maybe the note came from a bloke called Will.'

I stared at him. 'That's the most ridiculous thing I've ever heard.'

He pulled himself up, indignant. 'You do better, then. Or go to the Lion in Smithfield and ask if there's a bloke called Will there, then we'll see who's the clever one.'

'I'm not even going to consider wasting my – wait a minute.' I fished out from my pocket the other note, the one that began with the half moon. 'Tell me what this one means, then. Is there a place called Beechfield that you know of?'

He considered, with his same intent concentrating face. 'Shoreditch, you lummox.' He said it quite affectionately.

'I thought that was a ploughed furrow, in a field?'

'Or a ditch. See – there's the seashore, there's a ditch. And this time it's the Half Moon. Sent by a girl called Rose.' He beamed up at me, like a star pupil expecting a prize. 'I like this game, can we do another one?'

'That's all I have. So there's an inn called the Half Moon in Shoreditch?'

'Yeah. You want to go there?'

'I'm not riding all the way to Shoreditch to see if they've ever met a girl called Rose.'

He shrugged. 'Suit yourself.'

Ben's interpretation was absurd, but he was right – I didn't have anything better. The Half Moon Shoreditch note had appeared twice – once in Clara's locket and once in Titch's room, and Robin Poole had appeared surprised by the one in the locket. Perhaps it was worth a try. I shook my head and laughed.

'What's so funny?' Ben demanded.

'Nothing. You're a bright boy.' I was picturing Phelippes,

with all his treatises on cryptography and his prodigious memory, struggling all night to make sense of a picture puzzle that a child had solved at a glance. 'Can we borrow your dad's horse, do you think?'

'Course.' He jumped up and waved down a wherry. 'I reckon that's worth an extra sixpence?'

'Let's see if your mad idea is right first,' I said. 'If I find a woman called Rose at the Half Moon in Shoreditch, you'll get a shilling.'

'Deal,' he said, spitting on his hand and holding it out to shake.

'I'll trust your word,' I said, as the boat pulled up to the stairs.

On the way back to the Saracen's Head, he told me of his discoveries at the Unicorn: as far as the stable lads knew, there was a network of cellars beneath the main building, an attic and any number of mythical hiding places in the walls, including a cupboard behind the chimney breast in Madam Rosa's parlour where she supposedly kept all the jewels and money stolen from customers while they had their breeches down, and a secret room behind a beam on the top landing that was haunted by the ghost of a dead virgin who had been bricked up alive because she refused to give in to a rich nobleman's wicked desires. All that I discounted; I no longer thought Ballard was the killer, and therefore it was unlikely that Joe would be imprisoned somewhere around the Unicorn. More useful was the stable boy with the skin condition who said he had seen Joe leave with the tall man he was talking to at the gate; the boy had told Ben that Joe had appeared to go willingly, and he had seen no sign of the child being dragged or forced. None of that led us very far. By the time we reached the Saracen's Head, I was certain that all the evidence led to Robin Poole. I even wondered – with a strange, dizzying sensation – if Walsingham had suspected Poole's loyalty all along, and brought me into the conspiracy to spy not on Babington and his friends, but on his own man.

The courtyard was quiet, awaiting the midday rush. Ben went to ready the horse; I made my way to the tap-room to ask Dan's permission. I found him drying plates at the serving hatch.

'Fella to see you,' he said, in a low voice, nodding. I turned, one hand already moving to my dagger, and to my amazement saw Thomas Phelippes, sitting bolt upright at a corner table, his face fixed straight ahead but his eyes flicking anxiously left and right as if he were about to make a dash for the door. He was right; I had never seen a man look so out of place in a tavern. I slid into the bench opposite him and raised an eyebrow.

'I thought we weren't supposed to be meeting?'

'Yes, but there's been something of a crisis.' He said this in his usual, expressionless tone; he might as easily have been telling me discreetly that I had food down my shirt.

'You sent Clara Poole to the Cross Bones that night,' I said through my teeth, before he could launch into his crisis.

He quirked an eyebrow. 'How do you know that?'

'Never mind. To meet a man with a white feather in his hat. Who was he?'

He adopted that prissy face that drove me mad. 'Not your concern.'

'Listen here. I was asked to find out who killed her. The next day she turned up dead in the place she was supposed to meet this man, at your request, which you didn't think to mention to me – you don't suppose there might be a connection?' I jabbed a finger on the table, half-forgetting in my irritation that Clara was not actually dead.

'No. Now you listen—'

'Explain first. If you want me to find this killer, you need to tell me everything. I've wasted a lot of time trying to figure out what on earth she was doing in Southwark in the first place.'

He made a little impatient huff, but he steepled his fingers together and looked at them, so he didn't have to meet my eye. 'The man with the white feather – I'm not telling you his name – was bringing me something urgent from Flushing.'

'From the Low Countries? Why?'

'That's where Flushing is, the last time I looked. There's a war on. This man had extremely sensitive military intelligence.'

'What had Clara to do with that?' I had visions of this business spiralling out beyond the Babington group to encompass the fate of armies across the Channel; if I had not been feeling out of my depth before, I certainly would by now.

'Nothing at all. But I didn't want him bringing it to any of my regular contacts, in case they were being watched. It had to be someone fresh. I thought no one would pay attention to a man meeting a girl under cover of darkness in Southwark. I asked Clara, she was happy to oblige. All she had to do was take some papers from him and carry them back to Seething Lane.'

'And when she was found dead, you didn't for a minute think it could have been him?' The question was partly a test; I wanted to work out if Phelippes really believed that Clara Poole had been killed.

'For the first day I wondered,' he said. 'It did seem too much of a coincidence. I even worried that a third party had followed him, and killed her to get the papers after he left. But then I received a message from him – Mr White Feather – to say that bad weather had delayed his ship by half a day. So he hadn't been there at all that night. But someone else obviously followed her to the meeting point, and took advantage of the remoteness of it to kill her.'

'That's what you believe – that one of the conspirators knew she would be at the Cross Bones that night, and murdered her because he suspected her of being a spy?'

His face twitched with impatience. 'You know that's always been the theory.'

We watched one another for a long moment, until his eyes flinched away. If he suspected that the dead girl was not Clara, or that her brother had anything to do with it, he was not giving it away. I decided not to share what Lady Frances had said about Clara until I had better evidence. 'Anyway,' he continued, before I could interrupt again, 'we've got bigger problems right now. Father Prado has escaped.'

'*What?*' I glanced at the door, as if the priest might come bursting through at any moment demanding his clothes back. 'How did that happen?'

Phelippes frowned; the question clearly touched a nerve. 'Incompetence. He was being held at Barn Elms, in the cellars there. Master Secretary was away at court, his steward took Prado some food this morning. The priest said he had lost all feeling in his arms and asked for the restraints to be removed briefly so that he could stretch, the steward is a soft-hearted man and indulged him. What happened next is unclear, I suspect because the steward is embarrassed. He was hit in the head with the pitcher of water he had brought and doesn't remember much, except that when he came round the priest was gone.'

'Were there no guards?'

'On the outer doors of the house, not on the cellar door. Apparently Prado went out a back window and stole a boat.'

'And he was in a fit state to row it?'

Phelippes blinked, offended. 'He hadn't been *racked*. There was no need – he was offered a choice and gave us everything we wanted, willingly.'

'So where is he now?'

'If I knew that, I wouldn't be here. The supposition is he'll either be on his way to the conspirators, or – more likely – to find his friend Father Weston.'

'Yes, it would have been useful to know they were friends. I've met Weston.'

'I see. So he knows you are not Prado?'

'Obviously.'

Phelippes gave a brisk nod. 'Right. Then it's time to pull you out. It's unfortunate – you were doing a good job – but with Prado and Weston at large knowing your identity, it's only a matter of time before the conspirators learn it, and they will kill you. We'll keep you safe somewhere for a few days until they are all arrested, and then get you back to France.'

'No.'

The small vertical crease above his nose appeared, as it always did when he had to confront a difficult person instead of a difficult cipher.

'That's an order from Master Secretary.'

'Then you can pass my reply back to him. Look, Thomas' – I leaned in – 'the killer has taken a child, to keep him from telling what he knows about the murder. And he's done that because I've come around asking questions. I don't know if that child is still alive, but I promised his mother I would find him, and I can't walk away until I do.'

'That's not my problem. If you continue to associate with the conspirators, your life is in danger. That is Master Secretary's second priority, after the integrity of the operation. You know more than enough, if they decide to torture you, to compromise other people and possibly the end goal.'

'I'm touched that you don't want me getting hurt. But I'm not giving up. I'm *this* close, Thomas.' I held my thumb and forefinger a pinch apart to demonstrate.

'You know who the killer is?'

'I think so. But I need to make certain.' I did not want to accuse Robin Poole to people who had known him far longer than I had, without compelling evidence. If I could track Clara down and make her confess the whole story, that would be enough.

'Here is the difficulty,' Phelippes said, touching his fingertips together and not looking at me. Even with his expressionless demeanour, I could tell he was angry. 'At this stage, we don't really care who killed Clara. What we want most urgently is the latest letter from Babington to Mary Stuart, setting out the new plan for the assassination in detail – Master Secretary does not want to move against the conspirators without that. But if they learn there's a spy in their midst before we get our hands on that letter, we may not have evidence to convict all of them.'

'Wait – you don't have the letter?' I was briefly confused, before I remembered that Gifford had fled before Babington had written it. 'Did you catch up with Gifford?'

Now it was Phelippes's turn to look puzzled. 'Gifford? What do you mean?'

'Last night – did you find him? I don't think he took a horse from the Cavendish stable, he must have had one ready elsewhere, unless he's lying low somewhere in London.'

'What are you talking about – Gifford has taken a horse where? Not to Staffordshire – he can't have done, he hasn't brought us the letter yet—'

I looked at him, trying to work out why he was being so slow, and then it dawned.

'Robin didn't come to you last night?'

'No. Should he have done?'

'*Merda.*' I thumped my fist on the table. 'Gifford has packed up and run. Robin said he would go straight to you with a message, so you could set out after him. You're telling me he didn't? You were definitely at Leadenhall Street last night, sometime around midnight?'

'I was there all night. No sign of Robin. You mean to say he's playing us false? And Gifford too?'

We exchanged a glance.

'It looks that way.'

Phelippes nodded. 'I wondered. Robin's father did the same. These Catholics – the guilt sucks them back, in the end.'

'Not all of us,' I said, affronted.

'No. You have other weaknesses. We're well aware of them.' He stood, pushing the table back. 'I must take this news to Master Secretary immediately and set about finding Gifford and Poole, as well as Prado. You should go to Leadenhall Street and wait there, out of harm's way. I'll give you a key.'

'I've said I'm not going.' There was no chance I was planning to spend the day skulking in Phelippes's rooms while Joe was missing. 'Look, I have an idea. Don't go after Robin for now. I don't think he's guessed anyone suspects him yet, so he has no reason to run. I might be able to make him talk.' The scene I had walked in on last night in Babington's room, and the fact that Clara was alive: I guessed Robin would go to some lengths to stop Walsingham – or Ballard – finding out those little secrets. 'Let me have one more day,' I said. 'The Queen is safe enough for now, as long as Bessie Pierrepont is kept out of her private chambers. Robin is the only one who can get Babington's letter for us, with Gilbert gone. I promise if I haven't found the child by tomorrow morning, you can go after Robin.'

'You can leave Bessie Pierrepont to us. But we may not have another day. If Prado gets to Ballard before we get to Prado, the conspirators will scatter, and they might come for you on the way. We have spent months setting this up to get the words we need from Mary – we can't let you mar it now.'

'It won't be me who mars it. You're the one who's missed two double agents under your nose.'

He flinched; criticism of his professional competence seemed to be the only thing that really stung him. 'My orders are to send you to Leadenhall Street.'

I stood up, set my shoulders back and clenched my fists. 'What are you going to do, Thomas, arrest me?'

He took a deep breath and looked me up and down as if he were seriously weighing up whether he could bundle me on to a horse. 'Not personally, no. But if you refuse to stand down from the operation, I will report you to Master Secretary and he may well decide to send armed men for you. There is too much at stake.'

'One more day, Thomas. I promise I can look after myself. Haven't I always, in the past?'

'As I recall, you have usually relied on Philip Sidney to get you out of trouble, and he is not here.' Touché; he was right, and I was the one looking down in shame. He sucked in his cheeks. 'Master Secretary won't like it.'

'Then don't tell him.'

He lifted his eyebrows, as if such a breach of protocol was beyond the reach of his imagination. 'Let's say until the end of today. Report to me at midnight at Leadenhall Street. Regardless of what you have found out by then, if Robin Poole is not loyal to Her Majesty, then he is an immediate danger and must be contained. Or you will be.'

I hesitated, before nodding a curt agreement; it was the best I was likely to get. Ben put his head around the door of the tap-room to say the horse was ready; his eyes widened when he saw Phelippes.

'Ah, Ben. Good. I need you to take some messages for me,' the cryptographer said.

The boy's gaze flitted anxiously to me. 'But I have to go with him – he promised a shilling if I'm right—'

'You'll get your shilling, Ben,' I said quickly, before Phelippes could ask what he was right about. 'I'll see you when I get back,' I said in a low voice as I passed him. 'Don't tell him about the puzzle, or no shilling.'

He shot me a scornful look. 'As if,' he said. I smiled to myself on my way out to the yard; if there was anyone unlikely to be intimidated by Phelippes, it was Ben. I found myself unexpectedly disappointed not to have his company on the ride.

* * *

I took the road out through the Bishopsgate and past the Bedlam, as I had the other night when I followed Gifford to the theatre. Overhead the sky was a high blue chequered with small, scudding clouds, though there was a snippy wind that kept people in their jackets and hats, as if England couldn't offer summer without a grudge. Before I reached The Curtain, I saw the sign I was looking for on the right-hand side and nudged the horse into the yard through the coach gates. The Half Moon was a run-down place, in need of a good coat of paint; the sort of inn you often saw on the outskirts of London, used by travellers who couldn't afford to stay closer to the centre. I tied the horse to a hitching post, threw a coin to a stable boy and headed inside.

Though the tap-room was shabby, it was full, and a savoury smell of home cooking drifted through from the kitchen; to judge by its popularity, the food must be better than the décor would suggest. I found a table in a corner with upturned casks for seats, and looked around. A cheap copy of Queen Elizabeth's portrait hung above the fireplace. It occurred to me as I sat there, with my Mediterranean face and my foppish Parisian clothes all screaming for the wrong kind of attention, that this was a spectacular waste of time. Ben's say-what-you-see approach to solving a cipher was a child's game, and while I chased after it like a fool, Joe was still missing, and Prado, Ballard and Walsingham's armed guards might be, even now, tracking me down with the aim of spoiling my afternoon. I almost stood and left before anyone realised my folly – I would give Ben his shilling anyway, it was Walsingham's money after all – but I reasoned that since I was here, and had missed my breakfast, I would at least stay for something to eat.

A broad-hipped woman with floury hands and a grubby apron wove her way with surprising agility between tables, plates balanced up her forearms. '*Rose!*' she yelled, over her shoulder, at a volume that threatened to crack the plaster on the walls, as she set the food down in front of four men in work clothes nearby. 'Go and wipe them tables out the back when you've brought these gentlemen their ale.' I tried to follow the direction of her shout, but the room was too busy. I wished I could have seen Ben's told-you-so expression.

Turning to me, the tavern keeper smoothed her apron and moderated her tone. 'What can I get you, love?'

I ordered bread and cold beef with a mug of small beer, and sat back to watch and wait.

When a serving girl brought the food to me, I kept my eyes on the table. As she set the plate down, I noted how the fingernails on both her hands were bitten down to the quick, to the point of drawing blood.

'Anything else?' she asked, forcing a note of brightness into a weary voice.

I reached out and closed a hand firmly but gently around her slim wrist.

'No, thank you, Clara.'

The noise she made was as sharp and sudden as if she had stood on a splinter of glass; she snatched her arm away and I raised my head to look at her. For a brief moment she met my eye, and I saw a strikingly pretty face, pale with delicate bones and bow-shaped lips, and light greenish-brown eyes wild with fear. Perhaps Lotte had looked something like that, before her face was smashed. Clara's famous auburn hair was all bound up and tucked under a white linen cap, and her figure was neat and trim under the shapeless grey dress and apron, no sign of a swelling belly yet. She wore a white linen scarf around her neck, presumably to hide the birthmark. It took her only a moment to master her shock, before she turned on her heel.

'I'm a friend of Titch,' I hissed, and she whipped back to me, eyes even wider. She pressed a finger to her lips and motioned to the yard with her head, holding up a hand with the fingers splayed to indicate five minutes. I left it two; I thought there was a good chance she might run.

But she hovered by a gate in the side wall that led out to a lane. I followed her and she pulled the gate to behind us. Her face was rigid with fear; either she didn't believe me, or she thought I could only have come to bring bad news. She would have been right on both counts.

'He told you I was here?' Her voice was soft and educated, and I could hear the fear fighting with anger; I guessed he had sworn to keep it secret.

'No. I worked it out all by myself, from your notes. I'm afraid I didn't tell the truth, back there – I'm actually a friend of Frances Sidney.'

She breathed hard for a moment, then tried to slip past me; I caught her wrist again and held it harder this time.

'I'll scream,' she said, glancing at the gate, her face bone white.

'You do that. Bring your employer out here, she seems like a woman who keeps a respectable house and loves the Queen. Does she know Rose is the pregnant slut of a Catholic who plans to kill Her Majesty?'

She lifted her free hand to slap me; I grabbed her other wrist and she struggled, before the fight went out of her and tears sprung to her eyes.

'Do you work for *him*?' she asked, slumping against the wall when I let her go.

'Who?' I affected innocence.

'You know who. Frances's father.'

'Yes. But it's true that I am also her friend. And she has been going out of her mind with grief over your cruel murder. Did you not think how your little stunt would leave her?'

I could see that she was fighting to keep the tears under control. 'I was going to write to her and explain. When everything was sorted out . . .' she let the sentence fall away.

I could barely contain my incredulity. 'Sorted *out*? Sweet infant Jesus, Clara – how exactly did you think this story was going to end? You bide your time here wiping tables until your lover sweeps you off to a lovely Catholic wedding before the baby starts to show, and then you get front row seats as man and wife at Mary Stuart's coronation? Is that how you think it plays out? Where would Walsingham's daughter be in that scenario?'

'*No.*' She pressed her knuckles into her eyes. 'It was nothing to do with Mary Stuart – I knew that would never succeed. But he *is* going to marry me.'

'He's already betrothed to someone, as I understand. An heiress.'

'He's going to break it off with her, he's writing to his parents—'

'More pressingly, he's on the cusp of being arrested for treason and carted off to Tyburn, so he won't be marrying either of you. You'll both be blowing kisses to his head on London Bridge.'

'You know nothing about it.' Though thick with tears, her voice was low and determined; I could have admired her resolve, if two people hadn't already died for it.

'Then why don't you put me in the picture? Before anyone else is killed.'

'Because I don't know who you are, or whose side you're on.'

I laughed. 'No one in any of this mess knows whose side anyone else is on. Put it this way – at the moment, I'm one of a very few people who are aware that you're not dead. If you want to keep it that way, you need to explain to me who the others are, and how exactly you thought this would play out when you decided to have another girl murdered so you could live happily ever after with Titch.'

She flinched as if I had struck her, and swallowed a sob. 'I never agreed to that. I didn't know that was the plan, I swear – I would never have wanted – but Robin said—' She shook her head and dissolved into incoherent sobs; I was in danger of losing her, just as I was drawing close to the prize.

'I need you to pull yourself together for me, Clara,' I said, with a stern note in my voice. 'What did Robin say?'

She looked up at me and I saw again that spark of terror in her eyes. 'Does he know I'm here?'

I stared back, wrong-footed. 'I don't know – does he?'

'I mean, did you tell him I was in Shoreditch? Did he see the notes too?'

I remembered Robin's face when Phelippes had opened the secret compartment of the locket; I would have wagered that he had no idea the note was there, nor how to read it, but it would be a mistake to underestimate his capacity for deception. 'Where does Robin think you are, if he doesn't know you're here?' I asked, avoiding the question.

'He thinks I'm on the road to my father's cousin in Essex,' she said. 'He paid a wool merchant to take me on his cart. I paid the man double to let me out in Shoreditch and keep quiet about it – I couldn't leave Titch. If Robin finds out I'm still in London, he'll kill me. I mean—' Her hand flew to her mouth as she realised what she had said.

'No – he'd just kill someone else and pretend it was you,' I said pointedly. 'Why don't you start at the beginning?'

'Goodwife Bailey will come looking for me in a moment, wondering why I'm shirking,' she said, with an eye on the gate. 'It's the busiest time of day.'

'Then you'll have to talk fast,' I said, barring her way.

She sighed. 'I told Robin about the baby. God forgive me, I never should have said a word, but he was so vexed with me about Titch. He only brought me into the group in the first place so that—' she stopped and bit her lip, careful of her brother's secret.

'So you could pretend to have a dalliance with Babington, to make sure Ballard and Walsingham didn't realise it was actually Robin bedding him,' I said bluntly. Her eyebrows nearly reached her hairline, but she nodded.

'I see you know a lot. That shouldn't surprise me, if you work for Sir Francis. That was the idea and I said I would do it to protect Robin, but I hadn't counted on meeting Titch.' Her eyes glazed over and I remembered what Frances had said about her dreamy expression. The boy must possess some subtle charm that had passed me by.

'You fell in love with him?'

'Completely. It was so unexpected, and it changed everything. Before, I'd have sworn I would do anything for Sir Francis – he's been so good to me and Robin, he became my father when our father died, and Frances has been like a sister to me. I told him I would be proud to do my bit by bringing him information about the conspirators, but I was so naïve. I thought it would be a question of copying a few letters, reporting conversations. I don't think I had really understood what it meant to be an informer.'

'To become friends with people, earn their trust and their affection, trick them into confiding in you, so that you can betray them to the cruellest possible death?' Walsingham had reminded me of the same reality. It had not been necessary; I remembered it all too well.

She gave one miserable nod. 'I see you understand. Once I met Titch, I realised I couldn't do it. I wanted to get out – but I wanted Titch out of it, too. He was never as fanatical for Mary Stuart's cause as the others, he only went along with them at the beginning for Anthony's sake. I thought with enough time I could persuade him it was a bad idea, without giving away that I'd been spying for Sir Francis.' Her voice wound tighter and higher with distress. 'But we didn't have time – Robin said as soon as Sir Francis got the letter he needed from Mary, the whole group would be arrested. I wanted to warn Titch, but I knew he would tell Anthony, who would tell Ballard, and then I would be in danger, and Robin too. When I found out about the baby, I thought that might be reason enough for Titch to give up the conspiracy.'

'So you told him?'

'Yes. I was afraid of how he would respond, but he was delighted.' She wiped a tear with her sleeve. 'He promised we would be together, he would tell Anthony he was out of the plot and we would leave London – he could see by then that the Mary Stuart business was built on delusions, even without knowing it was being monitored. But he didn't want to leave Anthony to Ballard's influence – he wanted to try and convince him to abandon the plan too. And I did what I have always done when I'm in trouble and worried.' She chewed savagely at her fingernail; I wanted to slap her hand away like a nursemaid and tell her to stop.

'You asked your big brother for advice,' I said heavily.

She examined the remains of her nail and nodded. 'I told Robin about the baby, God forgive me. I should never have said a word. He went mad. Called me all kinds of names, said I'd disgraced my father and mother, he told me he would drag me by the hair to this woman he knew of in Southwark to get rid of it. When I told him Titch was going to marry me, he laughed like a lunatic and told me I should be in the Bedlam as I was clearly insane. He said I had no idea what danger I was in.' Her eyes darted again to the gate.

'From whom? The conspirators?'

'No. Though I think Ballard would have been furious – Titch and I had been careful to keep our affair secret, just as Robin and Anthony had. No – Robin was afraid of what Sir Francis would do.'

'Because of your father?'

She stared again, as if trying to fathom me. 'How do you know all this?' When I didn't reply, she looked down and ran a hand thoughtfully over her almost flat belly. 'My brother was convinced that Sir Francis would have me killed if he knew about the baby, because he would think it meant I had gone over to the conspirators. Robin had this crazed idea that our father was murdered on Sir Francis's orders because he was really on the side of the Catholics – Jack Savage had heard this in prison from some old papist and Robin swallowed it whole.'

'But you didn't?'

She looked away. 'Our father drank. You probably know that too. He had a hard time recovering after his first wife died, Robin's mother, but when my mother died too, something broke in him, I think, that's when he really took to the bottle. You can't sustain the life he was living – lying to everyone – when you're never sober. I was amazed it took him so long to fall in the river. And it's just as likely that in his cups he told one of his Catholic friends he'd been an informer and *they* pushed him. But Robin didn't want to think about that, so he was thrilled when Savage handed him a reason to blame someone else. He turned against Sir Francis as soon as he heard that story.'

'When did Savage tell him about this?'

She considered. 'About six months ago, something like that?'

'But Robin carried on working for Walsingham?'

'He said he was waiting for the right opportunity to avenge our father. An eye for an eye. I thought he had gone a bit mad.' She pushed back a stray lock of hair that had come loose from her cap and gave a dry laugh. 'He sounded like something from one of those awful revenge plays they have at The Curtain. I told him to find better proof before he turned so dramatic.' A spot of colour had appeared on her high cheekbones.

'And he thought Walsingham would want to be rid of you the same way?'

She pressed her fingers into her eyes for a moment, as if that might make me go away, and seemed disappointed to find me still there when she opened them.

'Once I told him about the baby, he became *obsessed* with getting me out of London before Walsingham made sure I disappeared. I told him he was overreacting, I didn't think that would happen, but he wouldn't listen. He didn't want me going anywhere alone, he kept calling round to Seething Lane to check on me, it was making Frances suspicious. So to stop him, I said I would be happy to leave London in secret, as long as he gave me time to persuade Titch to come too. But he wanted me to go immediately. Robin can be very . . .' She pulled at the lock of hair again, twisting it around her finger. 'He likes to be in control. It's easier if I do as he says. He's been like that since our father died, he feels it's his job to protect me. I think he partly blamed himself for taking his eyes off me long enough for *this* to happen.' She patted her stomach.

'When did he go from wanting you out of London to killing another girl in your place?'

The colour drained from her face at that, and I began to believe that she had truly not intended Lotte's death. I could use that guilt, I thought.

'I had a note from Thomas Phelippes.'

'Asking you to go to the Cross Bones to meet a contact.'

She no longer looked surprised at my knowing so much. 'Yes. I showed it to Robin. He pounced on it, said there you have it, there is your death warrant. They must have found out about Titch and the baby, he said, why else would Sir Francis be sending me to Southwark in the middle of the night, if not to be killed? He was so intent, by that point I even started to think he might be right. Robin said we would use it to our advantage. He would go to Southwark and meet this man, and fix it so that Sir Francis and Phelippes believed I was dead. I was to leave London the same night to stay with our relative, to keep me out of harm's way while the business with the conspiracy played out. I agreed, but I made him promise to tell Titch that I was safe. I gave Robin my locket to pass on to him as a gift, and I'd hidden the note inside, in case for any reason Robin decided not to tell him after all. I knew Titch would understand and come to me – it was our code.'

'Adorable.'

She blushed, and darted me a shy smile. 'Oh, I know it was silly, but isn't that part of being in love – behaving like you're fourteen again with your first sweetheart? It was how we arranged places to meet, and false names – the picture codes. Guessing was part of the excitement. I was a Lily once, and a Daisy – he was Tom, though we did laugh about that, because he'd drawn a cat and I thought it would be Kit, so I was in this inn near the Black Friars asking was there a Kit waiting for me, when—'

'Yes, charming. But Robin didn't deliver the message.'

The smile vanished at my brusqueness. 'When I'd heard nothing for a few days, I realised he probably hadn't. He had lied to me about that, just as I had lied to him about leaving London. So I sent another copy of the same message via one of the delivery boys here.'

'And last night Titch found you.' Her fierce blush told me that I had guessed correctly. So the boy had not been entirely untruthful when he said he had been with a barmaid. 'When Robin said he would fix it so that Walsingham believed you were dead, what did you think he meant?'

'I thought he would pay this man off, to say the deed was done. I swear, I never imagined—'

'But he must have asked you for one of your dresses?'

She took a deep breath and ripped at another nail with her teeth; I clenched my jaw. 'I thought he meant to leave it by the riverbank or something, to look as if I had gone in the water.'

'So when did you learn that he killed another girl so people would think it was you?'

She levelled a fierce stare at me. 'Do you know for certain it was Robin killed her? Has he told you he did?'

'Well, someone killed her, and made sure she looked like you. He even got her to draw a stain on her neck with henna paste, to mimic this' – I reached out with one finger and pulled the scarf down to show her birthmark – 'so that Walsingham would identify the body as you. He took the trouble to smash her face up just enough that no one could say she wasn't.'

Her fingers strayed to her neck and she closed her eyes. 'Titch told me last night. I can't believe Robin could do that to a woman though.'

'Oh, it gets better,' I said, aware that I was inflicting punishment for something that was not wholly her fault. 'He also killed the friend of the dead girl, in case she gave him away, and he's abducted a young child who got the henna for them, who might also be dead by now. All so you could get safely to Essex. How will he feel when he learns you didn't even do that, after all he's risked for you?'

Clara made a small, strangled noise, and appeared to crumple at the knees as a great racking sob burst out of her; I stepped forward and caught her under the arms and she slumped against my shoulder while I held her up.

'I had no idea,' she whimpered. 'I swear to it, God knows I never meant for anyone else to get hurt. Once, when I was fourteen, just after Father died, there was a boy I liked.' Her voice disappeared, muffled, into the padding of my doublet. 'It was nothing, just children practising how to flirt. He was fifteen, he worked in the gardens at Sir Francis's house in Barn Elms. My brother saw me talking to him one day, just chatting and laughing, all very innocent. Robin was furious with me – he said I was simpering like a whore, our father would be disgusted with me and if I carried on, I would destroy the family name. Later, he beat the boy black and blue, and told Sir Francis it was because he'd caught him stealing. The boy lost his job.'

I remembered again the way Walsingham had said that Robin Poole loved his sister, the words so weighted with meaning. I had wondered if he was implying something improper, but it seemed the truth was more complicated.

'It sounds as if your brother would go to any lengths to protect you,' I said carefully. 'Or at least to make sure he is the only person you love.'

I felt her nod against my shoulder. 'I think he is afraid I'll leave him. Because he will never have a wife, you know – he wants me to be there, always. He was against my first marriage, but he couldn't defy Sir Francis, who gave it his blessing. But he was delighted when my husband died and I came back to Seething Lane, dependent again.'

'Listen, Clara,' I said, holding her gently by the upper arms so that I could look her in the eye. 'What is Robin's plan? You said he talked about revenge against Walsingham – does that mean he is now on the side of the conspirators? Will he try and find a means to make the plot against Elizabeth succeed?' I couldn't see any way this could work. Even if Robin had transferred his loyalty to Babington and his friends, there was not much he could do at this stage to prevent their arrests; Walsingham knew their names and had copies of their plans in writing, and even if Robin was now keeping details from Phelippes or feeding him false information, they had other sources inside the group – me, and Sophia watching Bessie Pierrepont. The realisation made the skin prickle on my neck, so that I glanced instinctively over my shoulder; either one of us could be Robin's next target, if he thought that in some way he could allow the assassination to go ahead.

'He's never spoken like that,' Clara said, wiping her face again on her sleeve. 'I don't think he gives two figs for Mary Stuart, or being Catholic for that matter, except in so far as it's a badge of loyalty to our father. But I know he thinks Ballard is an unhinged fanatic, I can't see that he'd want to support him to the bitter end. So, no – I don't think he would throw England into chaos just to spite Sir Francis.'

'Then what did he mean about revenge?'

'I don't know. I can tell you only that it's not religion that matters most to Robin, it's family.'

A flicker of fear started up somewhere at the base of my skull.

'But he has never threatened anything specific?'

She shook her head. 'I thought it was just a way to vent his anger. I didn't really think he would do anything. But now . . .' She let the words tail off, and went back to chewing her nail.

At that moment, the gate in the wall banged open and the innkeeper filled the doorway with a face like storm clouds.

'Rose Sidney, I'm run off my feet in there, customers are screaming for their dinner and you're dallying out here with another fancy man like a hussy – *oh*.' She noted Clara's tear-stained face and redirected her fury instantly to me. 'Have you been bothering this girl, you filthy Spanish whoreson?'

'No, Goodwife Bailey.' Clara reached out a hand to pacify her. 'This man is a friend of the family, and he has just brought me some sad news of a bereavement. But I am fine now. I'll get back to work.'

The goodwife shot me a look that contained all her feelings about men and foreigners. 'Right. Well. I'm sorry for your loss. *You* still haven't paid for your dinner,' she added, poking me in the chest.

'My apologies. I hope this will cover your trouble.' I bowed low and gave her sixpence. It occurred to me that I should have asked Phelippes for more money earlier – though I supposed he would be reluctant to grant it, now that I was defying an official order to stand down from the operation.

'Where can I find your brother?' I hissed to Clara, as she made to follow the woman back into the yard.

'His lodgings are in Long Lane, by the Charterhouse, above the stationers' shop. But please don't tell him I'm here – you swear to it?'

'If you promise not to go anywhere. And don't tell Titch that we've spoken, if you see him again. I'll be back.'

'I don't even know your name.'

I hesitated. 'You can call me Prado for now.'

* * *

I was familiar with the streets around the Charterhouse; the printer who had published my books had his press here, and the sight of the old monastery buildings, their pale yellow stone warm in the sunlight, skewered me with a pang of nostalgia. If I acquitted myself well in this business and Walsingham gave me the means to stay in England, I might even find myself knocking at his door in a few months' time with the manuscript of a new work. I dismounted and tethered the horse in a shady square, reprimanding myself; the conspiracy was not over yet, by a long way, and I must not allow myself to be distracted.

Long Lane ran alongside the churchyard of St Bartholomew the Great on one side of the road; the other was lined with smaller shops and businesses, some with their goods displayed on tables outside. A few customers loitered, browsing, making conversation; I wandered along the street, picking up occasional items as if I too were out shopping. I was pleased to see that the stationer's was busy; if the proprietor was attending to customers, he would be less likely to notice anyone poking around the rest of the property. At the side of the house a narrow passage led to a flight of steps up to the door of the first-floor lodgings. I drew my dagger and knocked sharply.

There was no response; I strained to listen for any sound of movement from inside, but heard nothing. I tried one more time; when I was satisfied that no one was in, I took out the folding penknife from my boot heel and crouched to pick the lock with its thin blade. The mechanism was new and not yet crusted with dirt and rust; it yielded with little effort, and I almost wished Savage had been there to admire my skills. I pushed the door open and closed it quietly behind me, treading as carefully as possible in case my steps could be heard in the shop downstairs.

Robin Poole's lodging was clean and sparely furnished: a truckle bed, a table with a few personal belongings – a comb, an earthenware jug, quills, penknives and a supply of paper, though no letters left out. A pair of breeches was folded neatly on top of a chest at the foot of the bed; the chest was unlocked and contained only clean shirts and underhose. I felt around the corners and rapped my knuckles on the base in search of a false compartment, but the wood sounded solid. I stood and let my gaze travel around the room. The place had a temporary air; there were none of the little touches of a home, no ornaments, no flowers on the windowsill. No sign of a woman, in other words. Robin Poole lived like me, and the thought struck me as sad: a single man in his thirties, whose whole life could be packed up in a travelling bag in a couple of hours. But, like me, he also lived a double life, which meant he had secrets to hide, and if we had anything in common, that ought to give me the insight into where to find them. In my rooms in Paris, I had kept the papers I did not want anyone to find under a loose board in the rafters. This was an old building, though clearly kept in good repair; I could not see any tell-tale gaps in the ceiling beams, but the walls were panelled with wood to waist height, and I began to work my way around knocking gently at intervals, trying to keep the sound down and stealing anxious glances at the door as I went. In the corner by the bed I heard the unmistakable hollow ring that told me there was a cavity in the wall; I pulled the bed out, felt around the panel with my fingertips and eventually located the tiny depression that allowed me to insert my knife and pry the panel until I could lift it free.

Inside I found a strongbox, locked. This lock took more work to pick; the box was of the kind purpose-built to keep money safe, and the mechanism was complex. More than once I was afraid I would snap some delicate moving part and the whole thing would break beyond repair, meaning the box would have to be forced; there was no time to risk that, and I doubted I would get very far if I tried to leave with it under my arm. But after a great deal of frustration and a couple of near-misses, I heard a small, satisfying click and the lock sprang open.

There was not much inside. A small purse of coins; a couple of sheets of cipher in Phelippes's distinctive, crabbed writing, and two miniature portraits, cheaply done. One was a bearded, smiling man in his forties, hair greying at the temples, his thick brows almost meeting in a V above his nose, as Robin's did; there was no doubting that this was George Poole as Robin remembered him. The second was easily recognisable; Robin himself, as a gawky youth of about twelve or thirteen, holding a delicate, smiling little girl with a mass of auburn curls. Though the artist had no great skill, he had managed to capture an expression of mutual delight on the children's faces as they looked at one another; Clara was reaching a hand up to touch her brother's cheek. For a moment, I felt an unnerving sense of loss; Robin lived like me, I thought, except for one thing: he had family. He had someone he believed depended on him, someone he would go to any lengths to protect, no matter how twisted that sense of duty had become. At the bottom of the box I found a folded sheet of paper, and a small charge, like the air before a storm, flashed up my spine.

Unfolding it, I saw the floorplan of a house, such as master builders use. Entrances and exits had been marked with arrows, the rooms labelled and two of them shaded. Along the top of the paper a sentence had been written in cipher, though I could see it was not Phelippes's writing this time. Beneath this, a single word, also in cipher, and a crude drawing of a gallows. Some of the characters looked familiar; I focused and tried to pull up from my memory the codes Phelippes had given me in the past, wishing I had the cryptographer's gift for memorising alphabets at a glance. But as I stared at the paper, I realised that I had seen at least one of the words before, in this same cipher; Phelippes must have been getting lazy, as he had evidently given the same key to me and to Robin. And the word I recognised was 'Elizabeth'.

My mouth dried; I slowed my breathing and shut out all other thoughts, working my way back through my memory system until I could see the alphabet as if it were written on the inside of my eyelids. When I was sure I had it, I looked back at the plan and deciphered the remaining words. It read: *Justice is the Daughter of Time*; a curious variant on Bloody Mary's motto. And underneath: *Elizabeth*, and a gallows.

I exhaled slowly, my hands shaking. So Robin Poole did intend to kill the Queen after all, and clearly in some manner unconnected with the rest of the Babington group and their clumsy plot, which he already knew was doomed to failure. When I had asked Robin what exactly he did for Walsingham, he had laughed and replied, 'talk to people'. That could have meant anything; it was possible that he had clearance to carry sensitive messages to Walsingham at court, and might therefore be admitted to the heart of the palace. But that must have been the case for some time; I wondered why he had not moved before now. Perhaps he intended to wait until the arrests of Babington and his friends were occupying all Walsingham's time and attention, and Queen Elizabeth believed the threat was past, before executing his own, private plan. I stared again at the drawing of the house, willing it to give up further information. It was not a plan of any of the royal palaces, that much was clear; the building was too small. I wondered if it might be one of the private manor houses the Queen had intended to stay in during her royal Progress to the countryside later this month. Walsingham would no doubt recognise the layout. I needed to get this paper to him as quickly as possible. I folded it again and tucked it into the lining of my doublet, before replacing the strongbox inside its cavity and pushing the bed back into place. The most obvious course was to take the paper straight to Phelippes at Leadenhall Street, though there was a good chance he might be away, trying to organise the separate pursuits of Prado and Gifford. If I didn't find him, I could try riding direct to the palace at Whitehall and asking for Walsingham in person, though I had experience of the layers of security at court when the Queen was in residence, and without a seal or any token to prove my right to speak to Master Secretary, I could be waiting for hours to be vetted.

Perhaps the best option would be to ride to Seething Lane and ask Lady Sidney to accompany me; if anyone could get me straight into her father's presence, it would be Frances. As I decided on this course, I turned and it was as if my mind caught up with my eyes; something clicked into place, like the mechanism of a lock, and I scrabbled to take out the floorplan and open it again. I looked at the rooms that had been marked up – study, parlour, kitchen, master bedroom, nursery. *Nursery.* A sensation like ice water sluiced through my veins; now I recognised the layout of that study, that corridor, that dining room. This was a plan of Walsingham's house at Seething Lane. An eye for an eye, Clara had said. She had also told me that Robin didn't care about religion; the only thing that really mattered to him was family. If he believed Walsingham had killed his father, what would he consider appropriate justice? *Elizabeth*: not the Queen of England, but her namesake, baby Lizzie, Walsingham's granddaughter.

I put the plan away, checked that I had left nothing out of place in the room, and pulled the door closed silently behind me. I had never learned the art of locking a door without a key, only opening one; it would be obvious to Robin as soon as he came back that someone had been in his lodgings, but so far there was no reason for him to imagine it was me. In any case, there was no time to worry about that; the paper gave no indication of when he might carry out his plan, but I knew I needed to get to Seething Lane as quickly as possible and take Lady Sidney and the baby to safety.

I raced the length of Long Lane towards the square where I had left the horse and at the corner almost collided with Anthony Babington. He did at least have the grace to look shame-faced.

'Father,' he muttered, shuffling his feet.

'Anthony.' I bobbed him a little bow, and we stood in awkward silence for a moment while I willed him to hurry away.

'I suppose you were visiting Robin?' He gestured down the street.

'I went to look for him, but he was not at home.'

'I did not expect you, last night.'

'You asked me to call on you,' I said.

'Oh. So I did. But it got so late, I thought you had forgotten. And then Robin knocked, and I thought he had bolted the door behind him . . .' He let the words drift, his eyes on the ground. 'Will we go to Hell, Father?'

The simplicity of the question made me think of Joe. I laid a hand on his arm; I no longer cared whether my response was consistent with Father Prado's character.

'I think God has bigger things to think about,' I said. Relief washed over his face; it had not escaped me that he was still addressing me as if he believed I were the priest. Wherever the real Prado had got to, he did not seem to have reached Babington yet.

'I'm glad I ran into you, though,' he said, falling into step beside me with a last yearning glance back towards Robin's lodgings. 'I came to call on you earlier, at your room – I was hoping we might talk without Gilbert there. But you were both gone.' He sounded peevish.

'I don't know where Gilbert could be,' I said truthfully. 'Did you finish your letter to Mary? Was that why you wanted him?'

'I did, but it's not ready to send yet – there may be further developments.'

'Is that right?' I said, apprehensive.

'Yes, Savage came by this morning – Ballard has called an emergency meeting at the Unicorn. Something about agreeing the exact date for the execution – apparently he has procured the poison. If we settle upon that, then I can let Queen Mary know of it in my letter, and tell her to prepare imminently for escape.' His eyes were bright with excitement, despite his previous reservations. I marvelled again at his naïveté in setting every detail down in writing.

'You really think Bessie will go through with it?' I asked, curious, though I wanted more than anything for him to take his leave.

'It sounds that way,' he said. 'She is a reliable girl, as far as I know. Anyway – we can go to Southwark together now. Do you have a horse?'

'Yes, but – I must run an urgent errand first. I'll meet you there.'

'Then I'll come with you. Savage was quite adamant that we should all be there as soon as possible – he's out looking for you himself. He might even catch up with us in a minute.'

I shot him a sidelong glance, wondering if he had been told not to let me out of his sight. It smelled like a trap. Babington may not yet know I was an imposter, but if Ballard had called a meeting, it was quite possible that he did. I hesitated. One good punch to the head and I could knock Babington out long enough to gallop away to Seething Lane; would it be worth it? Hardly, if Savage was somewhere around the corner. And of course there was always the chance that Prado had not yet found the conspirators, that the meeting was not a ruse, and I might be about to find out their exact plans for assassinating the Queen; Walsingham would not forgive me for letting that slip through my hands, and giving myself away needlessly.

'Is Robin going to the meeting?' I asked.

'We are all needed,' Babington said. 'He's probably already on his way, if he's not home.'

'Good, then,' I said brightly. If Poole was heading for Southwark, he could not also be at Seething Lane; I could even intercept him on the way back, find an excuse for a quiet word alone, knock him out and deliver him to Phelippes, bound and ready for questioning. I could not help wishing I had brought Ben with me; it could be useful to have someone knowing my whereabouts.

Babington said little as we rode side by side to Southwark

and he seemed edgy and uncomfortable with me, though I supposed this was because of what I had witnessed the night before. He was not such a skilled dissembler as Poole or Ballard, and I was sure that if he had learned the truth about my identity, he would have given it away somehow. My gut wound tighter with every yard we rode away from the direction of Seething Lane. When we left our horses at the Unicorn, I half expected to see Joe appear, palm out for coins; his absence only served to sharpen my fear and guilt.

Madam Rosa greeted us cheerfully, relieved us of our weapons, and the servant girl Dorothy escorted us to Captain Fortescue's room on the top floor. The door cracked open and Ballard's face appeared, smiling.

'Gentlemen! Thank you for coming at such short notice. Anthony, would you go down and wait for the others in the tap-room? I just need a quick word with Prado. Priestly business,' he added in a low voice. Babington looked somewhat put out, and all my muscles tensed.

'I'm sure there's nothing Anthony can't hear,' I said, matching Ballard's smile. Babington flashed me a look of pure fear, and I realised he thought the priest had somehow found out about his sins of the flesh.

'It won't take long,' Ballard said. 'Anthony doesn't mind, do you? Don't get distracted by any of those lovely ladies on the way, now.'

Babington gave him a sharp glance, unsure if he was being mocked; he muttered something disgruntled and set off towards the stairs. I should have run after him then, or slammed the door on Ballard's hand, anything that would have bought me time to run, but I hesitated a moment too long; I was not yet certain I had been discovered, and any sudden moves would have given me away. In the moment that I turned to watch Babington, Ballard seized me by the arm and pulled me inside the room; the door was slammed and bolted behind me and I knew instantly that I had made a terrible mistake.

Two other men were present. One was Father Weston, watching me from a window seat, his expression more of sorrow than anger. The other, standing by the fireplace, so taut with rage that his lips and knuckles had turned white, was a man of around my own age and height, with the olive skin and black hair of those who grew up in sight of the Mediterranean. He glared at me with eyes dark as my own; he could have been, if not my brother, then at least a cousin. Apart from a bruise on his cheek, he appeared in good shape.

'He doesn't even look anything like me,' he remarked to the room in general, in barely accented English.

I did not have a chance to reply because Ballard swung his arm and crashed a fist into my ribcage. I stumbled back and he took another swing, this time to my jaw; I felt the warm spill of blood bubbling in my mouth and down my chin. The Spaniard yelped.

'Get my clothes off him before you do any more,' he squealed, and I had time to think *dandified little prick* before Ballard landed another punch to my stomach and I dropped to my knees, holding up a hand weakly to shield my face, but the Spaniard leapt forward and grasped both my arms behind my back.

'You were good, Bruno, I'll give you that.' Ballard leaned down, his breath hot in my ear. 'I'll hold my hands up and say, you fooled me.'

I stared back at him in silence, blood running down my chin.

'You're wondering how I know who you are. I worked it out. That conversation we had on the way to Paul's about the Italian heretic in the French embassy – you couldn't let it go. You kept asking questions – you hinted that you understood his books. Your intellectual vanity was your downfall.'

Not for the first time, I thought, cursing my wilfulness. He wrestled with the doublet, hauling it off me until I was left in my shirt, then he hit me again in the side of the head, and something exploded in my ear.

'How much do they know?' he said, clamping a hand around my throat.

I turned my head and spat a gobbet of blood on to the floor.

'Why don't you ask *him* how much he told them?' I said. My voice came out thick and clotted.

The real Prado leaned over my shoulder, still holding my arms. 'You want to hear what your friends did to me? You'll find out, because I'm going to do it to you in return.'

'What happened to turning the other cheek, Father? They didn't do anything to you. I heard you cried for your mama before they'd even asked your name. Jesus would be proud.'

I flinched as he spat in my face. 'I take no pleasure in knowing you will rot in hell, dog. But you will have the chance to repent of your blasphemies before you die.'

'That's good of you.'

Ballard gently ushered Prado back, and tightened his grip on my throat, his face so close to mine that I could almost feel his beard tickling my skin.

'You know what disgusts me the most?' he asked softly, managing to sound regretful and menacing at the same time. 'I let you give the sacraments to my flock. An excommunicate heretic. A good woman died taking the host from your hand. Where is her soul now, thanks to you?'

I tried to speak; he eased his fingers so that I could get the words out.

'I wouldn't claim to know. But she died at peace,' I croaked. 'And if your God is so petty that he would damn a faithful old woman for my deception, I'm glad He is no God of mine.'

'You have no God, you atheist bastard.' He slapped me in the face with the back of his hand; the crack sounded like a pistol shot. 'I'll ask you again, Judas – how much do they know, your friends in the government?'

I forced my swollen lips into a smile; he followed up with another punch to the gut that made me retch.

'John, you promised,' Weston said, half-standing, a warning note in his voice.

'You're right.' Ballard stood, rubbing his knuckles, then aimed a kick at my ribs; I toppled on to my side and curled into a ball, bracing myself, thinking of Anneke's story about the man he had beaten to a pulp to protect Joe. 'I will have it out of you, but time is pressing – I've got to find Gifford urgently and send him to warn Mary. Don't worry, I'm not going to kill you right this minute,' he said, looking down at me with a face of pure contempt. 'We can use you to bargain with, if it comes to it. We'll put you somewhere safe for a little while.'

'Why were you in London?' I managed to stutter.

'What? When?'

'You came back from France early and lied to your friends about it. You were here on the twenty-seventh – it's in the ledger.'

He crouched down and stared at me, as if he couldn't believe we were having this conversation.

'I came back to see my mother. If that's all right with you?'

'Your mother?'

'Yes. In Putney.' He stood, rubbing his knuckles. 'In case something went wrong with the plan and we were arrested. In case it was the last time.'

'Just as well you did,' I said, and he kicked me again in the stomach. I let the blood trickle out of my mouth and tried to focus on him; my right eye was beginning to swell and it was difficult to keep it open.

'Enough talking now. Hold him up,' Ballard barked at the Spaniard, who hauled me to my knees again, keeping my arms firmly behind my back. Ballard walked a few paces away, to the corner of the room; I could not move my head far enough to see what he was doing. He returned with a small glass bottle in his hand, and immediately I understood what he intended.

'This is so you don't cause any trouble while we decide what to do with you. Over here, Weston.'

Father Weston rose reluctantly from his window seat and stood beside me. 'Wait,' I said, 'one more question.'

'I'm not in the humour to indulge you.' Ballard unstoppered the bottle and gave Weston a nod.

'Did you give Robin a bottle of opium?'

He paused, watching me as if he suspected a trick. 'What is it to you?'

'I wondered where he had got hold of it.'

Ballard frowned. 'He had seen me giving doses to the sick – he asked me for some to help him sleep. His leg often pains him. It brings a sweet oblivion, as you are about to discover. Weston.'

'No.' I twisted my head away. If he gave me opium I would be helpless; they could take me anywhere, do anything, and I would have no chance of escape, no hope of getting to Frances and the baby. Weston pulled my head back; I struggled, but he pinched my nose tight until the lack of air forced me to open my mouth.

'Sorry,' he murmured, in a very English way, but whatever his reservations, he held my head fast as I tried to shake it to avoid the bottle. Some spilled down the sides of my face, but Ballard kept pouring and though I choked a little, I swallowed enough that in a few moments I felt my vision start to spin; the faces around me became blurred, as if I were seeing them through water, and a warm, gentle current carried me away.

TWENTY-FIVE

I opened my one good eye in a dark room, wincing at intervals as feeling returned to various parts of my body, pain shooting white-hot bolts through my neck, my shoulders, my side, my jaw. My limbs appeared to be paralysed; as my sight adjusted – one eye remained stubbornly swollen shut – I became aware of a dim glow from a candle somewhere behind me, and the quiet sound of someone breathing. A cloth had been tied around my mouth, pressing against my tongue; trails of spittle ran down my chin at each side. My head felt as if I had been drinking for a week. I looked down and realised that I was bound to a chair. The low light was enough to see, as the room swam into focus, that I was in a bare space like an attic, with no windows or doors that I could make out. In frustration, I wrenched my arms against the cords that held them fast behind my back; the chair rocked and I tried to move a foot to steady myself, only to find my legs were fixed too.

'Don't struggle, you'll only make it worse.' The voice spoke gently, and I recognised it as Weston's. I tried frantically to communicate through the gag. He moved around to where I could see him and looked at me with his head on one side.

'If I take it off, will you promise not to make a noise?' he asked.

I nodded furiously; this might not be as hard as I had feared. I was glad Ballard had not left me with the real Prado; I'd have been lucky to wake up with any fingernails left. Weston was a more English type of Jesuit; he regarded me now with an expression that suggested he was very disappointed in my behaviour.

He loosened the gag and I sucked in air; salt saliva flooded my mouth and for a moment I feared I would vomit. When I could raise my head, he crouched and took a long look at my face. I could see two of him, and both looked pained.

'Oh dear,' he said. I tried to give him a rueful smile, though my split lip and bruised jaw made this harder. I ran my tongue around my teeth to check whether I had lost any. Contrition was my best hope with Father Weston, I decided.

'Where are we?' My voice came out sticky and hoarse.

'It's a secret room at the top of the Unicorn. They've hidden priests here in the past.'

'Ironic,' I said. 'Are you going to interrogate me?'

'Oh, goodness, no,' he said, straightening up again. I caught a flash of something glinting between his hands, but could not focus clearly enough to see. I hoped it was not a blade. 'No – I persuaded Father Ballard that that was not what you needed at this point.'

I squinted and made out that the object he was turning between his fingers was a gold crucifix. 'What do I need, then?' I asked warily.

'Dr Bruno. I know all about you.'

'I'm flattered.'

He folded his arms, the cross dangling on its chain from his fingers.

'Heresies and blasphemies as severe as yours come from one source.'

'Copernicus?' My voice sounded slurred; my head felt too heavy, like a stone ball balanced on the slender stem of a plant.

He laughed uncertainly. 'No. Though he may have been seduced in his turn. I'm talking about the Father of Lies. Satan himself.'

'Uh.' I nodded; a dull pain throbbed behind my eyes.

'You're possessed by demons,' he said firmly.

'That explains a lot.'

'Well, don't worry – I'm going to perform an exorcism to drive them out of you, but it may take a little time. Yours is a severe case.'

'Where's Ballard?' I asked, stumbling over the words. Memories were beginning to gather shape through the fog in my head – I had to be somewhere—

'Father Ballard has gone to warn the others that the conspiracy is discovered,' he said, kneeling beside my chair. 'Pray God they have time to flee before the pursuivants go after them.' He laid a hand on my arm. 'But I know it's not your fault you have betrayed Christ and the Holy Church and your brothers.'

I nodded again, and looked humble. 'It was the demons.'

'That's right. And I'm going to cast them out, so you can be reconciled.'

'Thank you, Father.'

His eyes shone – for a moment I thought he might actually cry – as he raised his crucifix towards my face.

'Wait – might I kneel and pray with you?'

'Well . . .' He glanced over his shoulder. I could see no obvious door, but I guessed there must be some secret entrance hidden on the far wall. 'Father Ballard was quite adamant that I must not in any circumstances be persuaded to loose your bonds. He said you are a most devious and cunning man. Besides, it is advisable that you should be bound, in case the demons make you lash out during the ritual.'

'What if you just untied my legs, Father, so that I can kneel in prayer? Besides, I'm so weak from the drug I don't think I could lash out at a fly.'

He havered, obviously doubting my sincerity. Eventually, the state of me after Ballard's beating and the opium must have convinced him I was no threat. When he untied the rope holding my legs to the chair and they splayed out as if the bones had turned to jelly, I feared he might be right. He helped me to my knees, and I bowed my head, my hands still tied behind my back.

Satisfied that I would not attempt to kick him or run, Weston made the sign of the cross and took a vial from the purse at his belt. He sprinkled me with holy water and began intoning the Litany of the Saints; automatically, I muttered the responses back to him. While his eyes were closed, I bent backwards until my hand touched the heel of my right boot, and opened the compartment, coughing to cover any sound. I slid the penknife out, terrified that my sweating hands would cause me to drop it; once I had managed to unfold it and grip the handle between my shaking fingers, I worked the blade upright and began cutting through the rope that bound my wrists. Weston was rattling through the saints at an impressive clip; I took up a fervent prayerful muttering that I hoped would disguise the sawing. The pressure on my wrists eased little by little as the strands frayed.

Weston was rising to a climax. He placed a hand on my head.

'I command you, unclean spirit, whoever you are, along with all your minions now attacking this servant of God, by the mysteries of the incarnation, passion, resurrection and ascension of our Lord Jesus Christ, that you tell me by some sign your name, and the day and hour of your departure—'

I ripped my hands apart as the last strand snapped, and with all the force I had left, grabbed him around the knees so that, caught off-guard, he toppled forward and landed half on top of me. While I had the advantage of surprise, I flipped him on to his back and sat astride his chest, the little penknife pointed at his neck.

'My name is Giordano Bruno, and I'm departing now,' I said, through my teeth; pain was flaring up my right side in jagged flashes so intense I thought I might pass out.

'I am speaking to you directly, unclean spirit,' Weston spluttered valiantly, as I held his arms above his head. 'I command you to obey me to the letter, I who am a minister of God, despite my unworthiness—'

'I don't want to have to hurt you, Weston, you seem like a good man,' I said, grabbing the length of rope that had held my legs and pushing him on to his face. Though my sight remained blurry, I managed to twist his hands behind his back and secure them to his ankles with a knot that I hoped would hold until I had had a chance to get some distance away.

'I adjure you, ancient serpent,' he shouted, so I fastened the gag around his mouth with an apology, and tucked the knife back into my boot heel.

'You won't be here for too long,' I said, pulling myself to my feet for the first time and gasping as the pain needled its way into every part of my body. I leaned against the wall to steady myself, and began feeling my way along the upright wooden beams in the spot where Weston had glanced earlier. He carried on making outraged noises through the gag; I gestured to the wall and his eyes widened in righteous indignation, so I kept going. Finally, I felt a yielding; one of the timbers had been built on a pivot, and swung smoothly outwards when I pushed. I gave Weston a parting nod and crawled out through the gap into the top floor corridor of the Unicorn.

More than once on my way down the first staircase I had to stop and hold on to the wall as my legs buckled and the floor threatened to tilt and slide under me; my vision blurred and I gasped shallow breaths through the pain bursting up my right side. As I reached the next landing, I heard a small scream; the serving girl Dorothy stood clutching a pile of fresh sheets and staring in horror. I must have looked worse than I thought. I pressed a finger to my lips.

'What happened to you?' she asked, recovering a little as I limped towards her.

'I had a disagreement.'

She glanced at the stairs; I wondered if she knew Captain Fortescue's reputation. 'You should get that seen to,' she said, gesturing vaguely to my face. 'Shall I fetch Madam Rosa?'

'No,' I said quickly. 'Is Leila here?'

She hesitated, then nodded. 'I'll take you to her. Better use the back stairs – don't want the customers seeing you like that. This is supposed to be a respectable house.'

She led me down to the cellar, where she knocked on a closed door. After a moment I heard a lock turn and Leila opened it, took in my appearance with a practised glance and swept me inside, telling Dorothy to bring hot water as quickly as possible. I found myself in a small room lit with oil lamps; there was a bed against one wall, covered by a clean sheet; a table and a cabinet, much like the room she used for seeing patients at her home.

'Who did you upset this time?' she asked, guiding me to sit on the bed and tilting my face to the light with one hand.

'Captain Fortescue learned that I am not who he thought I was. He gave me some of your opium.'

'I see. Let's get you cleaned up.' She poured a liquid that smelled of pine resin into a basin and dipped a cloth that she pressed to my jaw with more force than I would have liked; I clenched my teeth and tried not to look weak.

'What time is it?'

'Gone ten,' she said. 'Keep still.' She felt along my jawbone. 'I don't think you've broken anything. Where else does it hurt?'

I pointed to my side as I tried to get up. 'Christ, I've been out for hours, I need to go. I don't suppose you've heard any news of Joe?' Seething Lane; Robin; Lady Sidney and baby Lizzie – it all rushed back at me in an instant. I might be too late already.

'Nothing. And you can't go anywhere in this state.' She pushed me back into the chair. 'You won't get far, you're too groggy. I've got something that will help.' She poked her way down my torso until I bit down on a cry. 'Hm. Cracked rib, I think. Can't do much about that, but we can clean up the rest of it.' She finished scrubbing at my face and dabbed a vicious stinging salve on the bruises, assuring me that it would feel worse before it felt better. A few moments later, Dorothy knocked softly on the door and brought in a pan of hot water before retreating; Leila turned the lock behind her and busied herself at the table, grinding something in a mortar.

'I have to go,' I said. 'Can I borrow that jacket again, the one I just returned? They took mine. And could you get my dagger? I had to leave it at the door.' I realised, too, that in recovering his doublet, Prado had unwittingly taken the floor-plan of Seething Lane, the one solid piece of evidence I had against Robin Poole. I could only hope the Spaniard did not find it in the lining before he was arrested.

'In a minute.' Leila had her back to me, but her tone pre-empted all argument. I heard the sound of water being poured and an unusual aroma filled the room, rich and savoury. I lifted my head and breathed in as if I might taste it. She turned back to me with a tiny cup of steaming brown liquid, which she stirred briskly with a wooden spatula. 'Drink this. It will help with the effects of the drug.'

I took a sip and grimaced; it was thick and bitter and tasted as I would imagine the sweepings of a fireplace might if mixed with water.

'God, that's disgusting. What is it?'

'The Turks drink it. They call it kahve. You're supposed to put sugar in but I don't have any. But you'll see – it has stimulating properties that can be useful. It's becoming popular in Venice, I hear. There's a merchant who brings it to London from Constantinople in small quantities, I know a man who buys it from him and is confident that one day it will catch on here.'

'I sincerely doubt that.' Even brimful of sugar, I couldn't imagine anyone touching the stuff out of choice.

'Finish it up while I fetch those things for you.'

I swallowed the liquid down, and when she returned with the jacket and my dagger I followed her as she led the way along a servants' passageway and out to the yard.

'This urgent task you have,' she asked. 'Does it have anything to do with Joe?'

I hesitated as I strapped the knife to my belt; I didn't want to get her hopes up in vain. 'I'll let you know the moment I find out anything,' I said. She nodded, and turned quickly away so that I could not see her face.

The night was clear and cold; a silver half-moon rose over the river among a scattering of bright stars. As I waited for the stable boy to bring out my horse, I realised that Ballard must have taken my purse as well as the doublet. All credit to Leila and her strange concoction; the feeling that my head was stuffed with wet wool had begun to recede, and my vision was sharp again. I could even open both eyes. Despite the pain in my side and my jaw, I felt a restless energy that had me tapping my foot with impatience. After this was all over, I thought, I might ask her if this man could get me some kahve; at that moment a hand touched my elbow and I leapt a foot in the air. A slight figure materialised at my side with a lantern.

'*Dio porco*, Ben, you scared the life out of me. What are you doing here?'

'Master Thomas sent me here this afternoon to follow that Captain Fortescue bloke. I saw my dad's horse and realised you must be here too. When I'd finished, I came back to find you. I wanted to know if I was right about the pictures – Shoreditch and Rose and all that. You owe me a shilling if I was.' He held the light up and scanned my face. 'The fuck happened to you?'

'Long story. You were right about the pictures, and you'll

get your shilling as soon as I get my money back. Where did Captain Fortescue go?'

'Went to Herne's Rents with his mate, the one with the funny eyes, and a dark-haired bloke, looks a bit like you. Fortescue went in and came straight out again, cursing.'

Looking for Gifford, I thought. 'Then what?'

'They walked west in a big hurry as far as the Charing Cross. Then they hired horses and rode out westwards, I couldn't keep up so I came back. I told Master Thomas all this.'

'Right.' At least Ballard and the conspirators were out of the way for now. 'Can I borrow your lantern? I have urgent business.'

'Where you going?' His eyes gleamed in the dark. 'I'll come too.'

'I don't know, Ben – it might be dangerous.'

'You'll need me, then. Look at the state you get in the minute I leave you alone.'

I smiled, and winced. 'You have a point. But it's late, I don't think your father would thank me—'

'He will if you pay me,' Ben said. I had started to find his pragmatism endearing.

'Do you have your knife?'

'Always.' He patted the back of his breeches. 'I'd better ride – you look like you'd fall off at a sharp corner.'

For once I didn't have the energy to assert myself. I climbed into the saddle behind him, taking the lantern, and when the stable boy held his hand out for payment, I told him to put it on Captain Fortescue's bill, as Ben wheeled the horse out of the gate.

Across the bridge, the City of London was quiet, the streets almost empty; Ben pushed the horse to a fast trot, slowing when we saw the men of the watch patrolling the streets. If they flagged us down to ask our business, he had a swift reply, delivered in such rapid London slang that I often didn't catch the meaning, but each time they nodded us through without question; many of them seemed to know him, and waved him on his way with a grin and a mock-salute. I realised I would never have made it across the bridge without being stopped if I hadn't agreed to take him.

We rode up past the church of St Dunstan in the East and along Tower Street to the corner of Seething Lane, where we tethered the horse and walked the rest of the way to Walsingham's house. I could see no lights visible anywhere, and this immediately sharpened my instinct for danger: it was possible the entire household had retired early, but I would have expected some signs of life even at this time of night, if only candles in the upstairs servants' windows.

'No guards,' Ben whispered. I had been thinking aloud on the journey how best to gain entry to the house. Robin Poole would have walked in without hindrance; he was known here, and trusted, the guards would have waved him through. I had doubted whether they would show me the same courtesy; if I was lucky enough to encounter one of the men who had admitted me when I first arrived, he might remember me and take a message, but since Walsingham would have a number of guards working shifts, the chances of that were slim. Given the state of my face and the fact that I already looked like a Catholic assassin, I had worried that I would be detained for a while at the gate, and had suggested Ben might try to find another way over the wall while I kept the guards talking. But it appeared no such strategy would be needed; the house was unattended, and my nerves wound a notch tighter.

I tried the gate to find it locked. It seemed unwise to climb over in full view of the street, in case any neighbours happened to glance out. Instead we followed a path around the garden wall and found a place to scale it towards the rear of the buliding, by a little side door. Ben scrambled over, nimble as a cat; I forced every aching muscle to obey as I got a foothold on the gate handle and hauled myself up, the edge of the wall scraping my cracked ribs as I rolled over and landed with a jarring thud that left me swearing and hopping in the shadows on the other side. Ben motioned for me to be silent; we waited a few moments, and when no one came, we crept across the lawn towards the back of the house.

I had not explained the full situation to Ben, only told him that I thought a woman and a child might be in danger. I had not expected chivalric instincts from him – I knew he was only in this for the money – but he had seemed indignant that anyone could want to harm an infant, and spurred the horse on faster. He had put out the lantern at the foot of the wall, and now we had to feel our way as our eyes grew accustomed to the dark. The house remained ominously silent.

'Where do we go?' he hissed.

I paused, trying to bring the image of the floor plan back to my memory. Rooms had been marked; which ones?

'I'm not sure,' I said. 'Let's see if we can get inside first and who we can find.'

A gravel path led around to the rear courtyard, though we kept to the grass verge alongside it so our footsteps would not be heard. As we rounded the corner, Ben grabbed at my sleeve and yanked me back; his young eyes had spotted what mine had not.

'On the ground,' he whispered. I leaned around the side of the building and saw what he meant: a long, dark shape sprawled on the flagstones by a rear door. When I was satisfied that it was not moving, I nodded to him to follow me closer. The body of a man lay on the ground, his hands spread like white starfish against the stone. My throat tightened; I crouched to turn him over so I could see his face, pale as marble, the eyes unseeing. I recognised him as one of the guards I had met the other day. His sword remained sheathed at his side – he had not anticipated danger from this visitor – and the dark stain that spread over his livery suggested the stab wound had been swift and precise, under the ribs to the heart. The blood pooling underneath him was still sticky and his limbs had not yet had a chance to stiffen, meaning he had been killed within the past three or four hours.

'Shit,' Ben said, with feeling.

'Come on.' I drew the man's sword and gestured towards the door. I was under no illusion about my skill as a swordsman – I knew the basic techniques and Philip Sidney had tried to teach me some finesse – but the weapon would at least allow me more space to confront a potential attacker than my short dagger. I was braced to put my shoulder to the door, dreading what it would do to my ribs, but before I could try, Ben turned the handle and found that it opened smoothly. We exchanged a glance as I stepped into the dark corridor.

I could make out no sounds from anywhere; only the soft echo of our footsteps along the passage, which ended in a door that opened on to the high entrance hall and the main staircase. Moonlight fell in faint diamonds through a mullioned window over the stairs.

'Where are all the servants?' I whispered, looking around, the sword held out. 'They can't all be in bed.'

'Try calling.'

I shook my head. 'I don't want him to know we're here. Let's look upstairs.'

'For what?'

I closed my eyes briefly and tried to summon the image of the floor plan Robin had marked up, but it remained stubbornly submerged in the dregs of the opium haze; at that moment I would have given anything for another cup of Leila's kahve, even though it seemed to have made my hands jittery and my heart race faster. All I could recall of the plan was that one of the rooms had been labelled 'nursery'.

'Try to find the nursery. I'll take these stairs, you go along that hallway there, you should find the servants' stairs around the corner. I'll scout the first floor, you go to the second. And be careful.'

He gave a scornful snort and disappeared into the shadows. I climbed the main staircase, flinching at every creak in case it gave us away. I turned each door handle slowly and silently, springing into the room with the guard's sword drawn, only to find a succession of dark, empty parlours and bedchambers, nothing that looked like a child's room. As the silence grew, so too did my apprehension; I began to form terrible visions of opening the next door to find the entire household slaughtered. But by the time I was satisfied that I had tried every room on the first floor, I had seen no sign of life – or death. I was about to go up and find Ben when I heard footsteps and a small cry from above.

I took the stairs two at a time, no longer caring about the sound, and found Ben on the upper landing, a hand to his mouth, standing over another body laid prone on the carpet. I bent to turn it over and saw the staring face of the steward Marston, his clothes also soaked with blood on the left side where he had been stabbed.

'Did you find the nursery?' I asked Ben.

'Empty,' he said, looking at the body. His face appeared deathly white; I began to wish I had not brought him to witness all this. 'There's no one here.'

'He must have taken them somewhere. But – all the servants? Surely one of them would have tried to stop him.'

'Looks like this bloke did,' Ben said. 'Where do you think he's gone?'

I shook my head. 'I haven't a clue.' If Robin had managed to kidnap Lady Sidney and baby Lizzie, I could not begin to imagine where he might have taken them. I tried to think clearly. 'We need to get word to Walsingham at Whitehall. You take the horse and ride there, you're in better shape than me. I'll go to Phelippes at Leadenhall Street – he might have an idea. We'd better make haste.' I turned towards the stairs when the boy suddenly laid a hand on my arm.

'Wait – what was that?'

I froze, hearing nothing. I was about to move when he squeezed tighter.

'There – listen.'

This time I heard it – thin and distant, as if it were coming from somewhere far outside, but unmistakable none the less.

'That's a baby crying,' Ben said. 'Coming from downstairs.'

I cocked my head and listened again. 'Oh God. The cellars.'

He looked up at me, catching my expression. He would not have known that Walsingham had had the cellar at Barn Elms adapted to hold prisoners too sensitive to be seen at the Tower – especially suspected priests and Catholic spies, like the real Father Prado. It was possible that the same arrangement existed beneath this house too.

'Change of plan,' I said, grasping Ben by the shoulders. 'I need you to take a message for me. You'll have to ride as fast as you've ever ridden – can you do that?' There was only one person who could help us now. I gave Ben the instructions and he listened, nodding, eyes intent and serious. When I had finished, he spat on his palm and held it out to shake. This time I did the same.

'Godspeed,' I whispered as he scurried away, his feet soundless on the stairs.

I made my way down to the ground floor and followed the passageway back to the kitchen. In a house such as this, I would have expected to find the door to the cellar here, but if Walsingham used the underground chambers for detainees, it seemed likely that he would have had a separate entrance constructed so that they didn't have to be paraded through the house. I groped around the kitchen in the thin moonlight until I found a candle and tinderbox on a dresser; it was not much against the darkness, but better than nothing. I paused at the door that led out to the gardens; here the child's howling sounded closer, and more frantic. For as long as she was crying, though, she was alive, and there was a chance of saving her. The kitchen door opened on to a small yard planted with beds of herbs; on the far side I saw an outbuilding jutting at right angles to the house. I tried the wooden door and found it bolted from the inside, so there was no hope of picking the lock; instead I smashed the small window to one side and, stifling whimpers of pain, pulled myself through the gap into a storeroom piled with barrels and sacks. As I had hoped, there was a wide wooden hatch set into the floor at one end; I lifted one half and was surprised to find it unlocked. Inside it, a flight of stone steps led down into blackness.

I lowered myself in gingerly, holding the candle aloft in one hand and the sword in the other, and hoping that the baby's protests would have drowned out the sound of breaking glass and the hatch creaking on its hinges. The crying grew closer as I neared the foot of the stairs and reached another door. This one was locked, and I had to stop myself thumping it with my fists in frustration. But I could not give up now; I set the sword down, took the metal penknife from my boot heel and inserted it into the lock. It was difficult to see with only one candle, and my fingers shook badly from the combined effects of the opium and the kahve, but I had barely tried to move the knife before the door swung open smoothly and I fell through on to my knees, to find myself staring at a pair of boots.

'I wondered when you might join us,' Poole said, over the baby's screams. 'I didn't want you to miss it. After all, we're here because of you.'

I looked up to see him standing over me, baby Lizzie strapped to his chest in a kind of cloth sling; he was jiggling her up and down, but to little effect. His face in the shifting light appeared empty of expression. I could not see if he was armed.

'Get up,' he said, kicking the sword away and pulling the door shut behind me. 'Throw your knife down in that corner. And the one at your belt. Now, or I'll snap her neck.'

I stood, wincing, and did as I was told. The weapons fell

with a ring of steel on stone and I glanced around to find myself in an underground room well lit by torches in wall brackets. The chamber was lined in brick, the vaulted ceiling twice the height of a man, supported by stone columns at intervals, like the crypt of a church. Against the far wall, I could see three figures seated with their legs out, hands bound before them, gags around their faces. I recognised Alice, Lady Sidney's maidservant; the second was a plump, round-faced woman in a linen coif. The third person – slight and hunched in the shadows – was Joe. My heart leapt to see the child alive; his big eyes widened at the sight of me, though I could not tell if it was in hope or fear. But I could see no sign of Frances Sidney.

'God's blood, will this child never stop?' Poole said, exasperated, to the room in general. An urgent sound came from the large woman next to Alice, though none of it was intelligible through her gag.

'She's probably hungry,' I said.

'Oh. Lucky the expert has arrived.' He gave me a look from the tail of his eye. 'Stand against that wall and don't move a muscle.'

I did as I was told. He crossed the room to the women. 'You,' he said to the one who had been trying to speak, who I guessed was the child's wet-nurse. 'Feed her, shut her up. You know what will happen if you try anything.'

I saw the woman's eyes flit with terror to the right-hand side of the room; I tried to follow her gaze but whatever she was looking at was obscured from my view by pillars and shadows. Poole untied the plump woman's wrists and set the baby awkwardly in her arms; she undid her bodice and the baby snuffled her way inside the folds of cloth. The silence that fell when the screaming stopped felt like a reprieve.

'Thank God, now I can think.' Poole massaged his temples and returned to me. 'So I realised when I returned home this afternoon that someone had paid me a visit,' he said. 'I guessed it must have been you. Walsingham always said you were quick. I was almost jealous, he seemed so impressed by your talents.'

'Not quick enough,' I said, through my teeth.

'No, he overestimated you. I thought you'd have been here sooner – I began to fear you'd gone to tell him what you'd found. But I should have known you'd want all the credit for resolving the business single-handed. I'm guessing Ballard got to you first.' He looked me up and down. 'So you know about Clara. Frances told me.'

'Where is Frances? And the rest of the household?'

'I instructed Marston to send all the servants home immediately. I said it was Master Secretary's order. He gave them the night off and tomorrow, as long as they didn't ask any questions.'

I nodded; it was at least some relief to know I wasn't going to find any more murdered servants. 'Then you killed him.'

'Don't feel sorry for him. He was a lecher. Clara said he made her uncomfortable, since she'd been living there – always finding excuses to come to her room late at night and ask her something, standing that bit too close to her.'

'Did she say he touched her?'

'No, but I'm sure he would have tried, given the chance. I saw how he looked at her, filthy old hound.'

'God forbid anyone should look at your sister. And the guard outside – did he dare to look at her too?'

'No, he was in my way. I sent his colleague off to Barn Elms with an urgent message for Sir Francis, but that one still made a fuss about letting me in.'

'I thought Walsingham was at Whitehall?'

'He is. So that should keep the guard out of the way for a few hours.'

'What are you going to do about Clara's lover – kill him too?'

'I think Walsingham will do that for me,' he said with a

faint smile. 'They'll have scattered, but they won't get far. They won't escape punishment.'

'Not even Babington? Don't you care about him?'

He shrugged. 'He was diverting, while it lasted. I tried to persuade him to leave London before the plot was discovered. He didn't want to hear it – he's too much in love with the idea of his own heroism. Leave him to it – there are other pretty boys in the world.'

'And you? Do you seriously think you'll escape punishment?'

'I'll be long gone by the time anyone realises what's happened. There's a boat waiting for me at Tilbury. I'll sail tonight and be with Clara by tomorrow. Then we'll both leave the country.'

'What about the baby? And the rest of us?'

'The baby's coming with me. The rest of you will be found eventually, I suppose. Whether you're all alive depends on you.'

'What will you do with her?'

'Elizabeth?' He glanced back at the child, nuzzling contentedly in her nurse's arms. 'I haven't decided yet. Maybe I'll drop her in the river, eh. Then everyone can say she must have fallen in and drowned.' His attempt at calm was cracking; there was a febrile rage in his voice that I needed to keep at bay for a while longer, in case he did anything impulsive.

'Why are you doing this, Robin?' I held my hands out, palms up, in a gesture of submission. 'I understand wanting to protect your sister. But to harm a child – I find it hard to believe of you. Otherwise, why have you kept Joe alive?'

'Because I knew you were looking for him, and you'd find a body sooner or later. And don't imagine you know me. You clearly don't understand Walsingham, that's for sure.' He took a step closer and leaned down so that his face was a foot from mine. 'He took my father from me, and he would have taken my sister. I want him to know how it feels to lose everyone you love.'

'You have no evidence that Walsingham would have hurt Clara, and only the word of one bitter old man in prison about your father.'

'No evidence?' He spun on his heel and laughed – a wild, manic sound. 'You saw it for yourself. How he responded when he thought Clara had been murdered. He didn't even intend to investigate her death. It meant nothing to him, compared to his precious operation. This girl who had been his ward since she was fourteen years old – he would have thrown her in an unmarked grave, in case her death hampered his obsession with convicting Mary Stuart. He refused to let me see her body. He treated her as if she were *worthless*.'

'But it wasn't her.'

'He didn't know that!' He ran his hands through his hair; he was growing agitated, and that would not help any of us. 'I feigned Clara's death because I knew he would have considered her disposable if he learned of her condition, and her change of heart towards the conspirators. And I was right – he did consider her less important than the Babington plot, even in death. When I saw how he treated her – that's when I decided he must be *made* to understand.'

'Understand what?'

'That people are not his chess pieces, to move around at his whim.'

'So – let me see if I have this right – you're going to kill his granddaughter, to punish him for being prepared to murder your sister, even though you have no proof of that, and then for not investigating her death, even though that's exactly what he asked me to do, and she's not actually dead?'

Behind him, the baby made a series of small whimpering sounds; Poole turned abruptly and the nurse shook her head in panic, holding up a hand to fend him off as she transferred the child to the other breast.

'I'm tired of discussing this, Bruno,' Poole said. 'I knew the moment he asked you to look into her death – which he only did because Frances nagged him, by the way, not because he cared for Clara – that you'd come to the truth sooner or later. I should have got rid of you too, but I was intrigued to see if you would work it out.'

'You need a better eye for detail, Robin.' I was determined to keep him talking for as long as possible; I did not want to think of what might happen to baby Lizzie, as well as to me and the other prisoners, if he lost interest in explaining himself. 'The henna was a nice touch, but your sister bit her nails badly, the girl you killed did not. Though that wasn't even your biggest mistake.'

'No? Then tell me what was. And make it quick – I have a boat to catch.'

'You should have made sure Clara was on your side. That locket you dropped in the Cross Bones for me to find – you didn't know she'd hidden that secret message inside, did you? Did Joe see you plant the locket that morning you took me there – was that another reason to keep him quiet?'

His eyes narrowed. 'You worked out the message?' He gripped me by the collar and pulled my face to his. 'Tell me what it said.'

'If you tell me what you've done with Frances.'

He released his grip and smiled. 'Oh, I was going to do that. Come and see.' He led me to the far side of the room, around the pillar. I bit down a cry. This was clearly where interrogations took place, or had done when Walsingham lived in the house. Frances Sidney was kneeling on the floor, unmoving, her head bowed and her hair hanging around her face. Something had been bound around her head. Her wrists were tied with a leather strap behind her back, and attached to a length of rope that extended overhead and passed through a pulley fixed to the ceiling.

'Are you familiar with this?' Poole asked, indicating the contraption.

'*Il tormento della corda*,' I whispered. I felt my stomach

rise and clenched my teeth hard in case I vomited. Frances stirred at the sound of my voice; she lifted her head and I realised that she was wearing a scold's bridle – a metal frame that compressed the tongue, to stop women talking. Her eyes met mine but she seemed to have trouble focusing.

'That's right. *Strappado*, your people call it, don't they? Popular with the Inquisition, I believe – we learned a lot of techniques from them. You should feel at home.'

'*We*.' I looked at him, understanding. 'When you said you talk to people for Walsingham, was this what you meant?'

He smiled. 'Exactly. I turn the handle on the rack, so he doesn't have to get his hands dirty. I tighten the thumbscrews. I pull the rope that rips their arms out of their sockets, the young priests, when they don't want to give up their secrets. But they all talk to me, eventually.'

'Did you give her opium?' I asked. I wondered how long he had kept her tied up like that. She would be uncomfortable kneeling there, but that was as nothing to what would happen if and when he pulled on the end of the rope and she was lifted in the air, left hanging from her arms twisted behind her back; her bodyweight would gradually dislocate her shoulders. If he felt particularly vicious, he could let the rope out suddenly in a series of drops that would tear the tendons and ligaments in her arms beyond repair.

'Only a little. She was making a fuss about the baby.'

'For God's sake, Robin.' I could hear the despair in my voice. 'Don't do this. She's your sister's closest friend.'

'Quiet, Bruno, unless you want some opium too. I saved a bit just in case. No? Good, then. Kneel beside her.'

I hesitated, casting around to see how I might find a way out of this. There were too many people's lives at risk if I refused, or angered him enough that he decided to dispatch me with a quick knife-thrust, like Marston. I knelt, praying as I had never prayed before that Ben would return in time.

'I have something special for you,' he said. 'Hands behind

your back.' I obeyed, and for the second time that night I found my wrists bound behind me. This time, though, there was no prospect of cutting through the cords. He turned to a chest against the wall and brought out a metal object that he held up against the light for me to see. 'Do you know what this is?'

It was an iron implement about seven inches long, with two razor-sharp prongs at either end and a ring in the middle.

'*Dio cane.*' I heard how my breath shook as I exhaled. 'The Heretic's Fork.'

'That's right. Appropriate, no? I believe this one was actually brought in from Spain. Master Secretary takes a great interest in the methods of the Catholics, for all that he despises their doctrines.' He threaded a leather strap through the ring in the centre. 'Head back. Do as you're told, or I'll pull that rope and Frances can watch you from the ceiling.'

I tilted my head, trying not to shake. I had heard of this practice, though never seen it used. The idea was to force the heretic to look up at the heavens, while making sure he could not speak to repeat his blasphemies. Poole fastened the strap around my neck; with my head strained back as far as I could bend, the two top prongs pricked the skin below my chin, and the bottom ones pressed into my collarbone. As he pulled the strap tight, I felt all four points puncture the skin; there was no way I could speak or move my head without one end or both piercing deeper into the soft tissue. If I lost my balance or let the weight of my head fall forward, the top would go straight through the underside of my jaw, the lower prongs into my breastbone. I tried to swallow and feared I might choke on my own saliva. I slid my knees further apart to steady myself, and fixed my gaze on a knot of wood in the roof beam directly above; if I could focus and keep still, I had a better chance of avoiding the worst.

'Right. Give me that child.' Poole strode across to the nurse and snatched baby Lizzie out of her arms. I could not move my head to see, but from the sounds, I guessed that the nurse tried to protest; I heard a slap and muffled sobbing, before he appeared in front of me again with the infant wrapped in the sling around his front, now dozing contentedly with a string of milky dribble hanging from her chin.

'Goodbye, Bruno. It's been interesting. If they find you in time, you can tell them the whole story. I'll be halfway across the sea by then.'

He walked around behind us and I heard a slow creaking, followed by a strangled cry as, at my side, Frances began to lift into the air.

'Where are you going?' I tried to say, through clenched teeth, without moving my jaw.

'Sorry, didn't quite catch that.' He pulled harder on the rope, and Frances screamed, through the bridle; the opium had not been enough to dull the agony in her arms.

'Clara's not there,' I said, and felt blood run down my neck as the tines bit deeper.

'What?' He tied off the rope to a bracket on the wall and came to stand in front of me; from the corner of my eye, I could see Frances suspended five feet or so off the ground, slowly rotating, quietly whimpering. 'Not where?'

'Essex,' I managed, forcing my jaw to stay clenched.

'What do you know about it? How did you know she was going to Essex?' He grasped a handful of my hair in his fist. 'Tell me or I'll push down.'

Before I could speak, we both caught the click of the door opening; he twisted around, wrenching me with him.

'Robin?' said a woman's voice. I could have cried with relief. He let go of me and walked around the pillar.

'Sweetheart? How in God's name did you get here? I thought you were—'

'What are you doing – the boy said you were going to kill Lizzie?' Clara's voice trembled; I wondered if she had not believed Ben's story until she saw for herself. 'Oh, dear Jesus. Robin, give me the baby. Now.'

'Darling, you don't understand – you shouldn't be here. Why did you disobey me?' Though he was clearly reeling from shock, his tone had grown harder; I hoped to God I had not simply led another person into danger. At that moment, Frances let out another groan; Clara must have pushed past Robin, because she appeared suddenly in front of us and screamed.

'Oh, *God*, Robin, what have you done to Frances? What have you *done*? Let her down, now!'

'I can't. And you need to come with me. We're going to Tilbury.'

'Have you lost your mind?' Clara took a step towards Frances; Robin reached out and grabbed her arms to restrain her, and – though I could not quite see what happened next, with my eyes forced to the ceiling – a small figure materialised out of the shadows, I heard the slash of a blade through cloth, and Robin Poole crumpled to the ground with a cry, like a marionette with its strings cut. Clara dived forward and grabbed Lizzie from him, clasping the baby to her chest.

'Ben – get that woman down,' I said, my teeth gritted tight. 'Gently as you can.' He wiped his little knife on his breeches, looked from me to Frances, and nodded. I heard the creak of a rope as Frances was lowered carefully to the ground, where she slumped on to her face; Clara rushed to her and, with the baby over one shoulder, began undoing the ties that held her arms. Ben came round behind me, unbuckled the strap and removed the fork from my neck; I stretched my head forward gingerly as he began to saw through the cord holding my wrists.

Robin was writhing on the floor clutching the back of his thigh, howling like a wounded animal; blood pumped out alarmingly through his fingers and puddled on the uneven stones, but for as long as he wasn't putting up a fight, I thought he could be safely left. I hauled myself to my feet, found my knives in the corner where I had thrown them, and released Alice, Joe and the nurse, who swooped in like a Fury and gathered up baby Lizzie in her arms so that Clara could get the bridle off Frances, who fell sobbing into her friend's lap.

Robin tried to stand; he was bleeding severely, and he managed one or two staggering steps towards me, his face white as bone. I realised, belatedly, that his injury was more serious than I had thought.

'You fetched him a nasty cut there, Ben – what did you do?' I pushed Robin down to the floor again, found the gash in his leg and tried to press my hands against the wound to stop the bleeding.

'There's a vein in the back of the leg, if you cut it in the right place they bleed out in minutes,' he said, matter-of-fact as always. 'My dad taught me, he learned it in the army.'

'*Madonna porca* – we don't *want* him bleeding to death.' I pressed harder, but I could see that Robin's eyes were growing glassy.

'He was going to kill you and that girl, and the baby,' Ben said, indignant. 'I saved your bloody lives.'

'I know. But—' I ripped off my shirt, tore a sleeve from it and wound the cloth around Robin's leg, hoping to staunch the flow. He raised a hand and gripped my arm.

'Where is Clara?' he said, his voice hoarse.

She raised her head and looked at me, a question in her eyes. Alice crouched beside them and took Frances in her arms so that Clara could go to Robin.

'Quick,' I said. 'I think we're losing him.' I kept my shirt sleeve pulled tight around his leg as she leaned down and took his face between her hands.

He held his hand over hers. 'It was all for you,' he whispered.

'He didn't kill Father, Robin. And he wouldn't have killed me. You've destroyed everything.' Tears streamed down her face and fell on his as she shook her head.

He struggled to speak; I pressed with all the strength I had left, but I could see there was no chance of saving him. Clara leaned her ear to his mouth to catch his final words.

'I love you too,' she murmured, through quiet sobs, as he stopped moving and his stare fixed on somewhere far beyond her. 'And I hated you,' she added, when she was sure he could no longer hear, before a fresh wave of tears overtook her.

'I didn't think it would work,' Ben said in a small voice. 'I haven't really killed a man before, I just said that. Will I be hanged?'

I picked up my knife and smeared the blade with Robin's blood. 'Ben. You've done a phenomenal night's work. All of us owe you our lives. I know you've ridden all over London today, but this is your last job – you're going to take your dad's horse, and bring Joe back to his mother in Southwark. Ask her to put you to bed for the night – I'll get a message to Dan. Give your knife a good wash. I killed Robin in self-defence, if anyone asks.'

He looked at Poole's body a moment longer, as if both terrified and amazed by his own handiwork. 'Do I still get my shilling?' he asked.

'You'll get a lot better than that.' I pulled on my doublet over my bare chest and limped across to Joe, who was cowering against the wall. 'Did he harm you at all, Joe, while you were here?'

The child shook his head. 'No. He told me I had to be quiet or he would have my mother sent to prison and tortured.' He was biting his bottom lip; suddenly he pulled away from the wall and flung his arms around my waist. I placed a hand on his head to steady him until his breathing calmed.

'Your mother is quite safe – just worried about you. Go with Ben now, he'll take you to her.'

I watched as the children left together, Ben with his arm around Joe's shoulder like a big brother.

Clara had helped Frances to a sitting position; though the

opium had not quite worn off, and her jaw and shoulders clearly pained her, she did not seem to have sustained any lasting injuries. The nurse placed the baby in her lap and she looked up at me, her face drained.

'Bruno. We have to tell my father.'

'I'll go to Whitehall if you lend me a horse, but I'll need some kind of seal to take – they'll never let me near the palace looking like this.'

She shook her head and stood shakily, the baby over her shoulder. 'We'll all go. I'm not staying here alone with no guards. The conspirators are still out there, and they know there's been a spy among them.'

'My lady, you are not fit to ride that distance,' Alice said, alarmed.

'It's the only place I'll feel we're all safe,' Frances said, and a note of authority returned to her voice. 'You and Janet too' – she nodded to the nurse – 'or do you want to stay here all night with three dead men for company? No, I thought not. I'll fetch my father's seal from his study. Bruno, come with me in case I stumble in the dark.'

TWENTY-SIX

We took three horses from the stables; Alice and Clara helped me saddle them, since all the stable hands had been sent home. I rode with Frances behind me, holding me by the waist; Clara took another pony by herself, and Alice mounted the third, with the nurse riding pillion, carrying baby Lizzie in a sling. We must have made a strange party, traipsing through the midnight streets, bloodied and battered like a group of refugees; my face drew suspicion from the men of the watch each time they stopped us, but Frances showed Walsingham's seal and they immediately dropped back, bowing as we passed.

I had had less faith than Frances in our chances of being admitted to the palace at Whitehall, but at the Great Gatehouse, the seal worked its magic again. Alice and Janet were shown to the servants' quarter to rest, while Frances took the baby and insisted that she, Clara and I were brought straight to Walsingham. The vast complex of buildings was eerily silent at this hour; only tired-looking guards observed us as they fought to keep straight-backed and alert, while occasional figures in livery slipping through the courtyards glanced up briefly as they passed on their secret midnight business.

We were escorted along a series of corridors and up staircases, dimly lit as the night's torches burned down in their sconces. The rooms grew gradually more opulent and heavily guarded as we approached the heart of the palace, the Queen's private chambers. Finally we were brought to a stop outside a heavy wooden door, guarded by two men in royal livery, where a clerk with exhausted eyes sat on a chair with a portable desk around his neck, scribbling notes. At the sight of us, he stirred into life, and after a hasty whispered exchange with the soldiers flanking us, he stepped forward and raised a hand to bar our way.

'I'm sorry, but Sir Francis is in a most secret, high-security meeting and cannot possibly be disturbed.' His officious tone seemed intended to provoke; with Frances it succeeded. She knocked his arm out of the way and raised her voice.

'Listen to me, whoever you are. I am Lady Frances Sidney and this is my daughter, and these are my friends. We were all nearly murdered tonight and I need to see my father, so you can open that fucking door *right now* or I will kick it down.'

While the clerk spluttered, she marched straight past him and the stunned guards, and we followed her into a room that smelled of paper and leather and beeswax, the walls lined with wooden bookcases. Walsingham and his guest sat in high-backed chairs either side of a hearth where the embers of a fire flickered. Master Secretary rose at once; he took us in one by one, and when his gaze alighted on Clara he had to grasp the back of his chair for support. Meanwhile, I was staring with the same expression at the man he had invited for a clandestine midnight meeting in the heart of the palace. It was Archibald Douglas.

'Is it you?' Walsingham said wonderingly to Clara, holding out his arms to embrace her.

'It's you,' I said to Douglas.

'I *know*, me again – I turn up everywhere. Like a wee rat.' He grinned. 'What happened to your pretty face – did you get too fresh with one of your Southwark doxies?'

'Sir Francis, you know what this man is,' I said, amazed that Walsingham could have let him in.

'A man can be many things, Bruno,' Douglas said, cheerfully. 'Today I'm an ambassador of *l'amour*. I couldn't tell you before, it's a big old secret, but I am here about the business of true love. You'll know all about that, eh.'

I looked to Walsingham to demand an explanation, but he had turned to his daughter.

'*Daddy,*' Frances blurted, the word weighted with feeling, all her composure suddenly collapsing as she flung herself at him like a child. He wrapped an arm around her and the baby, the other around Clara, and folded them all into him.

'Oh, my girls,' he murmured, and I saw a tear fall down each cheek. I felt I was intruding on a private scene, and began to back towards the door. Douglas caught my eye behind Walsingham's back and mimed wiping his eyes; I almost slapped him.

'Robin is dead,' Clara said, after a moment, her voice dull. She was not weeping; she looked overcome by exhaustion.

'I killed him,' I said quickly, before the women could forget and mention Ben. Walsingham appeared to notice me for the first time.

'You killed Robin?' He sounded faint.

'He meant to torture me and drown Lizzie,' Frances sobbed, her voice muffled.

'Good God. You had better sit down, all of you, and tell me the whole story. Is Lizzie hurt?'

'No, Father – she barely knows any of it happened.'

Walsingham laid a hand on his granddaughter's sleeping head, and took a deep, shuddering breath as he composed himself, tidying away his shock and emotion and becoming Master Secretary again.

I kicked Douglas's legs to make him move; belatedly he realised, and jumped out of his chair to offer it to Frances. Walsingham called in the clerk and sent him for hot wine and bread, and told Douglas to wait outside. 'Our business will keep,' he said, in a tone that sounded like a threat.

'Aye, but not too long, eh,' Douglas said. 'She's no getting any younger.'

Before I could work out what he meant by that, Frances had launched into an explanation of everything that had happened since she and I realised that Clara was not dead; Clara and I filled in the gaps. Walsingham sat behind his desk, his fingers steepled together, tapping his lips with his forefingers, listening with that expression that always made you feel he could hear everything you were *not* telling him as clearly as the words that came out of your mouth.

'I saw the dead girl,' he said, looking at Clara in disbelief. 'I would have sworn she was you, even with the face . . .' He pointed to his own and left the rest unsaid.

'Robin would have chosen her well,' she said in the same flat tone. 'He was nothing if not resourceful.' The surge of fear and energy that had propelled us through the night's events had receded with violent haste, leaving us all grey-faced and drained. I sensed that Clara was only now properly understanding that she had lost her brother.

'That's why I valued him so highly,' Walsingham said. 'I wish I could have questioned him about all this. Did you have to kill him, Bruno?'

'It was not my intention,' I said, avoiding his steady gaze. 'I lashed out to save Frances – I must have caught a major artery in his leg. He bled out in minutes, I tried to stop it.'

'But I thought he had restrained you?'

'I cut Bruno loose,' Clara said quickly. 'To help me save Frances.'

Walsingham's dark eyes moved from her to me, opaque in the candlelight. He knew he was being lied to, but he also knew better than to push too hard.

'He was one of my most trusted men,' he said, shaking his head. 'I still can't believe he would have hurt Frances or Lizzie.'

'Believe it, Father,' Frances said, grim-faced, rubbing her shoulder. 'He put me in the *strappado*. It's only thanks to Bruno and Clara that Lizzie is not floating down the Thames at this moment. He meant to kill her, I'm sure of it.'

'Because of our father,' Clara added, turning to Walsingham. He nodded slowly.

'George was a good man,' he said. 'Too good, really. He didn't have the ruthlessness to be an informer. He wanted to please me, but when it came to it, he was reluctant to betray his friends, he didn't want the consequences on his conscience. So he was playing me false, passing misinformation – I discovered it, with proof, and he knew I had, but before I could confront him, he fell in the river.' He held his hands out, palms up. 'Whether that was an accident or by his own choice, we'll never know, but I swear this before God, Clara – it was not on my orders. Nor would I have punished you for getting too close to the conspirators – these things happen. I would have helped you, had I known. I wish Robin had understood that. He always had a tendency to believe the worst.'

'What will happen to them now? The conspirators, I mean,' Clara asked, barely audible, as if she hardly dared voice the question. I noticed how her hand strayed to her belly as she spoke.

'They have all fled – Prado's escape put them on the alert. Their lodgings have been raided and the pursuivants are out searching – they won't get far.'

'Will you show mercy, if they cooperate?'

He lowered his hands and gave her a long, steady look.

'You know I can't make those promises, Clara. We will see.'

She bowed her head without speaking. At that moment, the baby sneezed and woke herself up, looked around the company with wide blue eyes and burst into tears.

'You should take her to her nurse, my dear,' Walsingham said gently to his daughter, who was gradually slumping sideways in her chair. 'And get yourselves to bed. We can discuss the rest in the morning.'

Frances nodded, and rose to hug him; she seemed half-asleep already. Clara followed her, not looking at Walsingham.

'Not you, Bruno,' he said, as I pushed my chair back. 'A moment longer of your time, if you don't mind.'

When the door had closed behind the women, he drew up a chair opposite me by the fire.

'The truth now – did Frances kill Robin?'

'I killed him,' I repeated, hearing myself sound as drained as Clara had.

He smiled, but it didn't reach his eyes. 'Like all Dominicans, you are an accomplished liar. But I am well practised at spotting one.'

'You can ask me the same question every day for the rest of my life, with all the instruments in your cellar, you will get the same answer.'

'I know. You are a stubborn bastard. Let me see your neck.' He drew his chair closer and raised a finger to tilt my head back. 'Ah. The Heretic's Fork. I have never actually used that one. How long do you think you could have endured it, out of interest?' He sounded professionally curious.

'I wouldn't like to guess. But I'm sorry you missed the show,' I said, a little sharply; he inclined his head by way of apology.

'You're a brave man, Bruno. I would give my life for the Queen, you know that. But you risked your life to save the people I love most in the world, and I still have them because of you. I can never repay or forget that.' He looked away and coughed to hide his embarrassment.

'What could you have done with Robin, anyway, if he had lived?' I asked. 'You would not have tried him publicly for the murder of a Southwark whore – everything would have come out, about the Babington conspiracy. It would have become public knowledge that you allowed a plot against the Queen's life to flourish so you could entrap Mary Stuart.'

He sighed. 'I know. He could not have been brought to justice in the usual way, I grant. I only wish I could have questioned him. I was fond of Robin, and I believed he had some affection for me, after all I had done for him.'

'Maybe it was precisely because he felt dependent,' I said. 'It's a hard burden for a man to feel his life is always in someone else's hands. Perhaps he wanted to believe his story would have been different if his father had lived, so he turned the blame on you.' I did not suggest that the brutality of the work he had done for Walsingham must have affected him in some way: made cruelty a habit, or at least blunted his conscience.

'Perhaps. And what of you, Bruno? You're a man who needs patronage, you must know something of that resentment.'

'I hope I would not take innocent lives for it.'

'What would you most want, if it was in my power to give?'

I glanced sidelong at him, touching my fingers to the puncture wounds in my throat. 'To stay in London. Write my books.' And Sophia, I thought – but that is beyond the remit even of Master Secretary.

'I'll see what can be done. It's a delicate matter – there is only so much of this business I wish to reveal to the Queen, as you can imagine. But your testimony may be required when we bring Babington and his friends to trial, since you are the only one of my inside men who was not turned to their side. And you can't go back to France for the moment. My mole in the French embassy says that Prado managed to deliver a letter there before he went on the run. Mendoza will want your *cojones* nailed over his mantelpiece the minute you set foot in Paris.'

'You really think you will bring them to trial?' I asked, secretly delighted to have another reason not to go back to France.

'Oh yes. They can't run for ever, there are armed men with arrest warrants hunting them down. We've already taken

Thomas Salisbury on his way into London, complete with a list of Catholics who have pledged to help raise an army against the Queen. And we found drafts of new letters to Mary in Babington's rooms. I believe we have enough in writing to condemn every last one of them as a traitor.'

'What about Bessie Pierrepont?'

'Ah. Now that was an interesting business. Your Sophia did well there – she managed to copy a number of letters from Bessie's room at the Cavendish house. She's a natural at intelligence work.'

'She's good at deceiving people, if that's what you mean.' It came out with more bitterness than I had intended; Walsingham shot me a sidelong glance with a hint of a smile.

'Well, I shall make further use of her skills. You were right to suspect that Gifford was delivering letters to Chartley Manor, from Bessie to Mary's household, that he was not declaring to Phelippes.'

'So Bessie was writing to Mary? Sophia thought it was a man.'

'She was right. Mary's secretary, Claude Nau, to be precise. There is some kind of courtship between them, it seems. But the gist of his letters appeared to come directly from Mary – he was urging Bessie to petition Queen Elizabeth on Mary's behalf.'

'Petition for what?'

'Apparently Mary was ready to relinquish all claim to the English throne if Elizabeth would allow her to leave England and retire to *some solitary and reposeful place*, as she puts it.'

I let out a low whistle. 'So Bessie never intended to kill Elizabeth.'

'Far from it. She agreed to meet Babington and Ballard only so she could find out their plans and pass them on to her paramour, Nau, who is more cautious than Mary and was urging her to give up this fantasy of ruling England in return for her freedom. Your Sophia persuaded Bessie to tell me everything.'

I wished he would stop calling her 'my' Sophia; there was

something faintly condescending about it, as if he knew very well that she was not.

'So Mary Stuart was using Bessie to bargain with Elizabeth about giving up her claim to the throne, even while she knew Babington and his friends were risking their lives and fortunes to put her on it. Does she not care how many fervent young men go to the scaffold for her?'

He stroked his thumbnail along his beard. 'Last month she also wrote to Mendoza in Paris, telling him she would give her rights to the English crown to King Philip of Spain if her son James would not convert to the Catholic church. Mary grows ever more desperate – her health is failing and she is sick of incarceration. She is promising anything to anyone at the moment, with little thought for the consequences. I almost feel sorry for her.'

'And what of the consequences? Do you have the evidence you wanted against her?'

His mouth set in a hard line. 'I can work with what we have. The rest will depend on Queen Elizabeth. It won't be easy. I fear she will incline to mercy, even with hard proof in front of her.'

Proof which Phelippes partially forged, I thought, though I held my tongue. 'What about Tichborne? Will there be mercy for him?'

'Because he got Clara pregnant? In the scales of justice, that hardly tips the balance against plotting to kill the Queen and aid invasion by a foreign army. Besides, he's married.'

'Really? He told Clara it was a betrothal only.'

'Clara, like her brother, chose to believe what suited her. You should get some rest now, Bruno. I'll send a physician to you in the morning. I have business to finish.'

I glanced at the door and lowered my voice. 'With Douglas? You know he's a murderer – I'm amazed you would meet with him alone.'

Walsingham pressed his thumbs into his eyelids for a

moment, and I thought again how much he appeared to have aged. 'I know all about Archibald Douglas, far more than you do. Sometimes in politics, Bruno, you have to deal with people you don't like, some of whom certainly ought to be in prison.'

'But what is he doing here? What was all that business about love?'

At this he laughed, and some of the tension seemed to slide from his shoulders. 'He's telling the truth, for once. He comes as an ambassador from young King James of Scotland, with a proposal of marriage for Her Majesty. Do *not* repeat that to anyone.'

'You're not serious? James is, what, twenty? And the Queen is fifty—'

'About to turn fifty-three. We can safely say he's not driven by ardour, but it seems he's entirely serious. James is ambitious – he wants the English throne after Elizabeth, and it would be extremely convenient for him if his mother was taken out of the running. That makes Douglas our ally, for now, so you'll have to be civil to him.'

'I'd rather have the Heretic's Fork again. She won't marry James, will she?'

'Of course not. Though' – he dropped his voice to a whisper – 'I predict she will grant him the succession. But she'll make him wait.'

He showed me to the door. I stood, awkwardly, wondering how to take my leave, when he pulled me into a brief and very English embrace; barely any part of us touching, with a manly pat on the shoulder for reassurance, lest I become too emotional.

'I meant it, Bruno – I shall never forget the service you have done my family. When this business with the conspirators is over, I will find a way to recompense you. Now get some sleep.'

Outside the room Douglas was hovering, suspiciously close. As I passed him, he caught me by the wrist.

'I told you we were alike, you and me,' he said, with his wolfish smile, his face too close to mine. 'We seize our chances where we can.'

I pulled away and said nothing, because I had an unpleasant feeling that there was some truth in this.

'How's that lovely girl of yours, Bruno?' he asked casually, as I walked away. 'I often think of her late at night, when I'm alone in my bed, and even when I'm not.'

I wheeled around to point a finger in his face; the guards by the door gripped their swords tighter, anticipating a fight. 'You go near her and I will kill you.'

'You can't, I'm an ambassador now. Diplomatic immunity.' He gestured to himself and gave a little swagger. 'Until the next time, old pal. I'm sure there will be a next time.'

'You'd better hope there isn't,' I said, though in my present state, I could not blame him for laughing. He leaned in close again.

'And you'd better hope your friend Walsingham lives a good long life,' he whispered, 'because there's no one else in this whole damned country who's got your back.' He gave me a playful dig in my sore ribs as a parting shot, and disappeared through the door, chuckling as I doubled over in pain.

You're wrong, I thought, as I straightened up. When Philip Sidney returns from the war and learns that I saved his wife and daughter, he will petition the Queen day and night until she gives me some manner of official employment. I will be able to court Sophia properly then, and concentrate on my books. Mary will be executed, and the Catholic threat will die with her. England will enjoy a time of peace and prosperity, and I might finally feel that I had found a place where I could think and write freely, and call home.

I knew, even without Douglas's malicious laughter ringing in my ears, that it could never be as simple as that.

EPILOGUE

20th September 1586

A cold morning, overcast; it felt not so much as if autumn had come early, but that summer had given up before it arrived. The scaffold had been built especially at St Giles Fields, to allow for more spectators. Despite the chill and the early hour, most of London had turned out for the spectacle; pie-sellers and girls with pitchers of hot cider moved among the crowds, finding ready business. Fathers lifted children on to their shoulders for a better view, and the youngsters shrieked and pointed with all the excitement of a day out.

I stood on a rise at the back of the crowd, far enough away – I hoped – that I would not be able to see their faces. At my side, Sophia edged closer against me and I felt her shiver.

'You don't have to watch this, you know.' I put an arm around her shoulders and pulled her towards me. She resisted at the implication that she was not strong enough to endure it.

'Walsingham says I do,' she murmured, her eyes fixed on the platform where the executioner and his two assistants were preparing their equipment. I saw her take in the cross-frame where one of the youths, halfway up the ladder, tugged on the nooses to test the knots; the butcher's block in the centre, with its two cleavers and various metal hooks catching the sky's dull light; the iron cauldron at the back on its trivet over a low fire, steam already rising from the water where the entrails would be thrown. 'He says if I am to work for him, I must understand the end point. Intelligence work is all for the purpose of rooting out the Queen's enemies, he says, and if I can't stomach the result of my labours, I should not get involved in the first place. He says this is especially hard for a woman, but I must cultivate a certain ruthlessness, or I will be too easily diverted from my path.'

'You've never had any trouble with ruthlessness before,' I said.

She glanced up to see if I was joking.

'I'm glad you're here,' she said, slipping her arm around my waist. 'I would not have liked to do this alone, and I could not persuade Lady Grace to come with me, she'd have fainted before we reached the Charing Cross. I've never seen a traitors' execution before, though I know what it entails, of course.'

'Of course.'

A silence fell between us, as both our thoughts turned to the fate of her son's father – an execution that was the direct result of my investigations for Walsingham. She let go of my waist and moved subtly away from me.

'So he wants you to go on working for him?' I said, to change the subject.

'That's what he says. He is occupied with the trial of Mary Stuart at the moment, but once that is over he spoke of training me in the art of ciphers and placing me somewhere I can be useful.' She shrugged. 'It may come to nothing, I know. He is always so busy – I fear he will forget me.'

'He won't. He knows a good mind when he sees one, he won't let yours go to waste. And what news of . . .' I hesitated, unsure if I should ask about Phelippes's enquiries into the whereabouts of her son, since she had not mentioned it.

'My boy?' She looked down. 'Not yet. Thomas is trying to trace the couple who bought him from my aunt, through contacts in Kent. But I have faith, Bruno. If anyone can find him, Thomas will. I am closer than I have ever been.'

I said nothing; there was no need for me to point out all the many ways reality might turn out to disappoint her. She knew them as well as I did, but she needed to hold on to her hope, just as I needed to believe that one day I might live and write freely without persecution for my ideas, and Walsingham needed his dream that, with Mary Stuart dead, Elizabeth and her Protestant England would be secure.

'Look,' Sophia said, nodding towards the scaffold and pressing tighter against me as an eerie silence descended on the crowd. People drew back as the cart approached, pulled by two black horses with plumes in their harness.

A heavy drumbeat started up from somewhere near the front, slow and ominous, as if for a religious procession. The prisoners stood shakily in the cart, their hands bound, staring out with wild eyes; all except Ballard, who was tied to a chair. I could only guess at how badly he must have been racked; I wondered who had done it, now that Walsingham no longer had Robin Poole. Would he have turned the handle himself? They looked thinner, older, scoured-out; nothing left now between them and eternity but this short walk up the steps and minutes that would feel like hours of unimaginable horror.

A tremor of anticipation passed through the spectators as the conspirators were handed down and lined up at the edge of the scaffold; Queen Elizabeth herself had demanded a special degree of cruelty to this execution, in view of what they had planned for her, to strike 'more terror' into those watching. According to Phelippes, Babington had broken down and begged for mercy at his trial, blaming Ballard for everything. He and Titch had been captured to the north of London, in St John's Wood, where they had tried to disguise themselves as beggars by dressing in rags and staining their faces brown with walnut juice. They had held out for nine days, until hunger had forced them to beg food for real, and a householder had recognised them from the description circulated in the pamphlets Walsingham had distributed immediately after their flight. Ballard had not lasted so long; he and Savage had been taken after only a day, hiding in a priest-hole at the home of one of his Catholic flock.

I watched Babington turn to the guards to ask if he was standing in the right place, as if taking care to please his captors now might make some difference to the outcome. Ballard was half-carried to the platform by a sturdy soldier, who held him upright while he was allowed to make his final address to the crowd. Though his body was broken, something of his old defiance revived as he looked out over the mass of faces; his voice rang out clear and bold as he prayed that England would repent and turn back to the true faith. The crowd jeered and booed at this; he made the sign of the cross as best he could and was pushed up the ladder so the noose could be fastened around his neck. I wondered if anyone had told his mother in Putney.

He swung for a couple of minutes, eyes and tongue bulging, while the executioner in his black hood slashed the front of his shift and with one deft stroke cut off his genitals; the priest barely had a chance to scream before his stomach was sliced across and his guts spilled, steaming, on to the boards. At the sight of this, Babington began howling and convulsing as if he were already being butchered, and had to be restrained by two guards while Ballard was cut down and laid on the block so that the executioner and his men could set about winding out his entrails and hacking off his limbs. Sophia edged close to me again and I felt her body grow rigid against my arm, but she did not look away. I feared I might be sick, and clenched my jaw tight until the waves of nausea had passed; the stench of blood and offal reached us even at the back. The crowd had turned deathly silent; the only sound now was Babington gibbering and begging for mercy as he slipped in his friend's blood on his way to the ladder. When they came for him with the cleaver, Sophia turned her face into my shoulder and remained there, breathing hard. Behind Babington was a dark-haired young man I had not seen before, whose name was read out as Thomas Salisbury, and whose final prayer was barely audible; only days before he had been at liberty, riding about the country with the wind in his hair and no notion that he would arrive straight into the arms of the pursuivants. When they kicked the ladder away, his expression was one of indignant amazement, as if he still couldn't quite process how this had come to pass.

Titch, when his time came, seemed as if he were already elsewhere; given the chance to speak his last words, he began to recite a poem he had written in prison to his wife, but the presiding official cut him off, saying there was no time. I was glad Clara had not been here to witness it; she had travelled with Frances to join Philip Sidney in Flushing shortly after the conspirators were arrested. It was a difficult journey in her condition, but the child had not yet begun to show, and the intention was for Clara to wait out her confinement in the household of one of Sidney's trusted officers, to avoid any scandal. Her future after the birth was less certain, according to the letter I had received from Frances. Walsingham was willing to permit Clara's return to the Sidney household, but not with the bastard of an executed traitor in tow, and Clara insisted she would not be separated from her child, so for now the matter stood at an impasse. I stole a glance at Sophia and thought of her son, taken from her at birth for similar reasons, and how she felt his absence every day like an open wound that nothing would heal. I hoped Clara would find a better way to resolve her situation, though it was hard to see how.

Savage made no farewell speech; merely looked straight ahead as he was pushed from the ladder, and I recalled the catch in his voice when he told me the story of Ballard saving his life on the riverbank. For a moment I saw them all as they were around the table at The Castle, the night we swore our oath: their laughter, their nerves, their passion and faith and doubt and friendship. I remembered Ballard handing out food to the homeless men in Paul's churchyard, and the pure fury in his eyes when he swung his fist at my jaw; I pictured Titch, defiant and bright-eyed and smelling of sex, and the look of understanding I had exchanged with Savage, when he spoke of his dead child. I thought of Babington wrapped up naked with Robin, and the way he had raised his glass at The Castle with that tell-tale tremor, the candles gilding his hair as he declared 'perform or die' with a courage he did not quite own. All those dreams and fears and loves, brought to this chaos of blood and meat at the executioner's feet. I thought of Mary too, in her lonely room at Chartley Manor, pinning her desperate hopes on wild promises of freedom and finding instead the long, slow walk to the block. My legs buckled under me and I stumbled back. Walsingham was right; it takes ruthlessness to do this work. I was no longer sure I had the mettle for it.

'Are you all right?' Sophia whispered, looking up. 'You've gone deathly white.'

'I've seen enough.'

'Me too. Let's find somewhere to sit.' We walked away from the crowd to the churchyard of St Giles and sat on the ground under an oak tree. I placed a hand on my stomach and felt, with a kind of awe, the pulse of blood under the skin, the heat and strength of my aliveness.

'I wish I had not seen that,' Sophia said, her voice tight.

'Has it changed your mind about working for him?'

She shook her head, but her lips were pressed together in a white line. 'No. Because someone will always die. He told me that if they had succeeded, if Mary Stuart came to the throne and the Spanish invaded, they would slaughter innocent people in their beds. At least those men were not innocent.'

'Walsingham is wrong,' I said, and I heard the anger in my voice. 'It's not true that someone always has to die – only if both sides keep insisting that there can be no compromise. Do you think God sanctions what we just saw, any more than He smiled on the massacre of Protestants in Paris?'

She flinched at my vehemence. 'I was only telling you what he said.'

'Then try thinking for yourself. I had this same argument with Gifford. He wouldn't listen – just kept bleating about heresy.'

'What happened to Gifford?' she asked.

'He fled to France,' I said, glad to avoid an argument. 'He didn't want to testify publicly at the trial – he was afraid it would make him a target for revenge attacks by English Catholics. Walsingham thought it easier to let him go – this way the Catholics still think he's one of theirs. Walsingham says he might come in useful in Paris at some point.' Gifford had fled because he feared being rounded up with the others; whatever he was doing in Paris now, I imagined him always looking over one shoulder, wondering when his double life would catch up with him. Prado had also been sent back to Paris, bundled on to the next ship out, to avoid a diplomatic incident. Weston had been arrested and imprisoned at Wood Street gaol, where he would probably stay for years. At least, by keeping clear of the conspiracy, he had avoided the same fate as Ballard and his friends.

'What about you?' she said, leaning against my shoulder. 'Will you go back to Paris?'

'Not in a hurry,' I said. 'There are at least five people there who would kill me as soon as set eyes on me.'

'Only five? That's quite good odds for you, isn't it, Bruno?'

I smiled. 'Should I stay in London, then?'

In truth, I had no idea of what to do next; I was waiting for word from Walsingham, as always, like a maid hanging on in hope of a marriage proposal. He had made sure I was financially rewarded for the part I had played, which was something; I had stayed on in the rooms at Herne's Rents to see what more he would offer, but his time had been taken up entirely with the trial of the Babington group, and now there was the infinitely more significant matter of what their convictions meant for Mary Stuart. While I did not think he had forgotten me, I knew that it might be months before I had his attention again. I had tried to work on my book over the past few weeks, but my concentration was scattered and I ended up hating my own clumsy words, tearing every attempt at a beginning into shreds and throwing it into the fire. Alberico Gentili had written to me from the University of Wittenberg, reminding me that the offer of a position remained open, and I had begun to think, as so often in my life, that my best hope might be to move on. I still could not work out whether this was cowardice or optimism.

'If you stay in London, it should be because you want to,' Sophia said, carefully. 'Not because of Walsingham – or anyone else.'

'It wouldn't bother you, then, if I thought of going to Germany?' I tried to keep the hurt out of my voice, but whatever skills I possessed for dissembling had never worked with her.

She slipped her hand under my arm and twined her fingers through mine. 'You know that if they told me tomorrow that my son was in Scotland, or York, or Cornwall, I would pack up and leave in a heartbeat without saying goodbye. So I wouldn't expect you to stay here for me, if you have better prospects elsewhere.' She paused, her eyes on the ground. 'Don't pin your happiness on me, Bruno. I don't want that responsibility.'

I nodded. I did not trust myself to speak. There would be no cottage with roses and children playing at our feet, and perhaps it was time for me to accept that this was all we had. I could have told her again that I loved her, but she already knew, and I had some pride left. Instead I raised her hand to my lips and held it there, and we sat in silence, listening to the relentless thud of the execution drum.

I did not want to return to my empty rooms alone. After Sophia left for the Cavendish house, I decided to get drunk, though it was not yet midday. I walked back to the Saracen's Head to find the place deserted. Dan Hammett was in the yard, picking leaves from a bush in the small garden. He turned and wiped his hands on his apron when he heard my footsteps.

'How was it?'

'Brutal. Worse than usual.' I pushed my hair out of my eyes; it had grown long again in the past weeks. 'The crowd didn't like it, you could tell.'

He whistled. 'That's badly done, if you lose a London crowd. You look like you need something strong. Oh – there's a woman here to see you. She's a looker. Mind you,' he said, holding up the foliage in his hands, 'I asked her what she wanted to drink and she said an infusion of mint leaves. An *infusion*! What's that when it's at home, eh?'

I smiled and turned towards the tap-room. 'Just put them in boiling water and leave them to steep for a while.'

'Infusion,' he muttered, shaking his head. 'This is bloody *Holborn*.'

I found Leila sitting at one of the benches, looking out of the window, her hair falling loose around her face. She had put on a yellow dress to venture north of the river; I wondered if it was for my benefit. I had not seen her since she cleaned me up after Ballard's attentions that night at the Unicorn. She smiled when she saw me, rising to kiss me on both cheeks.

'I brought you a gift,' she said, holding out a small hessian bag that made a satisfying rattling sound as she handed it over. 'Kahve beans. The merchant was in town last week, I bought extra. You grind them up and pour hot water on. Take it with sugar, though.'

'Thank you.' I opened the bag and breathed in the scent. 'These could be useful. I could stay awake all night writing with this.'

'Writing.' She gave me a wry smile. 'That's not the first thing most men think of when they learn there's a drink that can keep you up all night.'

'I can see it would have other uses too.' I caught her eye and looked away, embarrassed. 'How is Joe?'

'He's well. Not stolen any horses lately – he's trying to keep out of trouble. Had enough adventure for one year, I think. He misses Lotte and Anneke, but he's happy to have his grandfather home. And they gave the old man a generous compensation for his wrongful arrest, so he can retire. Now I don't have to worry about either of them going to the Cross Bones at night any more.' She shuddered. 'Was that your doing?'

'Not directly. But I'm glad for him.'

'Joe told me everything that happened that night,' she said, leaning across the table and lowering her voice. 'I only wish—' She broke off, and her hand curled into a fist.

'What?'

'That he had suffered more. The man who killed Lotte and Anneke, and would have killed Joe, and the baby. He should not have got off so lightly.'

'He's dead,' I said bluntly. 'There's no point wishing he'd been punished differently.'

'Do you know what *qisas* means, in my language?'

I nodded. 'An eye for an eye.'

'Retribution,' she said quietly, looking at her fist closing and flexing on the table. 'My father spoke of it all the time. He was the leader of a Morisco uprising against the Spanish. When you have seen what I have seen, you start to believe that might be a kind of justice.'

'The man who would have killed Joe believed that too. But he was wrong.'

She pursed her lips and we sat in silence.

'I'm not Spanish, by the way,' I said, after a while. 'I'm not a priest, either. Not for many years.'

She smiled. 'I guessed all that. Where are you from?'

'Nola. Near Naples.'

'Ah.' She nodded. 'There were Neapolitan troops fighting for the Spanish when my parents were killed and I was captured.'

'My father was a soldier,' I said. 'I don't know if he was there – he never spoke much of his campaigns. I'm sorry.'

'Well.' She unclenched her fist and reached out to lay her hand over mine. 'You brought Joe back, so we'll say you've paid your debt. Look at us now. When my father was hiding in the caves of the Alpujarra, he could never have imagined that one day I would end up in London, friends with the son of a Neapolitan soldier.'

'Nor mine.'

She held my look for a long moment, and I wondered what we proved, if anything: that people could have more in common than the old enmities that separated us, that the endless cycle of vengeance over religious difference could simply stop, in one generation? It seemed too much to hope, especially after the official spectacle of revenge I had witnessed that morning. But perhaps this was how it began: one friendship at a time. I determined that I would finish my book and see it put into the hands of Queen Elizabeth. Hope was worth clinging on to.

Dan intruded on my thoughts, bustling over with a steaming mug full of leaves. '*Infusion* for the lady,' he said, as if the word denoted some exotic practice, setting it down with great ceremony in front of Leila. 'And this is on the house, mate. You've had a long day already.' He passed me a large tankard of wine and disappeared back to the kitchen.

'Well, I am glad of your friendship . . .' Leila picked up her mug and laughed, shaking her head. 'I don't even know your real name.'

'Bruno,' I said. 'My name is Giordano Bruno.' I raised my glass. 'To friendship. And to the end of division.' In that moment, I almost believed it.

Elizabeth by the grace of god Que

our right trustie and wellbeloved Co

marshall of England, Henrie E

Erle of Cumberland, Henrie Erle

the statute geven by yo[u] and others o

Quene of Scottes by the name of M

fifth late Kinge of Scotte commonlie

of Fraunce, as to you is well knowen

dyd not onlie deliberatelie with gre

sentence as iust and honorable but d

possible, at sondrie times require, s

publishinge of the same, and therupo

the person as they did adiudge her t

the forbearinge therof was and woul

not onlie to our owne life, but to the

state of this realme as well for the

of Christ, as for the peace of the

the same was with some delaye of tim

proclamacion and yet thinges to have fo

tisfaction of the sayd most earn